THE
Chosen Sin

THE
Chosen Sin

Anya Bast

HEAT
New York

THE BERKLEY PUBLISHING GROUP
Published by the Penguin Group
Penguin Group (USA) Inc.
375 Hudson Street, New York, New York 10014, USA
Penguin Group (Canada), 90 Eglinton Avenue East, Suite 700, Toronto, Ontario M4P 2Y3, Canada
(a division of Pearson Penguin Canada Inc.)
Penguin Books Ltd., 80 Strand, London WC2R 0RL, England
Penguin Group Ireland, 25 St. Stephen's Green, Dublin 2, Ireland (a division of Penguin Books Ltd.)
Penguin Group (Australia), 250 Camberwell Road, Camberwell, Victoria 3124, Australia
(a division of Pearson Australia Group Pty. Ltd.)
Penguin Books India Pvt. Ltd., 11 Community Centre, Panchsheel Park, New Delhi—110 017, India
Penguin Group (NZ), 67 Apollo Drive, Rosedale, North Shore 0632, New Zealand
(a division of Pearson New Zealand Ltd.)
Penguin Books (South Africa) (Pty.) Ltd., 24 Sturdee Avenue, Rosebank, Johannesburg 2196,
South Africa

Penguin Books Ltd., Registered Offices: 80 Strand, London WC2R 0RL, England

This is an original publication of The Berkley Publishing Group.

THE CHOSEN SIN

First edition: October 2008

Library of Congress Cataloging-in-Publication Data

Bast, Anya.
    The chosen sin / Anya Bast.—1st ed.
        p.   cm.
    ISBN 978-0-425-22356-7
    1.   Vampires—Fiction.   I. Title.
    PS3602. A8493C47 2008
    813'.6—dc22

                                                                        2008020314

PRINTED IN THE UNITED STATES OF AMERICA

10   9   8   7   6   5   4   3   2   1

THE
Chosen Sin

ALEJANDRO leaned against the bar and watched the crush of dancers gyrate to the pounding beat in the Blood Spot. Lights flashed through the dark interior of the building, periodically illuminating bodies clad in almost nothing.

Blood hunger stirred within him, restless for a drink that had nothing to do with the imported bourbon in the glass he held. This place was rich with promise for a vampire. All those young bodies flushed from the energy of the music and their dancing, it was nearly irresistible.

It would be so easy to pull one of the lush women from the crowd, lead her into the velvet darkness of the back of the bar, ease her head back, and drink from her throat. He'd make sure she liked it. He'd make sure she climaxed while he drew the blood from her veins. His *veil* was strong when it came to giving pleasure.

His gaze focused on a twenty-something brunette, whose hips twisted and snapped to the frenzied music. She had beautiful tanned skin—the kind of woman typically found out here on sunbaked Darpong. The dark part of Alejandro whispered, *You could make her beg for it.*

Hell, most of the patrons were here because they hoped they'd find a Chosen to bestow the dark kiss. The bite of a vampire was a rush to a human, like a drug. The venom secreted by a fully Chosen's fangs caused their victim to relax and become aroused. Too much of the venom could kill them, or turn them, but most were willing to take the chance for the high.

A Chosen's veil, their ability to twist and mischief a mind, further intensified the pleasure.

The Blood Spot was known as a place where willing human donors and vamps could meet up. The Chosen and humans alike came from miles around to this desolate location for just that purpose.

That little brunette out there would probably welcome his bite. In fact, she was probably looking for it. He could press her back against the wall, slide her skirt up to her waist, part her thighs, and ease his cock in and out of her hot little slit while he drank. She'd feel so smooth and soft around him, and her muscles would ripple and tighten as he made her come.

Alejandro swore under his breath and stared down at his glass to distract himself from the thoughts that assaulted his mind. He downed the remaining liquid, letting the alcohol burn down his throat.

Blood hunger twisted in his gut and he pushed it away. It remained tamped down for the moment, but he doubted his ability to keep it that way. He didn't deal well with temptation. Never had. Not even before he'd been Chosen.

He was here on business for the GBC, the Governing Body of the Chosen, not to avail himself of the willing donors who surrounded him. He could resist. He had to.

After ordering another drink, he settled back against the bar and watched the dancers with heavy-lidded eyes. The bourbon wouldn't make him drunk, but the enticing morsels shaking themselves in front of him could.

A redhead in the crowd caught his gaze and smiled flirtatiously. He looked away.

Maldita sea!

He was supposed to be meeting Daria here. Where the hell was she? If she didn't get here soon, all his self-control would dissolve.

Alliance law decreed that vampires were supposed to feed from only the *succubare*, the class of Chosen that gained their sustenance from sex instead of blood. They were humans who'd been Chosen, but hadn't made it through the arduous process. They were not *fully* Chosen, only halflings.

As long as vampires fed from willing human blood donors, the law wasn't typically enforced. Basically it was a consensual crime without punishment.

However, the Governing Body of the Chosen, the lawmaking organization for all Chosen, had the same law and they were strict. They were especially hard on the vampires who worked directly for the GBC. They were not allowed to feed from a human, no matter how willing that human might be.

He swirled the bourbon in his glass and tried not to stare at the redhead who still endeavored to catch his eye.

Yeah, he had a problem with the regulation placed on him by the GBC. He craved human blood, wanted to feel a human body crushed against him when he drank. He was driven to fill the hole it created inside him. Some humans found being bitten by a vamp an addiction, but he found taking their blood just as big an enticement.

Human blood was sweeter than the blood of the succubare and far more intoxicating.

The redhead broke away from the crowd and approached him on long, shapely legs. A short black skirt sheathed her from the waist to midthigh. Red stiletto heels, the same color as her filmy, almost see-through top, encased her slender feet.

The fashion was retro these days—Earth at the beginning of the twenty-first century. Out here in the Nabovsky Galaxy, named for the astronomer who'd discovered it, the settlers had a lot of nostalgia for the home planet.

An expensive ruby pendant nestled in the smooth hollow of her throat. More rubies hung from her delicate earlobes. The woman who approached him now was probably rich and slumming it out here in the outreaches of the lawless Logos Territory on Darpong, looking for a thrill or two. He'd bet any amount of money she had a wealthy husband back on Angel One.

"You look lonely over here," the redhead purred at him. She touched his chest with long, manicured nails. They scraped his skin through the material of his shirt. Her voice lowered predatorily, her eyes lighted with speculation. "You're a vamp, aren't you, handsome?"

~

DARIA Moran pushed the door open and stepped into the Blood Spot. Her pupils adjusted to the dim light and her nostrils flared at the heavy odor—a combination of Darpongese booze, the bitter smoke from *rashish* cigarettes, and the metallic scent of blood. The pounding beat of the club's music assaulted her eardrums.

There were vamps in here. She could feel them. This sleazy club in the outreaches of Darpong was well known as a place where *veilhounders*— blood donors who were psychologically addicted to a vamp's veil and physically addicted to the chemicals secreted by a vamp's bite—hung out, waiting for a vampire to grace them with their presence . . . and their fangs. The edges of her mouth curled down in disgust.

If it was up to Daria, veilhounding would be illegal everywhere. She found the practice abhorrent, despite the supposed joys of having a vampire sink his or her fangs into you and unfurl their illusions within your mind.

There were addiction clinics all over the Angel System. For the love of the quad planets, you'd think people would learn not to get their kicks this way.

There were even isolated cases of vampires trafficking in the sale of addicted humans they called blood slaves. Sometimes they abducted veilhounders from places just like this one and sold them into it.

She shook her head, glancing around at the people that filled the building. *The fools.*

Daria's hand rested on her patrol-issued pulse disruptor, a weapon capable of briefly preventing muscular impulses, or the cessation of synapses firing in the brain, depending on the setting. The weapon worked on most species, even the Chosen. She was not a willing blood donor and she'd be damned if anyone mistook her for one.

Her pupils finally adjusted to the dim light and she sought out Alejandro Martinez. She hadn't seen him in over seven years. All the same, she spotted him right away since he still looked like sin made flesh.

A black leather dune-biker jacket sheathed broad shoulders and his muscular arms and chest. Thick black hair framed a face hewn in masculine lines, with a strong chin, chocolate brown eyes, and a mouth made for kissing . . . and other things. She filled in from memory what she couldn't see, since his face was currently buried in the neck of a tall redhead.

Daria hung back, watching him sway and dip the woman in his arms, a veilhounder most likely, his pelvis moving sensually against hers. The rhythm to which they danced was a lot slower than the music. They looked like they were in the throes of a slow, pleasurable fuck, oblivious to everyone around them.

Daria shook her head. It had been far too long since she'd had one of those. Everything looked sensual to her these days. Of course, Alejandro had always exuded confident sexuality, even before he'd been Chosen.

What the hell was he doing biting a human? That was against GBC regulations.

She worked her way around the edge of the room, picking past entangled vampires and donors and stepping in sloshed beer and other substances she didn't care to identify. Finally, she entered the crush on the dance floor and elbowed her way to him.

"Alejandro?" she queried loudly, competing with the music. "It's me, Daria."

No reaction. Just that irritating sway and thrust.

"Alejandro," she repeated, louder this time.

He raised his head. His dark eyes were heavy lidded, and a hank of black hair had fallen across his forehead. Dark stubble graced the square jut of his jaw and shaded the skin around his well-formed mouth. Those beautiful lips twisted. "Your turn?" he drawled in his Spanish accent.

He released the veilhounder redhead, who stumbled back drunkenly with a smile on her face. Daria stepped away, but he grabbed her around the waist and drew her close.

Her protest died on her tongue as his hot breath caressed her throat. Some strange quirk of vampire chemistry made a Chosen's breath consistently sweet. Scientists had hypothesized that vamp breath acted as a mild tranquilizer, lulling their human victim and making them more susceptible to a bite.

Daria held her breath, trying not to inhale it. Alejandro bussed his lips across the bare skin between her collarbone and shoulder. The hard rake of fangs followed the sensation.

That broke her momentary stupor. She pushed him away and hooked her leg around his to sweep his legs out from under him. He went down hard on his back, scattering the bar's patrons around them.

Daria knelt beside him, drawing her pulser and pointing it at his temple. It whirred up, readying to fire. The light on top that was connected to her brain wave patterns flared red. "I told you, Alejandro. No fangs."

Someone to their immediate left gasped, another screamed. They all backed away. But Daria knew that in this place ruckus wasn't uncommon. They'd go back to their drinks and dancing soon enough.

Alejandro blinked. "Daria? Jesus, I didn't recognize you."

Self-consciously, she touched her hair with her free hand. She'd undergone a lot of cosmetic work for this operation. The face of the person she'd been when she'd known Alejandro was now permanently altered. Her dark chestnut-colored hair was now blond, and her jaw was square-shaped instead of delicately pointed. Her lips were fuller and her cheekbones more prominent.

The only thing she'd left untouched from the neck up were her eyes. They were still a dark blue. When she went undercover, she'd turn her blue eyes brown with an ordinary pair of colored contacts.

There'd be no way her quarry would recognize her even without the added precaution of the contacts, but there was no sense in taking chances.

Sante used to say he loved the color of her eyes, the bastard.

"*You* haven't changed at all," she said. "Don't sink your fangs into me, got it? No biting. No fangs."

"That's kind of ironic considering what you want me for. How do you think this is going to work, anyway? I can't Choose you without taking your blood."

A fine tremble in her hand shook the pulser. "I know." She was still in denial about that part. She'd do it, but until that time, she didn't want to think about it . . . or talk about it. "But that's for a good reason. I don't want you to bite me just for kicks. I'm not a veilhounder."

He stared at her for a moment before speaking. "You're not ready for this at all, are you?"

She ignored the question and cocked her head to the side. "What the hell are you doing breaking GBC law, anyway? Are you blood drunk?"

"What makes you think that?"

"You let me spill you on your ass, Alejandro, and me a puny human and all." She smiled. "You a lush now, big guy?"

With the kind of speed achieved by only the fully Chosen, he disarmed and flipped her in one smooth motion.

She tried to strike out at his throat and eyes, but he grabbed her wrists and pinned them to the floor.

"If I was blood drunk," he growled, "would I have been able to disarm and restrain an agent of the Allied Bureau of Investigation so easily?"

"You son of a bitch, Alejandro. I could've killed you if I wanted to. Your brain was only a trigger squeeze away." She lifted a brow. "If I didn't need you for this mission, I'd report you to the GBC for your little . . . *slip*. I wonder how often you're slipping these days."

Fear flashed through his eyes and he clenched his jaw before responding. "Such fire, Daria. I don't remember you being like this. It's so arousing." He lowered his mouth and brushed his lips across hers.

"I might have to change your mind about not allowing my"—he inhaled her scent and groaned—"*fangs* to sink into you."

His accent rolled over her and she tingled in places that hadn't tingled in a long time. God, she loved his accent and his voice. The two together were magic. She ignored her response. "Some things never change," she said. "Not after seven years, not even after you've been Chosen. You think all the women will just fall at your feet."

He smiled. "Didn't you?"

"That was before you were Chosen, and the circumstances were . . . strange. It wouldn't happen now."

White teeth flashed, making him look feral in the half-light. His fangs were retracted, thank God. "It would be even better *now*."

It had been fantastic before.

She could still remember that night, the taste of him in her mouth and the feel of him moving inside her. He'd brought her to climax hard and fast at first, and then he'd taken his time with her, drawing out two more orgasms before he was finished.

He'd been better than Sante had ever been, and Sante had been Chosen when she'd slept with him, even though she hadn't known it.

She'd used Alejandro that night. He'd known it and hadn't minded. She'd needed him to help her forget what had happened, to drown her in lust so she wouldn't drown in sorrow. He'd done a good job. For that one night, he'd been like a knight in shining armor to her damsel in distress.

Daria shivered as his mouth came down on hers. His lips slid over hers like silk, in just the lightest brush. Pure desire shot down her spine straight to her sex.

Damn you!

She was still attracted to him after all these years. And, of all the things he could be, he was a *vampire*. She bit his bottom lip and tasted blood. It spread across her tongue like the smoothest wine. She resisted the urge to spit.

Swearing, he jerked back, and Daria rolled away. She snatched up her lost pulser and stood, wiping the floor yuck from her clothing with a grimace. "Get up, Alejandro. We need to move." She offered her hand and he took it.

Once he was on his feet, she turned on her heel and headed straight for the bar. She needed to take a minute to settle her nerves, so she ordered a shot.

"Rocks?" the bartender asked.

She gave her head a shake.

The bartender served her the shot and she downed it. There was nothing like Darpongese whiskey. It was a little like Earth whiskey, but stronger, with a slightly bitter flavor and a smooth finish.

Alejandro touched her shoulder. "You okay?"

She shrugged him off. "I'm fine." She set the shot glass back on the bar and closed her eyes for a moment. It was a lie, one she was desperately trying to believe.

Two years of service in the Galactic Patrol, seven years in the Allied Bureau of Investigation, two medals of valor, numerous undercover operations, and hundreds of busts and she still wasn't sure she could handle what was to come.

2

T HEY stepped out of the dark bar and into the desolate, sand-swept terrain. The Blood Spot was located in the farthest reaches of the Logos Territory.

Alejandro scanned the horizon and saw nothing but the narrow road leading to Danpang City, surrounded by sand dunes in all directions. The Blood Spot had become a favored hot spot because of its secluded location.

The wind picked up, blowing sand across the road and sending an old can to rattle and scrape across the pavement. The lavender-tinged moon hung at half-mast in the sky and stars glimmered everywhere, sewn like diamond chips into black velvet cloth.

It almost looked like Earth's night sky, almost.

The Chosen had outed themselves the same year the first commercial space jaunts had become de rigueur in 2075. It had been something ancient, dark, and powerful meeting something new, shiny, and exciting. For certain, it had been a notable year in Earth history. The Chosen had known they were outnumbered by humans, known that when they exposed themselves there would be fear and bigotry. And there was.

Wasn't there always?

At the time, Earth had become overpopulated and unpleasant to live on. The Chosen had nursed dreams of finding another world to call home. It was a big universe out there and several habitable planets had already been discovered. Perhaps there'd be a place for them somewhere in the black?

But the Chosen had never managed to find a world to call their own. Outnumbered and outmaneuvered by human law, their requests had always been denied or they'd been stymied by politics and lobbying groups. They'd been forced to join in the rising tide of human immigrants leaving Earth to find a better world. A better world than one that had barely been saved from global warming and was stuffed to the gills with swelling humanity, locusts who devoured every resource in their path without thought for the future.

Then had come the big find of the Nabovsky Galaxy, and a solar system supporting not one, but four habitable planets in close proximity, some large, some smaller.

Angel One was perfect—lush, green, and verdant, like Earth before humans had messed it up. Though the sky was not blue, but a pale green yellow. That planet had become the "capital" of the Angel System and to this day was the most civilized.

Luckily there were strict environmental laws on Angel One that prohibited sprawl from the urban areas and protected the wild places. The urban areas, especially New Chicago, where he and Daria lived, were built high into the sky because of the anti-sprawl laws, though with ample areas of vegetation to enjoy within the confines of the city.

Another planet, Galileo, was small and covered mostly with water, though there were two sizable landmasses that had been colonized. With seas rich in edible fish and sea life, it was a place inhabited by fisher people and their families who worked for the two big food processing plants that served the quad planets, as they were called.

Darpong, where they were now, didn't have much water at all. It was a desert planet, hot during the day and cold at night. It was a medium-sized world and very friendly to humans, though the lack of water made it an unpopular choice. It was a vacation and party spot, mostly. Lawless and wild, it attracted the same. Nabovsky Galaxy's very popular gravsport competition was held here every year, an extreme sport spectacle with a high casualty rate.

With the amount of sun on Darpong, it was ironic that Sante had chosen it for his commune since vamps couldn't walk in sunlight, although if the stories were true, the dome protected the solar-sensitive occupants from the punishing rays.

Songset, named for the man who'd discovered her, was tidal locked. Without season, tide, or rotation, it simply existed. One side of the huge planet was caught in perpetual high summer, with temperatures reaching 120 degrees Fahrenheit nearly every day. The other side was caught in perpetual winter, temperatures dipping into the minus 50 region.

Most of the immigrants who'd elected to colonize Songset lived on the band circling the planet, where the climate was most hospitable, though some lived on the "day" and "night" sides under large man-made domes. Songset was a mining world, ravaged for its rich mineral deposits.

There had been noises about allowing the Chosen their own rock, perhaps the dark side of Songset, but, as usual, that had never come to fruition.

Alejandro watched Daria walk to her dune bike, which was a far more pleasing sight than their arid surroundings. Her newly blond hair was cut close to her head. It was so short you might think she was a man from behind, until you dropped your gaze and saw that long, slender neck, the delicate shoulders, and a nicely shaped ass. There was no mistaking her body for anything but 100 percent female.

Her face, as well as her hair, looked different. The surgeons had done a good job. Sante wouldn't recognize her. Her eyes were the same, although they held a hardness that hadn't been there when she'd been a newly graduated patroller.

Was it Christopher Sante who had stripped Daria of her youth so fast and hard? Or had it been one of the many other events that could befall a wet-behind-the-ears patroller in the barely settled Angel System?

Even after all these years, she intrigued him. When he'd discovered Daria was the agent selected for this assignment, he'd convinced the Council that he was the man to play her counterpart. He was still working out the *why* of that in his mind.

When they'd both been patrollers, he'd tried his best to protect her. Maybe a part of him felt like that job wasn't finished yet, although he knew what Daria would do if she ever found out he thought she needed protection. He'd be divested of his balls in about two seconds flat.

When they'd both worked at patrol headquarters, he had been desperate to get her into bed, but she'd only wanted Christopher Sante and had rejected all Alejandro's advances.

In the end, seduction hadn't been necessary. His efforts at consolation after Sante had done his number on her had turned into much more. He and Daria had their night together seven years ago and Alejandro had always thought that'd be the end of it. Until now.

Daria mounted her dune bike and started it. The shiny silver and black vehicle roared to life and then settled down to a kittenish purr. She reached for the helmet hooked behind her seat and pulled it on.

She shot him a look of impatience through the shaded visor. "Let's go. I want to get this thing over with." Almost imperceptibly, she shivered.

Alejandro knew it was probably because she was contemplating the Choosing that was to come. He could smell the little spike of fear in her even from a distance.

She shouldn't be doing this. She didn't want it and she wasn't ready for it.

He walked over and took his place on his own dune bike, the wide, silver machine that could speed over the heated sand of Darpong like a jet-powered cloud.

Before starting his bike, Alejandro studied her. Small lines of displeasure creased the skin between her midnight blue eyes. She'd set her shoulders, and every muscle in her body looked stiff. "How long has it been, Daria?"

She rolled her eyes. "How long for what?"

"Since you've been laid. You're a little bit on the cranky side."

"Shut up, Alejandro. Let's get going."

"A good three years, I'd say."

"Why do men always think every little thing revolves around them? My mood doesn't have anything to do with men or my sex life."

He put his helmet on, laid his thumb flat onto the starter, and revved his bike to life. "Sure, Daria," he shot back once his bike's engine had quieted. "Whatever you say."

"Alejandro—"

He kicked the throttle in and took off fast. His bike sped off over the stretch of desert. Out of the corner of his eye, he saw Daria coming up right beside him.

They sped over the sand at a rate that made speech impossible. It snatched their words straight from their lungs and scattered them to the wind. That was probably a good thing, considering the looks of death Daria shot him.

His bike hovered about three feet off the ground and clung to the contours of the sand dunes. Alejandro angled the bike toward his temporary abode deep in the desert. It wasn't very far from their final destination, the lair of the Shining Way.

Alejandro turned his head to watch her. Her hands were curled tight on the handles of her bike, her pulser tucked securely in the holster around her waist. He let his gaze travel down her shapely legs, clad in snug-fitting cream-colored pants. His body tightened at the sight of her, and he shook his head at the realization.

She still affected him.

Even after all these years. Of all the women he'd ever known, she was the one who had touched him the most. She'd always been tough, and he'd admired that in her, but she hadn't always been this *hard*. He remembered how huge and luminous her eyes had been after Sante's treachery had been discovered.

That night, so many years ago, Alejandro had wanted to take all that hurt away and bring back the fiery idealism that Sante had snatched away. Alejandro had pulled her aside to talk to her after all the *mierda* had gone down. He'd done it as a fellow patroller and without any ulterior motive. When she'd pushed him back in his chair and started kissing him he'd tried to stop himself, but his control had been shredded by her aggression and their shared attraction.

The morning had brought swift change for both of them. Disgraced and reprimanded for inadvertently aiding Sante in his masquerade as a patroller, Daria had been put on leave without pay, pending a further investigation. She'd left Angel One for a while in order to get her head together.

Alejandro had discovered soon after that he was one of the marked ones, a human with the genetic predisposition to vampirism, meant to be Chosen.

After that he'd had a short nightmarish period enslaved to his blood mother, Lucinda Valentini. When he'd been strong enough to break from her, he'd gone to work for the GBC. He'd had the perfect background to become a peacekeeper, one who took care of the vampires who violated Chosen law. It was a difficult job, and had brought out the darker side of his personality.

Finally, they reached his temporary dwelling, consisting of two tents, one large and one small, each of them camouflaged to look like a mound of sand when viewed from the air. The material of the tents concealed body heat to fool detectors.

Alejandro pulled his bike into the smaller tent to hide it from view and Daria followed. They grabbed their gear off the back of their bikes and headed into the larger tent.

"Hmmm . . . camping," murmured Daria with a raised eyebrow as she entered. She tossed her pack into a corner and removed her holster as she let her gaze flick over their surroundings.

He glanced around. The inside of the tent consisted of an inflatable bed in one corner and a smokeless kitchenette in the other, something he didn't have much use for beyond the small refrigerator that kept his supply of synthetic blood cold.

Multicolored pillows were scattered over the floor in one area, in front of a solar-powered commview. In the back was an enclosed area with an old-fashioned water shower, a sink, and a mirror. The heavy canvas floor covered the sand, and the sides of the tent rustled with the wind.

Yes, their surroundings were pretty meager, but you had to marvel at the tech that made the structure possible. All the appliances were freestanding and self-contained, powered by wind or the sun. The sinks in the kitchen and the bathroom were hooked up to a small water tank at the back of the tent.

"Home sweet home for now," he answered.

He popped out his PComp unit and Daria did the same. They wouldn't need them for a while since they couldn't take the communication devices into the Shining Way.

They put the units, about the size of his thumbnail, into a drawer in the kitchen. PComps fit into the bio-relay ports they both had at the base of their skulls. They downloaded information from the ABI or the GBC, or where they had uplinks, straight into their minds. The name for the device was a play on the name for the ancient device called a *personal computer*.

She turned to face him, one hand on her slim hip. "Do you even have a home? I remember you being quite the drifter. And now that you're working for the Governing Body of the Chosen . . ." She trailed off.

"I keep an apartment in New Chicago and a place on the dark side of Songset." It was true that his work didn't leave him a lot of time to spend at any one residence. They were places to stay, not homes.

"Songset? Near the dig?"

The colonists had wondered if they'd find alien life beyond Earth. They'd only found flora and fauna, no evolved beings. But not long after, there'd been an archaeological find on the night side of Songset, one that proved they weren't alone out here in the dark.

"My place is about one hundred clicks from there."

She nodded and kept looking around her.

He knew Daria had been born on Earth and had spent her childhood dreaming of the day she could become a Galactic Patroller, just like her father had been before he'd died. That's why she'd moved out to the Angel System. What she wanted Alejandro to do right now could destroy the career she cared about more than anything else.

He threw down his pack. "Why do you want to do this? It's obvious you don't have anything but contempt for the Chosen. Why do you want to become one?"

"I want into the Shining Way, Alejandro." Her eyes flashed angrily. "I want to take Sante down. I want—"

"To make him pay for what he did?"

"He deceived me and used me. He saw a brand-new patroller and he conned her. He made me love him, the bastard." Her voice shook with anger. "Then he used my connections to gain information and kill one of my friends. He ruined my reputation. He almost ruined my career. What? Have you forgotten all this? Yeah, I want to make him pay."

"He deceived all of us."

"Me worst of all." She looked away from him, and he saw her lower lip tremble. That glimpse of vulnerability was a telling sign. "He killed Julia," she said in a softer voice. "He killed her and he never saw a day of punishment."

He tried to make his voice comforting. "I know."

Sante was an old vampire skilled at hiding what he was. He'd become a patroller with the sole ambition of obtaining information regarding a witness who had been scheduled to testify against his blood mother, Maria Gillante, in a case of trafficking in blood slaves.

Specifically, Sante had used Daria to get the information, and he'd had a good time doing it. He'd wooed her and seduced her. He'd entered into a serious relationship with her under false pretenses. That had made what came next even more of a betrayal.

On the night Sante had finally obtained his information and located the house where the witness was being held, he'd killed Daria's best friend, Julia Harding. Julia had been one of three patrollers assigned to guard the witness that night.

Alejandro frowned. "You said he almost ruined your career, but I thought you were cleared of wrongdoing in that deal."

"I was, eventually. That still didn't stop everyone from blaming me for what happened. That still didn't stop them from thinking I was naïve and incompetent. It's taken me years to rebuild my reputation to an acceptable level."

Her eyes hardened. "He got away with it. *He got away with murdering* three patrollers and a witness. Do you remember their names, Alejandro? I do. Vincent Almeda, Trudy Horowitz, Stephen Miller . . ." Her voice shook with emotion. "And Julia Harding."

Alejandro sighed. "I know, Daria. I remember the trial."

They'd had no evidence to link Sante directly to the murder. He'd done a little time for impersonating a human, which was all the prosecutors could prove. It had been a slap in the face to both himself and Daria.

She turned away from him and crossed her arms over her chest. "And it was my fault," she finished in a whisper. "If it hadn't been for me, he never would've shown up at the house. Julia would still be alive."

Alejandro resisted the urge to comfort her. "It's not your—"

She whirled on him. "He's not getting away with this one," she said in a steely voice. "This time, we're getting him. I'm going to make sure we do."

Alejandro pushed a hand through his hair. "You know you're throwing your life away for this . . . for him? He was supposedly my partner. He betrayed me, too. I also want revenge, but I still wouldn't give up my life for the bastard."

Her eyes shuttered. "I'm not you."

"You're not marked, Daria. You have no genetic predisposition for this. That makes me Choosing you a risky proposition. You could end up succubare, forever feeding off sex, instead of life force. Worse, the Choosing could kill you."

"You ought to know I'm stronger than that. I'll push through the succubare and become a fully Chosen vampire."

Only a very small percentage of humans could push through. The odds were against her. "Okay. Let's say you do. What then? You hate the Chosen."

She turned and stalked away from him, to the bunch of throw pillows and back. "This may be my only chance. I might not get another. Sante fucked up bad this time. He's got the whole Interstellar Alliance pissed at him right now. They think he kidnapped Ari Templeton and they'll let us do anything to get her back."

Richard Templeton, Ari's father, was the head of The New Covenant Church, the largest religious organization in the quad planets. Templeton had been fighting to gain enough support to force the government to exterminate the Chosen. As radical as Templeton's views were, he was a powerful social and religious figure.

Templeton claimed his daughter had been abducted by Christopher Sante and taken to the Shining Way, the well-guarded fortress that was called a *community of Chosen*, but many thought was simply some kind of cult. The ABI thought perhaps Sante had done it in retaliation against Templeton and his hate-motivated movement targeting the Chosen.

Alejandro and Daria had been tasked with going undercover and investigating Templeton's claims. If they found they were true, their orders were to bring Ari home and Sante in, if possible. Kill him if it wasn't.

"The cost is too high," he answered.

She whirled. "Look, I want Sante. I'll do anything . . . *anything* to get him."

"That's good you'll do anything, because you know the other thing you're going to have to do in order to fool the Shining Way into accepting you as one of their own."

She turned toward him. Her big, midnight blue eyes shone with apprehension. "Yeah, I know."

Alejandro walked toward her. To her credit, she didn't back away. "You're going to have to be with me, Daria." He reached out and cupped her cheek against his palm. "Every inch of you from the top of your head to your pretty little toes will be mine once we reach the Shining Way."

The Shining Way was very restrictive about who they let in. Sante was allowing Alejandro in based on their past relationship. Sante had no idea that Alejandro was now a GBC employee. That information was secret. Alejandro had told Sante that "Valerie" was his mate and that he wouldn't come without her.

She clenched her jaw and swallowed hard, like she'd gulped down a bug, before speaking. He tried not to let his ego take a hit, but it was hard. "I can fake it." Her voice shook just a little. Only a Chosen would be able to hear that slight quaver.

He brushed his thumb over her lower lip. "You know as well as I do that we won't be able to fake it. We're going to have to make it real, *all* of it, for this operation. They have to be able to scent you on me and vice versa."

"Nice try, Alejandro. We don't necessarily have to have sex to accomplish that." Contrary to her words, desire flickered through her eyes. It rippled through his body and made his cock hard.

God help him, he still wanted her.

He wanted her stripped, wanted those long, strong legs wrapped around his waist while he eased in and out of her hot little slit. "That would be difficult."

Her eyes shuttered again and she knocked his hand away. "Yeah, I know, but not impossible." She pushed past him.

Alejandro raised a brow. "I guess you have a ways to go before you accept all this."

"Don't get your hopes up. I'll never *accept* it. I'm just going to *do* it." Daria turned and pushed a hand through her hair, making it stick up in little tufts. "Look, I had to fight hard to convince the bureau to assign me to this case. They thought I had too many issues concerning Sante to be objective."

"You do."

Daria ignored him. "It was my willingness to become a Chosen that swayed them in the end. I was the only one who would. So let's just do it, all right? If we don't do it now, I might lose my nerve. I can't think about it too much."

"You know I'm going to have to bite you, Daria. You're going to have to bite me, too." He took a step toward her and she backed away. He stilled. "Do you trust me?"

"No."

He shook his head. "You're not ready for this."

"Hell no, I'm not ready, and I don't trust you. Get it through your head that I will *never* be ready and I will never trust you. Just do it anyway."

Alejandro sighed. "I'm going to drink your blood, first. Let it combine in my veins before I give it back to you, blended with mine. That mix is going to cause drastic changes in you. You don't have a mark to smooth the way for you like I did. You were never meant to become a vampire and don't have the biological makeup for it. So, those transformations are going to be violent and occur in a very short amount of time. One of those changes will be a hormone surge—"

"I read about all this in the handbook, Alejandro," she interrupted.

"The handbook?" He snorted. "Come on, Daria, reading from the handbook and doing it in real life are two different things."

She shot him a very unfriendly look. "My point is, I know what to expect."

"So you know that from the time I Choose you until the time your body slides into unconsciousness you're going to want to fuck anyone within ten miles?"

Daria looked around the tent as though she could see beyond the walls to the hundred-mile radius of sand. She looked back at him, drawing the obvious conclusion.

"Yep," he said with a smile.

She shook her head. "I'll resist it."

He laughed.

3

ALEJANDRO sauntered toward her with a look of heat in his dark eyes. Daria resisted the urge to back away. He wanted her trust and she couldn't give it to him. All the same, she had to surrender herself completely to Alejandro right now.

Every fiber of her body protested that.

He put his hand to her cheek and she sighed at the heat his body gave off. When he snaked his other hand around to her nape, she winced and tried to back away. His grip tightened. Forcing herself to not fight him, she gritted her teeth and stayed in place.

"Are you absolutely sure you want this?" he asked.

A whimper lodged itself tightly in her throat. She nodded once.

He stepped forward, closing the slight space between them, and set his lips to her cheek. She flinched away, but he grasped her upper arm and held her in place. Drawing a deep breath, she closed her eyes and psyched herself up to be bitten. Every muscle in her body felt strung tight.

"Shhh," Alejandro soothed. He leaned in, bathing her lips with his intoxicating breath. Daria was sure he did it deliberately. It had a calming effect that she welcomed right now. She opened her eyes and inhaled, letting the serenity wash over her.

She was taking a huge risk here. If she were unable to push though the entire transformation, she'd end up destined to live her life surviving from the lust of others. The thought of being a vampire disgusted her, but the thought of ending up succubare absolutely terrified her.

"God, you smell so good, Daria," he murmured into her ear. "Remember that night right before you left the bureau on your suspension? Remember how good we were together? We were tangled together all night long, sweaty and oblivious to the rest of the world."

Despite her apprehension, the chemical in Alejandro's breath made her muscles languid. "Uh . . . huh. I remember," she murmured.

She stopped herself from purring at the memory of his bare chest rubbing against hers, how he'd pulled her beneath him and parted her thighs with his knee, the feel of his cock pressing into her pussy inch by delicious inch. She shivered.

He'd filled her so well, stretched the muscles of her cunt until she could barely take all of him. She'd felt deliciously possessed by him, overwhelmed by him.

God, she'd loved it.

She'd found comfort in Alejandro's arms for that night. Surely, she could find comfort there again.

"Just relax, and we can be that good during the Choosing, okay? *Relax*," he murmured.

Daria's body softened against his. Her fingers found his upper arms and gripped so she could allow herself to sag against him a little.

Alejandro trailed the hand cupping her cheek down her jaw, neck, and shoulder. It briefly caressed her waist, and then pressed against the small of her back. He brushed his lips lightly across hers but didn't linger. Instead, his mouth traced down over her jawbone to her throat.

The hand at her nape traveled up and twined in her hair. Using it as a grip, he slowly tilted her head to the side, exposing the vulnerable line of her throat. All the while he nuzzled her sensitive skin, raising goose bumps over her flesh.

Daria's heart rate and breathing sped from more than the impending bite. Even while her mind railed against the thought of sleeping with him again, her body primed itself.

The plain blue V-neck T-shirt she wore didn't impede Alejandro and he got right to business. With the sharp edges of his fangs, he lightly nipped the area where her shoulder and throat met. She shuddered in pleasure. Christ, she'd never get through this without spontaneously combusting.

"Alejandro, cut the foreplay. Just do it." At this point, she'd welcome his bite just to distract her from how bad she wanted him.

"Be patient." His tongue flicked out and sought her pulse, then settled in to lap at it. A tremor ran up her spine. Her legs suddenly unsteady, she twined her arms around him and held on.

Her voice shook when she replied, "I don't have all—" She gasped. Sharp fangs penetrated. Sweet, jagged pain made her stiffen.

The pain receded, and warm pleasure enveloped her. Somewhere in the back of her mind, Daria understood that Alejandro had rolled his veil over her. It was designed to mask the pain with pleasure.

Oh, and how it worked. Suddenly she understood the veilhounder's addiction.

Desire poured into her like thick, sweet honey, pooling in all the right places. Every time he moved, he brushed her hardened, sensitive nipples against his chest. The suction at her throat increased, causing the heady mixture of pleasure and pain to affect an area of her body much further south.

When he disengaged his fangs, withdrew his veil, and held her close, regret flickered.

With one hand he stroked her upper back. "Are you okay?" His voice sounded heavy, aroused, thick. It rumbled through her, and she fought the urge to lean against him and close her eyes. She needed to be able to stand on her own.

"I'm—" The word came out a strangled rasp. She pushed away from him and staggered back. "I'm fine." She reached up and touched the two puncture wounds at her throat to distract herself. "Wow, uh, I .

see what you mean about the lust." Damn it, her voice sounded quavering and thin.

He smiled. She noted uneasily that it seemed predatory. "I haven't Chosen you yet, Daria," he said in a purring, thick voice.

She felt the blood drain from her face. "O-oh."

"I thought you read the handbook."

"I did." Daria turned away from him and closed her eyes. She was not going to give in to him. She was *not*. A man like Alejandro was more dangerous than most and she wasn't going to let him in, not even if it was just for sex.

"Daria? Are you okay? You don't feel faint, do you?"

She turned, masking her worry with an expression of anger. "No, I don't feel *faint*." The word sounded like the lash of a whip in the quiet air.

Laughter lit his eyes but he obviously valued his balls enough not to let it slip from his throat. He was smart. "Good." He walked toward her, biting his wrist as he came. He twined an arm around her waist and pulled her close, placing his wrist to her mouth at the same time. "Then you can drink."

She eyed the blood dripping from the wound he'd made. "Uh."

"Drink, Daria. *This* is the Choosing."

She hesitated, then closed her eyes, screwed up her face—and her courage—and flicked her tongue out to taste his wrist. The flavor of his life force coated her tongue like aged, expensive wine. It had a silken texture with an edge of sweetness. It was a Chosen chemical quirk that made it taste so. She didn't want to spit it out like she had before. She licked his skin and closed her eyes.

It was irresistible.

Hold on . . . how could it be irresistible? Was he using his veil on her? Was Alejandro making her like it? No matter. She wanted, *needed*, more. Daria grabbed his forearm and latched her mouth to his wrist, licking and sucking.

His free arm tightened around her. "Daria." He let out a hard breath.

He didn't say anything more than that, but lust infused her name, letting her know he was feeling the desire, too.

Gently, he lowered her to the floor, keeping his wrist to her mouth and his arm around her waist. Daria was intensely conscious of the length of his hard body against hers. He cradled her in his lap.

Her body felt taut, ready to fire. His arm brushed her breast, and she whimpered. She didn't care about anything right now except her body's sudden intense demands. Daria let the blood fill her. It was as though she could feel it actually running through her veins, investigating her body, finding it suitable and infusing her.

"Stop. You're killing me," he groaned. "In more ways than one. You've had enough blood, Daria."

She relinquished her mouth's hold on his wrist. The wound seemed to close up immediately. In fascination, she watched it.

Alejandro pulled his hand away and she moved off his lap. He rolled onto his back with a guttural groan. Daria let her gaze travel from his head of thick black hair down the chiseled features of his face, to the rise and fall of that magnificent male chest, and to the obvious mound where his erection pressed against his pants.

She didn't know if it was an effect of the Choosing or if it was due to Alejandro's veil, but her mind felt folded under a thick cotton blanket. Daria fought for clarity, for logical reasoning, but it slipped through her fingers. All that remained in the wake of the fast departure of her senses were her body's needs.

Right now, her whole world was all about her overwhelming arousal and how Alejandro could take the sharp edge off of it. Somewhere in the back of her mind a whisper of remembrance lingered. She'd wanted to resist Alejandro, but the heavy spell of the Choosing trumped her former resolve.

She had to have him.

Daria shifted to her hands and knees and crawled up Alejandro's body. He opened his eyes and stared at her. Those dark brown orbs were heavy-lidded and appraising. Daria knew he wanted her as much as she wanted him. His muscles felt strung tight and he kept his hands carefully at his sides, as though he fought the impulse to touch her.

Daria wondered what she could do to make him lose that fight.

With confidence born of the knowledge of mutual attraction, she straddled him so he could feel the heat her sex radiated. One by one, she unfastened the buttons on his shirt, revealing his tan chest. She ran her fingers over his skin, tracing around his nipples.

He grabbed her wrists fast, making her gasp. "Daria, you're in the throes of the Choosing. What you're feeling is an effect of the chemical changes that are taking place in your body. I can't accept your invitation right now. I want to, don't get me wrong." He groaned. "*Dios*, I really do, but I can't."

Clarity emerged. She pulled her hands from his. He was right. He was so very, *very* right. What the hell was she doing? Then, as soon as it flickered, the thought was gone, leaving behind only her lust.

She traced one of his flat nipples lazily, and Alejandro shivered beneath her. Heat flared in his eyes. She wanted that heat to turn to fire, so she rotated her hips slowly, grinding her cunt down on his hard cock through their clothing.

"Daria," he rasped in warning. "Don't do that."

She only smiled. "Come on, Alejandro, I know you want to fuck me." Daria reached down between their bodies and rubbed his rock-hard shaft through his clothing. "You want to slide this cock deep inside me, just like you did so many years ago."

"I do." He flipped her and pinned her wrists to the floor on either side of her head. The hard press of his body wiped the smile from her face and heightened the need she felt. She squirmed beneath him, pressing up against the delicious, rigid side of his shaft. "I want to fuck you, but, Daria, please," he groaned. "You'd regret it in the morning and I don't want to be one of your regrets."

Despair filled her. He couldn't reject her now, not when this desperation for release seared her. She tossed her head and moaned, fighting the pleadings that crowded the back of her throat. She wouldn't beg him, but the need to do it felt almost irresistibly strong.

"Please." The word came out of her twisted, choked, desperate. "I need you, Alejandro."

Alejandro made a frustrated sound. His hand slipped between her thighs and found her clit. Methodically, he used the hard hem of her pants against the aroused bundle of nerves. Daria writhed on the floor beneath him, moving her thighs in time to his touch. "This will make you feel better."

"It's not enough. *More*," she moaned.

He hesitated, then his breath hissed out of him. "You're going to kill me with this, Daria." Alejandro undid the button and zipper of her pants and slid them down and off along with her panties. Cool air bathed her bare skin.

She thrust her own hands between her thighs, but he gently pushed them away. Dragging his strong fingers over her hot, flushed pussy, his breath hissed out of him. "You want my cock, here, baby, don't you?"

Daria bit her lower lip and nodded. *Oh, so bad . . .*

He slid a finger inside her, stretching muscles that hadn't stretched that way in a long, long time. With the pad of his index fingers, he rasped over her G-spot. Her breath shuddered out of her. "Just like that, *querida*? Is that how you want me to fuck you?"

"Yes," she breathed.

"Good. Spread those pretty legs of yours and let me make you come." His voice sounded ragged, hoarse.

She tossed her head as he added one more finger, stretching her muscles even more, but not as far as his cock would. He thrust in and out of her, making her body rock back and forth on the floor of the tent.

Her cunt was wet and eager, tingling with the erotic pleasure Alejandro bestowed on her. Daria was drunk on it, lost to it. She couldn't stop herself from digging her heels into the floor of the tent and moving her hips in time to his thrusts.

Daria's hands found the hem of her shirt and pushed upward,

finding her breasts so she could roll her nipples between her fingers. Her whole world was only about getting off right now, finding release for the intense sexual pressure the Choosing had built in her.

"Fuck, I can't take it," he growled. "I have to taste you."

He parted her legs and pushed her down, pinning her with strong hands to the floor and making her gasp. If she had wanted to move or get away, there would have been no way she could've. Her cunt was spread wide open for him, swollen and aroused with need.

Alejandro blew along the sensitive skin of her inner thigh and over her aroused cunt. Daria shuddered in delicious anticipation. Then Alejandro groaned and lowered his head, pulling her clit between his lips.

Her fingers found his hair and fisted. She watched his dark head bob between her thighs as he dragged his tongue up and down the length of her pussy. Alejandro acted like she was the best thing he'd ever had in his mouth.

He raised dazed eyes to hers. "You taste good. Sticky, hot, sweet heaven. Just like I remember." He removed one hand from her leg and slid two fingers deep inside her cunt, rasping along her G-spot as he rolled her clit back and forth with his tongue.

Orgasm swelled, receded . . . exploded. She tipped her head back and closed her eyes. Sweet release poured through her, drenching her cunt and making her spine bow. She gasped his name as it rippled through her. Alejandro licked over her as the waves eased and faded away, like he couldn't stop tasting her.

"I need more," she murmured, reaching for him after the waves of ecstasy had passed. "I need your cock inside me, Alejandro. I want you to fuck me."

Alejandro stared down at her sated pussy with carnal intensity. His fingers traced her labia, now red and swollen from his attentions, and she shivered and closed her eyes. "The process is faster than usual with you for some reason. It's almost time for it to start."

"What's *it*? What's going to start?" she murmured.

A tornado began in her mind.

She cried out. He released her and she rolled away from him, pulling herself into a little ball on the floor, not caring that she was half naked, not caring about anything at all beyond the sudden change in her mind and body.

Knowledge slammed into her, like a massive PComp download at the speed of light. Her body seemed to contract and then expand. Colors swirled through her mind, and sensations too numerous to register racked her body. She squeezed her eyes shut and lay panting under the onslaught.

Images from her childhood assaulted her mind's eye and battered her senses. The rubbery scent of her favorite doll. Her father's smiling face right before he'd died. The heavy weight of her mother's heirloom brooch in her hand. The sound of the crowd cheering the new class of Galactic Patrollers on graduation day.

The images faded, and she squeezed her eyes shut and fought the urge to vomit. Now she had the sensation of ascending, faster and faster. Wind ripped at her clothing and at her hair as she sped straight up through darkness with nothing to halt her progress. Even though she knew her body still lay on the floor of the tent, her mind had been launched like a rocket.

Something loomed before her, something tall and wide and shimmering in the black.

Daria screamed and arched her back as she hit it. The barrier shattered with a bright tinkling sound and crystal shards flew out from the impact. Her ascension slowed from the collision and, instinctively, she knew she had to speed it up somehow.

Writhing on the floor of the tent, she clawed out in front of her, groping the air in her search for more momentum. Another shining barrier glimmered up ahead. She knew she had to punch through it.

Panting, Daria used every last reserve she had to increase her velocity. *Almost there.* She was almost there, but she was so tired, so *tired . . .* She let her body relax.

"Fight, Daria," Alejandro whispered in her ear. "Don't give up. Don't give up now. Punch through."

Her eyes flickered opened, then closed again. He was right. She couldn't give in to the exhaustion now, but it was so hard. She felt like she'd been running in the desert for three hours. She couldn't take even one . . . more . . . step.

"Remember Julia," Alejandro whispered.

The name jolted Daria's body and an image of Julia filled her mind. Julia leaning across the lunchroom table, laughing, her badge glinting in the sunlight and her soft brown eyes crinkling at the edges with amusement. The next flash made Daria gasp—the sight of her friend sprawled on the floor, her eyes unseeing and glazed, the pupils blown.

Julia. She had to fight for her.

Daria sought way down in the recesses of her mind for her will. Her will had always been strong. One last burst of strength that poured pain through her body propelled her to the next barrier at an inching pace. She pounded on the wall until her fists in her mind's eye were bloodied and ravaged. She yelled and fought and kicked.

Finally, she punched her fist through the crystal barrier. A heartbeat later, it shattered.

The images flipped off like someone shutting down a commview and she went limp. Alejandro's warm body spooned her from behind and she was grateful for the support.

Apparently, that had been the *it*.

Her eyes fluttered open. The world looked so strange. She could see everything in minute detail if she concentrated hard enough. If she focused, she could pick out individual fibers in the tan-colored tent wall in front of her. If she concentrated very hard, she could hear each separate grain of sand blowing outside. She winced at the incredibly loud noise of it and ceased to put her attention there.

"Oh, my god," she breathed.

"Are you okay?" asked Alejandro.

"I–I don't know," she panted.

"Are you sleepy?"

"Yes." In fact, fatigue was starting to engulf her now. Her body relaxed involuntarily into exhaustion and it became difficult to keep her eyes open. Her body demanded rest. No matter the questions she had. No matter what her mind wanted. Darkness enveloped her.

"Did . . . I do it? Did I . . . push through the succubare?" she murmured as she lay on the edge of sleep.

His hand smoothed the hair back from her forehead. "We'll know when you wake up, *querida*." She floated away on the deep, sweet tones of his voice.

4

Daria roused and opened her eyes, immediately noting that Alejandro had laid her on the inflatable mattress in the center of the room and covered her with a light blanket. He'd dressed her again, too. Her head hurt and she felt weak, like she'd run thirty miles in the heat. She groaned, sat up, and looked around.

And suddenly felt much better.

Alejandro lay beside her, fast asleep. His black jeans were slung low on his hips with the top couple of buttons undone, revealing a little black hair and the jut of one lean hip. He was shirtless and one of his arms was thrown up over his head in a position that defined his biceps.

Smooth muscle rippled over the expanse of his chest and arms. A light dusting of dark hair tapered into a trail that went down his stomach, past the waistband of his jeans.

She really wanted to follow that trail.

Her gaze found the pulse in his throat and lingered there. Hunger started low in her belly and spread out. She imagined peeling his jeans off and stroking his cock to hardness, slipping her lips around his shaft, and rendering Alejandro helpless to her every carnal whim.

She envisioned him rolling her over, forcing her thighs apart and sinking his cock deep inside her, taking her slow at first and then faster and harder. She'd bite his throat as they came together and satisfy all her desires at once.

She stared hard at his pulse and her mouth watered.

Shit. What was wrong with her? Was the Choosing still affecting her? She winced, remembering how she'd acted last night. Man, she'd made a fool out of herself. She'd begged him to fuck her.

God, what he'd *done* to her! And she'd rolled there on her back, begging him for more.

Even though that radically slutty response seemed to have disappeared, the sight of him still caused her body to respond whether she wanted it to or not.

His dark eyes opened and he stretched like a cat, delineating every luscious muscle from the waist up. Daria looked away, trying to master herself.

"You're awake," he murmured. "Do you want sex or blood?"

Both, her mind screamed. *Both!* She looked back at him and desire tightened her body so hard she had to grip the blanket with both hands to keep from jumping him. Daria couldn't even form a sentence.

"Do you want blood at all?" he asked.

"God, yes." The answer poured from her lips before she could stop it.

"Good." He pushed up on his elbows. "You pushed through the succubare."

Relief washed through her as she remembered breaking through both the crystal barriers. "Whew. I didn't want to have to be a whore for the rest of my life to survive."

Alejandro held her gaze for a moment, a smile playing on his lips. He sat up and moved so close his body heat touched her. "Vampires are still very sexual, Daria. Sometimes we fuck for no reason at all."

She caught her breath at his proximity and her heart rate sped up.

"You put me through hell last night," he continued. "You were so tempting. I'm surprised I didn't give in to you." His voice was like dark, liquid silk pouring over her skin. It made her shiver.

Daria drew a breath and concentrated on gathering enough

strength to push away from him. How was she going to make it through this without letting him burn her?

"This is business, Alejandro. Remember? Business. I'm sorry about last night. I wasn't myself."

"I know and that's why I didn't take advantage." He brought his face close to hers. His hot, sweet breath stirred the fine hair around her face. He cupped her cheek in one callused hand and brushed his lips across hers deliberately. It was a gentle tasting, not a taking.

For one wildly insane moment she wished he would *take*. She wished he would crush her mouth to his and roll her beneath his body.

"Thank you," she whispered.

"Today you are yourself. So what's wrong with mixing a little pleasure with business?" he whispered against her mouth.

Daria inserted one hand in between their bodies and pushed him back . . . hard. She stood, and light-headedness washed over her, causing her to waver. Alejandro caught her and eased her down onto the mattress. A thousand pinpricks of pain assaulted her temples.

"You're weak from the Choosing, Daria. No fast moves or large bursts of strength. You need to give your body time to adjust to the changes it has gone through."

She fisted her hands against the pain and spoke through gritted teeth. "How *much* time?" She hated feeling so fragile, and right now she felt like prey to any animal that came along.

Alejandro shrugged. "You're still stronger than a human, but it will take a couple of days for you to start to feel comfortable in your skin again. It will take years for you to reach your full strength as a Chosen. Be patient."

She snorted. "Not one of my strong suits."

"Hey, be happy. You pushed through the succubare and you retained your sanity. You're one of the few unmarked humans to endure the Choosing and come out the other side a sane vamp."

"Yeah, I only have three hundred years until I lose my marbles now. I'll count my blessings tomorrow. I have room for procrastination."

Most Chosen went insane once they passed their third century. That seemed to be the breaking point for a person's mind when they lived so long. Most of them grew bored with existence. Became weary of watching those they loved pass on, the constant change of civilization, the beginning and end of wars. Eventually they started to feel the need for eternal rest, for escape, for renewal. All they saw stretching before them was a yawn of time filled with the same experiences over and over. That's why there weren't many old ones around.

Once a Chosen got to be about two hundred, their behavior grew erratic. Sexual appetites grew increasingly bizarre as they looked for new and different ways to amuse themselves. Some of them became sociopaths and serial killers. Still others took the path of monks and disappeared into the mountains of Darpong to become spiritual gurus.

Daria had heard the most common cause of death for the Chosen was suicide. Immortality wasn't all it was cracked up to be.

"Maybe you'll never pop, like Sante."

"Maybe he still will." She glanced at him. Sante was four hundred and hadn't gone insane yet. "What's your take on that?"

Alejandro shrugged. "I don't know how he's managed to retain his sanity. He's one of the few. However, his blood mother has not, and he remains unhealthily loyal to her."

Her hand fisted. "Personally, I don't care if he's sane or not. Either way, he's going down." She drew a shaky breath, calming herself before asking, "How do you think you'll handle immortality?"

He shrugged. "We'll see, I guess."

She chewed her lip, suddenly immersed in thought. "Yes, I will see, won't I? I might actually still be around three hundred years from now."

In that moment, Daria went just a little crazy herself.

She rubbed her eyes. "You have a shower in this sand trap? I need to bathe and change my clothes." Not to mention brush her teeth. It felt like she'd sleepwalked into the desert and gargled with sand.

"Hey, Daria, you know you're going to have to feed soon."

She suppressed a shudder at the thought. "Yeah, well, I'm going to put it off for as long as I can."

Alejandro shook his head. "It's dangerous for a new vampire to ignore blood hunger. You feel it, don't you?"

"Oh, you mean that persistent gnawing sensation in my stomach?" she shot back. "Yeah, I feel it." She started to stand, more carefully this time. "That was in the handbook, too."

Alejandro's hand clamped over her wrist like an iron band.

"Hey! Let go!"

Inexorably, he pulled her toward him, back onto the bed. "You have to feed *now*, Daria. I can't let you do anything else. It's very important. The Chosen who deny satisfaction of their blood hunger for too long can go into bloodlust. It's like going insane. Those vamps must be hunted down and killed by the GBC's peacekeepers. Was *that* in the handbook?"

Of its own accord, her gaze sought and fixed on the pulse in Alejandro's throat. The throbbing sensation in her stomach seemed to keep time with the beat of it. "You talk like the hunger is a beast within you that will devour you from the inside out if you don't keep it sated."

Even though she knew it was necessary for the fully Chosen, a part of her rebelled at the thought of taking blood. After all, this time it would be all her. She wouldn't have Alejandro's veil mischiefing her mind, making it sweet and irresistible.

The other part of her, the baby vampire part, she assumed, wanted it like nothing else. She tore her gaze away, but probably not quick enough to prevent Alejandro from recognizing her hunger.

"Your blood hunger *is* like a being that lives within you. One you must keep happy. If you don't, bad things can happen, especially to a brand-new vampire. Come on, Daria. Just give in to it. Stop fighting for once and take what you need from me." He drew her closer to him. "I'm willing to give."

"What about the synthetic blood in your fridge? Can't I drink that?"

He shook his head. "You're a new vamp, Daria. You need it straight from the vein, it's more powerful that way."

She looked back at his throat and the hunger roared through her body. Her head pounded with it. Hunger curled in her stomach and tightened like a fist. She'd been hungry before, but this was like nothing she'd ever experienced.

As much as she wanted to delay this initial encounter, she wouldn't be able to manage it. She licked her lips. The vampire part of her had won.

"Okay, but nothing sexual. Don't think of this as an invitation."

"As much as I might be tempted, I promise, Daria."

Another hunger pang pierced her stomach and she shifted on the mattress, her palm pressing against her abdomen. Alejandro took her hand and guided her to sit on his lap, straddling him. The position felt seriously intimate. She could feel the hard stab of his cock against her cunt. Suddenly, she was very thankful for the clothing that separated them.

Because he was *really* happy to have her in his lap.

And, *damn*. She was happy to be there, too.

He arched his neck, showing his jugular. Her canines lengthened into little points, as the manual said they would, at the mere sight of a feeding possibility. The sensation surprised her even though she'd been expecting it. "What do I do?"

"It's very simple. Bite me."

She blinked. "Then what?"

He let out a little laugh. "Uh, you start sucking. Trust me, instinct will do the rest."

The blood hunger bit into her stomach again and her vision swam. She had to feed, and she had to do it now. Daria took his head in her hands and lowered her mouth to his throat. She raked her teeth against his skin and felt him tense.

Her tongue stole out and licked the length of the vein, savoring the salty taste of him and feeling the prick of the stubble he needed to shave. Anticipation and arousal flushed her body and tingled between her thighs.

"What will it feel like for you?" she murmured, positioning her mouth over his vein. She didn't know how to control her veil yet, so there was no way for her to lessen the pain. "Will it hurt?"

"No, it will feel like sex." His voice was low, scratchy, and betrayed his arousal. "It will feel like sex, Daria, but without a climax. Just a tease."

She bit. Her fangs slid into his skin and found his vein like a heat-seeking missile. Sweet, hot blood coursed into her mouth, the combination of all the humans and succubare he'd fed from since he'd been Chosen.

It was ambrosia to her.

Alejandro's hands tightened on her waist and he let out a long, low groan. The sound of it went straight to her cunt, making her throb and grow slick. Alejandro's blood flowed into her, plumping her veins and satisfying her blood hunger.

Her eyelids fluttered closed at the ecstasy of it. Involuntarily, she thrust her hips forward, grinding herself against Alejandro's cock.

He gripped her waist, forcing her to cease the movement. "You're going to drive me insane," he bit off after he'd let out a stream of Spanish. "Stop that."

The ache in her stomach from the blood hunger eased little by little until it was completely gone. She released her hold on his throat and tipped her head back on a satisfied sigh. As much as she hated to admit it, she felt much better. Stronger.

She pushed off of him and stood. This time there was no wooziness at all. A hard flush enveloped her body as she glanced at Alejandro, who still reclined on the bed. Again she'd lost her control, and this time she didn't have the Choosing to blame.

"Next time try and unfurl your veil. You have one. You just need to learn how to use it."

She glanced at him. "I'm sorry. Did I hurt you?"

He shook his head and grinned. "You didn't *hurt* me, no."

"Can you tell if there's anything special about mine? I read that some vamps have different veil abilities."

"It's true different vamps have different flavorings to their veil.

Your specialized abilities probably won't develop for several years, though certain aptitudes may show themselves immediately."

"What are your secret ingredients?"

His fangs flashed as he grinned. "Pleasure. My bite gives more than the average amount."

Daria rolled her eyes.

"I also have the ability to tear down people's inhibitions with my veil. I don't advertise that skill."

"What do you mean?"

"My veil acts like a drug, or like alcohol on a human system. It frees the id, makes the receiver do exactly what they want to do, without the rational thought that would ordinarily hold them back."

"You can compel people? I see how you'd want to keep that on the lowdown."

He shook his head. "Not compel people. I can only free them of their inhibitions and make them do what *they* truly want to do. It's a rare ability, and only a handful of people know I possess it."

She considered him for a long moment. "Do not ever use that on me, Alejandro. I mean it."

"Most people get nervous when they find out I can do that. I felt you needed to know everything. I won't ever use it on you, Daria. Not without your permission. You have my word."

"Where's the shower?" she bit off.

"In the back."

"Thanks."

Daria gingerly made her way to the back of the tent and into the small bathroom. Catching her reflection in the mirror over the small travel sink, she stared. A small drop of blood dotted the corner of her mouth. Right before she licked it away, she caught herself. Her eyes widened as she realized that she had done it. She'd actually gone through with it. The blood drained from her cheeks.

She was a vampire. Immortality, whether she wanted it or not, was hers.

For a long moment, she gazed into her pale face in shock. Tears pricked her eyes. She ducked her head quickly and slammed on the tap to splash her face with water. She'd seen the tank at the back of the tent when they'd flown in. She didn't know how much water was in there and she didn't want to waste it.

After cupping her hands under the flow and taking a couple of gulps, she shut it off. Then she leaned her arms on the edge of the sink and listened to the *plink*, *plink* of water droplets dripping off her nose and hitting the porcelain. To her newly minted preternatural hearing, it sounded really loud. She closed her eyes.

What the hell had she done?

Even though she'd planned for this and had even fought for it, it seemed unreal to her now. Her thirst for revenge against Sante had been so much stronger than her will to live out her life as she'd been meant to. Her desire to take vengeance on him had eclipsed everything else, had driven her without thought or consideration. That was a frightening revelation.

How could she be capable of so much hatred?

She straightened and stared at her reflection in the mirror, wondering who it was she truly blamed, who it was she truly hated. Was it Sante?

Or was it herself?

5

Daria stepped out of her very short shower. The stupid thing had given her just a trickle of cold water. She stumbled on the canvas floor and caught herself on the edge of the sink. Gripping the rim of the cool porcelain, she closed her eyes for a moment. Her body felt weak, like she'd just recovered from a bad illness.

When she stepped away from the sink, she avoided catching her reflection in the mirror. Right now, she had to keep her mind on the job. The ABI had sent her to bring Ari Templeton home. That's what she had to concentrate on. When this was over, she could visit a psychiatrist for the rest.

Grumbling, she pulled a large white towel from the bar and dried herself. Voices from the room beyond the bathroom door made her fumble when she tucked in the flap of the towel over her left breast.

She padded to the door and pitched her new hearing outward past it. Alejandro's laughter boomed, and the sound of another other male laugh joined it.

Did they have neighbors way out here? She doubted it. She pushed the door open and stepped outside, really wishing she'd had the forethought to bring fresh clothing into the bathroom with her. Thinking straight hadn't been on her agenda after she'd taken Alejandro's blood. It probably hadn't been on her agenda for a while.

When she emerged from the bathroom, a man she didn't know stood from where he reclined in the jumble of oversized pillows on the floor. The man had shoulder length, wheat-colored hair and green eyes. He was as solidly built across the shoulders and chest as Alejandro, not someone she'd want to take on in a fight.

He was vampire. She could feel it with her shiny new vampire senses. Not only that, he felt old and strong. Apparently, this ability of sensing someone from afar had come with her new set of fangs.

She glanced at Alejandro. He still reclined on the bed, looking all shirtless and luscious. It was an eye-candy festival in here. Experimentally, she pitched her awareness toward him. He felt as strong as the other man to her, but not as old.

She wondered how she felt to them. Weak as a mewling kitten, maybe? Scowling at the thought, she narrowed her eyes at Alejandro.

Alejandro sat up when he saw her approach. An apprehensive look crossed his face.

Uh oh. She didn't like surprises, and it looked like she was about be socked in the gut with one that had light hair.

"Daria, this is Brandon Nichols." Alejandro motioned to the green-eyed man, who nodded slightly.

"Hey, Brandon." She cocked her head to the side and tried to look commanding, but that was hard to do when you were barefoot and wearing a towel. "What are you doing way out here?" She suspected strongly that she knew the answer to that.

Alejandro rolled off the side of the mattress and to his feet in a gesture that reminded her of a large cat. "I didn't tell you this last night because I didn't want to add to your stress, but the GBC has required he accompany us on this mission. He has a connection to Sante, so it wasn't that hard to work out. The GBC thought we could use some extra muscle and the knowledge of an older vampire. Brandon is over one hundred and fifty years old."

"Uh-huh." She tipped her chin at the two men. "So, what's your connection to Sante, Brandon?"

"We share the same blood mother, Maria Gillante." He had a charming English accent.

Daria raised an eyebrow. "That's a pretty damn good connection, Brandon, but I'll be honest with you. The fact that you share the same blood mother as Sante, the same woman who was the reason my best friend was killed, doesn't make me feel very warm and fuzzy." The words sounded hostile, but she didn't know any other way to sound at this point.

She glared at Alejandro. "It would have nice to have been told about this beforehand."

Alejandro sighed. "Look, Daria, this is a *joint* operation between the ABI and the GBC. The ABI didn't get to set all the rules. At the GBC's insistence, they agreed to Brandon being included. He brings skills we don't have to the table. You do want to get Sante, don't you?"

She gave him a withering look. "No, I wanted to grow a nice pearly white set of fangs for the hell of it."

Brandon glanced at Alejandro. "Uh, I'm just going to use the bathroom. Give you two a little time to talk." He pushed past her and headed toward the back.

Her pack leaned against the commview. She grabbed it and rifled through it for some clean clothes. "Why didn't you tell me about this last night?"

"Because I knew you'd react like this and you needed to be as relaxed as possible for the Choosing."

She turned and stared at him. "You don't know me that well. It's been seven years since we had anything to do with each other. I'm a completely different person now. There's no way you knew how I'd react."

"Yeah, okay, so I guessed." He grinned, and it infuriated her. "I guessed right, though, didn't I?"

Daria swore under her breath and turned back around to keep

searching through her bag for her clothing. She didn't want anyone else horning in on their operation. It would only complicate things.

~

ALEJANDRO'S mouth went dry as he watched Daria turn her back to him and drop the towel to her waist in order to pull on a bra and T-shirt.

His gaze followed the slender line of her nape down the sweet taper of her back to her narrow waist. *Dios*, he could see the curve of her breasts when she moved just right. The nipple he'd just been treated to a peek of was a pretty, suckable pink.

Dulce. Sweet. Just like he remembered it.

He wanted to walk over and cup her breasts in his hands, roll her nipples between his fingers. Wanted to do what she'd done to herself underneath her shirt the night before, while she'd been driving him insane as he tried not to fuck her right there on the floor. Last night she would've let him touch her, but if he tried now, he'd draw his hands back missing a couple digits. Although it might be worth the loss.

Even seven years later, he remembered her skin had been so silky and smooth under his hands and lips. He shuddered. Last night she'd been so fucking hot and tight when he'd teased her perfect little cunt with his fingers and tongue. The sexy moans and cries she'd made still echoed in his ears. Alejandro made fists as he remembered just how good she'd tasted, all spicy sweet. Her clit so responsive against his tongue . . . His fingers literally itched to touch her right now.

He looked away and rubbed a hand over his face, feeling stubble. He needed a shower and shave. "Daria, I had no say in the GBC's decision to include Brandon, but he'll bring benefits to the mission. He won't be a detriment."

"He'll have to convince me of that."

Keeping the towel around her waist, she slipped on a pair of white cotton panties, then dropped the towel and slid on a pair of blue jeans. There was heaven in the curve of that ass. He felt his cock stiffen.

She seemed completely unconscious of her sexual allure. It didn't even register that she was changing in front of a man who wanted nothing more than to pull her over to the bed so he could cover her body with his and kiss every inch of her, concentrating on that sweet, rounded ass and the smooth skin at the small of her back.

He'd lay her facedown, nudge her thighs apart, and press his cock against her, but not enter her. Not right away. He'd tease her nipples, lick and bite her throat until she pushed up and back. Only then would he grab her hips and cram his cock inside her tight cunt, take up a fast and hard rhythm to drive them both to bliss. *Fuck.*

Didn't she know she was driving him crazy?

"Don't like complications." Daria turned. "Alejandro?"

"Yes?"

"Did you just hear anything I said?"

"Uh."

She waved a hand dismissively at him and pulled on a pair of white socks and some heavy, black dune-biker boots. "Whatever. We're stuck with him, so that's that."

"There's that positive attitude I love about you," Alejandro shot back.

The woman could drive him insane in more ways than one.

The bathroom door opened and Brandon walked out. "What Alejandro didn't tell you was that I turned against Maria long ago. I left her right about the time she started keeping blood slaves in her territory because I was against the practice. It caused a rift between us. Sante stayed loyal to her, but I went back home to England and eventually started working for the Body. Sante has no idea I started working for the GBC. That makes me an excellent participant in this operation."

"How's that? It sounds like Sante wouldn't want you anywhere near him, let alone give you entrance into the exclusive community of the Shining Way," Daria reasoned. "I mean, he's still loyal to Gillante, seems like he'd be a little pissed at you."

"You're right that he's angry." Brandon smiled. "That's exactly why he was more than happy to grant me entry. Even though Sante has left Maria's territory, he's still close to her and he's miffed at me for turning against her. He's just itching to tell me off. We used to be close, he and I, before I left for England."

"Ah, England." Daria draped the towel over the commview and turned. "How are the merry ol' Brits these days?"

"Bloody overcrowded like everywhere on Earth," Brandon answered with a grin. "We still make excellent tea, however."

Daria smiled and extended her hand. "Welcome aboard, I guess."

Brandon shook her hand. "I've heard nothing but the highest praise of you from the GBC and from Alejandro. You're supposed to be a hell of an agent."

"Thanks, but at the moment, I only feel hellish. The Choosing walloped the piss out of me."

"You'll feel that way for a couple days."

"So they say," Daria muttered as she ran a hand through her damp hair. "I wish Alejandro and I could have had our party a little sooner than last night. I could've used some time to adjust before we headed to the Shining Way, but the schedule is tight. Everything's been happening really fast since Ari was taken. No time to lose."

Brandon turned to Alejandro. "We need to coordinate our arrivals. When are you two leaving here?"

"Later, *tio*. Daria needs to rest a little. The deadline is five a.m. Anyone on the list to be admitted who shows up after that time doesn't get in." The Shining Way grouped all the new members to arrive on the same day. Alejandro imagined there were likely more than just the three of them.

"Okay. I'll go in before the two of you."

Alejandro nodded. "Sounds good."

"The GBC told me no firepower. Is that true?" asked Brandon, looking from Alejandro to Daria.

Daria shrugged. "It's not like we can waltz in with a lot of weapons. That would look pretty suspicious. Hell, we can't even take in PComps."

"We can try to take our pulsers," said Alejandro. Everyone carried pulsers these days. "But my money is on the guards confiscating them."

"We're going to have to be our own weapons," answered Daria.

"This isn't going to be easy," said Brandon, "but I'm glad the GBC convinced the ABI that blasting their way in wasn't a good idea."

Daria walked to the edge of the bed and sat down. Alejandro watched her rub her palms on her jeans. She looked like she needed a few more hours of sleep, but he couldn't give it to her.

"That was just misguided," she said on a tired sigh. "The ABI would've had to use an incredible amount of firepower to simply break past the barriers of the Shining Way. It would've been like laying siege to a castle. Sante would've probably just found a way to smuggle Ari out in the melee, anyway."

"If she's still alive," said Brandon.

"If she's even there," Alejandro answered. "We don't know if she's being kept there yet. No one is even sure Richard Templeton's suspicions are true."

"Yeah," replied Brandon. "Imagine the scandal if the ABI sent forces blasting into someone's private property on a suspicion that turned out to be false. Sante would have a bloody sweet lawsuit."

"And the Organization for the Fair Treatment of Chosen would have a field day. They're always looking for a reason to accuse the ABI and human law of bigotry."

Daria nodded. "The bottom line is that the ABI knows now this isn't a job for an elephant. It's a job for three little mice."

"Hey, are you calling me a mouse?" joked Brandon.

"I can't believe she just called herself a mouse," muttered Alejandro.

"Yep, we're three lethal little mice," Daria answered as she rubbed her temples as though she had a headache. "Sante won't know what hit him."

The objective was to capture Sante alive if possible, take him dead if not. Alejandro suspected Daria might be looking less for a way to take Sante alive than dead. Considering all she'd sacrificed so far to get close to him, Alejandro wondered how she'd act when they finally had him in their control.

"Yeah, well, we don't kill Sante unless we have to," said Alejandro. "Remember, Daria, that's the deal."

She paused in the massage of her temples and looked up at him. Her eyes glittered. "I know what we're supposed to do, Alejandro."

"Anything we do, it's going to have to be subtle," said Brandon. The GBC and the ABI both agree that this is an operation that requires delicacy," said Brandon. He smiled. "You don't seem very subtle, Daria. No offense."

Daria dropped her hands to her lap and laughed. "Brandon, we've only just met and you already know me well."

~

DARIA staggered at the entrance of the tent and nearly fell. She went down on one knee and gritted her teeth. "I'm so weak," she bit off. Strong hands helped her to her feet.

"It's all part of being newly Chosen, Daria," said Alejandro. Both their packs were slung over his shoulder. "Consider yourself mine now, under my protection. I'll teach you what you need to know."

Was he deliberately trying to piss her off, or was he being sincere? She fought the growl in her throat and blew out a breath instead. If it was a goad, taking it was probably just what he wanted. Shit, she hated this, having to rely on someone else.

"I have a headache and the drug patch I put on isn't working." She bit the inside of her lip until she nearly drew blood at the whine in her voice.

"You're not human anymore, Daria. Of course it's not working." Alejandro's voice was gentle.

Dread curled in the pit of her stomach with the reminder. He was right; she wasn't human anymore. She'd forfeited her humanity. Forfeited it to get Sante. If she could attain that goal, maybe it would be worth it.

She pushed past him and walked into the small tent that housed their dune bikes. "Come on, let's get going."

Daria and Alejandro secured their packs, donned their protective gear, and mounted their bikes. Brandon had left not long after he'd arrived. He'd headed to the dome right after midnight and was probably already in.

Alejandro and Daria revved the vehicles' engines to life and flew off in puffs of sand, leaving the tents behind.

The moon hung like a lavender ball in the beautiful Darpongese sky. She'd never seen a more stunning night sky than she'd seen out here in the desert reaches of the Logos Territory, except maybe when she took the shuttle from Earth to the Angel System and back.

She should get used to the night sky since she wouldn't be seeing blue sky, not the *real* blue sky, anyway, ever again. Too bad, it had been too long since she'd seen the blue skies of Earth.

If all went well with this mission, maybe she could go back there on leave and visit her mother. She'd have to introduce the topic of her Chosen-ness slowly. Her mother would have a heart attack, thinking her daughter had joined one of those strange vampire cults.

They were the fad now. Simple humans—fed on the romanticism of the Chosen and hoping for immortality—joined them. Most of the Chosen themselves scorned the cults. They would Choose only those marked for it at birth, and in most cases no others. There was too much risk that unmarked humans would not be strong enough to breach the succubare stage. Now Daria could see why so many did not.

Even though vampires fed from the succubare and therefore needed them, the population was too large. Succubare sex workers littered the galaxies, feeding off their clients' lust and orgasms to survive.

Daria shivered. She'd been lucky to avoid that fate, though maybe what she'd done was even worse.

Alejandro angled his bike toward the east, and she followed suit. They weren't far from the protected space encircling the compound of the Shining Way. It lay in an area monitored heavily by armed guards and was sheltered under a dome that deflected air missiles. Purportedly, within the dome was a self-contained society of Chosen modeled to mimic Earth. It was probably the closest the Chosen would ever get to their own space.

Sante had amassed a fortune in the four hundred years he'd been alive. Many of the older vampires, if they were intelligent enough, had managed to make a lot of money through various means over the centuries. From her research, Daria knew that Sante dealt in antiquities on the side and had made quite a few good investments over the years.

His blood mother had even more money stashed away from her shady dealings. According to the information the ABI and GBC had, she'd helped him finance the construction of the Shining Way. The damn place was built from the blood of veil-addicted humans. Daria's glove-encased hands gripped the handle of her bike. It was time Sante paid his dues.

Silver glinted in the distance and Daria watched no less than five dune bikes approach them.

Halt. Stay where you are, commanded a voice within Daria's mind.

6

SHE jolted in the bike's seat, startled by the intrusion. *Shit*. She'd read about the vampiric ability of mind-speak in the handbook, but actually experiencing it was something else entirely.

Alejandro came to a stop, letting his dune bike hover above the sand. Daria pulled up on his side.

Sante's borderguards drew close, forming a circle around them. They all wore black leather uniforms and solid black helmets. All she could see were their mouths, drawn in tight, straight lines, and their strong, masculine chins.

There was one woman, as far as she could tell. One delicate chin among them. One slender body under the leather. The pulser she held looked as threatening as the rest.

Pulser fire would only kill a Chosen if the setting was on synap-cease, or if the pulse stream was very strong and the vamp very weak. If the pulse stream was set on low, Daria bet it would still hurt . . . a lot. All the weapons were aimed at Alejandro's and Daria's heads. She felt naked without anything to aim back.

"Put your hands up," one of them ordered. "Make any move besides raising your arms toward the sky and we'll fire."

Oh, good. The games have begun. She eyed the line of muzzles uneasily. If the pulsers were on the highest setting, she was probably the only vamp weak enough to be killed by the blast. Alejandro would likely only be knocked out, since the guards were a good distance away from them.

"What business do you have here?" the one in front of them asked.

"My name is Alejandro Martinez. Christopher Sante and I go way back. He's expecting Valerie"—he motioned to her with his elbow—"and I to arrive this morning. We should be on a list somewhere, guys. Watch those pulsers, okay? We're all friends here."

The guards' expressions didn't change as far as Daria could see. Not one of them cracked a smile. Apparently, they didn't think they were friends.

All the guards remained silent. Daria assumed they were communicating mentally with someone at the compound on some vampiric wavelength she wasn't on.

Finally, the first one spoke. "Both of you, lower your arms, take off your gloves, and hold your hands toward me, palms out."

They both did as requested.

The guard came closer and held up a small black box she recognized as a standard issue identification kit, an Identi Box. He pulled the long sensor free from the kit. He aimed it first at the pads of Alejandro's fingers, then at hers. The sensor emitted no light, nor any visible stream. It slowly scanned her fingerprints from a good five feet away. She felt a faint pressure on her skin.

Daria's fingerprints had been altered during her surgery. Valerie Hollan, her alias, would come up as an out of work waitress living in a community hostel in downtown New Chicago on Angel One. "Valerie" had been born in the Angel System and had lived there her whole life in relative poverty. Her blood father, Alejandro Martinez, had recently Chosen her and she was registered as a newly made vampire with the GBC.

The little light on top of the Identi Box blinked green. "All right.

We have confirmation," said the guard. "Follow us." The black-swathed sentries put their weapons away.

The guards powered up their bikes and sped off toward the horizon. Alejandro and Daria did the same. *These guys have lots of personality,* Alejandro said to Daria telepathically on their own private communication wavelength.

Yeah, I noticed, she thought back at him.

Telepathy was nifty, but she'd have to be careful she didn't broadcast thoughts she didn't want Alejandro to hear.

She'd have to be even more careful that she didn't broadcast her thoughts to any of the vamps inside the compound. That could be disastrous. She'd been instructed in how to shield her mind and she felt locked down tight, but sending thoughts still made her nervous. There had been no way to practice before she'd been Chosen and there'd been no time afterward.

Soon the dome of the compound came into view, glowing blue black in the moonlight. It was enormous, much larger than Daria had expected. The guards flew into a tiny opening at the base of the dome and Alejandro and Daria followed them.

Daria choked back a gasp when the dune bike cleared the doorway. It was daylight here.

Beside her, Alejandro visibly jerked in surprise. A Chosen's pupils never dilated, so she knew his reaction wasn't from the sudden influx of sunlight. Likely it was because he hadn't seen a day—even a vampsafe simulated one—in nearly seven years.

Lush green grass spread across the ground, dotted through with many different colorful flowers. Stone walkways and streets dotted the thriving greenery. The walkways led to a series of white buildings with high, arched windows and tall doorways. She looked up and the sight stole her breath. Blue sky with soft, scudding white clouds spread across the underside of the dome.

Earth sky during the day.

Hadn't she just been thinking it'd been too long since she'd seen the blue sky of Earth? Here it was, right in the middle of the Darpong Sector. No travel agent needed. No monthlong hyper-sleep journey on a high-speed ship to get you to a polluted, overpopulated planet that gave you only glimpses of this kind of sky on a good day.

She'd known that the Shining Way had this kind of artificial reality since the vamps who'd left this place had spread the tale. Experiencing the extent of it was another thing. There were a few corporations that had campuses like this. She'd been in them, but they weren't nearly this realistic. Daria had never dreamed Sante would have the resources to create this kind of state-of-the-art authenticity.

Where was Sante coming up with the cash for this?

She slanted a look at Alejandro. She wanted to ask him if he was suddenly as suspicious as she was, but she didn't trust her telepathic ability enough yet. Anyway, Alejandro was probably still too daystruck to be thinking that way.

The first guard hovered near them, but the others sped away, out the doorway and back into the dark desert wastes of the Logos Territory. The remaining guard lowered his bike onto a wide paved parking pad and Daria and Alejandro followed suit.

The guard dismounted and removed his helmet, revealing a blond head of hair and a face with vibrant blue eyes and a square jaw. "Leave your gear here. Follow me," he said and walked toward the largest of the structures, the one to which it seemed all the paths led.

The building appeared to be the central point of the campus. It was long, white, and rectangular, topped with a white dome. Tall, shimmering blue black windows lined the sides. Skylights were set in along the sloping length of the roof. Looking around, Daria realized that was true of all the buildings—better to soak in the fake sunlight, she'd make a guess.

Daria and Alejandro divested themselves of their helmets and leather jackets and followed. Daria's boots crunched over the pebbles that comprised the path. As she walked, she studied the perfectly manicured green grass and the well-maintained buildings that scattered the area. It was like Earth, only without the overpopulation and the pollution that came with it.

Earth, but five hundred years ago. To an Angel settler, even one used to Angel One, it was paradise.

They approached the white-domed building. The guard pushed open the heavy wood and metal double doors and they entered. The floor and walls were made of blue black marble, and the ceiling arched high above their heads. It reminded her of a church.

A large fountain dominated the entry room, overflowing with pale emerald water. It looked unpurified, chock-full of the minerals that gave it that distinctive shade. The pure drinking water was one of the reasons that Logos Territory had been the place the settlers had decided on two hundred years ago. It looked as if Sante had found an underground water reserve to service the dome residents.

Daria looked up. The arched ceiling was painted to look like the night sky—dark blue and scattered through by glittering silver stars. Aside from the fountain in the middle, the room was devoid of ornamentation. With the polished blue black marble walls and floor, much more decoration would have been overkill anyway. The sound of Daria and Alejandro's bootheels on the floor echoed throughout the chamber as they walked.

A door leading to what Daria presumed was the main part of the building whined open. A man with shoulder-length glossy black hair and deeply tanned skin entered, followed by five men who looked like muscle. More guards.

The black-haired man smiled as he approached them. He shook Daria's hand first, then Alejandro's. "Valerie, Alejandro, welcome to the Shining Way. I'm Carlos Hernadez. I'll be helping to orient you to your new surroundings."

Daria smiled and nodded like a good little Valerie would. Carlos Hernadez. He was one of Sante's inner circle, one of his most trusted. No one knew his age for certain, but it was reckoned to be close to two hundred. His records had come up clean, but she didn't like this man.

She had an instant gut reaction. When she tuned into him he felt really strong. Her intuition said *dangerous* and *sleazy*.

Carlos clasped his manicured hands in front of him. "Please. Remove your weapons."

She held her arms up and out. "We didn't come in with any weapons."

"We thought about bringing our pulsers, but figured you guys would search us and take them away," said Alejandro.

"You were correct." Carlos glanced at the guards and flicked his wrists toward them both. The guards moved toward them. "I believe you are unarmed, but please understand that we must still search you."

Three guards surrounded Alejandro. Two others approached her. Their eyes seemed to say, *fresh meat.*

Daria braced herself for the inevitable. The guards grabbed her roughly, hustled her up to a wall and pressed her face-first against it. Her breath *oof*ed out of her at the impact. She gave a bark of laughter. Now she knew how her prisoners felt. "This is quite a welcome, Carlos."

"I do sincerely apologize. It's necessary to preserve the tranquility of the Shining Way," he answered.

He *really* didn't sound sorry.

Daria couldn't tell what they were doing to Alejandro since her face was becoming so intimately acquainted with the wall. The guards slapped her palms flat on the cold marble and one of them moved behind her and kicked her feet apart. The other stood to the side and looked on.

The guard's hands were all business as he patted down her arms, but when they dropped to her waist and slid up, his motions slowed. All of a sudden, her mind was all on her own body and her personal space, instead of what was going on with Alejandro.

The guy searching her pressed his body up against hers. His hot breath stirred the small hairs at her nape as he slid his hands up way too slowly over her breasts.

The bastard is feeling me up.

Panic and rage filled her as he groped her breasts, running his fingertips over her nipples. Then he dipped down with one hand and slipped between her spread thighs to rub her clit through the fabric of her pants. Daria fought the urge to bring her elbow back into his face, turn around, and nail him in the balls. That's what *she* wanted to do, but what would *Valerie* do?

"Hey, I'm not your girlfriend," she snapped and tried to turn around. The guards forced her back into position. She struggled against them, but they held her tight.

Horror choked her for a moment as she fought for control over herself. Even if she fully let loose on these guys, she could sense they were far stronger than she was. Especially now, since she'd barely cut her new fangs.

7

From across the room, Alejandro watched Daria protest the guards' treatment and try to turn. Both men grabbed her arms and pushed her up against the wall. When she tried to twist away from them, they struggled to control her.

The guards near Alejandro hadn't touched him yet, so he stalked toward the assholes harassing Daria, but didn't get far. The men surrounding him grabbed him by his upper arms and wrists. He jerked free of one, only to have the hands of another clamp down on him.

Enraged, he pulled away from all of them. They scuffled. Alejandro brought his fist up fast and hard and punched one of the guards in the mouth, bloodying him.

"Zap him," said Carlos.

Pain assaulted his head as one of the guards hit him with a low pulse stream. He went straight down on his knees, stunned. The world went dim for a moment. The guards pushed him down, and he hit the floor, hard, on his stomach. One of the guards wrenched his hands behind him and cuffed them at the small of his back. As an extra torment, the guards held him down so he couldn't thrash.

Apparently, they wanted him conscious, or they would've used a higher setting. They'd effectively prevented him from aiding Daria, that was for sure.

Well, hell.

Alejandro glanced at Daria for a moment, but just for a moment because in this position it was hard to hold his head up. The guards held her firmly by her upper arms, but the assholes weren't fondling her now. "Are you okay, Valerie?"

"I'm fine." Cold rage, tightly restrained, seemed woven through those two syllables.

"Bastard," Alejandro swore at Carlos. He pushed up, trying to dislodge the strong grips of the guards. "You let them hurt a hair on her head, and I'll have your throat for dinner."

Carlos clucked his tongue. "Don't make threats when they're uncalled for. She's fine, Emanuel. That's your true name, isn't it? Emanuel Alejandro Martinez?"

"I'll judge whether or not she's fine."

"Emanuel, I don't want her hurt, either. If I don't want her hurt, she won't be."

"Call me Alejandro."

"I prefer your first name. You were born on Earth in the country of Spain, isn't that correct? Madrid is your city of naissance and where you spent your childhood. Your parents were both unmarked and live there still."

"Yes."

"Your father is a commview repairman. Humble beginnings, Emanuel."

Alejandro stilled for a moment under the restraining grasps of the guards, fear flickering through him. How deeply had they researched them? If the GBC's protections for their peacekeepers hadn't held up, he was dead. If the ABI hadn't provided a convincing background for Valerie, so was Daria.

Alejandro grunted as one of the guards decided to press his knee into the base of his spine. "There's nothing wrong with humble beginnings."

"No, not at all. I come from humble beginnings, myself. Many of us do." Carlos walked toward Alejandro and paced slowly in front of him. His boots clicked with every step. "You are young," Carlos continued. "So very young, yet exceptionally strong for a vampire who is only seven years of age. Your blood mother is Lucinda Valentini, yes? She holds a GBC seat and a territory in the Barand sector. An Italian by birth, I believe. She offered you a coveted place in her inner circle, but you declined."

"That's right."

He clucked again. That was really starting to get on Alejandro's nerves. "That's not very loyal, is it? Or smart. Lucinda is a very powerful Chosen. So, I wonder, is it a problem with loyalty that you have?" He leaned down near Alejandro's face. "Or brains?"

Alejandro felt his jaw lock. "Neither," he ground out.

He straightened. "Really? Then tell us the reason. We want to comprehend."

Rage seared his veins. He gritted his teeth, then snapped, "Rampant and resilient heterosexuality."

"Ah. That I understand." Carlos laughed. "You may have to explain it to your lady friend, however. She looks confused."

"Let us go and I will."

Carlos ignored him. The clicking of his boots on the marble began again. "So you left Lucinda to return to Danpong City where you work in personal security. Or, at least, you did until you decided to bring your new love here to live." The clicking of Carlos's heels stopped in front of Daria. "Your girlfriend's name is *Valerie*."

"Not so nice to meet you," Daria replied.

"Who is even younger than Alejandro, a newborn infant, in fact, and has a mouth on her that, in my day, would have been very unbecoming on a lady."

"Yes, and I come from New Chicago. Humble beginnings. Yadda, yadda. Can we cut the drama and get on with whatever it is we're doing here? I'm getting bored."

Silence.

Daria *really* needed to learn to control her mouth.

Alejandro wrenched his neck to see what was happening. Carlos stood in front of a very angry Daria. She was probably scared. When Daria was frightened, she became infuriated.

Carlos tipped his head back and laughed. "Fine," he said finally. He stepped away. "You're lucky I find your insolence amusing, Valerie."

The guards slammed her back up against the wall, which had Alejandro struggling again. These assholes wanted to play patty-cake with him while Daria was being felt up against her will. He hated being over here and unable to do anything about it. If they'd been human men, she might have been able to throw them off on her own, but they were Chosen and she was weak right now.

Hands tapped down his arms and legs, then up his torso. Alejandro fought them for every inch, kicking and using his elbows. Then, they simply uncuffed him and backed away. He lay sprawled on the smooth marble floor for a heartbeat, stunned that he didn't have to fight anymore.

"Get off me!" he heard Daria yell and then a thump of flesh meeting flesh and an *oof*.

Alejandro shot to his feet. Daria stood unrestrained near one of the guards who'd searched her. Her newly brown eyes shimmered and burned with anger. The offending guard leaned up against the wall behind them, holding a hand to his solar plexus.

He slid his gaze down Daria's body. She was clearly pissed, but seemed fine physically. She looked a little unsteady, but maybe that was because she'd just expended far more energy than any new vamp should.

Alejandro swung around to stare at Carlos. "I don't know what game you're playing here, but I want it understood now that this woman is mine. No else is to touch her. We don't stay at the Shining Way unless that is *comprehended* right here and now."

Carlos blinked slowly. "Living here in paradise is an honor for any Chosen, Emanuel. If you don't like the way we do things, you can leave."

"Doesn't seem much like paradise to me," said Daria. She'd wound her arms over her chest in a protective gesture.

"It was a test for you, Valerie," said Carlos. "You are maybe a week or so old, correct? According to our records you were an unmarked human, yet you got past the succubare stage. That's a very rare thing. We needed to check your strength."

"Why can't you just feel my strength from a distance?" she asked.

Carlos smiled. "That can be misleading. Don't you agree that strength is often something more mental than physical? It's in the mind, in the *will*. I suspected you had an exceptionally strong will, and you do. Sometimes, even weak people, when put in a situation they find untenable, become strong. You're newly Chosen, yet you threw off Austin." He motioned to the injured guard. "He's not easy to deter when he's allowed to frisk an attractive woman. I sent him to you for that very reason. I wanted to see how you'd react."

Alejandro's gaze sought Austin. Right now, he was the source of all of his frustration and anger. No one tried to stop Alejandro's stalk toward him. Austin watched his progress across the chamber with growing horror in his blue eyes.

Alejandro grabbed him by the front of the shirt, pulling him away from the wall. Satisfaction coursed through Alejandro as he sent him to the floor with a punch so hard it made pain flare through his hand and up his arm. Austin groaned and fell silent.

He turned and crossed the space separating himself from Carlos and got right up in the other man's face. He heard noise at his back and knew the guards had moved in to flank him, in order to protect the older vamp. Carlos held up a hand, telling them to stay back.

Alejandro's fangs lengthened as they did when he was exceptionally pissed off and he let a growl trickle through his lips. "I never, *ever* want Valerie to be tested like that again." He turned and stabbed everyone in the room with a cold stare. "Understand? Back off and leave us alone."

Carlos smiled. "That's the reaction we were looking for from you, Emanuel. You were also tested."

Alejandro spoke in a deceptively quiet voice. "Pull that shit again and I'll give you a reaction you'll never forget."

Carlos held his gaze for a long moment, still smiling, though it didn't reach his eyes. The look on Carlos's face was more threat than anything else. "Gordon, show them to their quarters," he said finally. "I think they've had enough for one day."

Alejandro turned away, seeking Daria. One of the taller guards Alejandro presumed was Gordon motioned for them to follow. Neither Daria nor Alejandro looked back as they left the building.

Once outside, he looked up into the "sky" and saw that the sun was going down. At least, whatever it was that passed for a sun. It seemed a little late for that, if they were trying to keep pace with Darpong. Obviously they could make their own rules in a domed environment.

"I think that went well," Daria muttered under her breath as they followed Gordon down one of the narrow pathways that led to a round building that looked like an apartment complex with only one floor.

Alejandro wondered if Brandon had been "tested" upon his arrival, too. "Are you okay?"

"I feel like I need a long, hot shower and a strong bar of soap, but other than that, I'm okay, I guess. The asshole just groped me. I've been groped before. I feel really tired, though."

She should be feeling tired. New vampires didn't have energy to burn. "They were putting us in our place," he answered. "Making sure we know where we stand."

"Waaaaay down at the bottom."

"Right now we're their toys, but we don't stand at the bottom. Not anymore. *Mierda*, I know the drill. It's like a dog pack. You have to show your strength to get any respect. We just showed strength."

Still simmering with rage over Austin, he barely noticed that they'd entered the building and had come to a stop in front of a door.

Gordon unlocked the door and handed the key to Daria. "Here's where you'll be staying for now. The walls are soundproofed for your privacy. There should be enough towels for you. There's toothpaste and soap, everything you should need. Return to Sante Hall tomorrow morning for your initiation ceremony."

"*Sante* Hall?" asked Daria. "Was that where we just were?"

"Yes. Return there in the morning, undergo the initiation ceremony and you'll finally truly be a part of our community."

"We'll be there," Alejandro answered.

Gordon nodded his head and even smiled. "Welcome. We're glad to have you here."

After Gordon left, Alejandro pushed the heavy door open and they entered the chamber. A large, four-poster bed stood in the middle of the room. The opposite side of the apartment was a wall with windows and French doors that opened into a lush, Earthlike garden. Leaf-bedecked vines snaked their way through the open window and curled all the way around the walls of the room. A small beverage panel that would dispense water, coffee, and other refreshments was built into one wall. The place was small, but beautiful.

"Oh, God," breathed Daria. She whirled toward him and thought, *Doesn't this seem a little suspicious to you? Where's he getting the money to do this?*

Maybe we can find out while we're looking for Ari. Maybe there's more going on here that the ABI and GBC would be interested in.

Without a word, Alejandro and Daria instantly started exploring the room, checking for listening devices. It was unlikely there were any, since vampires and succubare could communicate on private telepathic wavelengths. It made bugging a room a waste of energy.

Still, they might have the room under surveillance since Alejandro was a former patroller. There was reason for Sante to be suspicious of him.

Alejandro stood from checking the base of the bedside table. "There's nothing. It's safe to speak in here." He pushed his hand through his hair and winced. His hand would be black and blue soon, but would heal quickly enough. It was a small price to pay for the satisfaction he felt.

She walked to him and took his hand in hers. "Was that guy's face made of steel?"

"No, I just hit him really hard."

She traced a finger over the top of his hand. "This is going to hurt."

"Vamps heal fast. It'll be fine by morning."

She stroked her fingers along his palm and the tingling sensation of her touch went straight through his body. He fought the urge to push her back onto the bed. Hell, they'd needed to get their scent over each other anyway. He could think of a number of different ways he'd love to do that.

She raised an eyebrow. "By the way . . . *I'm your woman*? Could you get any more macho than that, Alejandro? The force of all that testosterone you released in there nearly knocked me over."

"I had to assert myself, Daria. Paint some boundaries for them."

A huge boundary was Daria. No one was going to be able to cross that one without making him dangerously crazy. He hoped he'd made that clear to Carlos.

"You had to piss on your fire hydrant?"

"Kind of. It's like I said on the way in. Unless you want to be everyone's little froufrou boy, you've got to let them know up front that you're not going to take any shit."

Her eyes shone. "You learned that in Valentini's territory?"

"I learned a lot from her."

Was that jealousy that flared across her face? *Interesting . . .*

"Thank you for defending my honor, kind sir," she purred and batted her eyelashes. "You're my hero."

He curled his hand around hers and pulled her flush up against him. Twining his arms around her, he dropped his mouth to her throat and laid a kiss there. He groaned as he inhaled the scent of her skin.

"How ever will you repay me?" he growled and lightly nipped the place where her shoulder met her neck.

She shuddered against him, and the faint scent of her arousal teased his nose. With a little sigh, she rubbed her cheek against his upper chest. "Maybe I can figure something out," she said in a breathless voice.

Well. This was a nice change.

Someone knocked on the door and Daria backed away from him. *Maldita sea! Damn it.*

"Come in," Alejandro shouted, trying really hard to keep the snarl out of his voice.

Gordon stuck his head in. "Your bags." He dropped their packs and jackets on the floor near the door and disappeared.

When Alejandro turned back around, Daria was out in the small garden. She stood in the center of the greenery, hugging herself and looking like she was deep in thought.

~

DARIA studied the small, enclosed area. She guessed every apartment had one of these flourishing gardens. Ivy climbed the stone walls and flowers bloomed in profusion. A small table and two chairs stood in the corner, flanked by two statues of angels reaching their little porcelain arms toward the sky.

A small bird landed on the top of the wall and chirped at her. "Wow," she breathed in amazement. It took off with a soft flutter of wings.

Above her head, the twilight deepened to early evening darkness much quicker than was natural. The falseness helped destroy the magic of this place a little for her.

Life under this dome was very seductive, even for her. It had to be even more so for a Chosen who hadn't had the sunlight on his skin for years.

She watched as faint little stars began to twinkle. Somewhere under the dome, Sante could be looking up into that same artificial sky this very moment. It brought home how close she was to him now.

She walked to the wall and reached out to brush her fingers across the ivy. Amazing. *Perplexing.* This dome probably could be called paradise, but it wasn't. It couldn't be. Financed and run by Sante, it had to be more like hell than heaven. They just had to uncover the reason for this place. It had to benefit Sante in some way. He was not an altruistic person. That was clear enough. He was a cold-blooded murderer who would do anything to get what he wanted.

Anything.

Daria closed her eyes as she remembered Julia's pleasant round face smiling at her, her eyes sparkling with mirth. The image faded to Julia with her throat black-and-blue, her eyes vacant, cold and dead, brown hair plastered to her forehead and limbs at unnatural positions where she'd fallen to the foyer floor.

Daria opened her eyes, feeling that familiar burst of rage running through her veins. Anger had become a close friend since Julia had been murdered.

She rested her head against the wall, letting the cool stone ground her and calm her. "I'll get him for you, Julia," she whispered. "I promise."

Vengeance for Julia's death was so close she could taste it, like something bittersweet on the back of her tongue.

Noise came from the room behind her. She turned in time to see Alejandro pull his shirt over his head. As it did every time she was treated to that tanned expanse of smoothly muscled chest, her mouth went dry. Even though her mind and emotions screamed, *No, look away*, every last of inch of her body cried out, *Yes, please fuck me now* when they saw that man's chest bared.

It humbled her to realize how much a slave she was to her hormones. Alejandro Martinez had always had a fine body and he still did. A prime male specimen that would make any woman drool.

"Overhead, off," he said. The bright light in the ceiling flipped off. The softer bedside table lamp remained on.

He sat down on the edge of the bed and pulled off his boots, leaving him in only his jeans. After he got the second boot off, he flopped back on the bed. His dark skin looked sinfully good against the red comforter.

Daria had an urge to go in there, climb on the bed, and lick every available inch of him. She was pretty sure he wouldn't push her away. No, she knew he wouldn't. Alejandro wanted her and she wanted him, but she had damn good reasons to resist.

He turned his head to the side and caught her gaze. All-consuming heat glowed in his eyes. He was being careful with her, giving her room to breathe. It was clear all he really wanted to do was strip her clothes off and act out every one of his carnal thoughts.

She should let him.

They needed to make this convincing, after all. They were supposed to be a couple. Not only that, they were supposed to be mated—the Chosen's equivalent of marriage. Mated pairs slept together, exchanged the oils of their skin, the scents of their bodies. She and Alejandro already had the scents of each other on them from the Choosing, but they had to make sure it stayed that way.

Through this, she could rationalize fucking Alejandro. It was for the mission. For the job. It was a sacrifice that had to be made for the ABI.

Yeah, right. She rolled her eyes. *What an inconvenience.*

She walked into the room and closed the garden doors behind her. As she passed the foot of the bed, she tried her best not to allow her gaze to eat up every square inch of him.

Yes, please fuck me now.

God, she was pathetic.

She picked her bag up off the floor. It looked like there was running water in the bathroom and a shower. All she wanted was a shower and to get into her pajamas. It was early, but she was so damn tired.

Alejandro sat up on the bed and turned toward her. "Are you changing your clothes?"

Oh, yeah, those already-warm brown eyes were smoldering.

"Yes." She took a step toward the bathroom.

"You didn't change in the bathroom this morning. This morning, you did it right in front of me."

"And your point is?" Casting an annoyed glance at him, she halted in the middle of the room. "Brandon was in the bathroom," she replied with patience. "I didn't think you'd mind. It's not like it's anything you haven't seen before."

He gave a short laugh. "You have no idea how bad you tempted me this morning, do you?"

"What does that mean?" She canted her hip and let her bag hang at her side. "Do you think I owe you something now?"

"No, that's not what I think. I'm pointing out that you don't know you're catnip to me."

She drew a careful breath. "Look, I won't do it again, okay? Both of us are in a bad situation right now. I said I wanted to try this with as little intimate contact as possible, but—"

"We have chemistry, and we're both attracted to each other."

Hell yes.

She nodded. "Yeah, but that doesn't mean I want to fall into bed with you."

"Again."

She shrugged and sighed. "Again." The weight of the bag grew too much and she let it fall to the floor.

He frowned. "You look tired. Do you need to feed?"

"The hunger is gnawing a little," she admitted. She was doing her best not to think about it.

"Go take a shower. You need to feed and then sleep. When I was first Chosen, I had to feed at least twice a day."

"Alejandro, what was that whole thing about your blood mother that Carlos was talking about? 'Rampant and resilient heterosexuality'?"

A dark expression crossed over his face and he looked away. "There's not much to tell."

That meant there was a lot to tell. She just stood there waiting for him to spit it out.

He glanced at her and sighed. "She was into some really kinky stuff, that's all. Lucinda likes men to be . . . together. She likes to watch. If you're a man in her inner circle, you're expected to play her little sexual games."

"What? You mean, like perform for her pleasure?"

He nodded. "Yeah, she's got a whole *playroom* set up. Whips and chains, you know. Everyone watches." His fangs flashed. "I'm not the submissive type. But sometimes she'd lock a man or a woman in place in that room and let everyone play. They were like a thing to her, a thing to tease. She got off on watching them get fucked."

"Were you ever one of her . . . *things*?"

He shook his head. "Like I said, being submissive isn't my deal. Demanding it from others . . . yeah, that's more my speed. So I played once in a while."

She shivered, imagining letting Alejandro play with her. Letting him do whatever he wanted. Oh, yeah, *that* was a worthy sexual fantasy. "So, uh, did you ever *play* with a man?"

He gave her a look so violent that she took a step backward. "I wasn't lying to Carlos when I told him that's why I didn't take her up on her offer. I have nothing against homosexuals. Whatever makes you happy. I *do* have something against being made into a sexual submissive and being treated like a trained dog."

"I believe you." She raised her hands. "Hey, even if you'd done it, I'm not the type to judge."

"Go take a shower so you can feed and go to sleep," he said carefully.

Grumbling more at the fact that a feeding sounded really good to her than at the fact she had to do it at all, Daria picked her bag up and headed into the bathroom.

8

AFTER a long, hot shower with the mineral-enriched water of the dome, Daria emerged from the bathroom wearing a pair of briefs and a tight T-shirt. She hoped it wasn't too catnippy since she didn't have much else to wear.

The pulsing heat of the water had made her body tingle and relaxed her muscles. All she wanted was to crawl into bed and sleep. "Bathroom light, off," she mumbled as she yawned.

Alejandro had turned off the bedside table lamp, but artificial moon glow lit the room. She found she had excellent night vision now anyway.

He'd slipped into bed and pulled the covers back on the side closest to her. He looked luscious lying there against all those crimson sheets and pillows. In fact, the sight stopped her dead in her tracks. "Can't we do this somewhere other than the bed?" It was far too suggestive.

"The only chairs are the heavy wrought iron ones out in the garden. Do you want to go out there, or sit on the floor? It won't be as comfortable." He patted the mattress. "Come on, Daria, you need to feed and sleep. Anyway, remember we need to be exchanging our scents as much as possible. We need our skin touching."

Work, work, work.

She climbed into the bed. His body heat had already warmed the mattress and the spicy male scent of him enveloped her. He pulled her toward him and wound his arms around her.

Ah, heaven.

All he wore was a pair of cotton boxers she could feel rubbing against her skin. His luscious, fantasy-inducing chest now lay flush up against her. Her nipples tightened and her cunt grew wet and warm. She wondered if Alejandro understood the power of his chest. Hell, he could succeed in world domination if the planet in question was comprised mostly of women.

Despite herself, she let out a shuddering sigh at the sensation of his body against hers. She would never admit it aloud, but being with Alejandro made her feel safe and protected.

She snuggled herself against him, finding a place for her head under his chin where she lay her ear to his chest. Daria closed her eyes and listened to his heartbeat. Every muscle in her body seemed to go limp as though she'd just had a massage. Exhaustion stole into her mind and made her thoughts come sluggishly.

Alejandro brushed his hand through her hair. "Hey, Daria," he murmured. "Don't go to sleep. You still have to feed."

It took her a moment to answer. Her eyes fluttered open. "Uhn. I know."

The hunger and her fatigue warred within her body, but it was a struggle that barely registered in her mind. Her arm lay across Alejandro's strong, warm body, her own body cushioned by the soft mattress.

Fatigue was winning.

If she hadn't been so physically shattered from the changes the Choosing had wrought in her, she would have regarded Alejandro as far more of a stimulant than a relaxant. The hard planes of his body invited further exploration. If she'd been anything but completely whipped, that would have excited her sexually and upset her psychologically because of the conflicting desires between her body and mind.

As it was, all she could do was lie in the protective circle of his arms and let his heartbeat lull her into the exhausted sleep her body demanded. She felt so heavy . . .

"Daria?"

"Mmmm?" She let the undertow of her weariness pull her under.

~

ALEJANDRO lay awake, staring into the darkened room, with one of the biggest hard-ons of his life. Daria had fallen asleep in his arms. In her drowsiness, she'd inserted a long, slender bare leg between his thighs. She probably wasn't even aware that she'd done it.

Her smooth skin rubbed very close to his cock and every single muscle of his body had sprung to awareness because of it. One of her hands rested on his side, and his nose was buried in the scent of the damp hair at the crown of her head. Her luscious breasts pressed against his chest. Almost every part of their bodies touched.

"*Shit,*" he muttered under his breath. How the hell was he supposed to sleep while this aroused? This woman would drive him insane before they could see the mission through.

Temptation lay in his arms, but he would do his best to resist it. The Choosing had exhausted Daria and she needed sleep. She needed to feed, too, but sleep seemed to be her body's priority at the moment. Because of that, Alejandro couldn't indulge his desires.

You could make her beg for it, the darkest part of him whispered. He had the right veil for that. Alejandro suspected Daria really did want him. All he had to do was exert the right kind of veil . . . and she'd be his. Willingly. Wantonly. Hell, she'd beg him to fuck her until she couldn't see straight.

Even without his veil, he could do it. He could roll her over and cover her body with his, kiss her awake. Kiss her until her body woke up and her sweet cunt primed itself for his cock. He could pull off her clothes and trail his tongue down her body until he hit her creamy pussy. Lick her until she moaned for him, until she shuddered and came for him. She'd beg for him to take her then. Beg for him to part those endless legs of hers and sink his cock deep inside her. With or without his veil.

He'd get everything he wanted.

He curled his fingers into the sheets and gritted his teeth at the thought of her hot, wet flesh gripping him. Temptation murmured into his mind, *You could make her body want it even if her mind doesn't. You could leave her pleasured so well she'd ignore the part of her mind that fights your seduction. You could make every one of her fantasies come true. If you did that, she wouldn't hate you in the morning.*

He squeezed his eyes shut as he fought to listen to the part of himself that reminded him that she was fatigued, weakened, and any effort on his part now would be taking advantage of that.

He looked down at her. Her dark lashes were swept down over her creamy skin, her full lips parted in slumber. God, he wanted her, but at the same time he felt this ridiculous urge to protect her.

If there was one thing Daria Moran could do, it was protect herself. She didn't need him to do that.

Yet, there it was, that image of her after Sante had betrayed everyone. Her big eyes luminous and vulnerable. Her heart grieving the loss of her friend.

She'd come to him that night to lose herself. To forget, just for a few hours, the horror of what had happened. He'd done that for her, had obliterated the pain with his body. Turned grief to passion. Though it had only been temporary, since in the morning the anguish had returned.

She moved in her sleep, turning over onto her back. He regretted the loss of skin-to-skin contact, even though it was driving him mad. The moonlight silvered her silky-smooth shoulder and kissed her face where a curling lock of her damp hair had fallen across her forehead.

Ah, damn.

Alejandro rolled off the bed and headed for the shower. He kicked on the water and stripped off his boxers. Then he climbed into the shower and let the hot water sluice down his body. He pressed one palm against the wall and stuck his head under the flow, letting a groan escape him.

He needed sexual release. Alejandro knew he could find it in ample supply here under the dome. Chosen women typically were up for a good fuck, no strings attached. The problem was that he didn't want just any woman. He wanted Daria.

Alejandro reached down and curled his fingers around the root of his cock with his opposite hand and stroked himself from base to tip. Pleasure shuddered through him as he imagined it was Daria's sweet little cunt he thrust into instead of his own palm.

He couldn't wait to feel all that slick, hot flesh closing around his shaft tighter than a fist. Couldn't wait to feel her soft skin against his, her moans and sexy little cries in his ears. He wanted nothing more than to feel the way her sex would pulse and ripple around his thrusting cock. Hear the hard slap of flesh on flesh as he drove her harder and faster.

Just the thought was enough to make his climax explode through him. He shuddered and groaned as he came with only the thought of Daria in his mind. Breathing heavily, he rested his head against the wall and let the water course over him.

He wanted Daria Moran with a carnal intensity that he couldn't control. The woman would be his, one way or another.

Two days, three at the most. That's how much time he'd give her to adjust to the Choosing. That's all she should need.

After that, all bets were off. After that, she became his conquest.

~

DARIA awoke to a morning-lit room with hunger rumbling through her body. She'd fallen asleep last night without feeding. Remembering the warmth of Alejandro's body against hers made her feel its absence now.

She turned toward the garden side of the room and spotted him out there, face raised to the sky. Nothing but that pair of tight-fitting jeans clothed him, strong muscles of his back rippling as he reached up to rub his face. He seemed tired.

As if sensing her gaze on him, he looked at her and walked back into the room wearing a stormy expression. "Hungry?" he asked.

She placed a palm flat to her stomach. Her need for sustenance cramped her belly. "It's time for me to feed. I can't deny it anymore."

He turned away and mumbled something.

"What did you say? I don't think I could've even used my new superhearing to catch that."

"Gordon stopped by this morning. Told us not to feed. He said the initiation ceremony involves food."

Well, that sounded ominous. Something other than hunger tightened in her abdomen. "Gee, do you think there will be a buffet?"

"Doubt it." He shot her an unfriendly look. Hmm, someone had gotten up on the wrong side of the bed.

She pushed up into a sitting position and yanked a hand through her unruly tresses. Ah, nothing like pillow-styled hair. She'd be the envy of all the other women today. "Did he clarify that comment at all?"

He shook his head. "Makes you wonder, doesn't it? There are succubare here. Lots of them. Maybe they're a part of the ceremony."

"Possible. Maybe there really will be a buffet." She rubbed her eyes and stretched. "So I slept through his visit, huh?"

"Seems like you could have slept through an earthquake."

"How about you? Did you sleep okay? I didn't steal the covers or anything, did I?"

He took a step toward her. Heat flashed through his eyes, and then was gone. "I didn't sleep well, but it wasn't because you stole the covers."

She climbed out of bed. "I wonder if Sante will be at the ceremony," she said almost to herself as she reached for her bag and pulled out a pair of jeans and a black T-shirt. "Give me five minutes and I'll be ready," she said as she headed into the bathroom.

She emerged minutes later with her hair looking a little better than it had when she'd awoken. At least it was combed.

Alejandro had pulled on his boots and a dark brown shirt that set off his eyes. As if his eyes needed something more to make them look deep, seductive, and heart stopping.

They left the apartment and headed over for the initiation ceremony.

The walkways leading to Sante Hall—she choked on that name when she merely thought it—were dotted here and there with other members of the Shining Way.

It was like they were back on Earth, and everyone was going to church on Sunday. The Church of Sante. Daria winced.

If she concentrated on each individual in turn, she could sense whether they were a vampire or a succubare.

The succubare seemed to vibrate—which was the only way she could describe it—at a lower rate than the vamps. Like the very molecules that made up the vampires moved at a faster velocity.

Each vamp she sensed remotely seemed old or young, strong or not so strong. Yet, as the oh-so-helpful Carlos had pointed out colorfully the day before, judging people that way could be deceiving.

All the Chosen around them were entering the hall on the opposite end of the doors they'd gone through yesterday. When she veered down a path to go in that direction, Alejandro caught her arm. "Gordon told me the front doors."

When they pushed open the heavy doors, Daria saw why. Carlos stood at the opposite end of the room, by the entrance to the rest of the building. Beside the fountain stood Brandon, along with three other vamps, two female, one male. One male succubare also stood there. All new initiates, she'd make a guess. She locked gazes briefly with Brandon.

Carlos walked toward them. "Good. You're all here." He wore a long white linen shirt, tight-fitting gray pants, and a pair of black boots. His long dark hair was clasped at the nape of his neck. He opened his hands to them. "Welcome."

Several of the initiates greeted him.

"You seven have been selected for various reasons to join us here at the Shining Way where we live in the benevolence of Christopher Sante. Some of you were allowed in based on your reputations, or the reputation and request of someone who knows and sponsors you."

Carlos turned and smiled first at Alejandro, then Brandon. "Some of you are old friends." He looked at Daria and his eyes seemed to glitter. "Or are friends of old friends. This morning's ceremony is designed to welcome each of you into our embrace. May we all live in peace and harmony here under the blue skies of the Shining Way."

"Thank you," said a couple of the initiates. Others smiled openly. Daria tried for a contented, yet neutral expression. She feared that if she attempted a pleased look, her eyes might give her away. Anyway, it would only be natural she'd still be pissed off about what had happened the previous day.

Excitement and apprehension rolled and tumbled inside her as Carlos instructed them to walk to the doors at the far end of the chamber. Her thoughts and feelings were not aided by her blood hunger. It roiled in the pit of her stomach. Would there be more "tests" for the initiated to undergo?

Would Sante be on the other side of that door?

Carlos pushed the double doors open. Alejandro grabbed her hand as they walked into the other room. They were the last two to pass through the doorway and into the darkened room on the other side. The light of myriad candles flickered around them, guttering from sconces on the walls and from containers set around the room that cast long shadows.

A high ceiling arched above their heads. The walls appeared to be inlaid with an interlocking pattern of white crystal. The tall blue black windows she'd seen from outside let in very little light.

The huge chamber was packed wall-to-wall with silent, motionless vamps, succubare and . . . What was the other energy she felt in this room? She scanned again. There were a small number of people who weren't vamp or succubare. They felt vulnerable to her, weak, young, and a bit slower in vibration than the others.

They felt like sheep in the middle of a pack of wolves.

Her mind clouded as her hunger surged. Not even sheep, more like veal. Tender, succulent, and perfectly prepared.

Her fangs extended into sharp little points in her mouth and the hunger hitched up a notch in her stomach. She tightened her grasp on Alejandro's hand in response.

He also trembled, a jarring reaction in a man as powerful as him. It was as if the scent of prey in the throng undid him, or perhaps tempted him so badly he fought to restrain himself. A glance at his face revealed nothing—he'd set his jaw and adopted a stoic expression.

Carlos started to speak to the crowd, introducing the initiates one by one, asking everyone to treat them well and help them become acclimated to their new surroundings. Daria caught a word here and there, but not all of it. The hunger pounded in her stomach, drowning out most thought.

Carlos repeated the short speech in Spanish, Mandarin, and then in Darpongese, a pidgin language that had developed in the sector. Daria spoke Darpongese, but couldn't concentrate on his words. She swayed, and Alejandro pressed her to his side, winding an arm around her to keep her upright.

She scanned the room, seeing faces all around her. Mostly, the vamps and succubare were off to the sides. All of them just stood there, watching them. Since they were all in one big mass, it was hard to get a fix on the group of the ones she couldn't identify.

Finally, Carlos turned toward them. "Our first gift to you" were the only words he uttered that really registered. The vamps in front of them parted.

There, before them, chained and kneeling on the floor, were the ones her mind had been searching for, the ones she'd been hungering for.

Seven human blood slaves.

9

Daria's mind stuttered for a moment as she absorbed three facts. First, she'd felt hunger for the humans who now knelt in front of her before she'd known what they were. Indeed, even now that she knew what they were, she still wanted them. Second, Carlos and the hundreds of vampires and succubare in the room seemed to want the initiates to feed from those humans right now.

Third, the new vamp in her liked that idea a lot.

Alejandro had gone rigid against her. He gripped her so hard he was cutting off the circulation to her arm.

Daria stared at them, taking a more critical look. Were they slaves or were they donors? The line was thin, but oh so important. Were they there by choice, addicted yet retaining their free will? Or had they been pressed into service, abused, and enslaved?

They appeared healthy, clean, and happy to be there. Their eyes lacked the rabid, mindless need for veil present in abused slaves. Yet, they wore chains. Maybe that was just affectation.

Daria just wasn't certain.

Carlos made a sweeping gesture, and said something she couldn't understand. The initiates all moved forward and she did too, propelled mostly by Alejandro's arm around her. She fought the urge to dig her heels in with everything she had.

Daria didn't want to feed from them, even though her hunger definitely thought she should. Damn it! She couldn't lose it now. She had to convince these Chosen she was one of them. She had to allow her hunger to win this battle.

A little hesitation could be explained by her being an infant vamp. A lot of hesitation would be suicide.

She watched the succubare male select a woman with long blond hair. She was perhaps in her twenties. When she realized she was being selected, the expression on her face became rapturous. Her beautiful features transformed into pleasurable anticipation and gratitude.

Was that her natural reaction? Was she so deeply veil-addicted that she would place herself in chains and allow a succubare male to feed from her lust? Or maybe these humans were under a veil right now. Carlos's, perhaps, or Sante's. A powerful mind trick to make them seem more willing than they were.

At the thought of Christopher Sante, she raised her gaze to search the crowd. Was Sante here right now, watching them? It was impossible to know. She didn't dare try to open her line of communication with Alejandro now, too afraid she'd slip and broadcast to the room at large.

The succubare drew the blond woman with the rapturous expression to her feet. After kissing her gently on the lips, he undid the ties of the long, multicolored skirt she wore. It dropped to the floor at her feet, revealing her smooth-shaven mound. She wore no panties. Apparently, they were going to go at it right here and now. *Great.*

In spite of herself, Daria's breath caught as the succubare's hand slipped between the woman's thighs and moved. He caressed her there until she moaned and her body tensed, until a needful expression enveloped her face. When the woman was ready, the succubare undid the buttons of his pants, pulled his hard cock out, and slid his hand under the woman's knee to hook her leg over his waist.

The muscles of his backside flexed as he pushed inside her cunt. Under the influence of his veil, the woman came immediately, her eyes rolling back into her head. The succubare kept her there in a state of ecstasy, fucking her until he'd drank his fill.

Someone in the crowd moved, catching her eye. Two men trapped a woman between their bodies, though she looked happy to be there. The man in back eased his arms around her, his hands finding the hem of her shirt and pushing beneath it to fondle her breasts. The man in front of her yanked her skirt up to her waist, revealing her mound. Apparently, she didn't believe in underwear. He undid his belt and lowered his pants, exposing the jut of his cock. While the Chosen behind her held her, the one in front spread her thighs and forced his cock deep inside her cunt.

Well. Not much foreplay there, but the woman looked like she was feeling no pain. Her face had relaxed into a picture of erotic enjoyment as the first man fucked her harder and faster while the second caressed her breasts.

In fact, now that Daria looked around, many of the observers had lapsed into erotic interludes of twos, threes, sometimes fours.

Oh . . . damn.

Daria couldn't stop the slow slide of her own body into arousal. Her mind knew it was wrong to be getting excited watching others go at it, especially under these circumstances, but she couldn't help her response. It was borne of her Choosing, of her new status as vampire. Her body felt ripe for sexual experimentation. Hell, she *craved* it.

One of the female vamps in Daria's group moved, breaking everyone's focus on the erotic displays around them. She knelt in front of a middle-aged woman with short dark hair. The other female vampire selected a man.

Brandon knelt in front of a young woman who had vibrant green eyes that seemed to retain a definite spark of free will. He stroked her face with his palm and she tipped her head back, offering her throat, and sighed in anticipation.

Veilhounders getting their fix. Honestly, they didn't look like they'd been forced to be here. She could scent no fear on them, nothing other than desire. Perhaps they were donors paid by the Shining Way, paid to be addicted toys for their members.

Carlos touched her arm, making her jump. "If you delay too long, you will be required to take the leavings."

Was that like table scraps? *God.*

Her gaze focused on the remaining slaves, hunger shooting pains through her stomach. She had to do this. There was no escape. She had no choice. A part of her, a deep, dark part, was happy about that. The rest of her was disgusted and resigned.

Alejandro released her. He walked to a middle-aged woman with long dark hair and drew her to her feet. She beamed like she'd won the intergalactic lottery and instantly offered him her jugular. Alejandro waited several moments before placing his hands to her upper arms to keep her steady while he fed. The woman whimpered, but Daria didn't think it was from fear. More like impatience.

She caught the eye of one of the remaining humans, who gazed upon her with undisguised lust. Clearly he anticipated her Chosen fangs upon him. Such trust the humans had in them. Their submission seemed so foolhardy. Weren't the humans afraid that they, the vampires, would go too far? That they'd drain them? Kill them?

Daria's breath caught in her throat. That was the very first time she'd thought of herself as a Chosen and not a human. It was the first time she'd put things in terms of *them* versus *us* and put herself on the bloodsucking side.

Alejandro tipped his head back. She watched his fangs extend. He lowered his mouth to the woman's throat and pierced her skin. There was no seduction. No prelude. This was nothing like what she'd seen him do with the woman at the Blood Spot. Alejandro was all about business today, though he hadn't hesitated even a moment before he'd bitten. The dark-haired woman moaned low in her throat and crushed herself against him.

A thread of something other than a thought came to her from Alejandro. *Euphoria. Ecstasy. Exhilaration.*

Daria took a step back, understanding that Alejandro took extreme pleasure in biting the woman. The hunger tightened in her stomach and she wanted nothing more than to deny it. She never, ever wanted to know the same kind of bliss from drinking a human's blood that Alejandro now knew.

She'd been a Galactic Patroller. Now she was an agent with the ABI. It was her job to protect humans, not treat them like cattle. This was wrong, *fundamentally*. Though her Chosen-ness disputed that truth, creating a war inside her.

Daria wondered if she'd feel differently if she'd been marked. Maybe if she'd been born with the DNA she'd be all right with treating human beings like food.

"Valerie." Carlos's voice close to her ear. "Time to feed."

She closed her eyes for a moment. Was this another test? If it was, she could not fail it.

Focusing her attention on a thirty-something man with auburn hair, she walked to him and sank to her knees.

The expression on his face remained neutral, but his dark blue eyes shone brightly. With what, Daria didn't know. Fear? Anticipation? Resignation? She wished she could ask him, but that would not be wise. She could feel Carlos behind her, watching.

The man's lips parted and he tipped his head to the side, offering her his throat. So meek. So submissive.

She wanted an answer to that indefinable emotion in his eyes before she bit him. Reaching out with her mind, she sensed the man as she did the vampires and succubare around her. A tendril of eagerness and hope wrapped around her. She sipped his expectancy like a fine wine. It spread over her tongue and made the hunger scream. He wanted her to bite him. He couldn't wait for it.

This was a donor, not a slave.

There was no pain here, no limp lack of will. Addiction, yes, but this man still retained his sanity . . . and he knew what he desired.

In response, the hunger speared through her belly and she drew him into her arms. His chains jangled as he reached out and twined his fingers into the material of her T-shirt. "Please," he whispered.

What about the veil this man so desperately wanted? She didn't know how to use hers. She didn't even know if she had any. When she caught sight of the pulsing vein in his throat, the question ceased to be relevant. Daria leaned in, set her fangs to his flesh, and bit.

Her fangs found his vein easily and his hot, sweet blood poured into her mouth. He tensed against her, as if in pain, and she remembered her veil. At the mere thought of it, she felt a little *tick* in her mind and it unfurled on its own, covering over the man she held in her arms.

The man relaxed into her, molding himself against her. The blood flowed easier, and suddenly Daria understood the biological reason for the veil. It was a little like a spider's venom, incapacitating her victim.

His blood filled her, sating the hunger. Daria closed her eyes and immersed herself in the experience. When she'd been human and she'd tasted blood, it had always been salty and metallic. Disgusting. Certainly nothing to savor. This was nothing like that. It was nothing like Alejandro's blood either, which had tasted silky and elegant. This blood was sweet, delicious. Like an after dinner sherry. Like laughter on a rainy day, or an unexpected commview from an old friend. Simply pleasurable.

Somehow, being Chosen had changed the flavor of human blood for her. Or maybe it was just that she knew it for what it was now. Humans might be fragile, but their capacity for life was endless. Perhaps that was the element in the blood that she focused on. Perhaps that ingredient tasted the strongest to her and drowned everything else out.

Whatever it was, it was ambrosia, and Daria drank her fill of it, letting the warm liquid pour down her throat and allowing it to replenish her.

The moment the hunger was satiated, she released the man. She did it so fast that he swayed and had to hold on to her to keep from falling backward. Daria had an instant to stare into his heavy-lidded eyes. He looked drugged and happy to be that way. He looked like every other veilhounder she'd ever picked up off the floor of a club or helped up from an alley in New Chicago.

Masking the horror she felt at having caused that reaction in him, she stood and backed away. Carlos's gaze was on her. Daria glanced around, realizing she was the first one to have ceased feeding, and knowing she'd been the last one to begin.

Carlos walked over to her slowly. "Your technique is shaky and amateurish, but I suppose it can be forgiven considering how new to Chosen-ness you are. That was the first human you've ever tasted, wasn't it?" he purred into her ear.

Not trusting herself to speak, she just nodded.

"Lovely, aren't they?"

She was saved from having to respond by the breakup of several of the vamp–blood donor pairings. One by one, the vamps separated from their victims and stepped back.

Alejandro was the last to stop feeding. The woman staggered back and sank to the floor, looking well satisfied, like a woman who had just been fucked to several climaxes. Having been on the receiving end of Alejandro's veil, Daria knew how strong it was. Of all of the victims, Alejandro's looked the most affected.

Alejandro turned toward Daria with his fangs still extended. When their gazes collided, heat flared fast in his hooded eyes. In that moment, Daria didn't need telepathy or any other means of communication to know exactly what Alejandro wanted to do to her. Consuming human blood had aroused him. She looked away.

The succubare and his donor simply never returned. Daria didn't want to know what was going on there.

Carlos mouthed some closing remarks that Daria heard but didn't care about since her mind was working over the implications of blood donors here at the Shining Way, the fact that feeding from a human had excited Alejandro, and the undeniable fact that humans were inherently irresistible to a vampire. Before, of course, she hadn't known that. Or, at least, the knowledge had been theoretical.

The group of initiates broke up and started to filter into the crush of the crowd. The lights grew brighter and talking and laughter began to reach her ears. The solemn atmosphere transformed to a festive one and a Latin beat filled the air.

Daria blinked, watching as Carlos and Gordon ushered the blood donors to their feet and out of the room.

Alejandro grasped her arm and whispered in her ear, "They're having a party here now, Valerie, but I suggest we go back to our room for a while." *We need to talk,* he finished telepathically.

He pulled her against him and twined a hand to the nape of her neck, the other around her waist. His mouth came down on hers without warning. Her hands found his shoulders and hung on to prevent her knees from buckling under the unanticipated impact of his lips on hers.

He kissed her lightly at first, tasting her. Their breath mingled as he brushed his lips back and forth over her mouth. Alejandro nipped at her lower lip, then slipped his mouth back over hers. The sensation shot straight to her sex, making her feel hot, swollen, and achy, and had her gripping his shoulders even harder.

That turned out to be just foreplay.

Alejandro slanted his mouth across hers, parted her lips, and slipped his hot tongue in to tangle. Deep. Possessive. It made her think of ways Alejandro could invade her body that had nothing at all to do with her mouth and everything do with places lower down. All traces of the blood he'd consumed were gone. He just tasted like pure, unadulterated sin.

All Alejandro.

He nibbled, sucked, and consumed her mouth. If there was anyone around them, Daria didn't know and she didn't care. Her whole world was suddenly all about Alejandro's mouth on hers.

Her sex felt hot and achy with the need to be filled by him. Her breasts were sensitive and tingled where they brushed against his chest. His hard cock pressed against her and all she wanted was to stroke it, lick it. She wanted it thrusting inside her, wanted his hard body over hers, driving into her.

When he pulled away, she lost her breath. He set his forehead to hers and groaned. "This is hell, you know that? I'm in fucking hell."

He grabbed her hand and guided her through the crowd and out the door. She did her best not to stumble and fall behind him. The man was a menace. Pure and simple.

Neither of them said a word until they reached the room. By then, Daria was back to simmering with anger instead of from Alejandro's kiss.

She closed the door behind them and fisted her hands. "Blood donors," she said quietly. And she'd fed from one and reveled in it. "Do you think there could be blood slaves, too?" They couldn't be far behind, not here, not when Christopher Sante came from a tradition of transporting them.

Alejandro walked to the windows and back. When he turned, Daria glimpsed a riot of emotion on his face before his expression settled into a neutral mask. "Yes. I would expect it of him. It's an easy way for Sante to afford all this. It's a business he knows. Why would he avoid it if it makes money?"

"Maybe the donors are just for show and the blood slaves are the private side business of Sante and his inner circle." Daria chewed the edge of her thumb. "Maybe the donors are just a cover."

Alejandro nodded. "It's definitely possible. It's probably not something he'd reveal to the world at large. Not even here, where he probably feels safe."

"You think he's collecting them and selling them off?"

"It would make sense, wouldn't it? Hell, the GBC has suspected it for a while now."

"We'll need proof. We'll have to find where he's keeping them." Besides snooping around for Ari Templeton, she'd be keeping her eyes open for anything linking Sante to blood slave trafficking.

Alejandro stared at her for a long moment, his expression turning grim.

"What's wrong with you, Alejandro? You're acting pissed off. What the hell are you thinking about?"

He shook his head. "Nothing's wrong."

"Bullshit."

10

ALEJANDRO fought the urge to round on her and snarl. He closed his eyes instead. There was plenty wrong, but he didn't want to talk about any of it. He didn't want to explain to her how his heart had gone pitter-patter when he saw those humans spread out before him like a goddamn feast.

He couldn't tell her that his fangs had extended instantly at the prospect of feeding on one of them, or how good it had tasted to have that woman's blood flow into his mouth. He couldn't reveal that, if given the choice, he wouldn't have stopped with just her. He would've fed from any of the others he'd been offered.

Daria couldn't know about the part of him that didn't care that the humans they'd fed from had an addiction to a vampire's veil the way some had an addiction to heroin or carmin. He knew those veil addicts would do anything to get a fix, including allow themselves to be chained for the pleasure of their addictors.

A dark part of him, the Chosen animal part of him, was simply a predator that didn't care about the state of his prey. Would Daria understand how badly he fought that side of himself? Would she understand that some days the animal side won? Alejandro didn't think so.

"It was the theater of the whole thing," he said finally. "The way they chained them up like that and presented them as a gift of welcome."

Daria didn't say anything for a heartbeat. Then finally, "Was that what bothered you, or was it the fact you wouldn't have been able to resist them, even if you could've said no?"

Daria had never been tactful.

He turned away from her brutal honesty and pushed a hand through his hair. "Didn't you feel them? Didn't you smell them? They wanted us to taste them more than anything in their little fucked-up worlds."

"Yes, I did, goddamn it," she said softly.

"Maldita sea! *Damn it!*" He rounded on her. "Could you have resisted humans so willing?"

"Yes, I could've. Even with the hunger burning a hole through my stomach, I could've walked away." Her voice rose. "The difference between you and me is that I *wanted* to walk away." A shadow moved through her eyes.

Alejandro pounced on that flicker of doubt. "Are you so sure? You're a Chosen now; we're meant to feed from them. That hunger you felt today is a part of us, like an arm or a leg. It doesn't care about the welfare of its food. Are you so sure you could've denied the hunger just like that?" He snapped his fingers.

"I'm not saying turning away would've been easy," she fired back. "But I *am* saying I could've done it." She paused, staring at him with narrowed eyes. "You've got a blood addiction, Alejandro. Admit it."

He made a frustrated sound and turned away from her. "Daria, you're newly Chosen and you don't have the same genes I do. Damn it . . . it's different."

"Have you killed, Alejandro? Have you ever been so caught up in the throes of bloodlust that you took too much and drained your victim?"

He jerked, unable to look at her, unable to respond.

"Alejandro?" Her voice sounded shocked and disbelieving, as if she'd asked the question expecting him to say no right away.

"Once," he answered, turning toward her, "once, I almost did. After I was newly Chosen. Lucinda brought in some addicted humans as *toys*, that's how she termed it. My control wasn't very good and I almost killed one. At the end the human woman fought me, knowing I was going too far—" He broke off, remembering her hands pushing him away. Her strength was a gnat's compared to his. "I just ignored her."

When Daria spoke again, her voice trembled. "I saw you today, Alejandro. I felt your bliss and the strong drive you had to feed from that donor. You have a problem."

"I might have a problem, but I also have strong control, Daria. I might have an addiction, but I won't hurt anyone."

"How can you be so sure?" She shouted it.

He rounded on her. "Do you think I haven't thought about it? Do you think I haven't had nightmares about that human I nearly killed? I know I have an addiction, but I have it under control. I *will not* harm any humans when I feed."

"I wish I could believe you."

Someone knocked on the door, but neither of them moved to answer it. They stood, staring at each other. Daria's eyes snapped with anger. Finally, she whirled and opened the door.

Brandon entered the room, glancing back and forth between them warily. "Well, I either interrupted a lover's spat or some really good foreplay." He paused thoughtfully. "Maybe it's both."

"Never mind that." Daria shut the door behind him. "Did you come from the hall? Is Sante there?"

Brandon gave his head a shake. "No. Bastard's nowhere around that I've seen yet."

Daria turned and stalked toward the garden, swearing under her breath as she went. "Where the hell is he?"

"We've been here less than a day," said Alejandro. "Relax."

"I don't think Sante rubs elbows with the peasants on a daily basis," answered Brandon. "We may have to wait awhile to see him."

Daria spoke toward the window, her back turned to them. "Maybe I'm just being impatient."

"As are we all."

"And disturbed by what just happened," added Alejandro.

"What we just saw may have been for my benefit," said Brandon. "That whole show. Sante might have been in there, watching me obliged to feed from those blood donors."

Alejandro frowned. "You think he'd want to see you squirm because of your disagreement with him over Maria Gillante's blood slaves?"

Brandon nodded. "It's possible. I asked around. Technically they're considered donors, not slaves. They're employed, with official labor contracts. According to the Chosen I spoke to, the donors have residences here at the dome and a nice fat paycheck every week. All the same, they chained them up, made them look like blood slaves. Unless they get off on that kind of playacting, it could have been for me."

She turned back toward them. "If that's true, Sante might be there. He'd want to see your reaction." She went for the door. "I have to go see for myself."

Brandon put his palm on the back of the door before she could open it. "The scorching kiss you two shared after that thing they called a ceremony has everyone thinking you nipped back here for a little one-on-one. You don't want everyone thinking he's a minute man, do you?"

Daria glanced at him. "I really don't care what anyone thinks." She tried to open the door again, but Brandon kept it closed.

"Please, try to act like a good little Valerie," Brandon said. "At least stay here for another half hour before you go back over. Bloody hell, you two put on a convincing show, let me say. You probably burned anyone within a three-foot radius. If you go back now, it will look suspicious."

Alejandro sat down on the edge of the bed and stared at Daria. "She wants to leave because she's pissed at me. She's good at running away, our Daria."

She whirled. "I want to leave because we have a job to do. Don't make this about anything personal."

Brandon raised an eyebrow. "Okaaaay, well, I guess I came by at the wrong time. I just wanted to let you know that I heard something."

Both Alejandro and Daria gave him their full attention.

"I heard someone say Ari Templeton's name in a conversation," said Brandon.

"What do you mean? That's all you heard?" asked Daria. "In what context? What did they say about her?"

Brandon shrugged under the liberal peppering of questions. "I didn't hear the whole thing and I don't know what they were talking about, but it's something. It means she might really be here. I just thought you should know."

"Or it could mean they were talking about The New Covenant Church and Richard Templeton. I'm sure he's a frequent topic of conversation here," said Alejandro. "Especially lately."

Brandon nodded. "Sure. Or they could've been talking about Ari Templeton being kept here. We don't know."

Daria nibbled the edge of her thumb, appearing deep in thought. "Okay," she said finally. "It's not much, but it's something. We're going to stay here for a while, then head back over."

Brandon went for the door. He winked before closing it behind him. "Maybe you guys can find something interesting to do while you're waiting besides fight."

Daria stared at the closed door for a moment before turning to face him. "Brandon seems to think disagreement turns us on."

"I think anger is probably an aphrodisiac for you."

Her eyes snapped back to life. "And human blood to you is—" She snapped her mouth closed. "We don't need to be doing this."

~

"WHAT do you think we should be doing?" Alejandro said with silken menace.

Five hundred sweaty skin-against-skin things suddenly assaulted her mind. The kiss he'd given her back in the hall hadn't helped her sex drive much. "I think we shouldn't be fighting. I think we should be at the hall. We're not going to find anything out by hiding in our room. Why did you want to come over here anyway?"

"I thought you needed a moment to get your head together. I know I did. I thought we needed to regroup."

"What was with that kiss you laid on me?"

He shrugged. "I wanted to kiss you. I want to kiss you again right now."

Mouth. Dry.

She drew a careful breath. "Look, I've been thinking, and maybe we should just go ahead and have sex. I mean, like you said, it's going to be hard to pretend otherwise. What we do here, it's all in the line of duty, you know."

Something dangerous moved through his eyes. He rolled off the bed and came toward her. "Just go ahead and have sex? In the line of duty?" he asked as he crossed the floor, his voice a threatening purr that raised the hair on the back of her neck.

I am not going to back away from him. I am not going to back away from him. I am not . . . Damn. Her gaze riveted on his chest, she backed up.

No one made Daria Moran retreat, except this man.

She didn't stop until she hit the wall behind her. All her attention was now focused on the six-foot, three-inch aroused and angry vampire in front of her.

"Daria." His voice was a low roll, treacherous and irresistible all at once. It stroked over her skin like a satin glove. It tingled her breasts and between her thighs. She fought a shiver.

She shifted uncomfortably. "Alejandro, come on." Did her voice have a quaver in it? *Damn.*

He reached out and rubbed her cheek with his thumb. Her lips parted and she quickly closed them. "You think we should take one for the team, then?" he asked in that velvet voice and his warm, rolling accent. "That we should sleep together out of a sense of responsibility? That it's just what we have to do for the job? Make a sacrifice?"

"Uh."

He dropped his hand to her waist and dragged her flush up against him. An uncontrollable quiver ran through her body when he dropped his mouth to her shoulder and brushed his lips very lightly across her skin. Her head fell back and lolled to the side to give him better access.

What was it about Alejandro that made her act like a cat in heat?

He laid a kiss on her collarbone, flicking his tongue out to taste her skin. Goose bumps pebbled her body as he drew those full lips up her throat. He lifted his head enough to ask, "Well, *querida*? What do you think?"

Think? It was hard to do that with his thumb under her shirt at the small of her back, rubbing back and forth, back and forth. It mesmerized her libido. All she could do was imagine him stroking her nipples like that, stroking her clit. Easing his long, broad fingers into her cunt.

"Uh," she breathed again. She couldn't seem to form a sentence. This was a full frontal assault, and the enemy was winning.

He licked the skin behind her ear, laid a kiss there. "Because here's the problem," he murmured into her ear. "I want you."

"You want me?" she murmured almost incoherently. She sounded drunk. No wonder; the man was intoxicating.

He kissed her earlobe and pressed her up against him so that his voice rumbled through her and his scent suddenly became her whole world. "I want to strip you out of these clothes, Daria, stretch you out on that bed over there. I want to kiss every inch of your body, and drag my tongue across your nipples one by one. I want to nibble each of them lightly, draw them into my mouth and suck on them like they're candy."

Daria was sure her face had flushed. She knew her nipples were hard at the thought of his lovely lips wrapping around them, pulling them into his hot mouth to be teased by his tongue. His words were quickly turning her bones to warm honey.

"I want to worship your body, Daria. Kiss your inner arms where I remember you're just the slightest bit ticklish, lick your inner thigh, the backs of your knees, and kiss my very favorite spot . . . the pretty little dip at the base of your spine where your back meets your gorgeous, rounded ass." He dipped his hand down to cup the curve of her rear.

He pressed her up against him. The rigid length of his cock pressed into her stomach and her flush faded into a flat-out fever.

"Then, when you're good and ready, completely primed and creamy in that perfect cunt of yours, I want to slide my cock deep inside you and take you fast and hard. I want to drive into your pussy over and over until you come, until you're screaming from the pleasure. That's the first time."

She licked dry lips. "The, uh, first time?"

"*Mmmm*, just to sate my appetite for you. The next time I'll want to take you slow." He gave a sexy little groan that made her knees go weak. "I like it slow, Daria, so slow and easy and deep. I want to savor every part of this pretty little body that I'm dying to have stripped and beneath me. And you know what?"

"What?" She hated that her voice sounded so damned breathless.

"For me, it isn't about obligation. It has nothing at all to do with business or the line of duty. I want you just because I want you, because you and I go well together and we always have. Now, what do you want?"

She *wanted* to protest his hands on her, *wanted* to yell and push him back. Wanted to run away screaming. The problem was, she couldn't move. Because what she wanted even more than all of that was Alejandro.

"You," she whispered.

He said nothing in response. He only laid a lingering kiss to her temple. It would be the most innocent thing he did for a while.

Daria swallowed hard as his hands ran slowly up her waist and over her stomach to cup her breasts. His thumbs stroked over her nipples through the cotton of her T-shirt and bra.

She closed her eyes, groped for control, and found none. "Alejandro," she whispered raggedly. Need slicked her sex, made a tight little ball of heat there she wanted assuaged.

"Let me touch you, Daria."

She'd told him yesterday she wanted to try this without actually having sex, and she'd meant it. Carlos had said she had a strong will. She did. Especially since she knew that sleeping with Alejandro would be every bit as much pleasure as it would be business. That made things treacherous for her.

Alejandro was a man more dangerous than most. The last thing she needed was another heartbreak. It was far better to keep things on this mission as professional as possible, no matter how tempted she might be to take advantage of the situation.

No matter how much she wanted him.

One of his hands dropped to the front of her jeans and undid the top button. "Daria?" he purred into her ear.

"Uh-huh."

"Let me help you out of these jeans."

Daria froze, fighting her need to touch and be touched, and not by just anyone. She wanted to touch Alejandro and be touched *by him*. Her fingers curled around his shoulders and she held on, caught between knowing she should push him away and wanting nothing more than to pull him closer.

He growled at her inaction and leaned in, capturing her lower lip and dragging it through his teeth. Her breath hissed out, and her sex grew warm and wet. All her careful reasoning for wanting to push him away went *poof*.

He spoke softly against her lips, "Daria, if you won't offer what I know you want to give"—he moved his hand between her thighs—"then I will convince you to let me take."

H IS smooth, rolling accent alone was almost enough to put her over the edge.

Alejandro pressed up and rotated, pushing the seam of her jeans against the side of her clit. Pleasure rippled through her, making her moan. "I don't think it will be too hard," he purred in a confident voice.

"Alejandro," she gasped against his lips.

"*Hmm?*"

"This is not fair."

He chuckled. "Just tell me to stop, if you want me to stop." He pressed and rotated, circling against her clit.

Her mouth went dry and she thought she'd swallow her tongue. Ripples of pleasure made her knees feel weak and swamped her thought process. His free arm kept her steady as he rubbed her clit methodically, *diabolically* . . . bringing her just to the edge of a climax and then holding her there. She creamed against her panties and wished fervently for less clothing between her cunt and his hand.

He leaned in and dragged her earlobe between his teeth. "Say you want me, Daria. I want to hear the words from your lips. Tell me you want me to take these clothes off you, spread you across the bed, and fuck you until you can't see straight. Say the words and I'll let you come."

Anger fought to rise from the depths of her drugged, sexual high but died a whimpering death when he kissed the sensitive place beneath her earlobe and scraped his fangs against her throat.

She made fists with her hands and gasped, "I want you Alejandro. You know I do." The idea of letting Alejandro have free rein over her body came to her again. *Just for one night*. Let him do whatever he wished to her.

She felt him smile against her skin in triumph a moment before he sank his fangs into her flesh, at the same time pressing just a little harder against her clit.

Daria gasped as her climax washed over her, the sweet, slight pain of his teeth's penetration playing counterpoint to the sexual ecstasy coursing through her body.

He drew out her blood while her orgasm went on and on. By the time the waves of pleasure had released her, her knees had completely given out, forcing him to hold her up. The aftermath of her climax swamped her muscles and her mind.

"Damn it, Alejandro," she slurred as though inebriated. "Who gave you the right?"

He released her throat and laughed softly. Setting her firmly on her feet, he looked at her. "You were mine the moment we set foot in this place. I'm fully within my rights." He paused, studying her. "Are you going to tell me you didn't enjoy it?"

She raked her gaze up his body, noting the way his cock jutted against his jeans. He was fully aroused, and a part of her had to stop herself from reaching out and stroking him, leading him to the bed and assuaging his need. She had trouble remembering exactly why that would be such a bad idea.

Instead, she pushed past him. "That's not the point."

"So you did enjoy it, then?" His sensual mouth curved in a playful smile. "Because from my end, it looked like you did."

"Alejandro, I don't remember you being this damn arrogant."

He caught her wrist and yanked her against him. His lips came down on hers in a possessive kiss that made her toes curl. Her breath caught at the sensual glide of his lips against hers and the swipe of his tongue into her mouth. He ended the kiss and she pushed away from him.

"I'm the same Alejandro you've always known. The same man who wanted you then and who wants you now."

She made a frustrated noise and headed for the door. "Enjoy your hard-on. I'm going back to work."

Right before she closed the door behind her, she heard him call, "Baby, everything about you is work."

She slammed the door extra hard.

Daria crashed out of the building and into the disconcerting Earth-like sunshine. Above her the sky shone a deep blue and white, puffy clouds scudded past. No one was around. Probably everyone was still in Sante Hall, at the party. She stopped for a moment on the path and closed her eyes, immersing herself in the moment in order to ground herself.

Her body still hummed and tingled from Alejandro's touch. As much as she hated to admit it, the man made her feel good. Being in his arms felt right.

Her ears filled with the twitter of the birds in the trees and a light breeze lifted the hair at the nape of her neck, drying the sweat on her skin. The fresh scent of grass teased her nose and Daria had to remind herself that she wasn't back on Earth. She was here on Darpong in the Logos Territory, at the Shining Way . . . and Christopher Sante was somewhere in the vicinity.

As she centered herself in the moment, the disturbing pleasure of feeding from the blood donor reentered her mind like a fever she couldn't shake. He had smelled so good and the thought of his life force, coursing strong and certain through the veins just under his skin, had called to her like the sweetest song. She'd known all she'd had to do was penetrate that thin, vulnerable layer of flesh to drink the goodness within.

Daria shuddered. So this is what it was to be a Chosen. Tears pricked her eyes.

Far away, the muffled sound of voices and music met her ears. Her eyes popped open and she headed toward it. *Work*. She could do work. It was Alejandro she had problems with.

When she reached Sante Hall and opened the door, the driving sound of digitized music mixed with an ancient tribal beat nearly overpowered her. They'd dimmed the lights, and the scent of human blood, sex, and the tang of tobacco fought for prominence in the room. Daria fought her way through the crush of people, seeking the back of the room where the music was less loud.

As she made her way through, skillfully avoiding being served anything to drink, she caught a glimpse of Brandon sandwiched between two slim, female bodies, his head buried in the throat of one and his hand down the pants of the other. As she glanced around, seeing more such erotic entanglements, her stomach tightened.

To her right a pair of three entwined in a dark corner. A woman between a man and another woman, all questing lips and exploring hands. The succubare in the middle was currently orgasming around some object the male was fucking her with while the woman tongue-kissed her.

All righty, then. That's how it was. That's how it always was here in Vamplandia.

She would have to be extra alert. She didn't want to do any heavy petting with anyone but Alejandro, and obviously she had issues about that, too.

Brandon apparently didn't have a problem with acting like a local. Of course, if push came to shove and her cover risked being blown, she'd have to join in, too. She just hoped push never came to shove. She'd do all she could to avoid that.

Carlos approached her and she pasted a welcoming look on her face for the oily vampire. She even managed to hold it when he moved to the side and she saw that he led the man she'd fed from earlier. The human stumbled along after him on a chain, looking dazed and confused.

"Valerie," he greeted her. "I saw you leave with your lover. I am glad you have returned." He made a show of glancing around. "But where is Emanuel? Did he not accompany you?"

"I'm sure he'll be along soon. He needed a moment to recompose himself after the excitement of the day." *Damn it.* Had her expression tightened just a bit? Had there been a note of sarcasm in her voice?

Carlos smiled knowingly. "Ah, Valerie, are you jealous he chose a woman to feed from? You must not be. The Chosen don't like to feed on the same sex if they can help it. Well, unless they *enjoy* the same sex. It was clear to all that the only one he wants is you."

She wanted to tell the bastard she didn't need her ego stroked, and she certainly wasn't jealous of Alejandro's choice of food. She also wanted to tell him that, by the way, his proximity creeped her out and could he please move away? Instead she unlocked her jaw and said, "I appreciate your reassurance."

He yanked the chain of the blood donor, who staggered forward a couple of steps. Blood marked the skin of the thirty-something man. His face was pale, his eyes heavily hooded, and his mouth slack. He looked drunk, drugged out of his mind with veil pleasure.

Daria made a tight fist at her side, fighting the obscene allure she had to biting the man again—fighting her newly born Chosen-ness. "Have you been allowing everyone to snack on him?" she asked in a mild voice, tinged with curiosity.

Carlos shrugged one shoulder loosely. "He enjoys it. We enjoy it. It's a win-win situation. He's a walking party favor."

She smiled tightly. "Is he a slave?"

Carlos's lips compressed. "No. He is a slave to nothing more than his addiction. Once he sobers, if he wants to leave the dome and return to New Chicago, we will allow that. He is paid to be here to *play* the role of a slave." He paused. "If you wish to see his employment contract, you may. We don't deal in blood slaves here, Valerie. We never have and never will. I find the practice abhorrent and would not allow it."

Right.

Daria's gaze scanned the donor. He would die if he lost much more blood. Daria had to hold herself back from taking his chain from Carlos's grasp and dragging him out of there. She couldn't do that. To act in such a way would blow her cover, it would endanger their lives, and, worse, Sante would get away. Again.

Carlos yanked on the man's chain again, not knowing he was also yanking hers. "Would you like another taste for your evening sustenance?"

The human's addiction-glazed gaze snapped to her face and a look of longing transformed his slack expression. The man was so out of it he didn't even know he was a breath away from death. Two more good pulls on this man's veins might very well mean his end.

She shook her head, searching for a response that would be plausible. "He looks dead on his feet. This man is playing fang roulette." God, she hoped those words got through to the human. "I don't want to be the Chosen who kills him and takes away a valuable Shining Way employee."

Two birds, one stone. She'd done what she could to warn the man while not acting overly interested in his welfare.

He nodded at her throat. "I see your lover has bitten you and you have lost blood. As a newly Chosen I am surprised you can resist the offer."

"As you have already pointed out, I have a very strong will. That's why I made it through the succubare." She gave him a cold little smile. "In fact, if you must know, I don't like dining from other Chosens' leavings."

The human reacted as if slapped. Awareness snapped to attention in his bloodshot eyes, and he speared her with a look to kill. Daria was surprised he still retained an ego to be bruised. Of course the man didn't know she was trying to save his pathetic life.

Carlos's gaze took her in from head to toe. "You have an attitude already and you are but newly born." A slow, small smile that turned her stomach spread over his face. "Perhaps you will do well here after all."

She returned his smile. "I'm pleased you think so."

Daria sensed Alejandro's approach behind her.

Carlos looked over her shoulder, glimpsing him. "Ah, and here is your Emanuel. I will take my leave." He turned away to melt back into the crowd, trailing the blood donor behind him. That poor man wouldn't last the night, voluntary service or not. Idiot.

She turned and caught Alejandro's gaze. His eyes were hooded and he looked pissed off. Of course, unless he'd taken himself in hand after she'd left, she wasn't surprised he was agitated. His cock had been like a steel rod, and she'd left him unsatisfied.

Anything? He'd opened a private mental pathway. Even in her brain, he sounded tense.

No. She paused. *Look, it makes me nervous to speak this way. I'm afraid I'm going to slip and broadcast all over the place.*

You won't. It doesn't work that way, but we'll work on it tonight in the room, okay? Let you have some practice before we do this anymore. He cut off the pathway so fast her brain practically spun. Yep, he was still mad.

She knew from the manual that the telepathic abilities between Chosen took a long time to master. It required several steps in order to address more than one person at a time, steps she wasn't ready to try yet. Steps she didn't even know. Still, she was shaky on her newly Chosen feet and didn't want to take any chances. Doing these things in reality was far different than reading about them in orientation.

Alejandro came to stand near her. His body heat radiated off him and she absorbed it with gratitude. Despite the press of bodies in the room, she remained chilled. In the distance, they both watched Brandon enjoying himself.

"I see Brandon has settled in well," Alejandro murmured.

"Yep."

"Sante's been here. I heard from someone in the crowd."

Her body stiffened.

"He's gone now." He took a swig of his beer. "Back into his hole here under the dome, wherever that is. People around here talk like he's a god."

Frustration at missing his appearance tightened her stomach. "To these people, he probably is."

Carlos climbed onto the podium, and everyone in the room clapped and cheered. Daria scanned the area near him, but saw no sign of the male blood donor. She hoped Carlos had sent him away. Or, even better, he'd left on his own. Carlos held his hands out in a gesture meant to quiet the crowd and the roar died to a murmur.

"Let us all give thanks to our benefactor, Christopher Sante, for hosting this gathering tonight. Without him, we would not have the pleasure of each other's company, sustenance in our veins, or a roof over our heads. We all benefit from his generosity."

The crowd went crazy, hooting and clapping. Daria tried not to gag as she applauded politely and smiled.

When everyone calmed, Carlos continued. "Tonight we celebrate to welcome new members into our community. We hope they are happy here . . . and are productive." The crowd cheered, and he made the hand gesture again. The boisterous Chosen again quieted. "So tonight, eat, drink, and be merry. Tomorrow we go back to work!"

Work?

Alejandro and Daria exchanged a quick look. The outside world knew next to nothing about the Shining Way. It was a theory that the commune produced some kind of product, origins masked by an unknown distribution company, in order to finance themselves. Or it could be some kind of work related to the trafficking of blood slaves, or drugs, or both. Really, it could be anything.

Daria eased the beer bottle from Alejandro's fingers and took a drink herself.

12

ALEJANDRO sprawled on the bed, dressed in just his jeans, and studied Daria across the distance. "Okay, open up a pathway."

Daria sat clear across the room from him, as far as she could get. That was probably a good idea. She'd left him with a rock-hard cock earlier that day and just about the only thing he had on his mind now was stripping her bare, spreading her across the bed, and fucking her until neither of them could think straight. Having her in this room with him, her scent filling his senses, was nearly more than he could bear.

It's open.

Good. Now I want you to bring an image of Brandon into your mind and open a pathway in the direction of that picture in your mind's eye. I want you to talk to both of us at the same time.

She concentrated. It took a few minutes, but she finally pinged them both. *Brandon, are you there?*

Silence. Then, *Busy.* His voice came terse and out of breath. The pathway collapsed.

Alejandro let out a bark of laughter, and Daria looked at him and threw up her hands. "You did it right. That's all I wanted. You felt the shift of your awareness, right?"

She nodded and rubbed the bridge of her nose. Daria did that when she was tired. "It felt far different talking to you alone than it did addressing two people at once. They talked about that during my training, but now I truly understand it."

"So you see that you'd need to specifically direct your intent in order to broadcast to a room at large, and, if you did, you'd know it. It's nearly impossible to do accidentally."

"How do you address people whose faces you've never seen? I still don't understand that. How did the guards speak to us as we approached the Shining Way?"

"All you need is an image to open up a pathway. The guards saw us, we were in their range, and therefore they could communicate with us even though they'd never seen our faces. If you had a picture or holo of someone you never met who was miles away, you could open a pathway. But you could not initiate communication with someone across a distance without knowing what they look like." He paused. "Well, you could try, but you'd probably get a wrong number," he amended.

"All that was covered in the training, but it's much different in reality."

He nodded, letting his gaze travel from her slim bare feet, up her long legs, to the press of her breasts against her shirt, to her face. Her body appeared tense, in direct contrast to the relaxed slouch he maintained on the bed. His fingers itched to massage away the stress she so clearly held in her shoulders. "Why are so far away from me, Daria? Are you afraid I'll bite you again?"

She made a frustrated sound and stood. "Not everything is about *you*, Alejandro."

Daria walked to the closed door of the courtyard. It was a beautiful night, but they kept the doors shut most of the time so they could speak freely. "I'm wondering where Ari Templeton is tonight. I'm wondering what happened to that man I fed from this morning. Are they both lying facedown somewhere, dead?" Her voice broke. "I couldn't do anything for that blood donor today. He was being passed around like an hors d'oeuvre and there wasn't a damn thing I could do to stop it."

He rolled off the bed and came up behind her. Knowing he probably risked a limb, he reached out and put his hand on her shoulder. She startled, but then relaxed under his palm. "Ever since I first met you, I've seen this desire in you to protect everyone in the world, Daria, most especially the downtrodden and weak. It's one of the qualities about you that I most admire, and it's something that attracts me to you." He paused. "But you can't take on responsibility for everyone you meet and still stay sane."

"Please don't tell me that man chose his addiction. Don't talk to me about consensual crimes." Her voice and body had gone bowstring tight.

He took a moment to answer. "I've known Chosen who have deliberately addicted humans. They held them captive and forcibly fed from them until their victim was under their thrall. It's the same thing as rape. So I won't say a word about choosing addiction. We don't know anything about the histories of the donors employed by the Shining Way. Knowing what I know, I won't make judgments about any of the humans I saw today."

She turned and looked up at him, studying his face. "You've seen that kind of mistreatment? Why didn't you stop it? Were you in thrall and unable to step in?"

He dropped his hand from her shoulder. "Yes, I was in thrall to Lucinda at the time. It was after she'd Chosen me, and I was still very weak. When I could help, I did, but Chosen hierarchy is a complicated thing. I was not free to act for the first three years after my making because she'd placed me under her dominion. I could do nothing without her consent. The minute I was strong enough to break away from her, I did."

"Why did you free me, Alejandro? Why am I not under your dominion? It seems like you'd enjoy that."

He shook his head. "Do you really think that of me? I would never hold another in thrall, *never*. Although I was urged to do so. Without sharing my energy from the dominion, many in the GBC figured you'd be weak as a newborn kitten and of no use to the mission. As usual, however, you've stood strong. I thought you would. That's why I didn't think twice about releasing you after the Choosing."

She stared up into his eyes, her solid resolve clear in her gaze. "I have no other choice but to stand strong." She pursed her lips, her expression hardening. "Tell me about Lucinda Valentini. How did she come to Choose you?"

He turned away and pushed a hand through his hair. "She saw me in a club one night and sensed I had the genes to make it through the succubare. She took a liking to me, and decided she wanted me for her own. So one night she cornered me outside a bar in New Chicago with three Chosen males. I was pissed drunk at the time, so I didn't put up much of a fight. By the next morning I was Chosen, had a lover I never wanted, and some shiny new mental tethers to her."

"Damn," she said softly. "I never knew. It's like you were raped and enslaved."

He turned back to her. "It wasn't all bad. I never asked to be Chosen, but I'm stronger now, faster." He turned and gave her a feral grin. "Not to mention immortal, if I can prevent the insanity."

"Yeah, I'm still getting used to that idea."

"I gave Lucinda as much hell as I could. I snapped at her from the end of my leash for all the years I was under her dominion. Once I could get out, I got."

"Good."

He studied her. "When will you tell your family?" He knew how close she was to her mother, but he also knew her well enough to understand she hadn't told anyone about her Choosing beforehand. That would've jeopardized the mission.

"After." She shook her head. "I don't think she's going to understand."

"She will. Remember, I've met your mother. She loves you and will accept you any way you come to her. You'll walk in and she'll be baking that banana bread of hers that makes my mouth water. She'll hug you, tell you she loves you no matter what, and that will be the end of it."

She smiled. "She always liked you."

He spread his hands and grinned. "What's not to like, *querida*?"

Her smile faded and she looked out the window, up past the opening of the courtyard and into the star-scattered sky. "We should get some sleep."

"You need to feed again, Daria."

He could only see her profile, but he still glimpsed her expression darken in her reflection. "I already fed, remember?"

"That was this morning. I fed from you afterward, weakening you. You're a new vamp and I know you need more sustenance than you're getting. Daria, you're strong, but you're not that strong. Stop jeopardizing the mission by resisting me."

He knew that last sentence would get through to her. *Jeopardizing the mission.*

Her jaw tightened, and she closed her eyes briefly. "I suppose if I must feed, I would prefer it be from you." Her voice sounded flat, expressionless.

"I'm glad you sound so excited about it." He turned, switched off the light, and lay back on the bed. Daria remained at the window, staring out. The moonlight bleached the color from her form. "Whenever you're ready, sweetheart. I would like to get some sleep, too."

In reality, he simply couldn't wait to get his hands on her. Couldn't wait to get the scent of her skin on his. Couldn't wait to share the warmth of her body.

She turned and came toward the bed.

"Uh, uh." He made a *tch tch* sound. "Clothes off. If we're not having sex, then we need skin-to-skin contact."

Daria hesitated, anger flashing over her features for a moment before she conceded defeat. She pulled her shirt over her head and tossed it to the floor, then kicked her boots off and shed her pants.

Clad in only her tiny blue panties and white cotton bra, she walked to the bed. Alejandro's mouth grew drier with every step she took.

Daria didn't need lace and silk to enhance her body's allure. Her curves and soft skin needed no embellishment to make his cock hard.

"Happy now?" Her gaze flicked down to his straining crotch and she raised an eyebrow. "Forget I asked. Clearly you are."

"I'm a man, what can I say?"

"How do you want me?"

Alejandro allowed his mouth to curve in a feral smile.

She rolled her eyes and climbed onto the bed. Even now he caught the subtle, intoxicating scent of her arousal. Daria controlled herself better than anyone he'd ever met. The woman had a will of steel. However, he knew she hungered for sex, knew it because he'd gone through the Choosing, too . . . and its hormone-filled aftermath.

He knew the score. Knew the empty place that had to be filled by questing hands and exploring lips. Knew that the only way to make the constant ache disappear was sexual contact—touching and being touched—on a regular basis.

He shifted, suppressing a groan, as she settled over his pelvis, the heat of her sex bleeding through the fabric of his jeans. In the darkness, her eyes seemed large and luminous, like the moon had been dragged into the room with them and split in two.

She gave one small sigh, maybe in resignation, maybe from hunger, or maybe even from passion, Alejandro couldn't be sure, then dipped her head and inserted her face into the crook of his neck.

He closed his eyes, enjoying the rub of her skin against his, and wanting her scent to be joined with his on an intimate level. Alejandro let his hands drift up and rub her back. Unable to resist, he undid the clasp of her bra. She stiffened, but then relaxed against him. When he pulled the article of clothing up, so her warm, heavy breasts lay against him, she went very, very still.

He threaded his fingers through the short hair at her nape. "Drink, *querida*."

Daria curled her hands around his shoulders and nuzzled his neck, making his throat go tight. He felt the hard brush of fang and braced himself for the first painful stab. It came, followed by the sweet rush of her beginner's veil blanketing him. She drew on him and his body went tight with need.

He slid his hand down her back, enjoying the smoothness of her skin and wanting nothing more than to run his tongue over every inch of it. She shifted against him and the heat of her cunt grew warmer. Taking that as an indication of her arousal, he dipped his hand beneath the elastic of her panties and cupped her delectable ass. Alejandro wondered if she'd ever had a man give her attention there and then swiftly decided *he* would, if he could.

Daria moved her hands from his shoulders to the spokes on the bed frame, rubbing her breasts against his chest. His cock was hard as a steel rod and he needed to come. Just touching her, making her orgasm, would make him happy. It would help her, too. So he eased his hand between her spread thighs, straight into heaven.

Ah, yes, she was aroused. Her cunt was like hot silk against his fingers. He found her clit, ripe, full, and swollen—like a decadent little cherry just dying to be nibbled at—and eased the pad of his finger over it and over it again, petting it. It swelled under his touch, growing larger and more needy. He took it between his thumb and forefinger and stroked.

She broke the bite and gasped. "Alejandro."

"*Mmmmm* . . . let me bring you ease."

He moved his head, finding her earlobe and dragging it between his teeth. She shuddered against him and rose up, but she didn't push him away. She only drew her arms from her bra and tossed it to the floor, baring her lovely breasts with their lickable hard, red nipples to his gaze.

Her eyes were wide and dark, the pupils enlarged from her arousal. She shifted against his hand, rubbing her cunt against it, and shivered. Still, something warred on her face and in her eyes.

"*Shhhh* . . . It's okay," he murmured. "I know you need it. Just take what I'm offering you, Daria." His voice sounded strained to his own ears. Fuck, he wanted her.

She slipped her hand between their bodies, pressing his palm against her and rubbing her pussy more firmly against it. He shifted his hand, letting two of his fingers penetrate her. She closed her eyes and groaned, began to rotate her hips, fucking herself on his fingers.

"That's it. There you go," he encouraged. "Ride them."

She tipped her head back and moaned. She was only using him to relieve herself of the sexual pressure of the Choosing. Alejandro understood that. One day maybe it could be more than that between them. Alejandro was surprised to realize just how much he wished for it. He wanted Daria to care about him. For the time being, he'd take what he could get.

His gaze dropped to where her pretty pink pussy lips slid up and down on his fingers. If only it was his cock sliding so snugly into her wet, velvet cunt. Daria could have no idea what doing this cost him.

He leaned forward and captured one of her nipples in his mouth. Latching on, he stimulated it with the tip of his tongue, while he gently rolled and pinched the other one between his thumb and index finger. All the while, Daria rode him, taking the climax he offered her.

Daria finally shuddered and came. He reveled in her pleasure as much as she did. The only thing that would have been better would have been to have his cock buried deep her sweet, tight cunt. As it was, he was still unsatisfied. Good thing he'd learned a lot of control during his years with Lucinda.

She rolled to the side the second it was over. "Damn it, Alejandro."

"Just accept that you like sex with me, Daria. Get it over with. Give it up."

"I never said I didn't like sex with you, Alejandro."

She tried to roll away, but he lunged across the bed, wrapped his arm around her waist, and dragged her back against him. Daria fought him for a moment and then gave up, relaxing into him like warmed butter.

He nuzzled the hair at the nape of her neck and slid a leg over her thighs, trapping her. "Sleep now."

"I don't take orders from you," she said with a tremble in her voice.

"Come on, Daria. Relax. We have a hell of a day ahead of us tomorrow. I wonder what we'll find."

She sighed, and took a moment to reply. "The theories out of the ABI are all dark—drugs, sense chips, or blood slaves."

Sense chips were microchips people could insert into special bio drives on their arms or in their necks that immersed them in a false real-life experience for a time. The most popular sense chips were porn, of course. They were illegal because they were addictive—not physically, but psychologically.

"I guess we'll see," he answered, closing his eyes.

"How can you be so relaxed about everything?"

"Why worry now about stuff that'll happen tomorrow? How can you be so uptight about everything?"

She turned in his arms. "I'm not uptight."

He laughed, letting his gaze trail over her bare breasts. His Daria had a good heart and would go to the ends of the earth to right a wrong. She was brave, beautiful inside and out, intelligent, and tougher than most men he knew . . . and she also was definitely uptight. "Then give me one reason you're turning down no-strings-attached sex with me when I know you're dying for it, Daria."

"Damn, you're so arrogant. It's incredible."

"Yeah, I'm arrogant. We've already established that. So give me a reason. Flat-out. Are you afraid of me?"

A small smile curved her sensual lips. She leaned in toward him, gathering his hand and pressing it to the mound of her warm, soft breast. Then she brushed her mouth across his. Alejandro's world spun for a moment. He went in for a deeper taste, hoping to finally get some ease for his aching body, but she pulled away.

"I'm not afraid of you," she murmured against his lips. "I just don't want you as much as you think I do." With that, she pulled from his grasp, grabbed her clothes, and went into the bathroom.

Alejandro collapsed back onto the mattress and covered his face with his hands. The woman was going to kill him with this shit. He had half a mind to tie her to the bed and just get it over with.

He didn't believe the line she'd just fed him. For some reason he scared the hell out of her, but he had no idea why.

～

"TEDDY bears?" Daria blinked, not believing her eyes. Mound after mound of fluffy brown teddy bears lay on the conveyor belt in front of her. Teddy bears, here, under Christopher Sante's roof. Something wasn't right.

That morning a woman named Guo Jia Ying had rousted them from bed at the crack of dawn to go to work. Daria had only grabbed a couple hours of sleep, since she'd spent most of the night trying to avoid Alejandro. She'd spent the bulk of it in the garden, looking up at the stars and trying to ignore the sight of Alejandro's nearly nude body sprawled on the bed.

He'd probably slept great.

When she'd finally broken down and climbed into bed, she'd only caught a few winks since she'd been fully clothed and curled up on the very edge of the mattress. It hadn't been a recipe for deep sleep and today she was a bit grouchy.

And flabbergasted.

Jia Ying smiled, her lovely brown eyes twinkling. She obviously loved her job here, loved life under the dome in general. Or maybe she was just a naturally happy person. Was it bad that Daria had taking a liking to the older vamp the moment she'd met her? "Not just any teddy bears. These are handmade teddy bears, collector's items. There's a demand for certain items that aren't bot-made. These teddy bears are famous throughout all the settlements."

Beside her, Alejandro frowned and scratched his head, probably just as confused as she was.

"So this is how the Shining Way supports itself? It makes, um, teddy bears?" asked Daria.

"It's not the only way. There's a honey farm on the opposite side of the compound and we also maintain a small apple orchard."

Alejandro blinked. "Teddy bears, honey, and apples?"

Jia Ying smiled. "Yes. We thought you and Alejandro would be happiest here in the factory but if you'd prefer to work the honey or apples, we can switch you."

"Uh. Teddy bears are fine," answered Alejandro.

A line of people worked the mounds of teddies in various stages of completion. Stations were set up along the way. One group of people stuffed them, the next sewed seams, the next added a bow or clothing, depending on the line of teddy bear. Finally, the completed product disappeared through an opening at the end of the line and into another room.

It had to be a cover. It just had to be. There was something else going on here, something illicit. No way was *Christopher Sante* running some crunchy granola commune for Chosen that supported itself through cute and cuddly handicrafts, honey, and apples. Sante didn't work that clean and wholesomely. Either they were stuffing the bears with something after they left the work area, or this was just an elaborate ruse meant to cover up the slave trafficking business they had going on the side.

"What happens in that room down there?" she asked, studying the people at the end of the conveyor belt who joked and talked as they worked. Just beyond them was the opening, covered by a large industrial flap, where the finished product disappeared.

"That's the packaging room," answered Jia Ying. "That's where the bears are stitched up, tagged, and put in boxes."

Daria frowned. "Why is there a separate room for that?"

Jia Ying laughed. "I wondered, too. They told me they want to make sure no one puts anything into the teddy bears that shouldn't be there before they ship. It's a safety thing, since the bears are ultimately meant for children."

Hmmm. Or maybe so they *could* put something into the teddy bears before they shipped.

"That room is full at the moment," Jia Ying continued, "so I thought we'd put you two on the line."

"Sounds great," Daria answered, but she still fully intended to investigate the packaging room when she could.

In fact, every inch of the factory was going to get her special attention. If there was anything illegal going on, they would find out about it and add it to the list of things to prosecute Sante for. She studied the industrial flap. It would be an easy way to get in there, as long as it wasn't the locking kind. Of course, with her luck, it probably was.

Jia Ying led them to the stuffing station and introduced them to the two other Chosen there. There was Rodrigo, a sultry-eyed, effeminate succubare, and Emmet, an older vamp with chocolate-colored skin who threw his head back and laughed with his whole body, typically showing fang while he did it.

"So, you two are new here?" asked Emmet.

Alejandro nodded. "Arrived the day before yesterday. Do they always throw parties for the new members?"

"Oh, yeah. Every time." Emmet nodded, smiled, and showed a disconcerting amount of shiny, sharp fang. "And sometimes they just throw them for the hell of it. Christopher Sante knows how to treat us right."

Hmmm. Indeed, thought Daria. She stayed quiet, continuing to stuff teddy bears.

"With blood slaves and everything?" Alejandro inquired.

"They aren't blood slaves, man," Emmet answered. "Those humans come of their own free will. They want to be here. They're donors and come because they crave the dark kiss."

"I'm not complaining," answered Alejandro with a grin. He could look so nonthreatening when he wanted to. "Who organizes all that? Man, I could get used to those parties, my friend."

"Us peon dome residents don't get a heads-up on any of that, *mi hermano,*" Rodrigo said. "That's all the domain of Christopher Sante and the Shining Way board of directors."

Daria frowned. "Board of directors?"

"They're not really a board of directors," answered Jia Ying. "We just call them that. They're the Chosen closest to Sante. Sort of his advisors. They make all the decisions around here. Pretty much, they run this place."

"Seems like they're doing a good job," replied Alejandro, lifting a teddy bear and examining its stuffing. "I noticed you don't see Sante much. Too bad. I know him from way back. I was hoping I might get to say hello, catch up on old times." Alejandro was good at this, making subtle conversation that drew answers from people.

Jia Ying shook her head and grabbed another bear. "He doesn't come out much. He's kind of a recluse. We see him once in a while, usually just on special occasions. He's got a house on the east side of the compound and it's heavily protected. He values his privacy. We're all very grateful to him, though, for providing this community for us."

Heavily guarded house on the east end of the compound. Maybe that's where Ari was. Daria filed it away to think about later.

"I bet *your* head is spinning," Emmet said, nodding at Daria. "I can feel how young you are. You're just days old, little girl. All this must be quite a change for you. You're lucky, though, getting in here. It can be a cold universe out there for Chosen. We're too outnumbered by the normals." *Normal* was a slang term the Chosen had for humans. "This place is a good community, like-minded, and close-knit. You'll see. You got lucky being let in here so soon after your Choosing."

Daria tried not to gag as she answered. "I'm thankful I got in here, too." She shot him a smile. Hey, it wasn't even a lie . . . mostly.

"So how did you two meet?" asked Jia Ying.

"We met in New Chicago about three years ago," Alejandro answered, sticking with the story they'd agreed upon beforehand. "At a party of one our mutual friends." He gave Jia Ying a playful sidelong glance. "Valerie was so into me. *Dios*, she couldn't resist. I had to fight her off that night. Remember . . . *baby*?"

Daria resisted the urge to kick him. Instead she smiled sweetly,

"You tell your version, honey, I'll tell mine." She put her hand to the side of her mouth and whispered at Jia Ying. "He followed me around like a lovesick puppy dog all night."

Jia Ying laughed.

"Anyway," Alejandro continued, "it wasn't long before things got serious. Eventually Valerie decided she wanted to take things to the next level and she demanded I Choose her even though she lacked the genes. I tried to persuade her it was a bad idea, but"—Alejandro shook his head—"Valerie wants what she wants."

"And you made it through the succubare?" asked Jia Ying. "That's amazing."

"You are brave, lady," Rodrigo put in. "You must really love him to take that chance."

Alejandro laid his half-stuffed teddy bear down and crushed Daria to him, tipping her back and kissing her hard. His tongue snaked into her mouth, rubbing up against hers with long, erotic strokes that made her tingle all over and made her think of lots of things that had nothing to do with teddy bears. Emmet and Rodrigo hooted.

He set her back on her feet and grinned. "She's head over heels for me. Aren't you, baby?"

Feeling disorientated, she forced herself to focus. "Head over heels," she echoed blankly, blinking.

Everyone laughed.

Flushing, Daria picked up a teddy bear and concentrated on packing stuffing in correctly. "I just knew that if we wanted to stay together, I'd have to be Chosen. Otherwise, he would've had to watch me grow old and die while he stayed young and good-looking."

"Not just good-looking—smokin' sweetheart," said Rodrigo with a leer in Alejandro's direction, which made everyone laugh again.

"Even if I'd ended up succubare, at least we could have stayed together," Daria finished.

Jia Ying nodded. "I know what it is to watch those you love pass into old age and die. I have done it often."

"How old are you, Jia Ying?" Alejandro asked.

"I'm nearly two hundred and ninety five." She didn't look a day over twenty. "I was the only one in my family to inherit the genes. Apparently they were a leftover surprise gift from somewhere far down my bloodline."

Daria dropped a finished teddy bear to the belt. "So you had to watch your whole family grow old and die. I'm so sorry."

"The worst was watching my daughter go. However, it's a part of being Chosen." Jia Ying smiled. "And, to look on the bright side, I got to watch her live a long, happy life and die a very old woman."

Daria returned her smile. She had a feeling Jia Ying could find the bright side of most things. Maybe Daria could learn something from her.

By the end of her shift, Daria hadn't forgotten she was there undercover, but she could have. She found she genuinely liked Jia Ying, Rodrigo, and Emmet. They were companionable and friendly. Daria couldn't remember the last time she'd laughed so much in one day. For the most part, she had the impression that none of them knew anything about illegal goings-on at the Shining Way. They just seemed glad to be able to call the place home.

Throughout the day, she heard each of their stories. Emmet had come to the Shining Way to escape his life on Galileo, where there weren't many Chosen. The climate was hostile toward the few that did live there. He was a young vampire, but had been Chosen late in life.

Jia Ying had been a successful attorney on Earth, specializing in representing the Chosen. It had been the latest in a string of careers she'd pursued. As she'd grown older, she'd realized she'd wanted to "retire" from working life.

Since she had enough money saved to do anything she wanted, she decided to seek out new experiences. Soon after the Shining Way had been created, she'd bought her way in. It was home to her now and she didn't want to live anywhere else.

Jia Ying was one of the original dome residents. Daria made a point of filing this bit of information away. If anyone should know what was going on here, it would be a longtimer.

Finally, Rodrigo had followed love to the Shining Way. He and his longtime partner had come to the dome to drop out of society and live a calm life. Happily ever after was not to be, however. When the relationship ended, Rodrigo stayed while his lover moved on. Here Rodrigo had many people from which to satisfy his needs as a succubare. Daria hadn't inquired further.

Even though the day had been enjoyable, Daria left the factory at closing time with disappointment weighing bitterly on her heart.

She stopped outside on the walkway, watching the fake Earth sky darken into fake twilight. The days and nights seemed to have odd lengths under the dome, but she supposed that Sante could make them whatever duration he liked best. Sante would enjoy playing god that way. As a result, it was impossible to know what time of day it was beyond the dome's walls, furthering the fantasyland feel of the Shining Way.

Daria could see the allure of this place, especially to the disenfranchised.

Jia Ying, Emmet, and Rodrigo all adored their current way of life and, as far as Daria could tell, had not one negative word to speak against Christopher Sante.

It left a bad taste in her mouth. How could someone as evil as Christopher Sante inspire such loyalty? How had he perpetuated such an illusion about himself as to make these people, who by all appearances seemed intelligent and rational, adore him and think he could do no wrong?

An image of Julia's broken body flashed into her mind and tears pricked her eyes.

Alejandro stopped beside her, slipped a hand into a pocket, and looked up at the same sky. "So, want to take a walk before we head back?"

"Sure." The thought of being crammed in that room with Alejandro didn't make her want to rush back. He was too much of a temptation and she was far too weak.

They strolled down the path toward the east, in perfect accord. They had every right to explore their surroundings, after all. They were new around here. Even if they should find themselves close to the famed house of Christopher Sante, their generous benefactor, no one would find it suspicious.

Their minds and intentions one, they headed in that direction.

By the time they reached the easternmost side of the compound, it was completely dark. The dome was a lot larger than she'd ever imagined and Daria was sorry they hadn't grabbed their dune bikes for the trek. Sante's mansion rose from a lush green lawn, dotted with towering trees and flowering bushes. A tall wrought iron fence rose around it all, to keep out his admirers and the curious. A guardhouse stood at the entranceway, complete with two muscular and armed Chosen.

Daria assessed the property as they stood looking on, just another couple of Shining Way members getting a glimpse of the famous Christopher Sante's abode. She knew Alejandro was doing the same beside her.

Was Ari Templeton somewhere behind those walls? Was Sante hurting her now? Did she even still live?

Because if Ari Templeton was anywhere in the compound, every instinct Daria had screamed the abducted woman would be here.

They'd stayed there for as long as they could, talking together and pointing like tourists, until the guards approached and asked them to move away. By then Daria had already devised several ways to get into the house.

On the way back to their room, Alejandro opened up a mental pathway and shared that he also had been figuring out various ways to break in. Together they settled on one.

Tonight? finished Alejandro.

Daria thought of Ari. *Yes. We can't get careless, but I don't think we have a moment to lose.*

13

DARIA dropped down onto the grass hard enough to make her teeth clack. She rolled to the side, and lay still for a moment, heart thumping in her chest. God, she hoped there were no dogs. She could handle almost any kind of alarm, but dogs were tricky. This had to be the fiftieth time she'd done B&E in the line of duty, and every time it gave her a case of nerves.

Alejandro had boosted her up over the fence, at the same time as Brandon had disabled—just for about ten seconds—the trip alarm that ran around the interior perimeter of the fence. It had given her enough time to use her shiny new vampiric strength and agility to get over the fence and roll to the side, away from the laser beam that, if tripped, would reveal her location.

Inhaling the scent of freshly cut grass, she waited for several moments. No barking met her ears. Oh, that was *so* good.

She pushed to her feet and made her way into the trees, knowing that Brandon and Alejandro, unable to hoist themselves easily over the fence because of their size, had melted into the shadows.

The place was guarded, but not overly so. As far as she could tell he had a standard security setup. It wasn't anything that, with her specialized training, she couldn't easily circumvent on her own.

Sante probably didn't feel he needed anything more than mild deterrents, just enough to protect himself from admirers. After all, the compound itself was a fortress. They handpicked and investigated every person before they allowed them through the front gate.

Lucky for her, since she wasn't equipped to break into an expertly guarded house right now. But she could do a run-of-the-mill alarm on her own with the tools they'd smuggled in sewed into the lining of their duffle bags.

Using the shadows, trees, and bushes, she made her way very slowly to the house. She was taking a huge risk because she didn't have any inside knowledge of the house or blueprints. It was a necessary risk, however. If Ari Templeton still lived, she may not have a lot of time.

Her eyes open and her senses completely alert, she approached the house and began looking for both a way inside and for any other security devices. Only one window on the second floor showed light or activity.

It was late, and she'd hoped Sante and anyone else in the house would be asleep. Once the Chosen adjusted to life under the dome, they started to sleep when it was dark and be awake when it was light. But apparently someone was still up.

She found an entrance point and wistfully touched the tools in her vest pocket that she wouldn't need. There appeared to be no other electronic security system in place for the residence. Sante apparently thought the gate, guard, and perimeter alert were enough.

This would be no challenge, but at least she'd be able to get in and out without raising any suspicion or leaving any trace of her presence. That was the best-case scenario, to be a ghost. In, check for Ari, and out.

Slipping a basic lock-picking tool from her pocket, she quickly used it on the lock at the back of the house. Slowly, she eased the door open and entered the kitchen on feet as silent as a cat's. Before she'd left the apartment, she'd washed her body thoroughly with a product designed to cleanse away all the scent. Daria hoped it had done the job. Otherwise Sante might be able to detect her in his home with his clever, ancient Chosen nose.

A dim light over the oven illuminated the large room. It was, of course, state-of-the-art. Nothing less would do for Christopher Sante.

A wine rack covered one entire wall, stacked high with bottles. Above the large cooking island in the center of the room hung fine crystal glasses and assorted cooking implements. Yes, Daria remembered well that Sante enjoyed his wine. They'd spent many cool evenings on the patio sipping glasses of fine red while watching the sun dip lower in the sky.

Bastard.

Shaking off the memory, she eased along the wall toward a door that was either a broom closet, bathroom, or entryway to the basement. Bingo, it was the basement.

She disappeared through it and made her way down into the dank-smelling lower level of the house. Every step she took into the darkness, she thanked her spanking-new preternatural vision.

One by one, slowly, silently, she explored every room. Having found only spiders and more dusty wine racks, she returned to the first floor and repeated her search. She found nothing that wasn't completely domestic. Nothing of an illegal nature. No drugs, no sense chips, nothing having to do with the illegal trafficking of blood slaves, and certainly no Ari Templeton.

Having satisfied herself that she'd thoroughly investigated all she could, Daria made her way up the stairs to the second floor, keeping well to the wall to avoid any creaks or squeaks.

She tried to suppress her bitter disappointment. Her desire to nail Sante to the wall was strong . . . and very personal, but she needed to stay neutral and objective. If there wasn't anything to implicate him in the house, there simply wasn't.

Anyway, it was a big compound and they had yet to explore it all. Evidence—and Ari Templeton—could be anywhere. Maybe her instincts about Templeton being in the house were simply wrong.

She reached the top of the stairs and found herself in a long corridor. Soft light spilled from under a closed door and pooled on the hardwood floor.

The scent of Sante's cologne lightly teased her nostrils, bringing a flood of memory to the fore that was so strong it bowed her knees for a moment. Images of the person she'd been before surged through her mind, from a time when she'd been younger and her heart lighter. She could still see Sante's laughing face above her in their bed, his lips tenderly capturing hers. She could still hear sweet, soft words of endearment flowing from his mouth.

Steps sounded from within the lighted bedroom, approaching the closed door from the other side, and Daria practically dove into the darkened guest bathroom in front of her. Immediately her mind worked through places to hide in the large room, in case this was the walker's destination. She opened a door, found a linen and toiletries closet and ducked within, leaving the door open just a crack so she could see out.

Sante walked down the corridor, past the bathroom, wearing only a pair of dark blue boxers. His body had changed little since she'd known him—he remained fit and well taken care of, a challenge to best in any hand-to-hand combat, with a strong chest and brawny arms. His hair was a bit longer these days, but other than that he appeared much the same.

Another whiff of his cologne sucker punched her in the stomach and made her remember how hard she'd fallen for him. Daria had really believed she'd loved Christopher Sante back then.

She'd believed he loved her back.

Sante disappeared down the stairs and returned a minute later with two wineglasses and an open bottle. When he reentered the bedroom, Daria heard the roll of soft, sultry feminine laughter. Her skin prickled with the feel of succubare. The woman very well could have been the one at the party the other day. Maybe she'd snagged Sante somehow as a snack.

Yuck.

She waited several moments, until things had quieted in the bedroom, before she exited the bathroom. Every nerve in her body demanded that she leave this place immediately and get as far from Sante as she could, but she knew it was just a personal reaction. Forcing it away, she finished her job and checked all the rooms on the second floor before giving in to her urge to flee.

Leaving the way she'd come in and relocking the door behind her, she snuck back through the yard, confident that she'd left no trace of her presence anywhere for Sante to find. She'd been successful.

Now, if only she'd found something.

Jumping up, she captured a tree branch and shimmied up the trunk to climb out on a limb high enough to avoid the perimeter laser detector and close enough for her to reach the top of the fence. Another few moments and she'd dropped onto the other side and melted into the shadows, bound for the room and her update, which was an annoying handful of nothing.

She stopped and turned in the darkness, staring at the house. Why, when she'd found no sign of any captive, did her gut still say Ari Templeton was there?

~

ALEJANDRO watched Daria disappear down the pathway toward the dorm, rubbing the back of her neck from a long day of stuffing teddy bears, pretty much the last thing either them of them thought they'd be doing here.

The entire week had been mostly just work and little progress on the investigation front. It was hard to get time away from the eyes of the other members of the Shining Way. The only way to explore was to do it after dark, and that was risky since it was hard to explain why they were walking around in the wee morning hours. No one seemed to be out then, though there was no curfew in place.

Daria had made it a personal goal to get into the packaging room at the teddy bear factory, but it was proving difficult. That raised red flags with all of them. What did they have to hide?

He felt Brandon come up to stand beside him. Together they watched Daria disappear into the apartment building.

"*Qué tal estás, tio?* How are you, my friend? How goes the honey making?" Alejandro asked him without turning his head, his thoughts still centered on his pretty partner.

Brandon slipped a hand into his pocket. "It's a laugh a bloody minute, but at least there are a lot of honeys around to make it worthwhile. No sense in letting all the pretty flowers go unattended. Why not have a little play on the side while you work?" He paused, then jerked his chin in the direction Daria had gone. "How goes *your* honey making?"

He growled his answer. "None of your fucking business, *tio*."

Brandon snorted. "That well?"

"Yes. That well."

"You know the women here look at you like you're some kind of god, Alejandro. Pick some flowers with me. There are plenty of women to choose from if you're in need."

Maybe, but he only wanted one of them. Brandon wouldn't understand that, so he simply didn't answer.

"Come on, let's go to the room," said Brandon. "I have something to tell you."

Once they got to the dorm, they found Daria just emerging from the bathroom in a puff of steam. Her long, lithe body was wrapped in a towel and her short blond hair stood up in damp tufts around her head. The scent of her freshly washed skin made his cock hard, but then a light breeze coupled with the thought of Daria made his cock hard these days.

She still fed from him every day, but she hadn't allowed him to touch her the way he had before. That last night had changed something between them and Alejandro wanted desperately to know why.

Worse, since they needed to carry each other's scent, she undressed to take blood from him. Every night they lay nearly naked together—skin touching, breath mingling. It was enough to keep suspicion from them; it was also just enough to drive him insane.

He masked his need for her, however. Daria didn't have any idea just how badly she was teasing him. She'd made it clear from the beginning that she'd wanted to pursue this mission while not actually having sex, and he didn't want to push her to do something she didn't desire with her heart. That would cause a larger rift between them. That was not his goal.

He wanted more than just sex from Daria Moran. Much more.

Alejandro knew he had to be patient. Even though all he really wanted was to strip her naked and tease her mercilessly with his lips, tongue, and hands until she begged him to fuck her.

Daria said her greetings to Brandon then snagged a bottle of lotion and began applying it to her long, bare legs. Alejandro sat across from her and watched with avid interest as she moved, occasionally giving him flashes of her naked sex, unbeknownst to her.

Yes, Daria had surely been put in the universe just to make him crazy. That had to be it.

"On the other side of the compound, there's some interesting things happening," Brandon began.

Alejandro dragged his attention away from Daria, with effort, and focused on their partner.

"Guards coming and going on the road leading past the beekeeping field. They were there yesterday and again today. This afternoon"—he paused dramatically—"they marched a group of veil-addicted humans right past us."

"A group?" Alejandro asked. Now Brandon had his full attention. "Where were they going?"

"It has been nearly impossible for me to slip the leash of the foreman over there, so I don't know, but I think we should check it out."

"Tonight," said Daria. She'd paused, rapt and attentive to Brandon, lotion pooled in one hand.

"Not if it's a full moon," answered Alejandro. "They don't have the moon phases here on any kind of a schedule, so we don't know what it will be tonight. If it's a full moon, we can't go. Too much light, too great a risk we'll be caught."

She nodded. "Fine. You're right. The first night there's no full moon then."

"There's a party at the Alhambra Building tonight," added Brandon. "We should definitely be making an appearance there. We need to mingle with the natives as much as possible."

Daria nodded. "Jia Ying told me about it today. I was getting ready to go over there. Sounds like Sante might even make an appearance. It's the event of the week and the whole commune is abuzz." She finished with the lotion as she spoke. "Dress in dark colors. If there's no full moon, we can head over toward the beekeeping fields from the party."

Brandon nodded and headed out the door. "See you over there."

Alejandro sat in the chair and glowered as Daria stood with her back to him and dropped her towel to dress. His gaze skated over her curves, centering on her lovely heart-shaped ass.

"Do you have to do that?" His voice sounded like gravel.

"Do what?" She pulled on a pair of white cotton panties, bending over just enough to give him a glimpse of sweetness. She cast an irritated glance at him. "Are you going to get dressed? I want to get over there."

No, clearly she had no idea. He moved lightning fast and without conscious thought. Alejandro had her on her back with her thighs spread in a moment. She let out a surprised yelp and fought him, but he'd gotten the better of her. He easily pinned her deadly arms to the mattress, so she couldn't hurt him.

"Eres lo mas lindo que he visto. Te deseo, querida."

Daria struggled against him. "I don't understand what you're saying."

"I said you're the most beautiful thing I've ever seen. I want you, Daria," he drawled, his accent thicker from his anger and arousal. "But if you are not going to fuck me, then do not tease me with your nude body."

She blinked, looking surprised. "But you've seen me many times, Alejandro. You've touched me. I put my skin to yours every night when I take your blood. What does it matter that I drop my towel in front of you once in a while to change my clothes?"

"I want to touch you more than you allow me. Don't you understand? Don't you see how much I desire you?" He nudged the soft, vulnerable flesh between her thighs with his hard cock. "You are making me absolutely insane with sexual need. Every night I must endure your body against mine intimately, yet I can't make love to you the way I want to. I cannot take any more additional teasing, Daria. Not one moment more."

Her blue eyes were wide and her breath came in labored little gasps. "I'm sorry, Alejandro. I didn't know."

The scent of her arousal teased his nose, made every muscle in his body tense. The press of her bare breasts against his chest didn't help either.

"I know you want me. I do not know why you fight me, but, you, Daria, are an excellent fighter. You have a will like I have never seen in all my life. You are winning this fight." With effort he released her arms and rolled off the bed. "You are winning this stupid fight between us, but we are both losing the war."

With that said, he turned and left the room to head over to the party.

～

YOU ARE WINNING *this stupid fight between us, but we are both losing the war.*

The words rang through her mind as Daria watched Alejandro from across the room, a death grip on her drink. The fight was obviously over sex, but what was the war?

Around her tittered Jia Ying and some of her friends. Jia Ying had taken Daria under her wing and introduced her to many people at the Shining Way. The older Chosen was friendly and good-natured, and everyone seemed to like her.

Daria had never been good at having friendships with women, especially not since Julia had died. She was used to dealing with men in her line of work and related to them better than she did to women, but she would do her best to fit in here. *Valerie* would be good at female friendships.

On the surface the Shining Way was a lot like an exclusive resort for the Chosen. It was an idealistic place in the minds of most and the people around her now had no idea anything illegal was going on here, of that Daria was sure. Sante obviously didn't broadcast his darker operations at large.

"Look at that one," said Marissa, a young, attractive succubare, pointing in Alejandro's direction. "I never noticed *him* before. I think I need to go and introduce myself."

Jia Ying laughed and caught Marissa's arm before she could get far. "His name is Alejandro and he's spoken for, so if you don't want Valerie to tear you from limb to limb, stay here."

"Oh, I'm sorry, but you must be used to it by now," answered Marissa with an apologetic smile. "How do you keep the women off him? He's gorgeous. Or maybe you two have an open relationship," she finished hopefully.

A flicker of unwelcome jealousy ran through her. The thought flashed—*Alejandro is mine. No one else is allowed to covet him.* But, of course, he wasn't hers. Not only that, she didn't want him to be hers. That was only some stupid, irrational feeling born from their current close work relationship.

Jia Ying hit her friend's shoulder. "Dumb question. You can smell Valerie on Alejandro, and Alejandro on Valerie. It's very obvious they're mated and they're only with each other. No other scents. Back off, Marissa."

Just then the far doors opened and a group of Chosen entered. A hush fell over the crowd, followed by an excited murmur that flowed like a wave to where Daria stood.

Christopher Sante had arrived.

14

ALEJANDRO turned and met her eyes meaningfully for a moment before slamming back the rest of his drink. Brandon was nowhere to be seen.

"Wow, the whole board of directors showed tonight," said Marissa, going up on her tiptoes to see over the crowd. Her long brown hair dipped into her drink as she moved from side to side in order to see better.

Daria was tall enough to easily see the small pocket of Chosen making their way through the crowd. "Do you know who they all are? The board of directors, I mean?"

Jia Ying replied, "Max Ortega, Sophia Helete, Carlos Hernadez, Eleanor Matthews, and Jillian O'Bryan."

Everyone who knew about the illegal activities at the Shining Way.

Daria said her good-byes and made her way over to Alejandro.

"He's coming in this direction," he said, snaking an arm around her waist and pulling her up against his side. She snuggled against him like she belonged there, or at least that's how she hoped it looked.

Indeed, Sante did appear to be making a straight line for them through the throng, stopping occasionally to greet someone or shake a hand like a freaking intergalactic politician. Seemed everyone wanted a piece of the owner of the Shining Way, yet no one was overly pushy. That might have something to do with the handful of badass Chosen bodyguards that Daria could see trailing the members of Sante's inner circle. Honestly, it was like waiting at court to be addressed by the king, and it made Daria's skin try to get up and walk away without her.

Sante spotted them in the crowd and did a double take. "Alejandro?" He walked toward them.

Daria pasted a smile on her face, even forced it all the way up to her eyes. Damn, she was a good actress.

When Sante reached them, Alejandro shook his hand, but, smiling, Sante pulled him forward into an embrace and slapped him on the back. "It's been a long time."

"Too long, *tio*," Alejandro replied, grinning.

"I knew you'd recently joined us here at the Shining Way. I confess I was looking for you this evening." Sante wore a huge smile. He turned to her. "This must be Valerie?"

Daria extended her hand. "Very nice to meet you, Mr. Sante. I've heard so much about you. Really, it's an honor."

"Call me Christopher," he answered. "You have shared the blood donors employed here at the Shining Way, that makes us family."

Oh, puke.

"This place is amazing. I feel so privileged to be here. I do feel like I've come home . . . to family."

"Indeed, that's why I created the Shining Way in the first place," Sante continued, "so we could have a place apart from the humans. Somewhere all our own, a community."

She increased the dazzle of her smile. "I appreciate you allowing me in . . . Christopher."

"I'm glad you're both here." He turned back to Alejandro. "How many years has it been? Five?"

"It's been seven years," answered Alejandro.

"Longer than I thought, then. I'd heard you were Chosen by Lucinda Valentini. You didn't win the luck of the draw with that one."

"You're telling me, my friend."

"A lot has happened since our days at the ABI."

"I left that life behind me after my Choosing. It never really suited me the first time around, and now that I'm living the life of the Chosen," Alejandro paused and added meaningfully, "I don't look back."

A slow smile spread across Sante's lips as the unspoken message registered loudly. *I have new allegiances now and understand the loyalty the Chosen have to their blood kin. I forgive you for the past.*

Alejandro tightened his grip around her waist, knowing how she must feel. Daria didn't flinch, didn't allow her smile to waver for even a moment as the memory of the past—Julia's death—flickered through Sante's eyes, accompanied by a slow smile of understanding. Her stomach roiled. The truth had glimmered behind his gaze for a moment, quickly covered by a dark lie.

Even though she wanted to lunge at Sante, close her hands around his throat, and squeeze, she didn't move a muscle.

Sante nodded, a warm, speculative look in his eye. "I appreciate that."

"I just want to create a new life for myself here with Valerie."

Actually, I want to rip his heart out for hurting you.

The comment, uttered on a pathway Alejandro had opened with her, made her hand tighten on her cup. She didn't respond, but she could see that Alejandro trembled subtly in otherwise well-concealed rage. His protectiveness warmed her.

And Daria understood. It was hard to stand there and smile into the man's face when all they both wanted was his throat crushing between their fingers.

They'd both done jobs like this a million times, but this one was personal.

Sante turned his attention back to Daria. "Have I met you before, Valerie? You seem familiar to me."

Her heart stopped, then thudded a little faster than normal. She fought to calm herself, knowing that the older vamp might be able to hear the increase in her heart rate, might be able to scent the startled thrill of fear on her skin. "I don't believe we have ever met, but it's possible. Ever spent any time in New Chicago? That's where I spent most of my life."

Sante studied her for a moment with an intensity that made apprehension curl through her stomach. Her surgery had been complete. There should be no way Sante could recognize her. *Her own mother* hadn't recognized her when Daria had called on the commview after the procedure.

Finally, Sante nodded and glanced at Alejandro. "I have. We will have to explore our possible mutual connections more thoroughly sometime soon." Sante moved to leave them. "Enjoy the evening."

Once they'd exchanged parting words and Sante had moved on, Alejandro and Daria shared one short look as the rest of his party flowed behind him like a wedding train.

Daria opened a pathway. *I have to get out of here for a minute.*

Go on back to the room. There's nothing left to do here.

She handed her empty glass to him and slipped from the grasp of the crowd with a relieved sigh.

Once out of the building, she glanced up at the sky and cursed. Full moon. Tonight there would be no foray to the other side of the compound. Silvery light lit the grounds almost like daylight, bleaching the color from everything around her. She drew a deep, shaky breath, trying to get her nerves under control from seeing Sante after so many years.

Movement caught her gaze and she turned her head to see a woman walking down a pathway at the end of the building. Tall, thin, long brown hair, nose a bit larger than what might be considered classically attractive.

Ari Templeton.

Daria took off, racing after the woman as she turned a corner, her heart pounding in her chest. She skidded around the corner of the building to find . . . *no one.* Daria scanned the area, looking for a side door into the Alhambra Building or somewhere she could have gone, but there was nothing.

"What the hell?"

She stood, staring down the pathway. Maybe she was losing it. Maybe there hadn't really been a woman at all. Perhaps she'd hallucinated the whole thing. She sniffed the air, trying to parse out the various scents with her new super-duper Chosen sniffer, but couldn't isolate the single scent of a person who'd recently walked through the air. Nothing. A creepy chill entered her bones, making her shiver.

Or maybe she was chasing a ghost.

It couldn't have been Ari Templeton she'd seen. She had to have been mistaken.

~

DARIA tried not to enjoy it when Alejandro slid into the bed beside her and pulled her against him. She pretended to sleep, so she had an excuse to stay that way—head against his chest and his warm, bare body tucked against her side.

Unable to fall asleep while she questioned her sanity, she welcomed the comfort of his scent and the silken solidity of his form beside her. Alejandro had stayed at the party until the morning hours, and she wondered what had kept him there.

The thought of Marissa flashed through her mind, accompanied by an unwelcome dose of jealousy. Stupid, since she really didn't care what—or who—Alejandro did. This assignment was getting to her. She was starting to believe her cover.

All the same, she inhaled deeply, searching for any hint of another woman on him. She got nothing, of course. The crowd surrounding them in the Alhambra Building masked just about everything, though she could detect the scent of herself on his skin—like a mark of ownership. It comforted her and, in turn, disturbed her.

Tomorrow she would tell Alejandro she saw a ghost . . . or something. Tonight she wanted to stay where she was. Perhaps now that he was here, she might be able to go to sleep.

He twined his arms around her waist and rested his chin on the top of her head. A groan rumbled from him, vibrating through her. The low, sexy sound, so much like the noises he made when aroused, raised goose bumps along her arms.

Slowly, relaxation finally settled over her limbs, chasing away the last of the thoughts that crowded her mind. Sleep teased her, drawing her under a little at a time until her eyelids drifted closed.

The sound of the door opening jerked her from her lazy almost-sleep. Daria and Alejandro both came aware and sat up with lightning-fast reflexes.

"Easy," said Sante as he came through the door. Two guards trailed him.

Alejandro sleepily pushed a hand through his hair, trying to look relaxed, but his body felt taut as a bowstring beside her. "Easy? What the fuck, Sante? It's three in the morning." He careened off into a stream of mutterings in Spanish.

Sante stood at the end of the bed. "We've had a complaint about you."

Daria shifted uneasily on the mattress. "About what?"

Sante motioned in his guards, and then ordered them to close the door. "Someone thinks you aren't really a mated couple."

"That's ridiculous," answered Alejandro. "You can see us right here in bed together."

"Yes." Sante paused. "But sleeping side by side is easy. Look"—he spread his hands—"I believe you're really mated, but you and I have a history, brother. Because of that history, I can't be too careful. You know what I mean?"

"What the hell do you want from us," asked Daria angrily. "How can we give you proof? I'm not much of an exhibitionist, so if you want to watch us have sex I'm afraid you're out of luck." Rage burned in her veins, but that was okay. Valerie would be pissed to have her sleep interrupted and her relationship questioned. It was natural.

"I'm no voyeur. Sex means nothing. Any two people can have sex and make it look like they mean it. I want to watch Alejandro take your blood."

Alejandro made a frustrated sound. "You know that feeding between a mated pair is almost always sexual. It can't help be anything but. So what was that part about you not being a voyeur again?"

Daria broke in and asked, "How does watching him take my blood prove a damn thing?"

Sante favored her with a slow smile, white teeth gleaming like wolf's fangs in the semi-light. "I have lived a long time, beautiful Valerie. I have been Chosen for four hundred years. When I watch a mated couple share blood, believe me, I can tell truth from fiction."

Beside her Alejandro went still. No sound broke the silence in the room for several long moments. Then Alejandro's voice flicked like the end of a lash. "I'm sick of being tested, Sante. Carlos tested us as soon as we arrived and it engendered ill will. Now this. When does it end?"

"Tonight. It ends tonight." Sante leaned against the wall across from the bed. "Prove your matedness to me now and I promise no more tests. I must make sure you're not lying to me, Alejandro. I have let you both in too close to my heart to take risks. I am fully within my rights to demand this."

Neither of them moved. Instead they stared at Sante, who gazed expectantly at them. His muscle had settled in to flank him. Daria had to bite her tongue to keep from offering them popcorn. The caustic words rose to her tongue with a bitter flavor and she choked them back down.

A tense silence settled over the room like a shroud. Daria didn't want to give Sante what he wanted, but she knew their hand was being forced. They couldn't endanger this mission over something so trivial. Yet, she wondered by the hard annoyance emanating from Alejandro if he would challenge Sante. Alejandro was not used to giving in to another's will. Especially on something so intimate. He had to hate this more than she did.

"No." The word slipped from Alejandro's lips and fell like a heavy stone into the quiet.

Briefly, she closed her eyes. *Damn it, Alejandro.*

Immediately, Sante twitched his hand. No hesitation, as if he'd expected Alejandro to resist. The guards sprang into action, capturing Alejandro and dragging him from the bed. Daria had to stop herself from fighting the guards, not wanting to give Sante any indication she was anything more than a down-on-her-luck waitress and newly Chosen vampire. Valerie wouldn't be able to fight men twice her size.

Alejandro fought, but was unable to throw off the two vamps who each had one of his arms firmly in their grasp. They muscled him up against the wall and pinned him there, where he seethed and glowered darkly at Sante.

Sante hadn't moved. His expression hadn't changed. The older vamp's gaze was centered on her. Daria's breath hitched in her throat. She didn't like having those keen eyes focused so intently on her face.

Keeping his gaze centered on her, Sante spoke. "Over these past few years, as I have moved into my fourth century as a Chosen, I have developed a new ability. I can sip from a person's veins, Chosen or not, and tell many things about them. You would be surprised at the secrets an individual's blood will tell. If you would like, I can spare you the embarrassment of taking blood from Valerie and simply do it myself."

Panic sliced through her. The implications were clear—if Sante tasted her blood, he might be able to tell they weren't truly mated. Her fingers curled into the blankets and fisted.

He might be able to recognize her.

Sante stood in one flowing, controlled movement. His gaze swept over her. "It will be no hardship. She's very attractive. You don't mind, do you, Alejandro?"

Alejandro exploded into action, fighting against the guards and swearing in Spanish at the top of his lungs. "You won't put a tooth on her, Sante." His voice came out a low, dangerous growl and his fangs had extended. The sharp white tips peeked from between his lips.

Sante took a step toward the end of the bed. "You said you wouldn't draw her blood while I watched, yet I must have this issue settled before I leave the room. What else do you expect me to do? She is very beautiful, your Valerie, I don't mind touching her."

This could not happen. Daria understood that Sante was deliberately baiting Alejandro, yet she could see the intention in Sante's eyes to truly carry out his threat.

Daria moved warily to the opposite side of the bed, but not far enough out of his reach. Sante touched her cheek, his thumb drawing a slow arc under her eye. She suppressed a shudder of revulsion, but couldn't avoid turning her face away.

"Don't touch her," Alejandro growled.

"Then agree to my request. It's such a small one."

"All right! Yes, I agree!" He jerked his arms from the grasp of the guards. "Call off the muscle and I'll do it."

Thank god.

Sante removed his hand from her cheek, his gaze still holding hers. "I admit I'm a little disappointed you gave in, Alejandro."

Gave in. The use of those words was not lost on Daria. Sante was trying to needle Alejandro's pride.

Sante turned and looked at his men. "Desist," he ordered tersely, and they backed away from Alejandro. Then Sante backed away himself, giving Alejandro room to move.

Alejandro immediately stepped between her and Sante in a protective gesture. He stood for a moment, staring at the older vampire, aggression and threat in his stance and, even though Daria couldn't see, probably on his face.

A slow smile spread across Sante's mouth. "Do you like it here at the Shining Way, Alejandro?"

"Not at the moment," he ground out in response.

Sante flashed fang and his eyes glittered in the half-light. "Come now. Being bound to Lucinda all those years must have broken the alpha in you at least a little."

"Apparently not."

"If you want to stay here, you must play by my rules. If you are deemed trustworthy, I may want you in my inner circle. I have always had high regard for you. I know what kind of a person you are. You hold strong ideals and loyalty. However, we need to get over this suspicion that has been placed on you first. Think of this as a test. If you pass, the rewards will be great. Do you understand?"

The possibility of Alejandro being included in Sante's inner circle practically made Daria salivate. She was certain the words had gone well marked by Alejandro also.

She risked opening a mental pathway. *Just do it.* He made no indication that he'd heard her.

Alejandro didn't answer Sante verbally. Instead he turned and fixed her with his intense gaze. His pupils were blown in his agitation and his fangs were still extended. Pissed-off resignation sat in the hunch of his shoulders and the grim set of his lips.

Daria held his gaze for a moment, communicating without words. They had to do this. *They had to make it look good.* The mission depended on it. Their *lives* depended on it.

He approached and leaned toward her. She had to fight her gut impulse to back away. Alejandro didn't give her a choice, anyway. He flipped the blankets off her, grabbed her calf, and dragged her toward him.

15

T HE boxer shorts she wore slid up as he pulled her across the mattress to lay prone beneath his big body. If Sante hadn't been in the room with them the action would've made her wet. As it was, it only made her uneasy.

Alejandro hesitated, noting the sudden stiffness in her body. He squeezed her calf and then ran his palm up her skin slowly, to the back of her knee. Her breath quickened, but it did little to relax her. Flicking her gaze to the left, she saw that Sante had resumed his position against the wall, settling in for the show.

Alejandro yanked her toward him again, this time a little rougher. It was an unspoken directive. He was right; she had to get her head in the game.

Daria sat up, curling one hand around Alejandro's neck and drawing him down over her as she sealed her mouth to his. A hungry sound rumbled out of him. He grasped her boxer shorts and jerked them downward, drawing a quick gasp of surprise from her throat.

Once he had the article of clothing down and off, leaving her in only her cotton underwear and the tank top she wore to bed, he inserted his knee between her thighs and forced them apart. Then he came down on top of her, dragging her leg up over his hip and grinding his cock against her.

Apparently Sante being in the room hadn't affected *his* sex drive.

Her entire body went taut. She drew a breath, trying to relax herself, trying to soften her muscles and command the soft, erotic wash of pleasure over her body that would be present if her mate was about to take her blood. However that kind of mood couldn't be commanded, not now. Not with Sante here. Not even for the kind of stakes they were playing for.

Thinking about her every move, she spread her legs for him. Alejandro's touch had produced somewhat of a reaction in her. Her breasts had grown heavier and her hard nipples pressed against the fabric of her tank top.

Alejandro's fingers fisted in her hair and he used it to yank her head to the side. He nibbled and sucked his way from her mouth, over her chin and then along her throat, raising goose bumps along her body. His fangs nicked her skin and a short burst of pain exploded, followed quickly by a rush of intense pleasure. Alejandro had unfurled a massive amount of veil over her, mischiefing her mind.

Ah, thank god . . . Even though she'd forbidden him, he was using his "special ingredient."

Normally it would have alarmed her, pissed her off. Now she relaxed into it gratefully. It filled her like a drug, erasing her inhibitions and making the threat of Sante in the room only a distant concern.

Soon all she could think about were her body's needs.

Her eyes closed and she shuddered in a long erotic sigh. Her whole world became Alejandro—his hands on her body, his cock rubbing rhythmically against her pussy through their clothes, his lips and mouth moving over her skin. Between her thighs, she warmed and plumped, knowing the scent of her arousal now filled the room.

He reached down and pulled her panties down and off, then dragged his fingers over her heated flesh, stopping to rub her clit until she whimpered against his lips.

Her cunt felt heavy and warm. Alejandro didn't ever have to do much to elicit that reaction in her. All he had to do was touch her, kiss her, look at her. Her breasts strained against her tank top. She whimpered, trying not to beg for his hands on her, the slow, long glide of his cock deep inside her.

Alejandro slid his thigh between her legs and pressed up against her sex. She let out a sharp breath at the contact, her fingers twining through his hair. He groaned against her throat and rocked his leg back and forth, stimulating that needy part of her anatomy.

He yanked her head to the side, exposing the vulnerable column of her throat. Keeping up the slow rock between her thighs, he traced his skillful lips over her flesh, raising more goose bumps over her.

All the world faded away, replaced by Alejandro's will and her wanting body. She opened her eyes briefly in a haze of lust as he brushed his fangs over her skin. He bit and a wash of orgasmic bliss flowed over her. She dug her fingers into his upper arms and hung on under the onslaught.

Alejandro made a low, pleasured sound of approval and moved from her throat, where a bead of her blood welled, down her chest. His hands found the small of her back, arching her up and into him as he nipped gently at each of her nipples through the material of her tank top, making them sensitive and erect. Her fingers fisted in his hair, twining through the silky strands as she fought the urge to move her hips to increase the delicious friction of him pressing against her sex.

Someone moved out of the corner of her eye, but she couldn't bring herself to glance over, couldn't bring herself to . . . *care*. Not when Alejandro was moving further down her body still, pushing up the hem of her tank top and dragging his sensual lips over her abdomen, stroking the pad of his index finger over her clit until she spread her legs for him. Under the heavy veil he'd used on her, she regarded nothing important but the pleasure washing over her and the anticipation of Alejandro's next bite.

He nipped at the place where her thigh met her sex, such a sensitive area, and she shuddered. His fingers grasped her legs and pushed them apart as he dragged his tongue down her skin to her inner thigh. There, he brushed his fangs—a slow, hard rub in amongst all the softness. It made her shiver, made her clit throb with the need to be touched. Alejandro did not oblige her. As much as she wanted it, some deep, buried part of her was grateful.

Alejandro's heavy, warm hand rested on her hip. His other hand braced against her opposite knee, forcing her legs apart and holding her down. Her hands fisted in the blankets on either side of her and her body tingled with awareness. He licked the area high on her inner thigh, laving it with his tongue. After he'd laid a lingering kiss, the sharp points of his fangs pricked her skin, a sweet hint of pain playing counterpoint to the pleasure.

Then he bit.

His fangs slid into her flesh and that familiar ecstasy enveloped her body, tingling along her nerve endings. It brought her just shy of a climax and left her teetering there, on the brink. He pulled on her blood, and his suction brought a new wave of pleasure. Her clit pulsed, swollen and throbbing with the need to be touched.

Daria arched her back and fought the rising whimper in her throat. She held on to the blankets with all she had, her body riding that leading edge of climax but, maddeningly, not tipping over.

Alejandro took his time, dragging out his feeding and keeping her there, hovering on the edge. By the time he'd finished, she was a frustrated mess from the sexual teasing.

He released her leg and climbed up her body, threading his hands through her hair and staring down at her in the semidarkness.

For that one moment, their bodies strung tight from sexual need, it truly was as if they were all alone.

Bare desire shone in Alejandro's eyes, touched with caring for her. It was the caring that made her want him. It was the leading edge of love that she could see glimmering in the depths of his dark eyes, like a velvet blanket brushing over her skin, holding her close and warming her on a cold, cold night.

"I've seen enough," said Sante from across the room. Neither Daria nor Alejandro moved or acknowledged his presence at all. "It is clear you are mated. This matter is put to rest."

Alejandro didn't break his hold on her gaze as Sante and his men left. Once the door closed, Alejandro lowered his head and kissed her. Passion coursed between the two of them, tangible as heat against their skin. Daria had to have him now, damn all else. Why had she rejected him before now?

He lifted his head. "Daria," he whispered.

She pulled at his clothing, trying desperately to free him of the fabric that separated her body from his. All she wanted was the sensation of his bare skin sliding along hers, his cock buried deep within her cunt.

"Daria!" He grabbed her wrists and pressed them to the mattress on either side of her head. "Listen to me."

Panting, she tried to focus on his face through the haze of lust.

"I tore down your walls with veil. I took away all your inhibitions to get you through that. What you're feeling now are your impulses free from your misgivings, your fears, and perhaps your better sense. Do you understand? I did the thing you told me never to do to you. Right now, it's like you're drunk. I can't do this while you're this way. It would be taking advantage."

She fought against his grasp until he released her, and she grabbed the front of his shirt, dragging him down nose to nose with her. "Alejandro, fuck your respect for me. Screw your honor. I want you. Veil or not. You will take away this need I have of you right here, right now."

"Daria—"

She pushed up, her fangs lengthening, going straight for his throat. Her fangs bit at the time she unfurled her veil. Alejandro's big body stiffened above hers and he let out a low groan of pleasure as she took what she needed from him.

To seal the deal, she reached between their bodies and found his cock through the fabric of his boxer shorts. She took the long, thick length against her palm and stroked it from tip to base, until he shuddered.

"Daria, I can't resist you when you do this." He sounded desperate and heavy with lust, his voice little more than a groan.

I know, she whispered in his mind.

He growled like the vampire he was, with a low and feral sound. His hand plunged between her legs to stroke and tease. Daria lost her hold on his throat and threw her head back on a moan.

His mouth closed around one nipple, then the other, sucking and gently biting. Daria struggled to gain control over herself, but couldn't stop the snap and twist of her hips as she rocked her cunt against his caressing hand. She wanted him inside her more than she wanted anything else in the world at that moment.

"Alejandro," she groaned, her fingers curling around his cock. "Please."

He yanked his boxers down to his knees, forced her thighs apart and thrust inside her roughly, impatiently to the base of him. The length and breadth of him stretched her deliciously, stroking deep places inside her that hadn't had attention in a long, long time.

She squirmed for a moment beneath him, her cunt crammed full with his cock. It was such a possession to have him inside her this way, like he owned every inch of her. She shivered.

She liked it.

Alejandro remained unmoving for a long moment, hovering over her and staring down into her heavy-lidded eyes. He murmured her name like a prayer, pulled out, and thrust back in. She closed her eyes, and stars exploded on the back of her eyelids. Orgasm poured through her body, dragging her into a sea of pleasure.

He took her hard and fast, pinning her to the bed as he slammed into her over and over. The slapping sound of skin on skin filled the room. Her climax went on for a deliciously long time, her cunt pulsing around his shaft that moved pistonlike within her. It wasn't long before his cock jumped inside her and she felt him come.

Together they lay tangled on the bed, a mess of intertwined limbs. Her body tingled nicely in places that couldn't remember the last time they'd received such erotic attention. She could tell she'd be sore in the morning, since Alejandro was not a small man . . . in any way.

And she wanted him again. Just the thought of it made her shiver.

Alejandro wrapped his arms around her and rolled to the side, taking her with him. She ended up with her legs still straddling his muscular waist, his cock still buried deep within her. His mouth found hers, his lips skating softly across hers. A sigh released itself from her throat and she tightened her arms around him.

"Again," she murmured against his lips. "Fuck me again, Alejandro."

He shifted his hips, showing her that he hadn't lost his hardness. It was a trait of some Chosen males, and one she was currently very happy Alejandro possessed.

"You're still veil affected."

She ran her hand down his hip and over one nice, muscular buttock. Squeezing, she pushed him against her. "Alejandro, I need to sate myself with you. Don't deny me."

He traced her collarbone with his index finger. "You're going to hate me in the morning."

"I don't care about the morning."

"I do." In one smooth, powerful move, Alejandro pulled out and flipped her. She scrambled for a moment facedown on the bedcover, surprised at the show of speed and strength that had so suddenly gotten her there. Then he grabbed her by the thighs and dragged her over the mattress to fit his cock once again to her pussy.

Her fingers curled into the blankets in anticipation, but she never expected the touch of his finger to her anus. She jerked on the mattress in surprise.

He clamped down on her, preventing her from moving away. "Hush, Daria, it's all right. Have you ever been touched here before?"

"No."

"A lover has never awoken all these sensitive nerves?" he purred as he stroked her.

Daria shivered in pleasure as her cunt suddenly gushed with moisture. There were, indeed, many nerves there. All of them felt delicious when stimulated.

"None of your lovers have ever penetrated both places at once, sweet Daria? Fucked your cunt and your ass at the same time? Tell me it isn't so."

Again, alarm flared through her briefly, but it was no match for her arousal. "No."

"What sort of men have you been with that they wouldn't do such a simple and pleasurable thing for you?" His silken voice rolled over her as he gathered slickness from her cunt and rubbed it over her anus. Slowly, carefully, he slipped a finger inside her.

She tensed. "Alejandro!"

"Relax, Daria. Just relax and let me do as I wish. I promise you will not be sorry."

He worked the digit back and forth, making a low moan rip from her throat. Then he added another, stretching those muscles that had never been stretched and stimulating her into nearly climaxing.

"Ah, you like it. I thought you would, Daria," he whispered in a ragged, aroused voice. "I like it, too. I like it because it is the ultimate domination." He paused. "You like it for that reason, too, I would guess."

He was right. Alejandro sliding into that most private, vulnerable part of her body *was* the ultimate domination.

"Now, feel what double penetration is." He eased two fingers into her cunt and thrust back and forth out of each orifice at the same time. It was . . . indescribable to have both places filled and stimulated at the same time. Overwhelming. He possessed every intimate inch of her.

"Oh, yes, baby, you like that, don't you? One day I want you tied up and at my mercy, *querida*. I want to fill this pretty little ass of yours and fuck your cunt at the same time."

His language, coarse as it was, made her shudder with pleasure. The image his words brought up made her body shiver on the edge of a climax.

"That's it, Daria. Come for me." He thrust into her ass and cunt over and over and she surrendered herself completely to the erotic bliss of it.

Daria clawed at the blankets as he rocked her body back and forth on the mattress. Her orgasm exploded over her, making her writhe and cry out his name. She gushed over his hand, her cunt gripping and releasing his invading fingers. Daria didn't think she'd ever come so hard.

Then, before the tremors of her climax had completely faded, his cock was deep inside her cunt.

But this time he took her slow.

Alejandro withdrew and thrust in again so leisurely she could feel every inch of his shaft as it glided inside her. With a strong grip, he held her hips, keeping her from moving as he slowed his pace even more.

God, he wanted to drive her crazy. That had to be it.

Yet he knew what he was doing, knew that the slow thrust of his cock was priming her body for another powerful climax. The man could play her body like a fine instrument, it seemed. He knew just which notes to play for greatest effect.

She clawed at the sheets in front her. "Faster," she pleaded. She knew he was building her up for a mind-numbing orgasm, but the time it would take to get there would kill her.

He jabbed into her in response. "No. I want you slow this time. I like the way you look in the moonlight, Daria. The arch of your back, and the curve of your hip. You're beautiful." He said it like he meant it, and, ridiculously, it made tears prick her eyes. "I won't go faster, not yet. I want to savor you."

Her breath hissed out of her as she found herself once again impaled and at Alejandro's mercy. She *liked* being at his mercy . . . at least in bed. She also liked the slide of his cock into her sex. Every inward stroke brushed the head against some sensitive point of plea-sure deep inside her.

Alejandro bent over her body, still shafting her slowly enough to make her lose her mind, and kissed the nape of her neck. She shud-dered at the way his body pinned her and how his lips brushed her skin so gently, so . . . *lovingly*. Something within her twinged a little, longed for that kind of touch more often in her life. Maybe even longed for it from him.

He trailed his tongue down her spine as far as he could, leaving goose bumps in his wake. Then he slipped his hand between her abdo-men and the mattress, delving down to find her clit and tease it.

His fingers slipped over the bundle of nerves, rotating and press-ing until her body quickened and her breath came in little pants. She tried to push up, but he kept her prone.

"Come for me again," he murmured. "I want to feel you come, *mi amante*."

As if purely on his command, she shattered once more. A primal yell ripped from her throat as another, far more powerful climax poured through her body. On the heels of her release, Alejandro found his. He groaned low and whispered her name as he spilled inside her for the second time that night.

After they'd tumbled together onto the mattress and lay for a few minutes, catching their breath, Alejandro rolled to the side, pulling her to curl against his body. Irrationally, she missed his cock when it pulled from her. Missed that intimate connection.

He didn't stop touching her, even though they'd made love twice. His hand caressed her breasts slowly, teasing her nipples, dipped be-tween her thighs to slick over her folds and over her sated, swollen clit. Soon lust tightened her body again and he brought her to an-other lusciously slow climax with his fingers—this one softer than the others.

Once she'd stopped shuddering and sighing against him, he cupped her face between his palms and kissed her for a long time. His lips skated lovingly over hers, his teeth nipped and his tongue stole within to brush against hers. The man almost kissed well enough to bring her to climax a fourth time.

Gentled by the residual effects of Alejandro's veil, Daria allowed it all. He touched her so much, it was like Alejandro needed the contact and assumed tonight would be the only night he'd ever get it. The thought fought its way through the haze of satisfied lethargy that had stolen over her body and mind.

She needed it, too.

When he'd finished making love to her mouth and nuzzling her throat, he pulled the blankets up over both of them and curled himself protectively against her. "Sleep now, Daria. When you wake, you'll be in control of all you faculties again."

Was there a note of regret in his voice? Daria had only a few moments to consider it before the heavy hands of sleep pulled her under.

~

CHRISTOPHER Alexander Julian Sante did not have the ability to recognize someone by the scent of their blood alone like some other Chosen did. Nor did he have the ability to taste a person's blood and tell their secrets, as he'd bluffed in Alejandro's room.

But he still knew a lie when he saw one.

It wasn't that the surgery that Daria Moran had undergone was ineffective. On the contrary, if he hadn't at one time been so in love with Daria, he never would have been clued in to her true identity. She looked nothing like she had.

And he'd never suspected from the scent of them that they weren't actually mates. In that area, they'd done a good job. She and Alejandro were probably sleeping together.

Still, there'd been no way for him to mistake Daria. None.

He entered his house and closed the door behind him. The guards had left him near the entrance of his property and he'd walked up the drive in the early morning, deep in thought. Making his way upstairs, he replayed the events of the evening in his mind.

At one time he'd fancied himself so incredibly in love with Daria

Moran that he'd memorized every inch of her body, every whisper of motion she made—from the way she tilted her head to the side when she was interested in something to the little hitch in her breathing when she was aroused.

He'd been watching the couple from the shadows ever since they'd arrived. The surgery hadn't changed Daria's mannerisms—the way she tilted her head, how her lips quirked in a smile, the exact way she gestured with her hands when she was upset or excited.

And he'd suspected.

Then last night at the party it had been one single movement of her right foot—an inch forward—as she shifted her weight *just so*. That gesture had cemented his suspicions even further. The movement had brought memories rushing back, filling his mind with Daria. The motion had been so *her* that it had made his heart ache.

And that was it. He'd arranged the visit to their room under the false pretense of the accusation in an effort to catch them unaware. His intention had been to study Valerie closer, to put his suspicion to rest one way or the other.

How she'd shifted and sighed. The way her face had slackened when she'd grown aroused under Alejandro's touch. How she'd moved and breathed—*Daria*. It was all Daria. It had brought the past crashing into him and even, for a fleeting moment, made him miss her, long for her.

He'd always known that Alejandro had wanted Daria. It had always been clear in the heat of his gaze when he'd looked at her that the man had coveted her. If the display they'd shown him just now was any indication, the lust was reciprocal. The heat that had come off Alejandro and Daria could scorch an observer at twenty paces. They were clearly having sex, at the very least. Perhaps they were even in love.

He'd seen love in Alejandro when he'd touched her.

A ghost of jealousy raised its head, but he knew it was just habit. He still cared for Daria, but that part of his life was over now and he'd put Daria behind him with it. After the incident, he'd mourned the loss of her. He'd been depressed by the knowledge of how much she hated him. But as the years had passed, he'd relinquished her hold on his heart and moved on. These days he had a new love, the last love he would ever have in his life.

"Christopher, come in here. I miss you."

She called from the bedroom, where the early morning faux-light shone in through the window and pooled on the hardwood floor. Emotion coursed through him at the mere sound of his name on her lips. He made his way into the bedroom and began to undress.

She lay tangled in the sheets, one long leg extended on top of the bedcoverings. Her silky hair cascaded over the pillows and she wore a small smile on her perfectly curved lips.

She was perfect, and she was his.

When he'd met his current lover, he'd discovered what undying and eternal love truly was. Compared to what he'd felt for Daria, *this* was an inferno to a flame.

It was fitting that Daria had come now to nail him—and he knew that was exactly her intention. If she'd arrived a couple of years earlier, he may well have turned himself in even though prison for a Chosen was a nightmare of eternal proportions. It was, for all intents and purposes, *hell*.

He'd mired himself in a large amount of self-hatred after the killings. The guilt had been so heavy, he'd been ready for punishment. He'd created the Shining Way as a retreat, a place he could separate himself from the rest of the world. All he'd wanted back then was to be a recluse. That's all he wanted still.

Then, on a trip to Angel One, he'd met his lady. He'd been immediately entranced with her and, while it had taken him a while to convince her she was entranced with him, had fallen deeply in love. After that he hadn't wanted to turn himself in anymore and the occasional urge he'd had to walk into the dawn—the *real* dawn—had completely faded.

His lady had saved his life. Nothing, no one, would take her from him or destroy their future together.

So, Daria had come back to him, dragging Alejandro along for the ride. The question was, what to do with them? He needed to know more about why they were here in order to make that determination. If they threatened him, threatened his woman or his current way of life, as much as he would regret it . . . bad things would happen to them.

He slid into his lady's welcoming arms.

"Where have you been?" she murmured into the curve where his shoulder met his throat.

He stroked her upper arm. "Just taking care of some business, my sweet."

Her arms tightened around him. "Don't leave me again."

"I won't."

As much as he still cared about Daria, he wouldn't hesitate to kill her if she threatened him. He would do anything to protect the woman in his arms.

16

DARIA sat on the edge of the bed, wrapped in a sheet, surveying the clothing strewn on the floor and remembering the events of the night before.

Oh, god . . . what he'd done to her. She'd never allowed a man to touch her that way, bring her to climax like that. Her cheeks burned. And she'd liked it, too.

Alejandro walked out of the bathroom, with only a towel around his lean waist. Water droplets beaded on the muscular expanse of his chest and on his powerful arms—arms that had held her down on the bed while he'd fucked her silly the night before. Twice. Forward and backward. While she moaned and begged him for more. She glanced up at him, frowning.

He spread his hands. "Look, Daria—"

"*Alejandro.*" She frowned even more. Soon her face would crack.

He sighed. "I'm sorry, but I had to release my whole veil over you. I couldn't hold anything back. You were too tense, understandably so. I had to do it."

She looked away. "I know."

"It was a necess—" He paused. "You know?"

"I don't like it, but I understand why you did it. I don't want anything to jeopardize this mission, Alejandro. *Anything.*"

"I did what I had to do." He took a step toward her. "But it was a risk."

She looked up at him, trying to meet his eyes, but failing. God, how many times had his name spilled from her lips the night before? "What do you mean?"

He shrugged a shoulder. "I played on my bet that you wanted me but had been holding yourself back for . . . whatever reasons you hold yourself back. I could have been wrong. That's why I mean it was a risk. Once I broke down your walls with my veil, you could have just as easily kneed me in the balls, if that's what you'd truly wanted to do." A grin spread over his lips. "I think that would have given us a fail."

She blinked. "Does it count that I want to kick you in the balls now?"

"Daria you can't blame me—"

"I don't. I'm glad you did what you did. The rest, well, those were my desires free from my misgivings and fears right? Can't blame you for those. Anyway, I know I pushed you . . . afterward. After Sante left."

"You did push me."

"I know. It was all my doing."

"I appreciate that."

"It's the truth." She dropped her gaze, feeling miserable. "So now you know just how badly I've wanted you."

"Yes." He grinned wolfishly. "Pretty damn bad."

"Yeah, but I've had you now. A couple of times." Anger flared and she narrowed her eyes at him. "Don't be looking for more where that came from."

All Alejandro did was grin at her response. Clearly, he didn't believe her. She looked away from him. Hell, she didn't believe herself. Just looking at him, standing there with water droplets running down his body, she wanted him. Wanted to lick every one of them off his skin. Wanted to take his cock into her mouth and see if she could make him as crazy as he'd made her last night. Heat flushed her body, and she closed her eyes.

"Daria, it's the Choosing that's making your libido run this hard. Damn, I've never seen anyone with as much control as you have. Your will is very strong, but it's not as strong as the aftereffects of the change." He took a few steps toward her. "Just give it up."

She sank her teeth into her lower lip. After a moment, she said, "I never give up."

He sat on the bed beside her and traced the bare skin of her back above the line of the sheet that wrapped her. "I gave you last night and, fuck, it was sweet. *Te deseo.* That means I want you. I want you now, I want you always." His voice was a low, silken rasp. It made her shiver and the hair on the back of her neck stand on end.

She wanted him, too. It seemed that having Alejandro once was not enough. Her body—if not her mind—desired him again.

The question was, what did her heart want?

"Maybe," he continued, still caressing her back, "maybe you should just let this be what it is, Daria. Just for now. Let this attraction between us play out for the duration of our time here. After it's over, we'll go our separate ways. No problem. The advantages are that we convinced Sante and the Shining Way that we are truly a mated pair and we also get to sate our lust for each other. No strings once this is all through, just lots of sex before we part ways."

"The disadvantages?" she asked in a hoarse voice.

"Disadvantages?" He laughed, and the sound of it rolled over her. "Honey, for me there are no disadvantages."

What if she fell in love with him? That was the disadvantage for her. It would be so easy to fall in love with this strong, good-natured, protective man. She drew a shuddering breath. "Let me think about it." She stood. "Right now I have to take a shower and get back to making teddy bears."

He nodded. "You think on it, Daria. Go ahead and think all you want, but I'm going to do my best to sway you in the direction I think you should go." He slipped a hand under the sheet. His palm was warm on her skin. "Understand?"

She tried to back away, she really did. In the end all she could do was stand there and look up into his warm, dark eyes.

His pupils dilated. "I had a taste of you last night and it wasn't enough. Not enough by a long mile. So the gloves are off. When I want someone, I go after them."

Daria forced herself to take a step back, away from that very dangerous hand and the more dangerous response her body was having to the look in his eyes and the words coming from his lips. "You can try." The words were good, but her voice was a bit shaky.

Leave it to Alejandro Martinez to make her feel vulnerable. She turned and escaped into the bathroom.

~

ALEJANDRO had every intention of busting down more than just the walls of Daria's inhibitions. He wanted more than just sex from her. He wanted her to look at him the way he remembered she used to look at Christopher Sante.

Alejandro wanted more than just her body; he wanted her love.

He watched her disappear into the bathroom, her conflicted emotions clearly displayed on her face and in her body language. He fisted his hands in his lap, forcing himself to not go in there and tease her into sexual submission once again. She was very susceptible to him right now. He knew he could do it, but Alejandro wanted her for the long haul, and therefore, he needed to show restraint.

Daria had been betrayed badly and it still affected her at a deep level. Alejandro knew he had to win her trust before he could win her love. In fact, Alejandro could sense the beginnings of that lofty emotion in her already. She fought it, but it was there. He knew he needed to seduce her, not overwhelm her, gentle her to him slowly and with patience.

Patience not being one of his better traits.

The water started in the bathroom and he shifted on the bed uncomfortably, his cock happy with the image of Daria in the shower, water sluicing over her curves, beading on her nipples, and running between her thighs.

It wasn't just her body that he loved. Daria was strong and intelligent, a woman who could meet him head-to-head and come out the winner. She was caring, too, beneath the gruff exterior. After all, here she was at the Shining Way, having altered her life irrevocably, in order to gain satisfaction for the death of her friend.

Long ago Alejandro had recognized that Daria Moran was the woman for him, and nothing had changed except his resolve. This time he wasn't going to let her walk away, no matter what he said about meaningless sex with no strings attached. With Daria, there was nothing *meaningless* about it.

With effort, he pulled himself away from thoughts about what might happen if he entered her shower. If he used his hands and mouth to physically show her just how much he cared about her. Sex was the only way he could do it right now without making her cut and run. He couldn't say he minded. Having her climax while he'd been sheathed deeply in her cunt the night before had been the best goddamn thing he'd experienced in years.

Daria was his. He'd make sure she was his, heart, body, and soul by the end of this game.

~

"So how much do you know about Sante?" Daria asked Jia Ying. They stood together on the line, stuffing teddy bears.

Jia Ying shrugged and shot her a shy smile. "Not a whole lot. I know he is one of the old ones and lucky he hasn't gone insane with the press of age on his mind. Know he's a little bit idealistic and that's why he created the Shining Way. He wanted to create a place just for Chosen, where we could be free to be ourselves. I respect his vision. Other than that, he's a private man. Talk is he's pretty serious about a woman right now." She smiled. "I think she's lucky."

Daria's head snapped up. "Really?" That was news to her.

"Oh, yeah, but they're being secretive about it. She stays in his house, never comes out, never sees anyone but him. No one at the Shining Way has ever even caught a glimpse of her."

Interesting. Sante was in love. Was he even capable of that? The idea didn't jibe with the Sante she remembered. Cold. Merciless. Murderer. Loyal to none but his bitch of a blood mother.

"Why is that?" Daria asked.

Jia Ying shrugged. "I don't know why they're keeping it so shushed. There's speculation, but I think he's just protective of her. Some of the members are overly zealous in their devotion to Christopher Sante. Personally, I think he's just trying to keep her away from all that."

"Sante's a real star around here, isn't he?"

Daria tried to keep the sarcasm out of her voice, but Jia Ying still caught the edge of it since her answer was a little on the defensive side. "With good reason!"

Daria put her head down and stuffed teddy bears, unable to answer that one and keep any semblance of *Valerie* in place.

"Where's your man today?" Jia Ying asked after a while.

"They needed some help with the bees, so he's spending the day out there. He'll be back tomorrow."

Brandon had hooked Alejandro with a temporary "in" over there, which was good since there had been a rash of full moons in the dome lately. They could have as many as they wanted, of course, and apparently someone wanted a bunch. It almost seemed like they desired extra light or something. Maybe to prevent people from sneaking around at night trying to see if they were trafficking blood slaves? It made Daria a little paranoid if she thought about it too much.

One of the factory managers approached them as they worked. "Your presence has been requested at Christopher Sante's home," he told Daria.

Her body jerked in shock and she dropped the teddy bear she'd been working on. She turned to face the foreman. "Excuse me?"

"It's just what I said. Sante requests your company. *Now.*"

"Yay!" Jia Ying clapped. "You get to see inside his house! You're so lucky! I wonder what he wants."

Yes, Daria wondered, too. "I feel like I'm being called to the principal's office."

"Oh, no, Valerie," Jia Ying replied with a warm smile. "Don't worry. Sante is no one to be afraid of."

If only Jia Ying knew.

A short time later Daria walked up the charming cobblestone path to Sante's front door. It all looked different in the daylight, when she wasn't sneaking around breaking and entering. The house was white, a throwback to Earth in the early twenty-first century, considered by most to be the planet's heyday. That bit of history fueled an enduring retro craze.

Daria knew Sante had been born during that time. So beyond the popularity of all things early twenty-first century, he probably had a preference for architecture of that style. Flowers bloomed along the path on either side of her, and overflowed from the boxes under the windows. Their scent drifted to her nose and calmed her a bit.

What the hell did Christopher Sante want with her? Alone. At his house in the middle of the dome's workday. *Gah.* At least, if Sante didn't kill her, she might get a glimpse of this woman he was hiding away. The female succubare she'd felt the night she'd broken in.

The door opened and Sante stepped out. "Valerie! Welcome to my home." He ushered her inside. "Would you like something to drink?"

"No, thank you." She gawked a bit at the retro furnishings of the living room, as though it was the first time she'd seen them. Valerie would be awed, of course.

"Come, sit down," Sante said, leading her further into the living room and motioning to a plush chair. "I just want to chat a bit."

Chat a bit? Daria tried not to look wary and sank down onto the expensive piece of furniture. "I appreciate you inviting me over, Mr. Sante. Frankly, I wasn't sure how I stood with you after the events of the other night."

"Please call me Christopher."

"All right . . . Christopher."

"That's why I wanted to talk. I know what I did was very intrusive, but you have to understand that I can take no chances here. I spent a lot of time and money building this community and must be very careful about who I allow to live here. There are those in the world who would like to see this place taken down, those who want to destroy all Chosen."

"You're talking about Richard Templeton and The New Covenant Church."

"They're one organization, perhaps the most activist, of several." He paused and pursed his lips. "I have many enemies, Valerie. People who want to destroy what I care about, those Chosen I have come to love. I cannot allow that to happen. Hence, the surprise visit to you and Alejandro the other night."

"I understand."

"I'm not a voyeur. I just needed to find out if the allegations lodged against you were true. That was the only way I knew, short of taking your blood myself, to determine if they were or not." He grinned. "Not that I didn't want to take your blood. You're a very attractive woman."

Hmmm. "Why didn't you have Alejandro meet us here, Christopher?"

He smiled. "I will meet with Alejandro separately. I thought you and I could get to know each other better if we were alone."

"I have no interest in sex."

Sante's body jerked a bit with surprise. His smile went icy for a moment. "I find you attractive, Valerie, but I don't want to have sex with you."

She tilted her head to the side. "Is it possible for a man to find a woman attractive and not want to have sex with her?"

His smile tightened. "For me it is."

She inclined her head a degree. "Then I apologize. I didn't mean to offend." Damn it. She'd gone fishing for evidence of the female secreted away in his house and had come up with nothing.

"No offense taken. I can understand why you may have thought that, but, really, Valerie, I saw ample evidence that you're mated to Alejandro the other night. I would never intrude on such a strong bond."

Daria blinked. If she hadn't known what a slimeball he was she might be inclined to like him. She saw how he could inspire loyalty at the Shining Way if he always behaved this way. Well . . . apart from barging into people's rooms at night and demanding he observe them in intimate acts.

"Now that we have that settled, tell me about yourself, Valerie. Tell me about your parents and your upbringing. As Alejandro's mate, I would like to get to know you better."

She'd been fishing, and now it seemed like he was, but she had no idea for what. Good thing she'd memorized Valerie's story front and back. "I was born and raised right here in the Logos Territories. My mother was a secretary for the water company in New Chicago and my father was a miner on Songset. He left early on and my mother died in a gravmetro accident when I was seventeen. To avoid being raised by my aunt, I quit school and went to work as a waitress."

"It's kind of a tragic story."

"I don't think so. It's just my story."

"But then you met Alejandro and fell in love."

She nodded and smiled. Frighteningly, it wasn't hard to smile when she thought of Alejandro. "Yes. I was very scared when he decided to Choose me. I didn't think I'd make it through the succubare."

He smiled. "And then you did. Quite amazing."

"And then I did."

"You know that only 1 percent of all humans lacking the Chosen gene make it through the succubare."

Oh, maybe that was why he'd taken an interest in her. "Yes, I've heard that. My mother used to always tell me that I had a stubborn streak. I guess it served me well during the Choosing. When I started to feel tired, started to feel like giving up, I forced myself to push harder."

"That kind of resolve is admirable. I may have need of you, if you don't mind playing a special role here at the Shining Way."

"I'm nobody special."

"Oh, I beg to differ." A slow smile spread across his lips. "I've never met anyone who pushed through the succubare and didn't have the gene. You're not just special; you're exceptional. In fact, I would like to have someone like you close to me, someone who has the drive and will that you do."

Her heart went pitter-pat. Getting into Sante's inner circle would be valuable. She'd thought maybe Alejandro had a shot, since he had a history with him. She'd never dreamed she'd have a chance, but she'd grab onto this one with both hands. "If you think I can be of value to you, Christopher, then I humbly offer my services."

"Good. I will summon Alejandro after you've left. When I need you, I will call."

That seemed like a dismissal, so Daria stood. "I'm glad we had this opportunity to talk."

Sante rose and escorted her to the front door. "I am, too." He clasped her hand warmly in his, and she suppressed a shudder of revulsion. "I'm very glad to have you at the Shining Way, Valerie."

Walking down the path away from the house, Daria couldn't stop the huge smile that had spread across her face. She was one step closer to her goal.

17

"WHAT did he tell you?" Daria asked Alejandro as she stared out the window of their room. Another full moon. She was really beginning to hate them.

"He apologized for the intrusion the other night, had me talk about old times with him. Then he asked me if I wanted to help him out with Shining Way business."

She turned. "Then we're both in."

"Seems that way."

"So you reminisced about old times? Those bad old days when you were both with the ABI and he was using me in preparation to kill my best friend, the guards, and the witness?" Bitterness tinged her voice.

Alejandro hesitated before answering. "He asked about you. I mean, about Daria."

She jolted in shock. "Please tell me my name did not pass his lips."

"He wondered if I kept in touch with you." Alejandro paused. "In a way, he has been keeping in touch with you."

"What?"

"Hell, Daria, he's been tracking you since the day it all happened."

Feeling oddly dirty, she sank onto the bed. "What did you tell him?"

"That I hadn't seen you since you left the ABI." Alejandro walked to the window and looked up at the moon. "He expressed sincere regret over what happened. He talked about it at length, saying he'd really been in love with you but that his loyalty to his blood mother came first. He told me that after he killed Julia, the guards, and the witness he was suicidal for a long time and that creating the Shining Way saved his life."

She simmered for a moment, shaking with absolute, pure rage. Then she rose and stalked to the window to stand near Alejandro. "Is that supposed to sway my opinion of him? Make me feel . . . *sorry* for him? That bastard doesn't get a moment of my thoughts beyond how I want to kill him."

Alejandro laid a hand on her shoulder and she started. "I just thought you should know."

She nearly shrugged his hand away, but the weight and heat of it was nice. "It doesn't change anything. Nothing he could say would change how I feel. I don't care if he felt guilty, or that it was an accident. I certainly don't care about his feelings for me."

"That goes without saying. If he can be taken down, we'll take him down. I'm committed to it."

Her voice was hard when she replied. "You better be. I don't want any good old boy Chosen connections to fuck this up."

He whirled her to face him, his mouth tight and his eyes flaring dark. "*Mierda!* Don't even suggest it. My loyalty is to justice first, not some romantic idea of Chosen allegiance above all else. I know you're pissed at Sante, Daria, but I'm not him."

At the moment every man was Sante. This time she did shrug him off. "I'll be in Brandon's room . . . if he's not screwing someone tonight."

He grabbed her upper arm before she could push past him. "Daria. Don't do this. Just calm down. Damn your temper. You need to learn how to control it."

She drew a shaky breath. "I just want this to be over. I want to get the hell out of this place, away from Christopher Sante."

"I know how personal this is for you. It's personal for me, too. Hell, I liked Julia a lot. She was a friend of mine. We used to have lunch together sometimes and talk about which gravball team traded which player, and if it was a good move or not."

"Yeah, but Sante never fucked you."

He released her arm. "Not physically. He fucked all of us, though, every one of us who he betrayed."

"Yeah." She paused. "Julia loved gravball." Daria couldn't help but smile at the memory. She was not a sports fan, but Julia had always tried to get her to go to the games anyway. "She was more than just a best friend to me, Alejandro. She was the sister I never had."

He nodded. "I remember how tight you two were."

"Anyway, I'm sorry. I know that anger is my Achilles' heel."

He reached out and touched her cheek. "Emotion in general is your downfall, Daria. You feel it all, don't you?"

She had an urge to turn her face away from his probing gaze. It was like he could see right into her soul. "I haven't had many close relationships in my life. Growing up, it was just my mother and I. We moved around a lot because my mom needed to find work here and there, so I didn't make a lot of friends. It wasn't until I got to the ABI that I formed any close relationships. Sante betrayed my first romantic one and killed the first real friend I ever had."

She'd never said those words aloud to anyone. Now that they had passed her lips, she wanted to call them back for how vulnerable they made her feel. She swore if she saw an ounce of sympathy in his eyes, she'd smack him.

But only warmth emanated from his dark gaze. "I know. I already figured all that out, Daria."

"You spend that much time thinking about me?"

He stared down at her for a moment. "And more."

Her lips parted. She was at a loss for words all of a sudden. A heavy moment passed between them. She smiled. "And here I've never ferreted out all the mysteries of Alejandro Martinez." She'd felt a need for levity.

His sensual lips twisted in a smile and she wondered what he was thinking. "Are you hungry?"

"What?" The question was pretty unexpected.

"Not for blood, but for old-fashioned food. I'm hungry for it."

"I miss it, honestly," she admitted. "Blood sustains me, and it's much nicer than I ever dreamed it would be, but I miss tangible food . . . different flavors."

He moved toward the door. "Stay here and I'll be back with food. Don't go to Brandon's. You know he's got some floozy Chosen in his room anyway."

She watched him leave and fidgeted, fighting the urge to flee Alejandro. The man made her feel things she wasn't sure she wanted to feel. It was nice . . . in a way, but uncomfortable. It challenged every solid wall she'd built around herself over the past seven years and she wasn't so sure she wanted Alejandro to go pulling them down quite yet.

In the end, she remained. When he came back, arms laden with things smelling so good it made her mouth water, she'd perched on the end of the bed. She'd changed into her pajamas—a tank top and a pair of boxers—while he'd been gone. Daria sat up a little straighter when he came and watched him lay the food containers on the table.

"Where'd you find all that?" she asked, rising and going over to take a curious look.

"There's one kitchen in the whole dome. Sante told me about it this afternoon. I got this stuff from there—fresh sliced peaches, a cold macaroni dish, Orbivian dates. I just grabbed some things that looked good."

She picked up a container with slices of fruit. "Ripe peaches? My god, I haven't had these in years. Where'd they get them?" She thought for a moment. "They're growing them here, aren't they?"

He nodded.

Entranced, Daria flopped down on a bed and popped the top. She inhaled deeply. "Oh, fuck. That's better than sex."

He raised an eyebrow. "Not sure if I should be offended right now or not." He picked up the package of dates and came to sit beside her.

Daria selected a peach slice and bit into it. Juice ran down her chin and the ripe, succulent flavor of the fruit exploded in her mouth. After she'd taken her time chewing and swallowing, she tipped her head back and groaned in ecstasy. "You should be jealous."

"I'll take that as a challenge." He bit into a date, eyeing her speculatively.

Ignoring that comment, she plucked a date out of the container and munched it. "So, did Sante say anything else?"

He shook his head. "No, but I don't want to talk about Sante tonight anyway."

"Fine." She shrugged. "Let's talk about you, then."

"Me?"

"Well, clearly you've plumbed the mysteries that are Daria. I have some catching up to do. For example, how did you survive those years with your blood mother? I still don't understand that."

"It wasn't that bad, Daria. I mean, it's true I was Chosen against my will, but in a lot of ways it was like coming home. I hated her for a time, then things got better." He paused, his face hardening. "Then, toward the end, I hated her again."

"Why?"

He shrugged and bit into another date. "She tried to push me to do things I didn't want to do."

He didn't seem like he wanted to talk about it, so she changed the subject. "You said it was like coming home? Not for me."

"You don't have the genes. It's probably a lot harsher for you. How are you doing, anyway?"

She studied a slice of peach. "I'm trying not to think about it. Just trying to take each day as it comes. I feel stronger than I did before, but I'm afraid it might make me too sure of myself and I know I'm still weak for a Chosen. Might get my ass kicked." She nibbled the peach. "And I miss food."

"Have you thought about what you're going to do when this is over?"

"Go home. Tell my mom I've been Chosen. After that, I don't know. I'm not sure I want to continue to work for the ABI."

"Why not?"

"Sante has been my goal for so long. Once we bring him down, I'll have achieved it."

"I'm sure the GBC would welcome your help."

"We'll see. I have some money saved up. I might want to do some traveling. I've never seen the moons of Songset. I've never visited the oceans of Galileo. It's a big universe out there."

"You going to do all that alone?"

She glanced at him. "Why? You looking for an invitation?"

"Maybe."

She dropped the rest of her peach into the container. "What is it you find so compelling about me, Alejandro? I'm prickly as all hell and I'm high maintenance. I'd never cook for you or pick up your dirty socks from the floor."

"I like prickly and high maintenance. It makes a long life more interesting. Anyway"—he turned her chin toward him—"I know what you're like under the prickly."

She knew she'd regret asking. "What's that?"

"Someone who is caring and loyal. Someone who would go to the four corners of the universe for a friend. Someone who would sacrifice their whole life for someone else."

"What if I'm doing all that for *me*?"

He shook his head. "It's all about Julia."

She swallowed hard. "Can I have a date?"

He smiled and handed her one.

Daria nibbled it. "So how many women have you seduced since you were Chosen, Alejandro? You seem pretty good at it."

"A few. Not as many as you might think. None as interesting as I find you."

She shot from the bed and crossed to the other side of the room. "Stop that."

"Stop what?"

"Stop acting like you care about me."

Alejandro stood and walked slowly toward her. Her stomach tightened increasingly as he approached. "It's not an act. I'm being honest. I told you I was taking the gloves off, Daria. I didn't just mean sexually."

He reached out and took her by the upper arm. Then he paused, as though expecting her to react in some way, perhaps pull away. Daria couldn't. She couldn't do anything but stand there, frozen and wondering at what she was feeling, wondering about the warmth that had spread through her chest. Then he pulled her forward, up against his hard chest and into the circle of his arms. He lowered his head and set his lips to hers. She could taste dates on his mouth.

Alejandro kissed better than most men made love. His teeth captured her lower lip and dragged, sending shivers down her spine. Then he growled a little and slanted his mouth over hers, sliding his tongue within to mate with hers. His kiss was at once possessive, ferocious, and tender. She rested her hands on his upper arms, feeling the pulse and bulge of the muscles there.

It took her breath away. Everything about Alejandro Martinez seemed to take her breath away.

It was like the first time he'd kissed her. Hell, it was like the first time she'd ever been kissed. It made her feel seventeen again, seemed to erase everything that had happened since that age when she'd been young, lush, and innocent.

Her hands floated up to smooth over his broad shoulders, finding his silky hair. He slid his hands up her back, letting one palm cup the nape of her neck. The kiss went on and on until her knees felt weak and her whole body shook almost imperceptibly.

Outside the window, in the garden, rain began to fall. The gentle pitter-patter of the raindrops was comforting, but the novelty of the occurrence wasn't enough to draw their attention. That was all centered on each other.

She thought about interrupting the kiss and stopping this whole thing . . . whatever it was. She *should*, really, but she didn't want to.

Fuck the shoulds. For this night she would let Alejandro lead the way. She was weary of fighting.

Alejandro broke the kiss and led her to the bed. Wordlessly, he turned off the light, stripped her clothes off and then his. They curled up together under the covers with as much skin touching as possible while the rain fell steadily outside. For the first time in years, Daria felt relaxed and content.

Alejandro's cock pressed against her leg, and she reacted to it. She responded to the scent of him and the heat of his body, her languor slowly turning into a lazy sexual desire. Her sex grew warm and she shifted against him, knowing very well that Alejandro could sense the change in her body.

She would like to have that cock in her mouth, to feel the way his body tensed as she pleasured him. Daria liked to have control over a man that way, knowing he lay at her mercy, helpless to the mere stroke of her tongue. The thought of making Alejandro that way made her cunt quiver with anticipation.

In a relaxed movement, she reached between their bodies and took his shaft into her hand. He let out a low, delicious-sounding moan as she caressed him.

If Alejandro didn't know before what she had in mind, he did now. Daria doubted he would object.

His cock was long and wide, any woman's dream. Dark, deep lust somewhere in the center of her cried out for her to have it in her mouth.

Daria hadn't been with many men. She could count all of them on two hands. Yet, her experiences hadn't been tame. There was little sexually that she hadn't done, aside from anal sex, but she couldn't ever remember needing a man like she needed Alejandro at this moment.

Maybe it was simply the desire to connect with someone. Daria didn't know and her body was far too needy at the moment for much introspection.

She dragged her hand up his cock and used his foreskin to pump him. Groaning, he tipped his head back.

"You're killing me, Daria," Alejandro murmured.

A small smile curved her lips as she leaned toward him and kissed his throat, allowing her tongue to steal out and draw small circles on his heated flesh. "Oh, I'm not done by half yet," she whispered, then disappeared under the covers.

After kissing her way down his luscious chest and over his muscled stomach, she found herself at the desired locale. Running her finger up and down his shaft, she explored every inch at her leisure, happy for the small amount of light being let in at the top edge of the blankets.

She leaned forward and licked the smooth crown, savouring the drop of pearlescent pre-cum that had slipped from the tip. Alejandro's body tightened and he groaned.

Acting as though she had all the time in the world and her body wasn't crying out for satisfaction, Daria traced over the length of his shaft, exploring every vein and teasing the small, sensitive area just under the broad, smooth crown. Every movement she made drew a shudder of pleasure from him.

Right when she sensed Alejandro was about to go insane, she engulfed him in her mouth.

18

ALEJANDRO's body jerked with pleasure as Daria slid her lush lips over his cock. He'd hoped she'd come to him again, initiate this without the help of his veil, but he hadn't expected it to happen tonight.

Not that he was complaining . . .

He fisted his hands in her hair and his breath hissed out of him. The hot, velvety interior of her mouth around his shaft made pleasure bunch in his balls. Impatiently, he flipped the blanket off, needing to be able to see her.

He fought the urge to bury his hands in the hair at her nape and thrust his cock deep into her mouth. Hell, he fought the urge to yank her up, spread her thighs as wide as they'd go, and sink into her warm, silky cunt.

He watched his length appear and disappear between her lush lips. With her tongue, she teased all the places that racked his body with erotic shudders. His fingers tightened a degree in her hair.

That was all he could stand.

He let out a stream of Spanish and gently thrust between her lips. Her tongue rippled and stroked him. It took only a few moments before pleasure exploded from his balls and he released himself into her mouth in a hot stream. Her tongue still bathed him after it was over, licking away every drop of his come as the shivers that wracked his body faded away.

Finally, she let him go, resting on her side and gazing up at his face with a hungry look in her eyes. His gaze traveled from her feet, up her smooth, shapely legs and curved body to her face.

"Get up here," he commanded in a hoarse voice. *"Vos necesito follar."*

"What does that mean?"

"I need to fuck you."

The slight smile on her lips faded and her pupils grew darker.

"Come here, *querida.*"

Moving to deliberately entice him, she traveled up his body slowly. Her hips swung and her shoulders rolled, a sultry expression on her beautiful face. She moved like a cat, a woman set on seduction. Here was the Daria he remembered from years ago—confident in the sexual power of her body.

If she meant to make him crazy for her, he was already there.

He rolled onto his side and pushed her to her back. With his index finger, he traced every hill and valley of her nipple until it tightened and grew hard. She closed her eyes and sighed, her body tightening with desire.

Alejandro dropped his hand between her thighs and teased her clit, rubbing it back and forth, until she moaned. "I want to watch you touch yourself."

Her eyes fluttered open. "What?"

He petted her cunt until she moved restlessly on the bed and she was so aroused he was sure she wouldn't deny him. "I want to see how you make yourself come. Don't tell me you never do it, Daria, when you're all alone and needing it."

She only stared at him, hesitation on her face.

He withdrew his hand. "Close your eyes and pretend I'm not here. Touch your breasts."

After a moment, she allowed her eyes to drift shut. Her hands moved slowly to her lovely breasts. Cupping them in both hands, she skated her thumbs over her nipples until they grew hard, cherry red—so suckable. As she caressed herself, her breath caught in her throat and her cheeks flushed crimson. Her hips thrust forward, as though looking for something to fuck.

Alejandro wanted to give her something, but first he wanted to see this through. "Now touch your pussy, Daria. Stroke your clit. Slide your fingers deep inside your cunt and tell me what you feel."

She splayed her hand on her stomach, just above her mound. It stayed there.

His Daria was shy, how endearing. Clearly she needed more detailed instruction. "Part your thighs."

Not opening her eyes, she did as he asked.

"Farther. Show me everything. Spread yourself completely."

She bent her knees, so her heels touched the backs of her thighs. In this position, she was completely open to him. Her cunt was swollen in its arousal, blushing a nice shade of pink. Her labia were flushed and pouting. Her clit peeked, engorged and begging for attention, from its hood.

"*Que lindo coño.* That means you have a pretty pussy, Daria."

His fingernails bit into his palms as he fisted his hands tighter, trying to resist touching her. He wanted to ease his fingers over her clit, make her come right now.

Patience. He needed more of it.

"You want to come, don't you? You want to feel my cock driving in and out of you, fucking your sweet cunt until you scream."

Her eyes flickered open. "Alejandro, you're killing me. Yes, I want you."

Alejandro fisted the blankets in his hands. "Make yourself orgasm for me. I want to watch. Do it slow."

Her breath came heavier in the quiet air of the room. She dragged the hand on her stomach downward. Letting it rest on her mound, she opened her eyes and raised her gaze to meet his. She dipped her hand between her thighs, keeping her gaze locked with his. With two fingers, she rubbed her clit. He watched in fascination as she caressed herself.

She gasped and arched her back. Alejandro reached out to cover her hand with his own, but pulled it away at the last moment. "Does that feel good, *querida*?"

Alejandro watched the slow rotation of her fingers around her swollen clit. Her labia looked heavy and he ached to lean in and take them between his lips. He wanted to nibble on them like candy.

Gently, he eased her other hand between her legs, to the entrance of her pussy. She spread her labia, giving him a glimpse of the heart of her. Then she dragged her fingertips over her entrance. Daria whimpered and her hips thrust forward as she unconsciously sought his cock to penetrate her.

Alejandro had to force himself not to jump on her and spear deep into her cunt. "One night, Daria, I want you to let me do whatever I want to you."

She tossed her head. "I want that, too."

"You do? Give it to me. Agree to give me one night. One night you totally give up control to me. Let me do whatever I want to this delicious body."

Her eyes flickered open and her gaze caught his. "Yes."

He growled in satisfaction. "Now . . . you want something to fill all that sweetness of yours?" He pressed her fingers inside her. They slid in easily, and she moaned his name. Dragging his fingers over her swollen flesh once, making her shudder, he forced himself to retreat.

She moved her hand and hips, fucking her own fingers.

"That's it. Can you feel all those pulsing muscles? That's what I feel when I'm inside you." He paused and when he spoke next, his voice shook. "You're beautiful, Daria. You're so fucking pretty."

She pumped into her sex, her other hand caressing her clit. Her back arched and she tossed her head as she drove herself closer and closer to coming.

Alejandro reached down and grasped his cock, stroking it from base to tip as he watched the erotic display before him. He wasn't sure how much more he could take before the tenuous grasp he had on his control broke.

Then her body went rigid and she whimpered, "I'm coming."

He placed his hand over her clit and pressed down.

"Alejandro!" Her body trembled and the room filled with the sweet, sweet sounds of her pleasure.

Before her orgasm had completely died, he removed her hands. He eased his own fingers deep inside her, feeling the hot, pulsing clasp of her still-climaxing muscles around them. Then lowered his head and sucked her clit between his lips to massage and flick with his tongue.

Daria cried out, her climax roaring back to life. He rode her through it, groaning at the erotic flavor of her spreading over his tongue.

Finally, she quieted and lay panting, but Alejandro wasn't finished with her yet. He licked her sensitive clit and then laved over everything else, too. He pulled her labia between his lips and gently sucked.

Daria writhed on the bed beneath him, her hands threading through his hair, as he drank his fill of her while he had the chance. This taste of her might have to last him a long, long time. She'd agreed to give herself over to him one night, but with Daria, he just never knew. Alejandro groaned deep in his throat.

Dios, *she tastes so good.*

When he'd satisfied himself, he didn't ask permission. He just mounted her fast and hard, pushing her thighs apart and sinking his cock deep inside her creamy cunt.

~

DARIA gasped and arched her back. Alejandro always made her feel so . . . *complete* when he was inside her. His cock stretched her so exquisitely it brought tears to her eyes and sent her body straight back to the edge of a climax.

He pressed his big body down on hers, his hands braced on the mattress on either side of her torso. "Alejandro . . ." She could say no more. Her eyes fluttered shut for a moment as pleasure pulsed through her. Then he began to thrust and it exploded.

She gripped his upper arms as he slammed into her with long, hard strokes. Every one sent a lightning bolt of ecstasy through her and pushed her toward a second, shattering climax.

They came at the same time, their pleasure reaching a shared crescendo. The first time he'd made her come, it had rippled through her long and gently. This time it rolled over her like a freight train, leaving her wracked, spent, and hoarse from crying out.

He came down over her, kissing her mouth and throat, threading his fingers through her hair. "Daria." He whispered her name over and over.

She buried her face in the curve where throat met shoulder. Closing her eyes, for a moment she wished he would never leave her body, *not ever*. Then as the aftermath of her climax faded, rationality flickered, and the thought faded away.

19

T HE building sat in the far corner of the dome, set along charming cobblestone pathways lined with flowering fruit trees. It was small, unassuming, yet was a beautiful example of modern architecture. Here Sante had not gone retro. The pointed roof was all unbreakable glass, reflecting the light of the fake sun on this lovely fake afternoon. Likely, as all the buildings in the dome had, there were solar panels embedded in the glass. Outside the walls of the dome it could have been midnight for all Daria knew.

The bottom half of the circular structure was creamy white *restao*, a building material they frequently used in the Logos Territories to aid in relieving the excessive heat. Wide, long windows were placed at regular intervals around the building. To serve as a transition between the white restao walls and the glass ceiling was a wooden lattice overhang, from which cool grapevines twined and lush, vibrantly green potted ferns hung suspended.

Here, apparently, was Sante's headquarters within the dome. Here would be where she and Alejandro would gain coveted membership in Sante's inner sanctum.

Sante had sent a messenger to their room that morning telling them to forgo their work at the factory and to come here instead. It looked as if they would not be returning to their daily factory shifts ever again, a fact which made Daria a little disappointed since she'd never reached her goal of attaining entrance into the packing room. However, this opportunity might offer her other ways to snoop.

Hell, who knew? Maybe Sante would show all his cards to them immediately and they could wrap this gig up. Daria and Alejandro could take this place down, put Sante in jail, and she could get on with her immortal, bloodsucking life.

It had been four days since Sante had called Daria and Alejandro to his home. He'd waited such a long interval to contact them again she'd begun to worry their chance had somehow slipped through their fingers. Likely it was just that Sante was a busy man—people to kill, women to kidnap, slaves to traffic, that sort of thing.

Carlos stood at the entrance, smoking a long, thin Darpongese cigarette. The acrid smoke floated a long way on the normally pure air of the dome, fouling it.

As she and Alejandro approached, Carlos's mouth twisted into a bitter not-smile. "For the record, I think it is too early for you to join us. In fact," he continued, eyeing Alejandro from toe to head, "I don't think some of us should have an in with Sante at all. It is a privilege and an honor to be accepted into this building. However, it is Sante who dictates membership, not I."

"Well, thanks for letting your preferences be known," snapped Daria. "You can be sure I made note of them."

"Carlos, let them in," called Sante from the interior of the structure.

Carlos gave them one last hostile look, then stepped aside to allow them passage.

They entered the cool, round room. The floor was of tan stone and covered with large area rugs. Potted plants stood at various locations, accenting plush, multicolored furniture with many throw pillows. Doorways led into other rooms at the back, and a large fountain burbled happily to itself along one wall. The wooden rafters above their head were home to a few vibrantly colored birds, which flitted here

and there, the soft *whirrr* of their wings playing nicely with the sound
of the water.

Daria wondered if it bothered the birds to see the sky above them
through the glass ceiling and be forever unable to reach it. Maybe that
amused Sante. It seemed like something that would.

The great man himself lounged on a bright blue and orange couch,
gazing at them lazily as though he had no cares in the galaxy. He
moved his hand. "Forgive Carlos. He has appointed himself my watch-
dog and he can be rabid in his protection of me."

Carlos, who had entered after them, didn't argue with this assessment. He only took a place at the back of the room and settled into a
gimlet stare at Alejandro. He wore a white shirt, open at the collar, and
had his hand tucked into the pocket of his beige slacks.

Daria wondered what Carlos had hidden in that pocket, a knife?
Carlos seemed the knife type. A thug. Although he was such an old
Chosen and had amassed so much power over the years, he could
probably kill them where they stood with his bare hands. Still, Daria
bet anything he preferred to use a knife—more blood that way.

"We understand," answered Alejandro diplomatically. Even though
she could feel the tension in his body, he sounded relaxed. His gaze
rested on the woman sitting on a nearby chair, the only other female
besides Daria in the room. "Nice to meet you."

"This is Eleanor Matthews. She comes to us by way of Songset. I
know her through our shared blood mother," Sante introduced. "Eleanor,
please meet Valerie and Alejandro."

"Pleased to meet you," Eleanor responded, sounding anything but.

Daria would have speculated that the tall blonde was the woman
Sante was in love with, if she hadn't recognized her as one of the inner
circle following Sante the night of the party. She knew her name, in
any case. Eleanor Matthews. She'd been in the file she'd received from
the GBC with the information on all of Sante's closest Chosen. The
ones he wrapped around himself like a warm blanket. It was true
Eleanor shared Sante's blood mother and had been with him from the
beginning.

Anyway, Sante's lady wasn't a moderately aged, moderately power-ful Chosen like Eleanor. She was a succubare, if Daria's little trip to Sante's house that night had given her any clue. Unless, of course, that woman had just been a snack on the side. That was always possible.

Daria glanced around the room and searched with her limited psychic sense to find other bodies in the building, but came up empty. *Damn.* She'd hoped to meet the mystery woman today.

"Please, have a seat," Sante said, motioning to the available furni-ture. "There are refreshments on the table if you desire something more than blood this morning."

"Thank you," answered Alejandro. They sat down.

Sante motioned to a bright red pitcher holding some unidentifiable cool drink that sat on a tray on the coffee table. Red glasses had been lined up on either side. "It's chilled blood wine." Sante frowned. "Some kind of fruit flavoring, I believe."

Daria shivered. She was Chosen now, but hadn't grown used to all a vampire's common dietary preferences yet. Blood wine was sought after in the Chosen community—blood mixed with wine and flavored with fruit. It was generally a very expensive refreshment. Something about mixing blood with strawberries or cherries made Daria's stom-ach unhappy.

Alejandro poured himself a glass and she relaxed, off the hook since one of them imbibed.

"I called you here so you could meet a couple of the people you may find yourself working with," said Sante. "I thought I would put both of you on my staff for community relations. You're new around here, so it will give you a chance to meet people."

Community relations. That didn't sound promising. She'd been hop-ing he'd appoint them to drug trafficking or something interesting.

"What exactly does the community relations staff do?" asked Ale-jandro.

Eleanor curled her long legs beneath her. "We organize parties and gatherings. Generally, we promote goodwill among our residents."

Holy shuffleboard on the lido deck, they wanted them to be party planners? Teddy bears, honey making, and goodwill. What was next? Organized rainbow chasing and bubble-blowing contests?

Eleanor smiled at Daria. "I see your expression, Valerie. It will be far more interesting than you think. Keeping the long-lived and generally jaded Chosen entertained is quite a trick. You haven't been here long enough to discover all our various gatherings."

"Valerie and Alejandro, my pet," Sante broke in, "are sadly monogamous. There will be no playing for them."

Oh.

Eleanor eyed not Alejandro with regret, but Daria. She made a moue with her rosy lips. "What a pity. Well, give them a hundred years of the missionary position with only one partner and they might change their tune."

"Eleanor, don't push," Sante said in a reproving tone.

She studied Daria. "But that still shouldn't stop you from helping organize the fetes, correct?"

Daria didn't like the predatory look in her eyes, as though Eleanor might be inclined to try and change her mind on the issue. There would be no changing her mind, *ever.*

"Of course not," Alejandro answered for them.

Daria nodded her assent. "We'd be happy to help out." They had no good reason to decline and, at this point, they had to take what was offered. "It sounds . . . fun."

"It's a lot of work," Sante broke in. "We take the happiness of the residents very seriously. Bored Chosen are dangerous Chosen."

Why did that statement seem so ironic coming from his mouth?

"All members of the board of directors, as they're called, are in charge of various things here at the Shining Way," continued Sante. "I switch members around sometimes, so you won't be doing this forever."

"What is Carlos in charge of?" Daria couldn't help asking. It just flew right out of her mouth.

Sante smiled wolfishly. "Security."

Color her surprised.

"Do you think we could get a formal tour of the dome?" Daria asked. "We've been here a couple of weeks, but we still feel like we haven't seen it all."

They would see only what Sante wanted them to see, but who knew what they might glimpse by chance? Who knew what new bit of information a tour might yield? Anything to break their consistent run of bad luck would be welcome, no matter how small.

Sante mulled that over for a moment. "I can have someone show you around, yes."

Movement drew their attention to the back of the building. The scent of the individual reached her before she caught a glimpse of the woman's multicolored gown—a succubare.

The woman bustled through the doorway, and Daria's heart stopped for a moment. Her vision blurred and it took every ounce of her will to not show her utter and complete surprise.

Ari Templeton.

20

S HE walked toward Sante in a smooth, graceful gait, a serene look on her face. The hem of her breezy long dress, a pleasing pattern of various bold hues, swirled around her ankles. She wore no shoes on her slender feet, only a small gold ankle bracelet adorned them. Gold glittered at each ear, on her fingers, and in the hollow of her throat, where an expensive-looking pendant lay, a diamond winking at its center.

This woman did not appear kidnapped, not by any stretch of the imagination. She did not look hassled. She did not look harmed.

She looked like she was vacationing.

"My love," said Ari, approaching Sante. Her voice was low and mellifluous. It was the voice Daria had heard coming from Sante's bedroom the night she'd broken into his house.

Sante smiled as warmly as Daria could remember him occasionally smiling at her—in another life—then reached up and pulled Ari down into his lap to kiss her. Across from them, Eleanor rolled her eyes like someone annoyed by the behavior of the newly in love.

Daria mastered her expression with effort, but managed to smile indulgently at the couple as she imagined Valerie would do. Within, her thoughts and emotions swirled in a confused tornado, threatening to overwhelm her.

Beside her, Alejandro controlled his reaction like the pro he was, though he had to be as shocked as she was.

Their acting ability was a good thing. Carlos watched them carefully from across the room with his beady dark eyes, measuring them, weighing them, as he *always* seemed to be measuring and weighing them.

Sante and Ari kissed for several moments. The kind of kiss that makes everyone around a couple feel like they're intruding on an intimate moment and are voyeurs. The kiss of a couple so in love they don't care who's watching; they simply have to touch.

Finally they broke their embrace and Ari slid to the side, still keeping one slim leg draped over Sante's muscular one. She glanced at Daria and Alejandro and smiled sheepishly, coloring a bit as she ran a finger around her lips to fix her lipstick.

Oh, god. The poor woman is like a besotted teenager.

"Forgive us," Sante said with a shrug and a pair of broad, upturned hands. "Ari and I are newly mated. I'm sure you can understand."

Alejandro made some polite sounds of assent, but Daria couldn't respond. All her energy went to masking her expression.

"In addition," Sante continued, "Ari is a new Chosen and her appetites are especially hearty. Not that I mind." Another wolfish grin. He nodded toward Daria. "My Ari did not make it through the succubare, as you did, Valerie. It is one reason I am interested in you."

"You're the human who made it through?" asked Ari suddenly.

"Yes," Daria answered smoothly. "It's a pleasure to meet you."

Ari slid from the couch and crossed the floor in a sensual movement. She knelt at Daria's feet and took one of Daria's hands between her palms. "I just had to touch you." The succubare were like that. "How did you do it? I tried and tried to push through, but I couldn't." Tears glistened in the woman's eyes.

"Like I told Christopher, I'm not sure. When I felt like giving up, I pushed harder." Daria paused, glancing at Sante. "You were Chosen voluntarily, weren't you?"

Ari bowed her head and nodded. "I knew the chances that I wouldn't push through were great. I took them anyway because I was so in love." She raised her head. "I don't regret it, but I'm sorry I wasn't strong enough to make it through."

Such a long life lived dependent on sex; Daria could imagine she was sorry.

Sante rose and helped Ari to her feet. She seemed like such a sweet woman, soft, and vulnerable. The total opposite of her father, Richard Templeton. How could she have fallen in love with Christopher Sante?

"How did you two meet?" Alejandro asked. *God bless him.*

Ari smiled. "He came into Rapid City one evening. I'd gone there to demonstrate against my father's latest crusade against the Chosen. You know my father, undoubtedly. He's Richard Templeton." She paused and waited for their reaction, which they gave in a couple of understanding murmurings. "Christopher was there that night, and it was love at first bite." She smiled and it lit her entire face. "We dated in secret for a long time, until we knew we had to be together as a mated pair. So I underwent the Choosing."

"That's a very romantic story," answered Daria.

"Please, her presence here is secret," said Sante. "She travels through the dome via underground passageways. No one sees her except my inner circle. As you can understand, her father isn't happy with this arrangement. It's for her protection."

"Of course," answered Alejandro.

"If you'll excuse us," continued Sante. "We're done here. I'll let you coordinate with Eleanor for the rest."

Alejandro and Daria watched Sante lead Ari away, her head resting on his shoulder and his arm around her waist in a loving and protective gesture.

Eleanor stood. "Well, I've got to go, too, but I'll be in touch soon regarding particulars. We have a gathering tomorrow you should probably attend, very erotic. Hope you don't mind. It's at the Alhambra Building at midnight. See you there?"

Oh, good. An orgy. Daria could hardly wait.

"We'll see you there," answered Alejandro.

They followed Eleanor out of the building, Carlos staring at them the whole time. The way he looked at her made shivers of revulsion rocket up her spine. Daria was just able to control herself until they were free of the building and Eleanor had walked in the other direction.

Alejandro took her arm, perhaps sensing her impending explosion. "Just keeping walking."

She did, concentrating on putting one foot in front of the other. They walked all the way back to the room and as soon as she closed the door she paced. "What the fuck, Alejandro? *What the fuck!*"

"I'm as confused as you are."

"Do you think she's being coerced in some way?"

Alejandro shook his head. "You saw her. Did she look coerced? I think Sante's got a lot of power, but not that much."

She chewed on the edge of her thumbnail. "He's got to have an angle. He's playing her like he played me."

"Maybe."

She looked up at him and stopped chewing. "*Maybe*? No doubt, Alejandro. Wooing and winning the daughter of Richard Templeton? Hell, and he didn't even have to kidnap her. All he had to do was turn on the charm and seduce her away. Charm and seduce her enough to *want to be Chosen*?"

Alejandro ran a hand over his chin. "It does sound like Sante."

"You think?" Bitterness gave the words a hard edge. "*Bastard.* He's making this twice as hard." It would've been easier to free Ari had she been willing to be freed. Sante had mind-fucked the woman but good.

"I'm calling Brandon in here." He concentrated a moment, communicating with the other man via a mental pathway.

"What's happened?" Brandon asked as soon as he entered the room. Apparently he hadn't left for work yet.

They told him.

He stood stunned for a moment, stymied for words. Finally he scratched his head, stuttered a moment, and then said, "We have to entertain the possibility she's here because they truly are in love."

Daria leaned forward. "He's not capable of it, Brandon."

Brandon fixed her with a steady stare. "You have personal baggage here. Don't let it affect the mission." His voice was as hard as she'd ever heard it.

"I'm not saying I don't have any, but this is not my personal baggage talking. Right now it's my personal knowledge of this man. I was with him intimately for years. I know him better than either of you."

"You knew the Sante he *chose* to present to you," Brandon spat back. "You didn't know the real man."

"Stop it!" commanded Alejandro in a low voice.

Both she and Brandon froze.

"Daria, I believe Sante did love you. He was sincere when he spoke about you the other day. I believe he is capable of emotion. So Brandon is right. We do need to entertain the possibility that Sante and Ari Templeton truly are together out of love."

Daria sat back in defeat. She couldn't believe his words, but she was outnumbered. She sighed. "Then . . . we need to investigate further."

But she knew what they'd find.

Brandon nodded. "It will be easier for you two to do that, of course, since you both have entrée into his inner circle." He paused. "Any chance of getting me in?"

Alejandro frowned. "We don't need you in, Brandon. You're more valuable where you are, close to where they might be trafficking blood slaves. We work this end, you work that one."

"Yes," Brandon answered. "But this is more important right now, and the more hands we have in there, the better."

"More important, *tio*?" Alejandro snapped. "I think finding out whether or not there are blood slaves here is pretty damn important."

"We can handle the Ari thing," said Daria. "Sante put us on the social patrol. That will give us lots of excuses to get friendly with people and ask questions. Anyway, we shouldn't put everyone in the

same location. If Alejandro and I get popped, you're still undercover."

Brandon fidgeted impatiently. "Ari Templeton is our number one
priority. I demand, as highest-ranking member of this operation, that
you try and get me in."

Daria looked at Alejandro for a moment in disbelief, her blood
pressure rising. *What a fucking snotty little control freak.* "Listen,
you—"

"Fine." Alejandro held up a hand. "We'll try, okay, Brandon? Happy
now?"

"Fucking ecstatic."

"What's with the tension?" Alejandro pointed at her. "I get yours.
What's up with you, Brandon?"

He yanked a hand through his hair. "Frustration. Today we're no
closer to getting anything on Sante than the day we came in here.
There are potential things, the trafficking in blood slaves, possible
smuggling. Now this damn trip up with Ari Templeton. It all costs us
time and I don't want to spend any more time here than we need to."

"You're singing my song, my friend," Alejandro answered. "But it
is what it is. Relax and we'll do our best to get to the bottom of all of it.
We caught one lucky break being let into Sante's inner circle. We need
to follow the trail of bread crumbs now."

"You mean the one that led to the witch's oven?" Brandon flashed
a grin.

Alejandro nodded. "Yeah, but Hansel and Gretel pushed the witch
in, right?" He shot Daria a glance, seeing the perplexed look on her
face. "Yes, I'm familiar with children's stories. I have a bunch of little
nieces and nephews."

Daria raised a hand. "I wasn't judging." She turned to Brandon.
"Anyway, I thought you liked the women here and all that. Why are
you in such a rush to get out of here all of a sudden?"

He shrugged. "There are women everywhere. I've got to go." He
pointed at them both in turn. "Get me into Sante's inner circle if you
can." He turned and left the room.

"He just flipped his asshole switch," muttered Daria once he'd left.

"No kidding. Look, are you okay with all this?"

"I meant what I said about not letting my personal baggage trip me up. I do have to admit I'm feeling a little for Ari Templeton right now if she is being duped, but that's going to help me, not hinder me."

"Get friendly with Eleanor."

She shot him an incredulous look. "Excuse me?"

"That woman is definitely bisexual and was definitely with Sante at some point. I watched her carefully when Ari came in. They didn't greet each other, and Eleanor was jealous as hell." Alejandro grinned. "She's attracted to you. It was all in her body language, so it should be easy."

"I don't do women," she stated flatly.

"Just be friendly with her. Use her . . . *appreciation* of you to your advantage. Get close to her and subtly pump her for information. Maybe she was Sante's last lover. Even better, maybe she's Sante's current lover, sidelined while he takes Richard Templeton's beloved daughter for a ride."

"I'll do my best." She sat for a moment, thinking. "Can you imagine what Richard Templeton would do if he knew his only daughter has fallen in love with a Chosen?"

"Worse, that she allowed herself to be Chosen? That she is now succubare?"

Daria nodded. "Imagine the shame he'd feel." She couldn't help a little smile. "God, that would be awesome."

"But would leave us nowhere closer to pinning Sante with anything."

Her smile faded. "Yeah." She stood. "I'm going to the factory."

"I don't think they want us back there anymore."

She shrugged. "Got a whole day to fill. Might as well stuff some teddy bears. I still want a shot at entry into that packaging room. Anyway, I like Jia Ying and the others."

His voice lowered. "I can think of better ways to spend the day than making teddy bears."

She smiled at him as she went for the door. "Work, Alejandro. *Work.*"

~

CHRISTOPHER gazed down at Ari as she slept, her long dark hair tumbling over her pillow and one creamy leg exposed. She always slept with her feet, at least one, sticking out from the bottom of the covers. It was one of many endearing qualities she possessed. He loved her so much.

But he could imagine what Daria was thinking right now.

He'd set up the meeting between Ari, Daria, and Alejandro on purpose, of course. Christopher needed Daria to understand they were truly in love, he and Ari. He needed to know what her reaction to that information would be before he took any further steps. If she backed off, fine.

If she didn't . . .

If Daria meant to split them up, bring Ari back to grovel at the feet of her hating, bigoted father, then his next move would be a violent one.

He supposed it had been a risk, showing Ari to them, but better that than having them sneak around the compound looking for an abducted woman. Even though Ari had told her father she was in love with him before she left Rapid City and was leaving volutarily, Richard Templeton had reported her kidnapped.

Sante reached down and fingered a tendril of Ari's hair, letting it slip through his fingers.

He hadn't told Ari yet, not about anything. He'd only told her, for her own protection, that she needed to stay well away from everyone in the dome but his inner circle, the so-called board of directors. He hadn't told her about her father, hadn't told her there were ABI and GBC agents here looking for her. She didn't need to know any of that. She was still recuperating from the Choosing and couldn't handle any added stress.

Anyway, he'd take care of her. Nothing would harm Ari. He'd die before he allowed her to be hurt.

His plan now was to make sure Daria understood Ari was truly here by choice, that he was in love with her. He knew Daria's doubting mind well enough to understand that she likely believed he was duping Ari, just like he'd duped her in the beginning.

Daria was a cynical woman, and Christopher knew that she'd probably only grown more so over the years . . . because of him.

The idea made his chest feel heavy.

So he turned his thoughts to the day he'd met Ari.

She'd been standing along the street in Rapid City, the sound of traffic, honking, and chanting filling the air. Ari had been among the hundreds who'd shown up that day in protest of Richard Templeton and The New Covenant Church, who had been meeting to figure out solutions to the Chosen "problem." Everywhere Templeton and his minions went, they were greeted with protesters.

Christopher had happened to be in Rapid City on Shining Way business when this meeting had occurred and had stopped by to see the circus.

Ari had just been standing there in the throng, hands thrust deeply into her blue winter coat to ward off the chill. Not holding a sign. Not chanting.

Even though she'd been wearing a hat and a pair of sunglasses, Christopher had still recognized her. It was her long hair that did it, the tilt of her full lips, the slightly larger than average nose. He'd seen pictures of the only daughter of Richard Templeton and thought her pretty . . . for being the undoubtedly twisted progeny of his race's worst enemy.

He'd strolled straight to her and asked what she thought she was doing there. He'd been pissed off, thinking she was spying for her father. She'd been nervous at first, shaken that he'd recognized her so easily. After all, her father did all he could to keep her out of the spotlight. Her face wasn't exactly a household image.

Then she'd been pissed he'd questioned her presence at the rally. She stood there on the street, went toe-to-toe with him and yelled into his face that she had a right to be there just like every other person who wanted equal rights for the Chosen.

Intrigued and wondering if she was telling the truth, Christopher had invited her for coffee. They'd stayed at the rally until it was over, then had walked to the nearest café and talked for hours.

That had been the beginning.

They'd dated for a long time. During that part of his life, Christopher hadn't spent much time at the Shining Way, instead giving over management of almost all operations to Carlos. Sante had wanted to be wherever Ari was, mostly at her place in Rapid City.

During that time he'd learned what a hard life Ari had lived under the iron fist of her father, the dreams she'd had of becoming an artist dashed by his controlling hand. Richard Templeton had his daughter's life mapped out for her and if she deviated, there was hell to pay.

She was a soft woman, strong-willed like her father, but in a quiet way. She had the temperament of an artist—she loved to do oil paintings— and was very emotional, sometimes scarily vulnerable. She was a woman who begged by her very existence to be cared for and protected.

Sometimes Christopher wondered if Ari hadn't fallen in love with him and decided to be Chosen all just to spite her father. If, on some level only a psychiatrist could plumb, she was using him.

He ran his finger down her cheek. Christopher was so in love with her, he wasn't sure he cared. Deep in his heart he knew it wasn't true, anyway.

This relationship was good and solid, not doomed to fail the way the relationship he'd had with Daria had been. He leaned down and kissed Ari's forehead.

He wasn't going to screw this up, and he *wasn't* going to lose her.

21

Daria stepped into the room and into candlelight. "Alejandro?" He stood in the middle of the room, holding something in his hand. "You gave me one night, Daria. Do you remember? One night to completely give yourself over to me." He paused, moving whatever it was he held from hand to hand. God, was that rope? "Tonight is that night."

She licked her lips as fear laced with desire rippled through her. When she'd masturbated for Alejandro, while she'd been in the throes of erotic bliss, she had agreed to that. If she hadn't been hopped up on hormones, she wouldn't have. The idea of being his object, letting him play out any fantasy he wished with her, would've stayed in the realm of her imagination, to be trotted out whenever she needed help bringing herself relief on her own in the dead of night.

But now the opportunity to make it a reality was at her fingertips.

"Don't say no, Daria." His voice was edged in steel. "I know you want it. Take it."

Arrogant. Except he was right, she did want it.

Alejandro took a step toward her, into a shaft of moonlight. She saw he wore only a pair of low-slung jeans, revealing the jut of his hip bones. The delicious expanse of his chest was bared, along with the trail of hair running down past the waistband of his pants that lead to his cock. His long, strong feet were bare, too.

"Strip out of your clothes and come here to me." He stared hard at her. "Do it."

Daria hesitated, then raised her gaze to his. She held it steadily as she stripped slowly, deliberately, revealing every body part to him in a tease. If she did this, it would probably be the last time she had any kind of control until morning.

His body had gone tight, his fingers clenched around the rope he held, by the time she stood in front of him, the soft air of the room bathing her skin and raising gooseflesh along her arms and legs. She walked slowly to him, rolling her hips, confident in her ability to arouse him.

Even in the mostly dark, Alejandro's gaze smoldered. He drew her against him and his mouth came down near hers, his breath branding her lips. He didn't kiss her, he only whispered close enough for her to hear, "Hands together at the small of your back."

Her breath hitched.

"You trust me, right?"

She blinked slowly and locked her jaw. That depended on what kind of trust he meant. Trust Alejandro with her body? *Yes.* She moved her hands to the small of her back.

He relaxed almost imperceptibly. Still with his lips just a breath's space from hers, he roped her wrists and secured them. *Talented.*

He took her upper arm and led her to the foot of the bed. After he sat down, he pulled her to lay facedown over his lap. His jeans rubbed the bare skin of her belly. Her gaze flicked to her left. There were items of an indiscernible nature lying on the mattress beside him.

Alejandro eased his hand down her spine and over the curve of her ass, then between her cheeks. He dragged his fingers over her flesh, gently forcing her thighs further apart so he could stroke her clit. She wiggled a little and moaned.

"Is your cunt wet for me, Daria?" His voice had a rasp to it.

"Why don't you touch it and find out for yourself?" she breathed.

He reached down and pinched her nipple hard enough to make her gasp. The slight pain of it quickly faded to erotic bliss, but she could tell he meant it as a rebuke. "You have no say in how I touch you tonight. Not when. Not where. Not *how*." He rolled her nipple between his thumb and forefinger. Pleasure jolted though her. "Do you have any objections?"

"No." She licked her suddenly dry lips.

"Good." He rubbed her clit again. "Do you want me to fuck your sweet cunt, Daria?"

Now her whole mouth was dry. "Yes."

"That was the right answer, *querida*. I will . . . in time." He went silent for a moment, then added in a soft, steady voice that sent shivers through her, "I'm making you mine tonight."

He caressed the cheek of her ass and then dragged his fingers down the length of her vulnerable, aroused sex and over her anus. She struggled for a moment against her bonds. It made her heart beat a little faster in panic even as it excited her.

"Scared, Daria?" He rubbed the pad of his finger around the entrance to her ass, making all the nerves there flare to life. "Afraid I'm going to do what, I wonder. Afraid I'm going to hurt you?"

"I'm not afraid," she answered in a steady voice, even though it wasn't completely true. She did feel the edge of fear mixing with the pleasure.

He gave a low, velvety laugh. "I know you better than you think." He slipped a finger inside her cunt and her muscles closed around the invasion, pulsing and rippling. "You'd never admit willingly to fear."

She let out a low moan. "I might be feeling a little vulnerable, but don't you dare fucking stop, Alejandro."

He laughed again and the sound of it in the quiet room made her shiver. "I couldn't stop now even if I wanted to, sweet Daria."

He added a second finger to the first and found her G-spot as he thrust in and out, making her see stars. With his other hand he rolled her nipple.

Daria let her body—and mind—relax, giving up to him completely.

Just until the morning. Just for sex. A soft cloud drifted through her thoughts. Giving in to Alejandro that way made her feel free, floating in a sea of perfect surrender. She had to be in control in her life all the time. Giving up now to a man she trusted, at least sexually, was a heady thing.

Alejandro eased a finger over her anus again and she jerked, cloud momentarily dispersing. "Easy, Daria. Remember, you're mine tonight." He slid a finger over it again. "Everywhere."

She relaxed once more, giving over to the experience. He did something she couldn't see and when he touched her there again, his fingers were slick with lube. Gently, he speared one finger deep inside her and worked it in and out until she was ready to take another.

There was a bit of pain as her muscles relaxed to accept the penetration, but it only served to make the pleasure more intense. Daria fought not to squirm on his lap. Her cunt felt heavy and warm but, most of all, needy.

Alejandro removed his fingers. A moment later a firm, smooth object pressed against her instead. Her breath hitched.

"*Shhh* . . . don't worry. You're excited and relaxed enough to take this."

She tensed a little anyway when he started to push the plug inside her. It was graduated in size, getting wider the farther he pushed it in. The slick end of the plug was sticky with the lubricant. When she moved, he slapped her ass. The stinging surprise of it faded to tingling pleasure that rippled through her cunt and she went still.

Little by little, he pressed it into her, filling her full of it and stimulating all her nerves so well she had to bite her lip to keep from screaming. There was a bit of pain, but only the barest of an edge. Only enough to sharpen the pleasure into a thing that swamped her mind and dominated her world.

She squirmed on his lap, heavy with the need to come, trying to get some kind of stimulation to her clit to manage it. His broad hand came down on her ass again in punishment, and she jerked, moaning, as orgasm flirted hard with her body and then retreated. If her hands hadn't been tied behind her back, she would have plunged them between her thighs and fucked herself to climax with her own fingers.

God, he was killing her.

Once in a while, he would ease it out a little and thrust it back in, letting her feel the ridges that ringed the plug. All she needed was a little stimulation to her clit, and she would come.

The experience was primal, erotic beyond anything she could have imagined. Having Alejandro exert this total, complete, and utter control over this part of her body was more arousing than she could have ever guessed it would be.

He thrust the plug in and out of her ass and she felt her juices drip from her empty, needy cunt. Then his fingers were there, stroking the entrance to her pussy, teasing her even further.

"Fuck me, Alejandro. Please."

"Stand up, Daria."

He helped her to her feet, but instead of easing his cock—which was rock hard—into her, he made her kneel on the floor. Her cheek pressed against the wood, filled ass high in the air, knees spread wide.

Alejandro circled her once, looking his fill. Then he bent and caressed her cunt, teasing her swollen clit unmercifully and rubbing her aroused labia. Her breath escaped her in a sobbing rush.

"You're very pretty like that. Should I keep you that way for a while?"

"Alejandro—"

He gave her no time to answer. He yanked up on her wrists, guiding her to her feet. Then he laid her face-first on the bed. Behind her came the blessed, glorious sound of his belt being undone. Was there a better noise in all the universe?

For several moments there was nothing, nothing but her body screaming to be filled even further than it was . . . screaming for Alejandro and for release. Then he came over her, his body pressing down against hers and warming her already heated flesh.

The slick, soft crown of his cock pressed against her cunt and slid in an inch. He did it impatiently, as if he was as much a victim of his sexual teasing as she was, and now his control was shredded.

Inch by long, hard inch, he fed his shaft to her. He thrust slowly in and out, every time driving more fully within her. As he moved, so did the plug, giving her the feeling she was being fucked in both places.

She fisted her bound hands, her mouth opening in a soundless scream of pleasure. Having both locations of her body filled simultaneously was nearly overwhelming. The sensations blended together, becoming one long buzz of bliss mixed with just a little bit of pain. Daria had always known she'd had a kink like this, a taste for utter and total domination in bed. Alejandro gave it to her now in mind-bending spades.

The sensations combined so well she couldn't separate the penetration of either orifice. It was just pure endless ecstasy, taking all of her thoughts, worries, and fears and throwing them to the wind. Her whole reality was her body and what Alejandro was doing to it.

His strokes became longer, harder, and faster, slamming into her with a ferocity that rocked her to her core. A powerful climax rose within her, unlike anything she'd ever experienced. When it came, it rolled over her like a wave. Sensation overtook her body, making her cry out. It possessed her body, tore thought from her mind, made her knees weak and her vision black out for a moment.

Alejandro yelled her name and came hard deep within her, his cock jumping against the walls of her cunt. His orgasm every bit as soul-shattering as hers.

Daria lay, breathing heavy, limp and sweating. She rested with her eyes closed, feeling and hearing Alejandro breathing hard, too.

After a moment, he released her wrists, though she still had no control over her limbs. He pulled his cock free of her body and extracted the plug as well. Still, she lay, shaking and spent, caught in the powerful throes of what had to be the best orgasm of her life.

Alejandro spoke softly to her, but she couldn't understand what he said. He slipped his hand under her pelvis and stroked her clit over and over, strong and steady, until she came against his hand once more, shuddering and sighing. Softer now. Easier. Bringing her back down to terra firma.

Finally, he gathered her up in his arms and took her into the shower with him. Coming alive once more under the hot stream of water, she stood and pressed her lips to his, giving him a kiss so sweet it stood in sharp contrast to the wonderful debauchery they'd just shared.

He slicked her hair away from her face. "All right, *querida*?"

"*Mmmm.*" She nuzzled the soap-smelling curve of his neck.

He chuckled. "I'll take that as a yes."

~

Music drifted around Daria in soft waves, the heady, sexy beat thrumming through her body. The room was outfitted with plush couches in dark reds and blues. An intricate area rug covered the hardwood floor.

Daria still hummed from the night before, when Alejandro had pretty much dominated every molecule—and orifice—of her body. Instead of sating her, it had only revved her libido, made her want more. That response could be a result of the Choosing, or perhaps this increased sexual appetite was simply a part of who she was now.

Whatever the reason, being in this place, where sex was treated so causally, sexual acts performed so openly . . . all of it heated her blood despite herself.

Around her Chosen laughed and talked in low voices in dim light. It was a party, a mixer of sorts for single Chosen and those couples with more adventurous tastes.

There were even blood donors.

The paid veilhounders were lined up against one wall, looking like sickly, painted, and dressed-up dolls. Like a fucking a la carte menu, the Chosen selecting which one they wanted a drink from.

Alejandro stood in the corner, trying valiantly to politely fend off the amorous advances of Jia Ying's succubare friend, Marissa. Apparently because they'd shown up at this party, that made him fair game.

If Daria had any claim on Alejandro at all . . . or wanted one, she supposed she should be over there getting possessive about her property. But she didn't have or want a claim. *Really.* Not even after sharing such intimate acts with him. It was just sex, nothing more. Alejandro could do what he wanted. If he wanted to do Marissa, so be it.

She stood near a couch, one eye on the couple all the same and hating herself for it.

Eleanor entered the room wearing a close-fitting, low-cut red dress that swirled around her perfect calves as she moved. Once within the room, she scanned the occupants, seized on Daria, and approached.

Daria glanced at Alejandro, who gave her a meaningful look. She shifted uncomfortably as the other woman drew near. *This* was something she'd never received training for at the Academy.

"Good evening, Valerie. I'm glad to see you and your mate could make it here this evening." Eleanor glanced at Alejandro, who must have just said something hilarious because Marissa was laughing like a hyena on carmin. Daria rolled her eyes.

"I'm glad we came, too, so we could see what these evenings are all about," Daria answered.

"It won't get really interesting until later when everyone's more relaxed and a little bit blood drunk. Please, sit with me."

Daria sank onto the couch beside Eleanor. Her gaze strayed to a couple near the wall. The male's hand was thrust up the woman's skirt and working back and forth. The woman's lithe body was taut and the slack look on her face made it clear that she was about to come right in the middle of all these people.

In another dark corner, two women writhed against each other, pulling at each other's pants and tangling their tongues, upthrust breasts rubbing together through the heated mesh of their clothing.

Yeah, Daria hoped to be back in her room long before things relaxed any more than this. She understood the sexual proclivities of the Chosen could sometimes be described as . . . *odd.* That was because they were so long lived. After a couple hundred years the run-of-the-mill sexual encounter just didn't cut it anymore. Vamps got kinkier as they became older. Succubare were kinky from the get-go. It was kind of in their nature.

Daria watched the male and female couple for a few moments, saw the woman shudder and tense against the man, her eyes closing in a fit of orgasmic ecstasy. The woman ground her pussy down on the man's hand, her own fingers rubbing her nipple through the material of her top.

Daria shifted uneasily, feeling the response in her own body. Watching the couple turned her on. It made her cunt tingle and pulse. Made her gaze stray to Alejandro and remember what he'd done to her the night before, the double penetration, the rope . . .

"I can see you're a little uncomfortable with it all," Eleanor breathed silkily, leaning in closer to Daria. Eleanor had successfully trapped Daria between her body and the couch's armrest. "But it's because you're new to Chosen life. One day you'll want to try new things, too."

"I guess we'll see." Daria's voice came out shaky.

"Like maybe even try a woman." Eleanor cocked an eyebrow and leaned in closer. It was hard for Daria to find fresh air now . . . and Eleanor's mouth was coming dangerously close to hers. "Have you ever?"

"No." Damn, did her voice sound shaky? She didn't want this, didn't want a woman. Er . . . did she? How could she turn away when she needed Eleanor to be friendly with her, give up information.

How friendly did she have to get?

Eleanor's lips pressed hers, soft and sweet, the breath of a Chosen nice and warm against her mouth. Daria returned the kiss, but when Eleanor's tongue fluttered against her lips, asking for entrance, Daria pulled away.

Whoa.

Across the room, she saw Alejandro staring at her and Eleanor, his glass held tight in his hand. Marissa was running her fingers up and down his arm and he wasn't even stopping her. Unexpected, hard anger flared.

Work, Daria. Focus.

Daria looked back at Eleanor, who appeared disappointed her attempt to woo had failed. She smiled coyly and allowed her hand to trail down the other woman's bare arm. "I'm sorry. I was distracted."

Eleanor's warm smile returned. "That's all right."

She tilted her head to the side and gave Eleanor the kind of grin that promised pleasure and erotic delight . . . a rusty smile normally used only on *men.* "Can we talk awhile?"

Eleanor instantly got the rest of her groove back, scenting blood in the water once more. "Of course. Shall I get us something to drink?"

"Excellent."

Daria tried to relax while Eleanor got two drinks from an alcove in the corner and returned.

Oh, good. Blood wine.

Like a good little Valerie, she took a sip and did her valiant best not to grimace. *Raspberry. Erk.*

Smoothly, Daria set the cup on the floor near her foot. "So how long have you been at the Shining Way, Eleanor?"

"From the beginning. I have always been with Christopher Sante, for as long as I can remember."

Bingo. It had been the right question and gave her a good segue into the information she truly wanted. She channeled Jia Ying for a moment. "Oh, you're so lucky! I mean, I've just met the man, but I can already tell that he's as wonderful as everyone says he is."

Eleanor's lips tightened. "He's a man, like any other man. Sometimes he's a good man, sometimes he's not."

"What do you mean?"

Eleanor traced a line on Daria's thigh . . . slowly. Daria had worn a skirt, one of the few times she'd done so in her life. Now she regretted it. Eleanor's touch on her bare skin sent confusing, erotic ripples through her. "I mean that, like all men, his dick has a mind of its own. That's why I like women, occasionally. They wander less."

"Were you with him . . . romantically?"

Eleanor laughed. "There wasn't anything *romantic* about it. It was just fucking." Her bitter tone suggested something else.

"Did you want it to be more?"

She traced another line on Daria's thigh, this time higher up. Unwelcome pleasure rippled through her. Eleanor tilted her head to the side as she answered, "You ask lots of personal questions."

Daria shrugged. "I'm just curious, just making conversation. Anyway, you don't seem to mind answering them."

A smile flickered over Eleanor's mouth. "I don't mind. You get to be a certain age and you don't care about being secretive anymore. In any case, most of the dome knows about it anyway. Yes, Sante and I had a very public affair. For him it was just sex. For me . . . I guess I wanted more. It wasn't to be, however."

"Because he met Ari Templeton."

Anger flashed through her eyes and she shifted away from Daria. Daria thought for a moment she'd pushed too hard, so she laid her hand on Eleanor's leg. The silk of her expensive dress cooled the heated flesh of Daria's palm. Eleanor relaxed a little and leaned in close again.

"I was with Christopher for years and couldn't get him to see me as anything more than a piece of ass. Then he meets a *human* woman, someone he's got nothing in common with at all, and he mates her within a year."

"They were together for a whole year before he finally Chose her?" That was news to her. Sante had really put some planning and time into this one. Of course, he'd put planning and time into her dupe, too. More than a year's worth.

"Yes, according to Christopher he's met his match for eternity."

Daria digested that. "You believe him?"

Eleanor shrugged a shoulder. "Christopher's got no reason to lie."

"But don't you think it's strange that she's the daughter of Richard Templeton, though? It's almost . . ."

"Poetic?" The word came out breathy. Eleanor leaned in closer to her.

Daria stiffened and forced herself to relax. "Something like that. I don't know. It seems . . . convenient." Fishing. That was a whole lot of fishing she'd just done.

Eleanor brushed her lips against Daria's cheek. Her warm, sweet breath bathed her skin. "I think it was an unfortunate coincidence. Not *convenient* at all."

Her lips neared Daria's and Daria froze, uncertain what to do. She didn't want to offend Eleanor, but neither did she want to kiss her again. Inevitably, Eleanor's mouth pressed hers once more. Her tongue fluttered, and Daria parted her lips, letting the other woman in to play. Eleanor's tongue brushed hers, sending an electric jolt through her body, straight to her cunt.

When Eleanor's hand closed over her breast, Daria didn't object. The woman's fingernail teased her nipple, the hard edge toying with the sensitive part of her anatomy through the material of her shirt and bra.

Daria soaked her panties.

Eleanor made a pleased sound in her throat and deepened her kiss, her hand straying to the hem of Daria's skirt and then pushing past it. Daria's breath came faster and she parted her thighs a little before she'd even realized she'd done it.

Maybe she was riper for sexual experimentation than she'd thought. "Valerie?"

Eleanor jerked away.

Slightly dazed, Daria looked up to see Alejandro.

"Get up." His expression was grim.

Eleanor backed away from Daria immediately after seeing the look on Alejandro's face. "I'm sorry. I didn't mean to trample any boundaries."

Alejandro only glared at her and held out his hand. "Valerie?" he snapped as if pissed off.

Daria took his hand and allowed him to pull her up from the couch and into his arms. He enveloped her and dipped her a little, letting his mouth come down on hers.

His lips slid like silk over hers as he sipped her for a long moment before going in for a deeper taste. His tongue rubbed against hers, making her body react instantly. Her sex grew warmer and her fingers dug into his upper arms for support, feeling the bunch and play of his muscles under her hands. Somebody whimpered, and she realized belatedly it was her.

When he finally set her on her feet, her knees were shaking and her facial muscles slack. Alejandro gave Eleanor a pointed look, having staked his claim on Daria, pissed on his territory, or whatever he'd done. But he wasn't finished yet.

He turned her to face Eleanor, who still sat on the couch, and yanked Daria's skirt up to her waist. Daria gasped in surprise, but when she tried to move away, he pulled her arms behind her back and bracketed them there. Then he pulled her panties down to her knees and slid his free hand between her thighs.

"You were mine to do with as I wish the moment we set foot here," he murmured into her ear. "Remember that. Remember you're *mine*."

"Alejandro—"

He brushed her clit, already swollen and aroused, and her back arched. A sexual haze, a familiar state these days, settled over her mind. She spread her legs as far as the panties would allow, not even caring she was displaying herself to the woman in front of her. Yes, of course she wanted him to touch her. She *always* wanted Alejandro to touch her.

Alejandro used her own moisture as a lubricant, circling her aroused clit until Daria shuddered and moaned. Then he slipped his hand down and slid two fingers deep inside her aching cunt. Her muscles clamped down and rippled around the invasion, pleasure coursing through her body. He started to thrust and Daria saw stars. The whole room and everyone in it disappeared as he slowly worked them in and out.

Since he no longer had to restrain her, he pushed his opposite hand under the hem of her shirt, yanking the article of clothing up enough to free a breast from her bra and gently pinch her nipple.

"Alejandro," she said breathlessly.

He said something in a harsh voice, but she couldn't make out the words. Daria was drowning. Eleanor answered.

"Come for me, baby," he whispered into her ear. He ground his palm against her clit. "Just let go."

She did. It coursed through her relentlessly. Her cunt pulsed and rippled as she climaxed against his pistoning fingers. Without shame, lost in the eroticism of the moment, throwing her head back and nearly screaming in release.

After Alejandro pulled her panties up and replaced her skirt, she slumped against him, shuddering in the powerful aftermath.

"I get it," said Eleanor. "I can look but not touch."

"Good." Alejandro nodded once, took Daria's hand, and led her from the building, back to the room.

On the path between the buildings, with the light of another damn full moon shining down on them, she was finally able to speak once more. "Thank you. That was a great performance. I doubt Eleanor will bother me anymore."

He glanced at her, his fangs extended and flashing white in the silvery light. "Who was performing?"

She stopped on the path. "You were mad that Eleanor made a pass at me?"

"*Maldita sea!*" He turned to face her. "I don't want anyone but me touching you. *Anyone.* I don't care what their gender is."

For a moment, she was pleased by his statement, pleased that he was jealous. She even smiled.

Then she was pissed.

"And what did you say to her when I—when I . . ."

He grinned, looking feral. His white teeth gleamed in the half-light. "When you were about to *come*? I said you were mine, no one else's. *Mine* to touch, mine to fuck." He paused. "I meant it, work or no. And not just for last night, Daria, I intend you to be mine forever."

She was speechless for a moment. "And what about you with little

Miss Marissa? She had her slutty succubare fingers all over you to-night. You get to touch anyone you want, but I can't? Is that it?"

"Did you want Eleanor to touch you? You looked distressed to me."

She had been, but not for the reasons she would have thought be-fore the other woman had touched her. Daria had never expected to like it. She changed the subject. "You ask me that and say nothing about little Miss Marissa?"

Any hope she'd had of continuing her denial of her feelings for Alejandro were pretty much dashed with the sharp stab of jealousy she felt.

He stepped toward her, caught her upper arms. "I don't want that Chosen. I only want you. Haven't you figured that out by now? Marissa saw what I did to you along with everyone else in the room. She saw the claim I staked on you, and she won't be bothering me anymore. I was just giving you room to get what you needed from Eleanor, but once it went too far, I went a little crazy." His face hardened. "I don't share well."

This was a dangerous conversation to have in the open. "Let's go back to the room for the rest of this discussion."

"You're right, we should."

He kissed her once, roughly, then backed away and led her back to their place.

Once he'd shut the door, Daria turned. "Eleanor seemed con-vinced—"

"Shut up."

He pushed her back onto the bed and covered her body with his. His mouth came down on hers and swallowed her gasp and all her words of protest. His erection pressed into her thigh and she realized belatedly that, yes, she'd received release at the party, but he had not. Now she had one hell of an aroused vampire on her hands.

Not that she couldn't handle him.

He eased her panties down and off even as she worked the buttons on his jeans. The part of her that had turned slutty after she'd been

Chosen couldn't wait to have him inside her, even as the other part, the *sane* part, worried she was getting deeper and deeper into this man emotionally.

Right now all she cared about was him getting deeper into her physically.

He snaked off his clothes from the waist down and forced her thighs apart. "Daria, goddamn it. You're like an addiction," he whispered a moment before his mouth came down over hers.

And she was happy to give him his fix.

He pushed her skirt farther up. In their impatience, she still wore all her clothing, even her heels. He'd only bothered to yank her underwear down and off. The head of his cock pushed at her entrance and she shifted, allowing him to slide deep inside her.

"*Yes*," she breathed against the curve of his throat. "Yes, that's it." With her fist balled, she gently hit his shoulder and fought the urge to bite him. His cock was lodged inside her to the base and her muscles rippled as she stretched to accommodate him.

Having him inside her was like coming home, like some part of her had gone missing and had just been found. That she would think that way was disturbing, but she would examine it later. Her hands curled around his shoulders and she held on while he pulled out then flexed the muscles of his buttocks and pushed all the way inside her to the base of him once more.

Oh, god. She closed her eyes in ecstasy. That was even better.

"You were excited when Eleanor touched you, weren't you, Daria?"

Oh, god, he wanted to make conversation? She wasn't sure she could manage that in her current state. "Uh, yes . . . I mean, I think so." She shook her head. "It's the Choosing, making me open to things I wouldn't have been okay with before."

His lips bussed her forehead. "Probably. It excited me to watch it."

"I thought it made you jealous." Her voice sounded all breathy and aroused. He'd lodged himself in her, long, hard, and wide. He touched every intimate inch of her, possessed her, pinned her. It was driving her crazy for him to simply remain that way without moving. She had to stop herself from moving her pelvis and forcing some kind of friction.

His fingers curled in her hair and drew her head to the side, baring the vulnerable column of her throat to him. Fangs flashed in the semi-lit room. "It did, but before I got possessive, I got turned on." He dropped his head and scraped his teeth over her skin.

Daria sighed and shifted beneath him. "And what about after, when you touched me that . . . way . . . in front of everyone."

"Are you trying to say when I made you come, Daria?" He growled and bit her a little. The prick of his teeth sent shivers down her spine. "That nearly killed me. That's why you're here now, beneath me."

She whimpered and moved her hips, managing to force his cock out of her and then back in a couple of inches. Pleasure spiked through her body, centering in her clit. "Then what are you waiting for? *Fuck me*."

He grinned ferociously. "Maybe I'm trying to make you feel as crazy as I did in there."

"You've done it. Fuck me now, Alejandro. Fuck me or I'll scream."

He braced his knees on the mattress and thrust. Daria closed her eyes and gripped his shoulders. *That* was what she wanted. He picked up the pace, harder and faster until her whole world was only the way their bodies connected, the hard, beautiful press of flesh.

Alejandro bit her throat. That now familiar burst of orgasmic pleasure at the strength of his veil and the pierce of his fangs rippled through her, sending her to the brink of a climax.

Her fangs also extended. Finding the perfect place where his throat met his shoulder, she sunk in deep. He jerked in ecstasy at the sharp penetration of the tips and the furl of her veil covering him.

Her climax rose slowly and went on and on. Over her, Alejandro also shuddered and came.

When their climaxes had both passed, Alejandro rolled to the side and pulled her near him. They lay tangled together, their breathing harsh in the quiet air. Being that close to Alejandro after such an intimate moment was too much like being lovers. Especially when he stroked her hair the way he was, and kissed her temple. Especially after he'd declared her *his* before all and sundry.

Especially since she wasn't sure she minded.

This was a pathway of thought fraught with danger. Daria pushed up and looked down at him. He looked taken aback at her abrupt movement. It was good they'd sated themselves. Now they could talk business without any distractions.

"I was going to say that Eleanor seemed convinced that Sante truly loves Ari Templeton. *Goddamn it.*" She paused. "And she knows him really well."

Alejandro sighed and pushed up. "Okay. It's one opinion."

"An informed one."

Daria rolled off the bed, took off her skirt, blouse, and shoes, and pulled on a pair of panties, sweatpants, and a T-shirt while Alejandro answered her.

"We have to start considering the possibility it's true." He sighed. "If it's true then we have to redouble our efforts at the factory and on the blood slave trafficking possibility, because we won't have a kidnapping case."

Daria turned and paced to the window looking out into the courtyard. "Even if Sante is duping her, kidnapping would be nearly impossible to make a case of." She let the truth of that sink in and then swore colorfully. "Either way we have nothing against Sante right now. We're going to have to let the kidnapping thing slide."

Alejandro nodded. "We have to look for other avenues to nail him."

She turned. "I feel like there's something, Alejandro. Don't you? It's not only that I think Sante can't run this place without some sort of illegal funding, it's that every instinct I have says they're hiding something."

Alejandro nodded. "I feel it, too."

"There's another issue, too—"

Someone knocked on the door. Alejandro jumped up, pulled on his jeans, and did up his belt before he opened it to admit Brandon. "I heard you two come in," he said as he entered. He favored Daria with an oily grin. "Thought I'd give you some time alone before I came knocking."

Daria looked away from him. She was liking this guy less and less.

"We were just talking about the fact we're going to have to leave off on the Ari Templeton kidnapping issue." Alejandro went to stand near the wall and crossed his arms over his chest. "Early indicators are that those closest to Sante believe he and Templeton are the real deal. That means that even if Sante is playing her somehow, we don't have a case."

"Either way she's here by choice," Daria put in bitterly.

"Who did you talk to?" Brandon asked sharply.

"I talked to Eleanor Matthews tonight. You probably recognize her name from the files we received. She was with Sante romantically, and has been loyal to him ever since he started the Shining Way. She and Sante share the same blood mother."

"Yeah." Brandon rubbed his chin. "Try Carlos. He's Sante's right hand, his muscle. If any of his people know his plans, it's that one."

"The thought occurred to me, too," answered Daria. "He hates us with the fire of a thousand suns for some unknown reason, but we can do our best. In the meantime—"

"Try to get me in," Brandon interrupted.

"We're working on it," Alejandro snapped in a voice with a subtext that clearly said, *Shut up about it already*. He stood in the middle of the room barefoot, shirtless, and with his hair mussed. He looked positively edible that way to Daria. "We're new to the inner circle and need to wait for the right moment. If we move too fast, we look suspicious. So, chill out on the issue, Brandon. We haven't forgotten."

"Yeah, don't."

"In the meantime," Daria continued pointedly, "I'll try and use my new position of honor to get me into the packing room at the factory."

Brandon walked to the door. "Good idea. All right, then. I'm out of here. I have some work to do of my own now." He lifted his eyebrows and grinned. "Of the female kind. Evening." They watched him leave, and Alejandro closed and locked the door behind him.

"Man, I knew my gut instinct about that guy was right from the beginning," Daria muttered. "He is a pain in the ass."

Strong arms took her from behind, his palm spreading flat over her lower stomach. The heat of his bare chest bled through the material of her T-shirt and warmed her back. His mouth came down by her ear and he murmured, "Forget about other men now, Daria. I want you to only think of me and what I want to do to you."

Daria ran out of breath. His silky voice and smooth accent rolled over her, making her cunt warm and wet. It didn't matter that they'd just had sex. She wanted him again. *Damn it all to hell.* It was like she was completely powerless against him. "And what, exactly, would that be?"

His hand slipped past the hem of her T-shirt and closed around her breast. With the pad of his finger, he teased her nipple back and forth. He dragged her earlobe between his teeth slowly, and then whispered, "To fuck you breathless. *Again.* You didn't think I was done with you yet, did you?" He pulled her sweatpants down and off. Hell, she'd just put them on.

"I'm already breathless." She could practically hear his grin.

~

THE sound of his belt coming free from his waist was loud in the quiet room and gave her shivers. "Get on the bed." His voice was already rough with lust.

Before she slipped from his arms and crawled onto the mattress, she fitted her rear into the curve of his pelvis and rubbed against his hard cock through his jeans, making him groan.

Oh, yeah, she was getting the hang of this sex thing again.

On the bed she lay facedown and listened to him strip the jeans off. The rustle of the garment hitting the floor was like a promise.

He hit the light and plunged the room into darkness, but for the moonlight glowing softly through the courtyard window. In the sudden silence, she waited, the air cool on her bare legs. She wore only her panties, having already discarded the rest.

Then he was there, breath warm and sweet along her skin. He had a long, thin piece of rope in one hand, which he looped around her wrists before she could say a word. She opened her mouth to protest, but he slipped a hand between her thighs from the rear and touched her clit. Pleasure flared through her body and she fell silent.

He placed his mouth to the sensitive skin beneath her ear. "Do you trust me?"

Again, *this* question. This complicated fucking question. It was one she had trouble answering fully. Daria trusted Alejandro to watch her back on this mission, or in a fight. She trusted him enough to let him tie her up and do delicious things to her body tonight in this bed.

But she didn't trust him with her heart. No. Not that. She didn't trust him not to mind-fuck her.

Daria didn't trust *any* man not to do that.

"Sometimes." The word floated out like a slap to Alejandro's face in the quiet air. "In some ways."

He hesitated. "It will have to be enough. For now."

Alejandro tied a knot around her wrists like a man who'd had a lot of practice securing women's wrists. Momentarily, she wondered about all the things his blood mother had made him do. Tying people up had definitely been one thing. It had to be. He took his belt, threaded it around a slat in the headboard, looped the other end around the rope, and secured it.

It left her on her knees, facedown, cheek against the mattress. He put his hand to the nape of her neck and massaged a moment, before running his palm down her back inch by slow inch, over her rear and then between her thighs.

Through the cotton of her panties, he found her clit fully aroused and practically panting for his attention. Taking it between two fingers, he rubbed it through the material until she moaned.

"*Mmm*, very nice. I'm going to enjoy having you at my mercy," he murmured. "Again." Then he tore her panties off, leaving her sex to be bathed by the cool air of the room.

22

S HE gasped. Damn it, she was running out of underwear with this guy.

Not, uh, that she minded at the moment. She could buy more.

Daria twisted her wrists in her bonds, wanting with every fiber of her being to touch Alejandro, wanting to feel his cock in her fingers and to trace over his velvety, muscular chest. "Alejandro," she breathed.

He didn't want her to touch him, though. That was clear enough when he swore low and mounted her. His body pressed her down against the mattress as the head of his cock found her slick entrance and pushed within. Daria gasped and cried out as he used her moisture to thrust balls-deep within her, stretching her muscles so deliciously it almost made her come.

He took her by the hips and rode her fast and hard, edgily, like touching her had driven him half mad and now he had to slake his need with her body. His cock slammed in and out of her cunt with an erotic ferocity that possessed her body completely and stole both her breath and her thought.

Alejandro slipped his hand down between her abdomen and the mattress to find her clit. He positioned it between his first two fingers and rubbed. The head of his cock dragged over her G-spot with every punishing inward stroke. The combination made a powerful climax slam into her body. Daria cried out from the intensity of it, the waves of pleasure swamping every part of her mind and making her knees weak.

He rode her through it, whispering low, dirty, sweet things. "You like when I'm inside your cunt, don't you, baby? You love it when I fuck you." She couldn't help that the coarse words excited her.

The orgasm stuttered to a halt, then flared to brilliant life once again. Her sex pulsed and rippled around Alejandro's thrusting cock. He groaned and let loose, his shaft jumping deep within her as he came.

He collapsed on top of her and she moved her wrists against her bonds, signaling without words that she wanted freedom.

"No." The word rang sure and low through the room. "Not until you admit you care about me."

She let those words—the last ones she'd expected to hear at this moment—sink in before exclaiming, "What?"

Alejandro used his full vampiric speed and strength and flipped her so she lay on her back, her arms bound above her head. "I'm not untying you until you admit it."

"Alejandro—"

He kissed her. A hot, mind-bending slide of lips over lips and the penetration of his tongue into the depths of her mouth. He didn't just kiss her, he ravaged her mouth. He tasted every bit of her that he could, almost like he tried to consume her.

Finally, he broke the kiss. "Tell me."

Daria could merely pant, unable to catch her breath. "Tell you what? What do you want to hear, Alejandro?"

He stared down at her. Her stomach did flip-flops. "The truth."

Her eyes widened. The truth about how she felt about him? Did he want to hear that she watched him sometimes when she knew he wasn't looking? That she loved the way his dark hair curled around the collar of his shirt, or how he drummed his fingers on his knee when he was deep in thought?

Should she tell him how much she loved how relaxed he was about everything . . . except when he got possessive about her and that, secretly, she loved it? Should she tell him there wasn't anyone she'd trust more at her back, with her life, than him?

There were many things she could tell Emanuel Alejandro Martinez, not the least of which would be that she thought she was falling in love with him and that, well, *that* . . .

"You scare me," she breathed into the short distance separating their mouths. She'd settled for the truth, part of it anyway . . . the most important part. "You confuse me."

He made a frustrated sound. With one harsh move he unbuckled his belt and rolled off the side of the bed. He walked a short distance and sank into a chair.

She pulled the rope from her wrists and propped herself up on her elbows to stare at his shadowed silhouette. "You asked for the truth."

He didn't say anything for several moments. Alejandro glanced at her. "And now I wish I hadn't."

Daria rolled from the bed and went to him. She set her hand on his bare thigh and tried not to let herself be distracted by the silver moonlight bleaching the warm gold color of his skin. All she wanted was to run her hands over it. Even now, after they'd made love, she still wanted—needed—to touch him.

She squeezed his leg. "I don't understand what you want from me."

He covered her hand with his own. "I'm in love with you, Daria."

She stilled as her mind tried, and failed, to process that simple sentence.

"You're a total pain in the ass, high-maintenance woman, *querida*. You're also passionate, caring, and the bravest damn person I've ever met." He leaned forward and captured her face between his palms. "I love you."

Daria swallowed hard, at a loss for words. "You want me to love you back." Her voice quavered on the question that wasn't really a question. Of course that's what he wanted. She was dangerously close to giving it to him, too.

Memory that was never far from her reach roared to life. Christopher Sante had said those words to her once, too, with that same sincere look in his eyes. He'd knelt on the floor and smiled up into her face one breezy, sunshiny afternoon with a bottle of champagne opened beside them on her kitchen table.

She had believed him. She had loved him back. Then he'd killed her best friend.

"I want . . ." He started and trailed off. "I just want you, Daria."

Heart. Soul. Body. Mind. Betrayal. That's how it had been the last time she'd loved.

Tears stung her eyes. Daria pulled away, stood, dressed, and left the room.

~

"LOVERS' spat?"

The toe of a boot nudged her side, and Daria's eyes flickered open. She'd gone to Brandon's room the night before to flee Alejandro, only to find Brandon was out. Since the door to his room was set into an alcove, she'd curled up on the floor. It was as out-of-the-way as she was likely to find under the dome, unless she found a place to sleep in the middle of a hedge somewhere.

She pushed up into a sitting position and ran her fingers through her hair. If she'd been human, she knew she would've been hurting from sleeping like that. As it was, with her body strong and supple from the Choosing, her neck just had a crick in it.

"Where were you all night?" she grouched.

Brandon keyed his security code into the pad beside his door. "I only answer to my girlfriend and my mother. Seeing as how my mother's dead and I have no girlfriend"—he looked down at her as the door clicked opened—"I have no one to answer to."

Daria yawned. "Fine, whatever."

"Come in and have some coffee. Tell me why you're sleeping outside my door."

Daria climbed to her feet. "I'll take the coffee at least."

He went for the console in the wall and got them both steaming hot cups. "Just don't let Sante see there's trouble in paradise."

"Look, couples fight sometimes, even mated Chosen." She took a grateful sip of the hot brew and closed her eyes for a moment, savoring it. "Even if anyone found out there were problems between me and Alejandro, it would be construed as a natural bump in the relationship."

He grinned. "Actually that was total bait. There's trouble between you and Alejandro, is there?"

"I wouldn't call it trouble." She set her coffee cup down and glanced at the unmade bed and clothes scattered on the floor. What a bachelor. "We're just having . . . issues."

"Issues, right. Well, a blind man could see Alejandro's crazy about you, and it doesn't have anything to do with the mission, either."

She jerked a little in surprise at his observation and turned away from him so he couldn't see her face. "Alejandro is a good man." He wasn't Sante. She knew that, but she'd thought Sante was a good man, too.

"He is. He's the best of men. Can be a bit intense, though."

Brandon was close to her, too close. She could feel his body heat. She turned.

He wore an expression on his face she hadn't seen before—interest in her.

God, she did not want more of that. Especially from him.

"But for a woman like you," Brandon continued, "maybe too intense. I get the sense you're too wild to settle down." He grinned and it struck Daria as a bit smarmy. "Maybe you just need a man to play with for a while, nothing more. Nothing committed, nothing messy."

She shook her head. Wow, Brandon had completely misread her. He didn't know or understand her at all. Alejandro had understanding her down to an art form. "You're right about me not wanting commitment, at least."

He spread his hands. "My door is always open."

"Actually, it's not. Last night being a case in point. Also, I'm not interested. No offense meant, Brandon. Lastly, while I was looking for a place to crash last night, I did have another reason for coming here."

He raised an eyebrow. "That being?"

"We have to leave off on the Ari thing for the time being. Even if Sante is playing her, she doesn't know she's being played. I'll still talk with Carlos, but we have a bigger issue on our plate now."

His expression had grown darker as she'd spoken. "What's that?"

"Why the hell is Richard Templeton having us hunt down a daughter he knows damn well went of her own accord?"

Brandon went very still. "Perhaps he doesn't know she went of her own accord."

Daria shook her head. "No way. Ari Templeton was bursting to get back at dad. No way she didn't tell him, which makes me wonder why he wants her back so bad."

"You don't know that for certain."

Daria went for the door. "You're right. It's only a strong hunch. I'm going find out if it's true."

He caught her arm before she could leave. "What are you going to do?"

"I'm going to go talk to her."

He glanced down at her rumpled clothing. "Better change first."

～

IT was easy.

When she presented herself at the guardhouse in front of Sante's house, she was on "the list." They let her right in. They even called Sante ahead of time, so he met her right at the door.

Luckily, Alejandro had been gone from the room when she'd gone back to take a shower and change. Now she looked sprite and charming as a daisy, rather than rumpled and well-fucked as she had that morning.

Daria put on her best nonthreatening smile. "Good morning,

Christopher. I thought I'd stop by and see how you and Ari were doing."

"That's very nice of you." He was smiling, but there was a note of suspicion in his voice. "Would you like something to drink?" He ushered her into the kitchen.

"No, thanks. Already had my morning coffee. Actually, I really came by because Ari seemed so interested in how I managed to punch through the succubare. I had some free time, so I thought I'd stop by and see if she wanted to talk with me any more about the subject. We're both so newly Chosen, I guess I feel a kind of kindredness with her."

The suspicion left Sante's eyes. He gave her the most sincere smile she'd ever seen on his lips. It made Daria's heart ache.

If only he'd ever smiled that way for her.

"I really appreciate this a lot, Valerie. It would be nice if Ari had a friend she could talk to. My female intimates here at the Shining Way, they've all been . . ."

"*Intimate* with you?" she ventured as he trailed off.

He nodded. "Makes friendship with my mate a little awkward on both sides."

How ironic, then, if she became bosom friends with Ari Templeton. "I think befriending Ari would be good for me, too. After all, I'm new here as well."

Just then Ari glided into the room with the liquid sexual grace of the succubare. "Valerie," she greeted with a smile as she slid next to Sante. Sante leaned over and tenderly kissed her head.

If Sante was faking it, he was doing a good job. But Daria knew all too well how good a faker he was, didn't she?

"What are you doing here so early in the morning?" Ari asked, her arms tightening around Sante's waist.

"I came by to see you, actually."

"Really?" She brightened. "Wonderful. Want to have breakfast with me? Food is a habit I'm finding hard to break."

Daria's stomach rumbled at the prospect. It was a ghost rumbling, of course, like an amputee might feel her missing arm. She didn't need to eat for sustenance now, but she still craved it. "Definitely."

Sante pulled away from Ari and walked toward the door. "I'll leave you alone, then. I've got work to do."

Ari pouted. "You don't have to go yet."

Sante returned and kissed her so well, so beautifully, and so full of love that Daria had to look away. He spoke some low words in Ari's ears that Daria tried not to hear, but with her superhearing did anyway. Then he left.

Ari stood for a moment looking out the door after him. Completely besotted. Daria had no doubt. Then she turned and went for the refrigerator. "Eggs?"

"Sounds incredible." Daria took a place at the breakfast bar. "Can I help you?"

"No, please. I love to cook." Ari threw a careless smile at her over her shoulder. "It's a last vestige from my life before." There was a note of wistfulness in her voice. Ari set a bowl of grapes on the counter in front of Daria, then turned to the stove to make the eggs.

"So, that begs the question. How are you doing with the adjustment to Chosen life?" Daria popped a grape into her mouth and nearly swooned when it burst against her tongue.

At the stove, Ari shrugged a shoulder. Her long hair was loose and shifting over her back. "All right. I mean, I'm very hungry." She glanced at her and grinned. "Of course, my hunger is different than yours."

"Of course."

Ari flipped the eggs onto two plates and handed her one, then moved to get them two glasses of orange juice. "Christopher is keeping me well sated, though."

Daria took a slow drink and formed her next question carefully. Beside her, Ari slid onto a chair and pulled her plate close. "But one day he won't be enough to sustain you, isn't that true? One day you'll have to go to others. Isn't that how it works for a succubare?"

She took a careful bite of eggs and chewed thoughtfully. "Yes, one day that will be true. I guess I'm not ready to think about that yet."

"Fair enough." Daria settled in to eat her eggs while they were still hot.

"And you?"

This time it was Daria's turn to shrug. "I feel stronger than I ever have before, but it's misleading because I'm still far weaker than the older Chosen. Blood is actually good, and I crave it. That's pretty strange. Otherwise, I'm doing pretty well. I'm here, with the false sunlight, so I haven't had to get used to nocturnal life yet."

Ari nodded. "We're lucky to have this place."

Daria agreed. As much as she hated Sante and despite the fact she knew in her gut there were illegal happenings here, this commune was a blessing to the Chosen.

"Christopher says this place saved his life," Ari continued. "That he wanted to walk into the dawn before he had the idea to create the commune."

"Why?" This aligned with what Alejandro had told her. She put her fork down.

"He told me he loved a woman, but had to betray her in order to fulfill a loyalty to his blood mother. He hurt her terribly in the process. From what I gather, from as much as he'll tell, he killed people close to her."

"And he got away with it?" Daria's voice sounded harsh to her own ears.

"He got away with it from the perspective of the human and Chosen systems of law. He didn't get away with it in his own consciousness. Guilt plagued him so badly he renounced his blood mother and nearly killed himself."

Poor, poor Christopher Sante. Daria thought she might weep from the violin music.

"He started the Shining Way as an effort to give back some of what he'd taken," Ari finished.

"We all have to pay prices for the choices we make." It was all the response Daria could muster. "I thought I saw you one night, when I was leaving the party at the Alhambra Building. Was it you walking the path there that night?"

She smiled. "I get around via secret passageways. Yes, it was me."

When she smiled Ari Templeton reminded her of Julia. There was a softness about her that Julia had possessed, too. Daria shook her head to clear the thought and keep her mind in the present. "I thought you were a ghost. I thought I was losing my mind."

"It was just me, sneaking around. In order to stay with the man I love, I had to completely alter my life. You should know since you did it, too."

Scenting a way to steer the conversation where she wanted it to go, Daria nodded. "Yes, we had to give up sunlight, give up every normal thing we ever knew." She paused and looked sad. "Give up family."

"You had to give up your family when you were Chosen?"

"My mother wasn't happy with my decision." It wasn't really a lie, just a slight misdirection of the truth. Her mother *wouldn't* be happy with her decision when she found out.

Ari threw her fork down onto the countertop so hard, Daria jumped. "The bigotry against the Chosen never fails to piss me off. All the Chosen want is the right to exist. We're not hurting anyone. This fear of the other, the fear of the more powerful . . . it makes humans crazy! They preach out of one side of their mouths about perfect, unconditional love. Then out of the other side they advocate for laws making the Chosen a hunted species . . . like an . . . *an animal!*"

Bingo.

Daria suppressed her smile of victory and turned in her seat. "You're talking about your father, Richard Templeton."

A pained look crossed Ari's face. She glanced away, but not before Daria glimpsed tears sheening the other woman's eyes.

Daria felt a pinch of guilt for getting her so riled up and deliberately pushing a button. Ari Templeton was an easily likable person, and Daria had no wish to cause her discomfort.

"Yes, I'm talking about my father. Damn him. He's the worst of the bigots. I'm ashamed to say I share his blood."

"Does he know . . . I mean, about you and Christopher Sante? Does he know you've been Chosen?"

She nodded and wiped a tear from her cheek. Daria suppressed the ridiculous urge to put her arm around Ari's shoulders. "I told him all about it before I was Chosen. Told him I'd fallen in love and nothing would keep us apart, not even his almighty church. He was so mad he almost backhanded me. Then he just turned his back on me and told me I was no longer his daughter."

The pain in her voice was so raw, so little-girl-lost. Daria suspected she truly craved the one thing she would never have—the unconditional love of her father.

What was Richard Templeton up to? Why had he lied to the GBS and the ABI? Why had he reported her kidnapped and cast all that suspicion on Sante?

Perhaps he regretted the harsh words he'd spoken to his daughter and was now attempting to get her back home without anyone knowing she'd been Chosen. That would be embarrassing to him, after all.

But that seemed unlikely. He'd disowned her, according to Ari. That seemed like a pretty final action.

Daria chewed her lower lip and frowned. Did Templeton have a darker scheme in play?

Ari's shoulders hunched miserably and a tear fell into her lap. Unable to resist any longer, Daria put her arm around her shoulders. Ari leaned into her and cried quietly.

"I'm sorry, Ari," Daria whispered.

She was. Sorry that Ari's father was such a horrific person, sorry she'd been duped by Sante. Daria vowed right then and there she would do all she could to protect Ari Templeton.

Someone had to.

~

ALEJANDRO watched Daria slick her hair back away from her head as she entered the room. It had been raining nonstop for a week, a necessity for some of the crops they grew in the dome. Her white T-shirt was soaked and clung to her in all the right places, revealing her dark, hard nipples through her white cotton bra.

He was a man, he noticed these things. Especially on Daria.

Even if he'd scared off Daria so skillfully she wouldn't even sleep in the same bed with him these days.

He had the magic touch, that was for sure.

She glanced at him, wariness in her eyes. Mostly she tried to be in the room when he wasn't.

"Where have you been?" he asked.

"With Ari this morning, then with Jia Ying for a while." Daria had been spending a lot of time with Ari lately. "This afternoon we're supposed to meet with Eleanor, don't forget."

He shook his head. "*Dios*, you're keeping a hell of a social calendar."

She went into the bathroom to get a towel. "It's work," she called. "I've developed a friendship with Jia Ying, it's true. That's not really work. But now that I've insinuated myself in with Ari, I need to stay close."

"I know." Even if he was a little jealous. "But you do like her. Ari, I mean."

She reemerged from the bathroom, rubbing the towel through her hair. "There's little not to like about her. She's got a fragile quality to her that makes you want to protect her."

"You've always been a protector, Daria. I wish you'd let someone protect you once in a while."

She gave him an irritated glance. "I don't need counseling right now, Alejandro, but thanks for trying to help."

Daria pulled off her soaked T-shirt and pulled a gray jersey from a drawer. "Anyway, I just stopped in for a minute. I'm leaving again to head back to Sante's house. Ari wants to have lunch with me." She pulled the sweatshirt over her head. "What are you doing today?"

"I'm with Carlos."

She stilled and looked at him. "Really?"

He nodded. "Sante put me on security detail."

"Shit."

"I tried to get Brandon an *in*, but it didn't work. I was shut down right away."

"Did you tell Brandon?"

Alejandro nodded. "He wasn't too happy, but he's got his hands full as it is. There's been more movement over by the honey fields. The supervisors there won't let him stray anywhere close, though."

She shook her head. "I think the best move for us is simply to get closer and closer to Ari, Sante, and Carlos. The rest will reveal itself eventually, once they truly begin to trust us. Brandon is just upset because he's out of the loop on this. He's a control freak, that guy. He doesn't like that we've taken the lead here."

Alejandro grit his teeth. "I don't like being that passive."

"It's either we wait for Sante to let us in on the true goings-on here, or we risk getting caught and blowing the whole operation. There have been full moons every night, extra guards over by the honey fields." She gestured impatiently. "I don't see a better option at this time."

"I'm not arguing. I just don't like it. Don't pick a fight with me, Daria. I'm not in the mood."

Her jaw locked. "Look—"

The door slammed open, and Brandon stood there, panting and soaked from the rain. "Sante's house was just bombed."

23

Daria stood stricken for a moment, and then ran past Brandon and out the door.

Alejandro and Brandon stared at each other for a moment. "Is he dead?"

"Don't know, but it's pretty bad."

Alejandro rushed after Daria and Brandon followed. Outside he saw that Daria had taken off on a dune bike, rushing across the surface of the ground at top speed toward Sante's house. He grabbed another and was off, leaving Brandon to fend for his own transportation.

By the time he reached the house a crowd had already gathered. Half the place was on fire, smoke billowing up in a heavy plume. Not even the steady rain seemed to be having an effect on the raging inferno that seemed as though it would engulf the rest of the house in no time.

In horror, he watched Daria jump from her bike before it had even stopped and go running past the guard gate, toward the burning house. The bike crashed into the heavy steel fence surrounding the house and whined to a halt.

Alejandro gunned the engine on his bike and sped after Daria.

Coming up alongside her, he grabbed her around the middle and slung her over his lap.

Daria slammed her fist into his gut. *Hard.* "Let me down."

He grunted. "*Mierda*, Daria! No way in hell."

As they approached the house, he began to believe they actually were in hell. Heat warred with the downpour, the flames licking dangerously close to them.

He veered the bike away from the house, but Daria was having none of that. She punched him in the gut again and at the same time bit his leg, fangs extended. It was not a love bite, and there was no veil. It was just pain, pure and simple. Blood gushed from his thigh and he loosened his hold on her just for a moment.

It was all she needed.

Daria yanked herself backward, using her foot on the edge of the bike to get leverage to propel herself away from him. She fell five feet to the ground and rolled.

"Fuck!" Alejandro pulled a hard right, just in time to see Daria hauling ass into the burning house. He pulled up and jumped off the bike himself. Alejandro hit the ground running, ignoring the pain in his leg where she'd bitten him.

Heat burned his face and exposed arms. He was grateful he was soaked, or it would have been worse. He had a split second to notice that near the house no rain fell; the heat of the fire made it evaporate before it even hit the ground.

Brandon came up behind him, but Alejandro pushed him back. "Get out of here! All three of us don't need to commit suicide."

"I can help!" He pushed past Alejandro.

Alejandro grabbed his shirt and flung him violently backward. Brandon ended up on his ass. They needed one agent still alive and kicking after today.

Smoke billowed around Alejandro as he entered the kitchen and he covered his mouth with his forearm.

"Ari?" Daria's voice coming from the living room. "Ari? Where are you?"

He ran after her. "Get your ass out of here. This place is going up."

Daria coughed and turned toward him. She shook her head. "I was supposed to meet her here. She's in this house somewhere and I have to find her."

He took her by the shoulders and shook her. "*No, Daria!* We have to get out of here," he yelled over the roar within the house.

"*I won't let her die!*" Tears ran down her soot-covered face.

He stared down at her for a moment, his lungs burning. Somewhere above them, timber cracked ominously. "Goddamn it." He released her.

Daria pushed past him, going for the stairs. Alejandro followed.

When they reached the top, they caught sight of a white bit of fabric on the floor just at the beginning of the upstairs hallway.

Ari Templeton.

Daria knelt and pulled her up, but the woman was out cold, maybe dead already. The Chosen were immortal, but that only meant they didn't age and had above average immune systems. Smoke inhalation could do them in the same as a human.

Daria struggled to get her down the stairs. Alejandro stepped in and slung Ari over his shoulder. Together they made their way out of the burning building as pieces of the floor above them began to rain down.

They both stumbled outside, coughing, and made their way down the path and past the gates. Behind them, the house collapsed in the middle. If they'd stayed in there just a minute longer, they'd be fried, flat Chosen pancakes.

Then Sante was there, pulling Ari from Alejandro's arms. Sante laid her on the ground while he and Daria collapsed to the grass, both wheezing in an effort to get air into their scorched lungs. Beside them, Sante performed mouth-to-mouth resuscitation on his lover.

Daria sat up and watched Ari with a desperately pained expression on her face.

Ari wasn't moving.

Alejandro reached out and pulled Daria into his arms. She came willingly, gratefully, snuggling against his chest as they watched Sante try to breathe life back into Ari Templeton. A crowd had formed around them, all keeping a respectful distance.

"Live," Sante murmured against her lips. Then louder, "Live!" He kept up the resuscitation, but Ari remained limp, lifeless.

Carlos broke past the circle of onlookers and came to stand near his boss. Alejandro was struck for a moment at the expression of utter horror on Carlos's face. It was as though he actually *cared* about Ari.

Carlos hesitated a moment, then stepped forward and touched Sante's shoulder. It was clear to everyone that Ari wasn't coming back.

"Leave me alone!" Sante snarled. Then he rested his forehead on Ari's, closed his eyes, and whispered, "Please, Ari. I can't do this without you. *Please live.*"

In that one unguarded moment, all doubts Alejandro had about whether or not Sante truly loved Ari Templeton vanished.

Sante sealed his mouth over Ari's once more and pumped her chest. Nothing. He leaned back, rain beating down, and looked at his dead lover.

All was silent but for the crack and burn of the house behind them.

Then Ari's chest heaved. She coughed and gasped. A look of absolute, pure happiness transformed Sante's face and he caught her up against his chest and held her. Ari grabbed his shoulders as he rocked her back and forth, murmuring things into her soot-streaked hair.

Daria turned her face into Alejandro's chest and breathed deeply, shuddering in relief against him.

Brandon stood near them, looking a little bruised from Alejandro's emphatic denial of his aid. A smile played on his lips. Maybe he wasn't such a womanizing bastard after all.

After several moments, Carlos drew Ari away to the dome doctors who had rushed to the scene. There was no way to put out the fire, though it did seem the rain was coming down even harder now in this area, perhaps engineered to do so.

Once Ari had been handed over for medical attention, Sante

stalked over and pulled Daria from Alejandro's arms and into his. "Thank you," he said as he embraced her. The sincerity of those words rang through the air.

Daria went visibly stiff in Sante's arms—probably shocked—and pushed away from him almost immediately. "I didn't go in to save Ari *for you*." It was a hostile comment, something that *Valerie* wouldn't say. It was the first time Alejandro had seen Daria's mask slip.

However, Sante didn't seem to notice it. He answered smoothly, "I don't care, Valerie. You saved her. That's all that matters."

Alejandro drew her back against him. Emotions were running high, and they'd just risked their lives. He worried Daria might slip even more.

"Who did this?" Alejandro asked, his voice rough from coughing and smoke inhalation.

Sante's lips pursed in thought. Around them Carlos had begun to shoo the onlookers away. "I have enemies. Many of them. We'll investigate, but it sounds like it was a bomb."

Alejandro stated the obvious. "You have someone in this dome who means you harm." Besides himself, Daria, and Brandon, that was.

"Wouldn't be the first time." Sante made a fist. "When I find them, and I will, they're dead for this."

"You were at your headquarters," Daria broke in. "It was public knowledge. Either the bomber wanted to threaten you and didn't know Ari was in the house, or they *did* know she was there and their intent was murder."

Sante's smile was cold and the look in his eyes brutal. Here was the Christopher Sante who had killed Julia and the guards and who'd taken pleasure in slowly torturing their witness to death. *Here* was the Sante who had slept with and romanced Daria for years under a pretense. "Either way, he's dead . . . slowly."

"Keep Ari safe." Daria's voice was hard. "Keep her guarded."

Sante cocked his head to the side a little and gave a curious half smile. "Why do you care so much, Valerie? You barely know her."

Daria hesitated a moment before answering. "She reminds me of someone I knew once, a friend."

His smile faded. "I'll take good care of Ari, don't worry."

~

CHRISTOPHER lay in the dark, in an apartment on the other side of the compound. Above him was a skylight, one of two large ones in this residence. Through it he could see the slit in the dome they'd opened to release some of the smoke from the destruction of his house. The dark, gaping opening looked like a crack in the illusion of their reality.

Daria/Valerie, who never missed a thing, asked how they maintained security when the dome was opened. He'd told her about the invisible energy barrier that covered the slit and about the quirk in the barrier's operation. The security mechanism shut down while the dome opened and closed, which took a little over a minute.

During that minute he'd set guards to watch for anyone who tried to get out of the Shining Way. It was bait. If they caught the person who'd almost killed Ari, he or she was slated for death in the most horrifying way he could imagine.

Sante had enjoyed planning that death, but he'd enjoy the actual killing even more. He imagined blood and flesh filling his mouth, and pure white-hot bliss filled him.

He closed his eyes for a moment, fighting the rising bloodlust within him, the leading edge of age insanity that ate at the fringes of his mind. He could control it. He had to control it for Ari's sake.

She lay next to him in the bed, her breathing finally deep and even. She was still a new succubare and her enhanced healing abilities hadn't fully developed, but she was doing much better than anyone had expected after her near brush with death.

Now she slept, and that was good. However, sleep remained elusive for him. His mind turned over the possibilities endlessly.

Who would want Ari dead? Who would dare threaten him?

The obvious answer was that someone under the dome was gunning for Ari and they were affiliated somehow with her father. Someone paid to be here. It could be anyone.

Alejandro and Daria were here at the behest of Richard Templeton and therefore were a threat to Ari. That's why he kept them so close. They would have been top on his list were it not for the fact they'd risked their lives to save her. He dismissed the notion. No, they were just good agents working under the notion they were doing good things.

There were some other possible suspects. Tomorrow he would set to work analyzing all the recent members once more, even closer, in an effort to discover who had done this.

He put his arm over his eyes and blew out a sharp breath. Ari reminded Daria of Julia. He couldn't get it out of his mind. There were parallels. Julia had been tougher than Ari physically, but they'd both possessed the same touching vulnerability, a quality that made you like them right away and made you want to draw them under your wing.

His memories flashed back to that night, when he'd gone to take care of the witness. When Julia had seen his face on the camera at the base of the high-security building where they'd been protecting Stephen Miller, she let him right in. All going according to his plan, she'd met him at the door and smiled, asked him why'd come so late at night. He'd given her a plausible excuse . . . then choked her to death.

Christopher could still see the look of surprise on her face after he'd snaked his hand out fast and hard and caught her in the foyer of the apartment. He could still feel the way her slender neck had cracked under the pressure of his grip. He'd gone for her throat, so she couldn't alert the two other guards.

He hadn't wanted to do it; he'd grown to like Julia. Yet there'd been an undeniable, feral part of him that enjoyed her soft skin squeezing in his palms. A violent, maybe even age-insane, part of him had gloried in the control he'd had over her and enjoyed it when the light of her fragile, human life had flickered and died in her eyes.

Once he'd had a taste of that murder and it had coated his tongue like a sweetly bitter sip of wine, he'd gone in and killed the two guards. Fast. Clean. Cut their throats with a blade and let their blood sink into the beige carpet. The sight of it, the scent had made him insane with hunger.

He'd found Stephen Miller, an aging human who'd been his blood mother's accountant, hiding in a closet. Before he'd pulled him out, he'd played with him a little, making him whimper and wet his pants.

Christopher had saved the best for last and had taken his time with the man. He'd tied him up and tortured him slowly, breaking each of his fingers and toes and biting pieces out of his arms, legs, and stomach until Miller had been insane with terror and only been able to babble.

Then Christopher had drained him slowly until Miller's life had slipped from his fingers and Christopher had been sated.

He'd left the apartment that night high on what he'd done, crazed by it. That night, even though he'd loved Daria, he'd fought the urge to return to her apartment before his kills were discovered and torture her, too. That's how much he'd wanted to do it again.

Christopher closed his eyes. Instead he'd plucked a homeless woman from the streets and sated his need.

That night he'd discovered a part of himself he'd always known existed, but had tried to suppress—the very edge of age-inspired insanity. One day Christopher knew it would come for him in earnest. When that happened, he would be a very dangerous Chosen.

Once the highs from his kills had worn off and the reality of what he'd done, and how much he'd enjoyed it, had set in, he'd sunk into depression.

After he'd served his short stint in jail for impersonating a human, he'd gone back to his blood mother and discharged himself from her forever. Then he'd disappeared for years, resurfacing only when the idea for the Shining Way had manifested itself in his mind and ultimately saved his wretched life.

There wasn't a day that went by that he hadn't seen the faces of Julia, the guards, or Stephen Miller in his mind's eye. The homeless woman had never bothered his conscience much. There wasn't a day he didn't suppress the sweet flush of excitement those faces created in him as he remembered the killings.

Every day was an effort to remain sane. He'd been doing better with it, but with the attempt on Ari, he could feel his bloodlust flickering to life.

And the lust wasn't very discriminate.

24

In appreciation for saving Ari's life, Sante flung open his arms and gave Daria and Alejandro everything they could want.

Even things they didn't want.

The morning after the bombing, three Chosen men had arrived at their room. Within minutes, they'd been packed up and moved across the dome to much larger and fancier accommodations—a three-bedroom, two-bath apartment complete with a kitchen, a luxury reserved only for the wealthiest of Chosen under the dome.

Packing up their stuff had caused Daria some concern—so had moving from their private area where they could speak freely—but it wasn't like they could refuse Sante's gesture. That would look pretty suspicious. Once Alejandro and Daria reached their new digs, they'd resecured it.

Daria had taken one of the guest rooms.

Alejandro didn't like it. He'd been brooding about it for two days now, casting only dark looks in her direction. But it had to be done. She had to distance herself a little from him.

A relationship was not what she'd gone into this mission looking for. She wasn't ready for one yet. Maybe she'd never be ready for one.

It was her desire to not complicate her life. Her choice to remain alone. She had made that decision many years ago and she intended to maintain it. She didn't need a man to be happy, or to complete her. She had her career. That was enough. Sex she could get anytime.

Not only had their rescue of Ari procured them nice new digs, they'd also gained a new respect around the dome. Entry to where they'd never been able to gain entry before.

Like at the teddy bear factory.

Now Daria was headed there on the pretense of visiting Jia Ying, as she did most days. However, today she had an ulterior motive, one she'd been setting up for a week. She wanted in that packing room.

Alejandro was focusing his efforts with Brandon down at the honey fields, though so far hadn't had much luck.

"Valerie!" Jia Ying greeted her with a warm hug as she approached her at the belt. "Have you come to visit with us peon minions again?"

Daria winked and glanced at Rodrigo and Emmet. "There are only a few peon minions I come to see."

"We're always glad to see you," said Emmet, "but we miss you down here on the lines."

She eyed the teddy bears passing on the belt, glancing down at their final destination, the ever-secret packing room. "I'm happy to visit, too. Today I actually came on a mission for Christopher Sante, though."

"Oh!" Rodrigo waved his hands with dramatic flair. "Madam is on official business."

Daria grinned. "I am, but as you've noticed I came right at quitting time. I'd hoped you'd all take a drink with me after you're done." The Alhambra Building had a disturbing melange of willing blood donors and actual alcoholic consumables. "Say the Alhambra, right after shift?"

A smile spread across Jia Ying's face. "We'll be there."

They said their good-byes, and Daria walked away from them, down the line past the other workers to the packing room and the manager she could see standing there. Even though her heart was pounding, she kept a confident look on her face.

She was about to take a risk, one she'd discussed with Alejandro and Brandon at length. Everyone agreed this was their best shot at getting into the packing room at the factory. It might be their only shot.

"Bennie," she said as she approached the Chosen male. He'd been in his midthirties when he'd been Chosen and was of a swarthy complexion, perhaps from some sort of Mediterranean descent. "You have a lot to explain, sir."

Bennie pushed away from the wall as she approached. As he recognized who she was, a look of alarm passed over his handsome face. "Excuse me?"

"Mr. Sante has heard some very disheartening things about what's been going on here in your packing room and sent me over for a surprise inspection." She came to a halt in front of the man who towered over her and stared up into his face with a severe expression.

"I–I haven't heard anything about Mr. Sante being unhappy with our work here."

She compressed her lips into a thin line. "You're hearing it now."

"But I—"

"I don't want to hear any excuses." Daria whirled and marched straight for the door of the packing room. "Open this immediately and allow me entrance."

A guard stood nearby. She'd always suspected he was there specifically to watch this door. Her suspicions were confirmed when the man's hand went to his waist, undoubtedly moving toward his weapon.

When the manager made no further move, she glared at him and barked, "Now!"

"This is against everything we've been told—"

Daria put a hand on her hip. "Should I call Carlos, then? I can buzz him right now—mentally, of course—and have him over here right away. Then you can deal with *him* instead of me."

Bennie blanched.

"Of course, neither Carlos nor Sante are in a very good mood these days considering the bombing of the house and near death of Sante's new mate." Her identity still wasn't being advertised, though there were plenty of rumors and suspicion in the dome these days. "Carlos might be a little more difficult to deal with than me."

"All right," Bennie said. "Okay, okay!" He walked toward the door. "I didn't mean to imply I didn't trust you. It's just that we have explicit instructions on the management of this room." He punched in the code to unlock the door. "But you're Valerie Hollan. We know you're close to Sante."

The door unlocked and swung open an inch. *Finally, I'm in.* For a moment, she savored her triumph.

She turned and looked at him. "I get that. Look, you made the right decision. I'll be a lot gentler in my assessment than Carlos would be." Then she pushed the door the rest of the way open.

The room was well lit. The belt continually brought teddy bears into the room past a line of four workers who stuffed small, white plastic pouches into the bellies of the toys before sending them down the line into a machine that stitched them up, tagged, and packaged them.

The workers looked at her curiously as she approached the belt, wanting to find out what was in those pouches. Boxes were stacked along the sides of the room and a desk strewn with papers stood in the corner. Otherwise, the room was empty.

"Looks efficient to me," Daria said to Bennie, who stood nervously beside her. "I wonder what the complaint was about."

She stepped closer to the belt and picked up one of the pouches. It was opaque, and there was no way to tell what was within. Palming it, she turned and did a tour of the room. "It's clean, seems well organized."

Bennie visibly relaxed. "We run things as well as we can down here."

She nodded, inspecting the equipment and then standing for a time, watching the workers.

Finally she turned and walked toward the exit. "I wouldn't worry,

Bennie. I think this was a waste of my time. This place appears to be running smoothly." She frowned. "Do you have any enemies who might be trying to get you into trouble?"

His mouth quirked in a mirthless smile. "I do."

There always were, weren't there? She nodded knowingly. "*Hmmm.* In any case, I'll be giving a favorable report to Sante. You can relax."

He opened the door to allow her to exit. "Thank you so much for your help, Valerie."

She turned and gave him a dazzling smile. "My pleasure."

~

BACK at the apartment, Alejandro opened the pouch Daria had procured while Brandon stood nearby. A crystallized brown substance lay within.

"Carmin," Daria and Alejandro said together. What a surprise.

Alejandro dipped his finger in and tasted it to make sure. The bitter flavor of it spread over his tongue, gradually turning into a slow burn as the organisms died. He made a face immediately and nodded. "Oh, yeah. That's what it is. *Dios*, I hate that."

Taking it on his tongue wouldn't get him high. Like some of the powdered drugs from Earth of old, it had to be inhaled to be effective. However, unlike the powdered drugs from Earth of old, carmin was actually comprised of microscopic, living organisms that found a comfortable place within their host's brain to live out their life spans.

In the process the parasite slowly destroyed tissues and released toxins into the bloodstream of the victim, toxins that gave the host a euphoric, invincible feeling. It was highly potent, very addictive, and eventually killed the host.

Carmin was a drug made from the carmilla plant, found only on Darpong until it had been exported and grown elsewhere. The plant was infested with the parasites, the only place, other than comfortable brain tissue, where the bugs could survive. Parasite and plant had become synonymous.

The early settlers in this part of the universe had wasted no time identifying the alien plants, and their bugs, that would get them high. Thousands of people on Angel One died every month from doing carmin.

It did well in sunny, hot weather and Alejandro would bet a million syscredits that Sante had a whole field of it here.

"Bastard!" Daria put the pouch down on the table and whirled, pacing away from Alejandro. "I knew the bastard was financing this place through illegal means."

Alejandro stared down at the pouch in his hand. "If what you say about the teddy bear factory is true, we've got enough to put him away for a long time just on drug charges."

Daria chewed the edge of her thumb. "Yes, and yet . . ."

Alejandro knew exactly what she was thinking. "We need to wait and see if we can get him on blood slave trafficking."

She halted and nodded. "That would put him away for the rest of his unnatural life. *Eternity.*"

"No," Brandon broke in. "We have the drug charge. That's all we need. We get the names of the manager, the guard, and the workers in the packing room at the teddy bear factory and we take Sante. Now. End of story."

"And the blood slaves? What about them?" Daria whirled toward Brandon and yelled it, her face going red. "That would give the inner circle plenty of warning before the ABI and the GBC arrive. Do we just let Carlos and god knows who else shuffle them away into a dark corner to prevent them from being discovered?"

"We have all we need, Daria!" Brandon countered. "See reason."

"See reason?" She made a scoffing noise. "Have you ever seen a blood slave, Brandon? Blood slaves are a far cry from your average veilhounder. Slaves are drugged into docility, physically abused, often raped, and starved half to death. We can't ignore an opportunity to help them."

"We don't even know if there are blood slaves," Brandon shot back. "What I saw by the honey fields may well have been simply the paid blood donors being shuffled back to their quarters."

"*Qué pasa contigo, tio?* What's wrong with you, man?" Alejandro rounded on him, patience at an end. "Then why all the guards? Why the seclusion, the secrecy over on that side of the dome?"

Brandon shook his head. "We take the bird in our hand and leave the rest. We take the sure thing and get the fuck out of here."

"You aren't making any sense," said Daria. "I *know* there are blood slaves just like I knew there was something illegal happening at the teddy bear factory."

"I don't want to waste my time trusting your gut, Daria!" Brandon spat in a low, dangerous-sounding voice.

Alejandro took a couple of menacing steps toward him. "I don't know what your problem is, Brandon, but you're outnumbered. We're in a good position right now, and there's no reason to move in quickly on Sante. We've got the luxury to wait a little and investigate the slave possibility."

"You're fucking her, so you're willing to go along with anything she says, is that it?" Brandon snorted. "Bloody hell, Alejandro, you're a pussy-whipped son of a bitch. You both do remember that—"

Alejandro cut him off. "I don't want to hear a fucking word about rank. It's two to one right now and we're miles from any ABI or GBC outpost."

"So it's to be mutiny, then?"

Alejandro flashed fang. "We can make it a violent one, if you like."

Brandon glared at them a moment, then turned on his heel and stomped out of the apartment, slamming the door behind him.

Alejandro vibrated with rage, staring at the door.

"Thanks for backing me up."

He glanced at her. "I trust your gut."

Daria made fists at her sides. "The sooner this mission ends, the better. I don't like that guy."

"What's to like?"

He glanced at her and did a double take. Damn it. She hadn't been feeding. "You're pale and shaking."

She turned away. "I'm fine."

"Fine, my ass." He took her by the upper arm and spun her around to face him. "You haven't fed. Fuck, Daria. I knew you weren't feeding from me, but I thought you'd have sense enough to feed from someone."

She yanked her arm away from him. "Leave off, I'll find a donor today."

Overwhelming possessiveness swamped his brain and shut everything else off for a second, including logic. "The hell you will. I don't want your fangs in anyone but me."

Daria glared up at him. "You just said you thought I'd been feeding elsewhere these past couple of days."

"That was then. Now that I know you haven't been, your sweet ass is mine."

"I'm not sleeping with you, Alejandro."

He hitched one side of his mouth up in a wry smile. "Isn't it a little late for that? That deed's been done." He paused and his grin widened. "Several times."

She turned away from him. "I can't."

The rejection stung. "Afraid you can't resist me?" He tried to sound cocky.

"Yes," she answered honestly. "My libido has had a good taste of you, Alejandro, and it wants more."

And, for whatever broken reason, she didn't want to indulge it. Daria didn't want a longer taste of him.

Alejandro went silent for a long time, processing her words. In a way, maybe he should be flattered. She considered him a threat to the walls she'd built around herself. That meant he'd done a good job with his original intention—tearing them down.

It hadn't been enough, though. Alejandro was beginning to understand that Daria was too damaged to accept his love.

Then he finally said, "I promise not to push you, okay? Take my blood, and I won't touch you in any way not related to the feeding."

She turned and looked at him.

"I'll be a perfect gentleman." He raised his hands, palms out. "Swear." He'd do his best, anyway.

"I would rather feed from you than a stranger."

"That's a point we can both agree on." He moved to sit on the plush, overstuffed burgundy couch. He stretched his large frame and groaned. "Better hurry up, though, it's almost time for us to head back over to Sante's."

They'd agreed to watch over Ari Templeton ever since the explosion. Tonight they would sit with her and watch the asteroid shower, a magnificent yearly event.

She glanced at him, hesitating.

"Daria, you're going to do the biting, not me."

She took a moment longer and then walked to the couch.

"It's not flattering to my ego to be treated like I'm an executioner."

She only lowered her gaze and straddled him tentatively, not meeting his eyes.

His breath rushed out of him at the sensation of her cunt pressed against him, the warmth of it bleeding through his pants and touching his hard cock.

Alejandro knew she fought herself over him. Obscenely, that made him want to push her even though he'd promised not to.

Daria rested her hands on his shoulders and stared into his eyes. Shadows and uncertainty lurked in their depths. He'd vowed that if there wasn't a way into her heart, he'd find another way to get under her skin. Apparently he'd succeeded. But it wasn't enough. Alejandro wanted her love.

"Come on, *querida*," he said softly. "Bite me."

Her eyelids lowered a little as the invitation settled over her, likely the result of the acute hunger she must have been feeling. She leaned in toward him and he tipped his head to the side, offering her his throat. Daria hesitated, her gaze flicking to his eyes and then focusing on his jugular. She dipped her head, and her fangs scraped his skin, making pleasure flare throughout his body. Two sharp punctures, a stab of sweet pain, and her veil unfurled over him, making his body tense with sexual need.

Was it wrong that he wanted to ease her pants off and tease her until she yielded to him? The urge was strong. To keep his fingers from straying, he fisted her shirt in his hands and held on tight as she took what she needed from him.

Alejandro would always let her take what she needed from him.

The suction on his throat intensified. Her body trembled. She shifted her hips against him, rubbing herself like a cat along his body. Her hands fluttered from their place on his upper arms and eased downward.

"Don't," he growled. The one word ripped through his throat.

He couldn't handle it if she touched him. He would strip her and fuck her right here on this couch for sure and break the promise he'd made.

She halted and a shudder ran through her body. Her hands gripped his waist and didn't move again.

Finally the suction at his throat eased, but not until he began to feel the strain of the blood loss in his body. Daria had waited far too long to feed.

She eased away from him, still not meeting his gaze. He grabbed her wrist before she could pull away.

Alejandro really didn't know why he did it, other than that he hated what lay between them right now. He wished he could force it to be another way, that he could erase parts of Daria's past and make her heart fit to love and trust again. He could feel her slipping away from him more and more.

Daria stilled, looked down where he'd trapped her wrist and then up at his face. Her color looked better now. She was flushed from the rush of his blood through her veins.

They remained that way for several moments, holding each other's gaze—his jaw locked and fear flickering through her eyes.

Finally he released her and she snatched her arm away as if he'd burned her.

And that was that.

Daria was lost to him. Maybe she'd been lost from the beginning, and he'd been stupid to try and make her see he loved her.

25

A RI and Christopher Sante had moved across the dome to a small house on a huge hill. Guards roamed the forested perimeter, armed with fangs and artillery.

Daria and Alejandro parked their dune bikes and entered the house with absolute ease. They were considered two of Sante's most trusted people these days, an irony not lost on either of them.

Daria entered the room to see Ari sitting with her legs folded under her in a chair near a huge window that looked out over the dome and under a huge skylight that gave an excellent view of the expanse of the universe above.

Her long hair was now clipped close to her head, since the length had been badly singed in the fire. She wore her customary long, flowing skirt and loose blouse, making her appear ethereal.

Bandages wrapped her right hand and forearm. Daria knew she had another on her calf, covering the place where flame had pressed against delicate flesh—a kiss even darker than the Chosen could give.

Ari turned, and her face lit up as Daria and Alejandro entered the room. She seemed emotionally unaffected by the ordeal and, thanks to her Chosen-ness, her physical wounds would quickly heal.

Daria smiled and started toward her, but movement out of the corner of her eye caught her attention.

Christopher Sante stood in the dimly lit room, near the long, elegant dining room table that separated the living room from the kitchen. Daria had assumed he'd already left.

She stilled, and suppressed a glare at him. Rage simmered under her skin. If it was possible to hate him even more now that they'd found the carmin, she did.

Daria wondered if Ari knew.

"Ah, my babysitters have arrived," said Ari. "You can leave now, my love."

Sante walked across the room and laid a gentle kiss to Ari's forehead. "Not babysitters—bodyguards, my dear. I'm not taking any more chances with your precious life."

"I'm not a bodyguard, you know," answered Daria. "Alejandro has the training, but I don't. I'm just an out-of-work waitress."

Sante straightened and regarded her for a moment. "You showed an incredible natural aptitude for it during the bombing. I trust you with Ari's life, Valerie."

Christopher Sante trusted her to guard his precious mate's life. *Oh, joy.* How had she gotten herself into this situation?

Sante's gaze rested on her and then Alejandro briefly. "I'll be back in a couple of hours. You can watch the asteroid shower together, perhaps."

The Aproheid asteroid shower was peaking tonight and Sante had ordered the dome opened for the spectacle.

Daria glanced up through the skylight. Beyond the limits of Sante's world, no moon shone in the night skies of the Logos Territory. The combination of the new moon and the complete and utter lack of light pollution created the perfect conditions for appreciating the beautiful flashes of light that zipped periodically through the atmosphere of Darpong.

Back on Earth, because of overpopulation, there were no spots to watch such displays without interference from mankind's need to push light into every corner of the world.

People paid lots of money to travel to the outreaches of the Logos Territory to watch them. Even on Angel One, only big money provided the kind of view they'd get tonight, courtesy of Christopher Sante and his penchant for windowed ceilings.

Because of the utter darkness, tonight was also the perfect night to go hunting for blood slaves near the honey fields. Unfortunately, they'd been charged with guarding Ari.

"We'll do that," Alejandro put in casually, coming to stand near Ari under the skylight.

Daria watched him for a moment as he looked upward at the sky. Alejandro was a great actor. He could appear so harmless, so non-threatening when he wanted to, as he frequently did around Sante. Yet, she knew all too well the temper he had when pushed too hard or when he was protecting someone from a threat.

She knew as well the power and speed housed in that long, strong, magnificent body. Her own body still carried the memory of the recent encounters they'd had. She responded from the mere remembrance of his breath along her skin. Daria shivered.

He was a dangerous addiction, one she couldn't afford.

"Will you walk me out, Alejandro?" asked Sante.

"Of course," Alejandro answered.

They fell into step and traveled down the short staircase leading to the front door.

Daria settled into a soft chair next to Ari and watched the two men leave, trying not to appear curious about what they discussed in such low, secretive tones.

"Alejandro loves you so much."

Startled by the sentence, she blinked at Ari. "Excuse me?"

"When you sat down next to me, he turned around and looked at you with the most loving expression on his face."

"Did he?" She paused, smoothing a crease in her pant leg carefully as she digested Ari's observation. "Some days I'm not sure I'm worthy of his love."

Any day, really. Why did he persist with her so when she'd made it clear she just wanted to be left alone?

"Love doesn't recognize our self-perceptions. You may feel that way sometimes, but it's clear that Alejandro doesn't. He looks at you only with eyes of love."

Alejandro was blind.

Ari went silent for a moment, then added, "Look at Christopher and me. By all rights we never should have fallen in love, but love is wild and uncontrollable. You might try and plan out your life a certain way, but once you find the man or woman who is meant for you, you can forget about planning anymore. When that happens all you can do is relinquish control, hold on tight, and hope everything turns out all right." She smiled. "And enjoy it while it lasts."

"I loved once and when it ended—" Daria broke off. She couldn't tell this to Ari.

"It hurt?"

Hurt was far too mild a word.

Ari nodded and continued. "You put your love into someone else and trust them to carry it carefully, like a fine china vase. But you know that if they trip, if they shatter it, after you've put the pieces back together you'll just end up giving it to someone else again." Ari shrugged. "That's the nature of love. It's a beautiful insanity."

Daria stared wide-eyed into the darkness, absorbing what Ari had said. Truth glimmmered there, a truth that was uncomfortable and made places low within her ache. Made parts of her psyche cold with fear.

When Daria didn't reply, Ari added, "You have to love like you've never been hurt, because life won't be worth much if you don't." She paused. "Are you all right, Valerie?"

Daria was saved from having to reply by the reemergence of Alejandro through the front door. He sank down onto the couch opposite her, giving no indication he'd discussed anything of importance with Sante.

"You look cold, Valerie," said Alejandro with a grin. "Come over here and sit near me."

That was sneaky. Daria hesitated, but in her role she had to go over. She moved to sit beside him and he put his arm around her. Daria breathed in the scent of him—the spiciness of his soap and the indefinable aroma that was simply Alejandro.

Together the three of them made small talk and relaxed on the comfortable furniture, while above them the universe exploded with shimmering light. After an hour, Ari laid her head down and fell asleep.

Daria fought the fatigue that threatened to pull her under as well. Sleeping was not an option. Both she and Alejandro had to stay alert, even though this visit felt far more like pleasure than business.

The alarm on the door buzzed, jarring all of them from their states of relaxation.

Daria rose and went to check the security screen by the side of the door. She pressed the Receive button and one of the guards' faces outside popped onto the screen.

"I have a Chosen here named Brandon Nichols who says it's urgent he talk with you and Alejandro. I won't let him through the perimeter until you give the okay."

Daria frowned at the screen for a moment, wondering what the hell Brandon could want in the middle of the damn night when they were at Christopher Sante's house. It had to be important for him to be doing this.

She pressed the Send button. "He's all right. You can let him through."

This had better be good.

A few moments later Brandon parked his bike outside. He stepped into the foyer with a smile and a greeting on his lips. "Where's the woman?" he asked in a low voice.

"*The woman* is in the living room with Alejandro. What's the deal, Brandon. Why are you here?"

"It's important, or I wouldn't have come. It's too important even for mental pathways, that's why I came in person. Is there anyone else in the house?"

"No. Listen, just tell me what you came to say and get out."

"Okay." Brandon pulled a long, sharp knife from his sleeve and sliced her throat.

26

THE tip grazed her skin, sending white-hot pain through her. Her blood gushed. The only reason he hadn't slit her throat clear through was that she'd been backing away from him at the time, unwilling to share personal space with him.

She gasped and held her neck, feeling her hot blood well. Her mind whirled fast and hard at the sudden turn of events. Instinct and training taking over, she turned and threw her booted foot back with the intention of catching Brandon's wrist. She connected and the knife sailed out of his hands and slid across the floor of the foyer.

Then Alejandro was there, drawn by the scent of blood and the commotion. He sailed past her with a snarl and slammed into Brandon. Together they hit the front door and rolled to the floor, fangs extended.

Blood coursed down the front of Daria's shirt, soaking the material with her warm life's essence. Perhaps the slice had been deeper than she'd thought. She took a staggering step backward, holding her throat, and Ari appeared at the top of the stairs.

"Valerie!" Ari gasped.

Daria waved her back. "Get back, Ari! Get away from here." Her voice sounded strange and her throat was now going from numb shock to sharp, blooming pain.

She had no time to wonder if Ari had obeyed her or not because Brandon slammed his elbow into Alejandro's head and wrenched himself free. Alejandro fell back heavily against the wall and lay still.

Daria spotted the cool glint of a blade on the floor near her feet and saw Brandon also glimpse it. She dove to the floor, catching up the handle. Brandon's heavy body landed on her a moment afterward.

He grasped her wrist, holding the knife she wielded to the floor, and straddled her waist, pinning her immobile beneath him.

"I always wanted to get you into a position like this," he murmured.

She punched his gut as hard as she could, struggling for upward traction so she could target his throat and eyes. He calmly reached down with his free hand and closed his hand around her throat—and squeezed.

Her legs kicked out and her eyes bulged. Brandon was strong, much stronger than she was as a newling Chosen. Her throat compressed, cutting off her air so that she couldn't even gasp.

The slice on her throat still bled, now made worse from Brandon's grip. The pain was nothing compared to the choking sensation. She dug her nails into his forearms in an effort to dislodge his grasp out of a purely desperate panic to live. Rationality flickered and she punched her hands upward, gouging at his eyes.

At the same time, Alejandro regained consciousness, grabbed Brandon from behind, and wrenched him off her. Daria rolled to the side, gulping huge amounts of air. It tasted like the finest wine.

Furniture crashed, and the two men grunted as they fought. As soon as Daria could function, she pushed up to see Brandon fleeing out the front door, Alejandro close on his heels.

"Ari!" she cried hoarsely.

Ari appeared at the top of the stairs, pale and shaking. "I contacted Christopher right away. He should be here any minute."

Daria pushed to her feet and headed out the door, giving tense, staccato instructions as she went. "Find a weapon. Lock yourself in a room right now. Don't come out. I'm sending guards in."

Not waiting for a reply, she ran outside and glimpsed the back end of Alejandro's bike as he sped after Brandon.

She grabbed up her own bike, jumped on, and kick-started it. The engine purred to life and she was off.

Guards were already arriving at the house, saving her time since she didn't have to instruct them. She had no doubt Sante would be there shortly. Ari would be protected.

Her mind raced as fast as her dune bike as she pushed the vehicle to catch up with Brandon.

Damn, they'd both been blindsided!

Brandon had set the bomb at Sante's house. He'd been gunning for Ari Templeton all along. All the pieces started to fall into place—why he'd wanted them to get him into the inner circle so badly, why he'd wanted to move on the carmin right away and forget the blood slaves.

Daria would bet any amount that he'd been paid by Richard Templeton to murder Ari, for what reason she could only guess. Perhaps to further his agenda against the Chosen? Perhaps to silence her on some issue he was afraid she'd talk about? Pure, unadulterated hatred? The possibilities were endless, but it was clear now that Brandon's only objective from the start had been to gain close proximity to Ari so he could kill her.

He'd intended to do to her and Alejandro what Sante had done to Julia and the guards all those years before. He'd taken advantage of the trust he'd built to surprise them and kill them. If Daria hadn't been feeling uncomfortable with Brandon's come-ons and hadn't been backing away from him a little when he'd slashed at her throat, he might have succeeded in his goal.

Luck.

She was alive out of pure luck.

She touched her throat. The blood there was sticky and hot, but had stopped flowing. That was one bit of good news at least.

Her bike sped past the guards going the other direction. She dodged trees and bushes, coming up fast on Alejandro, who was right behind Brandon. Brandon suddenly directed his bike straight upward, toward the diamond-strewn expanse above.

For a moment her mind fumbled, then she realized what Brandon must be trying to do.

She opened a pathway with Alejandro. *He's going to try and time his exit for when the security grid snaps off while the dome is closing.* She'd shared that information with Brandon and Alejandro, thinking it was pertinent they both know.

Shit. When is that?

She had no watch, but it had to be soon. *Sante said it would happen at three a.m., when the peak of the asteroid shower was over.*

He planned that as his getaway. He'd kill Ari and then slip out in the gap during the brief time when the dome wasn't protected.

That seems likely. Wonder how he planned to avoid the patrols outside the dome?

Alejandro answered in a low growl inside her head. *An experienced GBC agent can shoot them easily enough. Daria, let's break this bastard's wings.*

Sounded good to her.

He shifted his angle upwards, above Brandon's bike, and she did the same. They had to keep him away from the slit in the dome, where he was angling his bike.

Together they arched above his bike and then angled downward in a synchronized move, forcing Brandon to change direction. Brandon tried to swerve from side to side, but every time either she or Alejandro intercepted him. They herded him like a wayward cow, toward the ground. They'd entered a desertlike section of the dome and Darpongese sand covered the ground below them.

From their left came a flash of silver and black. Sante rocketed toward them, headed straight for Brandon.

Sante's bike slammed into his, forcing both Daria and Alejandro to disengage and fly in opposite directions. Sante grabbed Brandon from his bike, and they plummeted like mating birds toward the ground while their unpiloted vehicles crashed and toppled end over end, transforming into chunks of mangled metal.

Below her, Sante and Brandon also made hard landings in the sand, where they both lay stunned and sprawled.

She swerved her bike around and dove in. Alejandro did the same. By the time they'd set back down on terre firma, Sante had recovered and pinned Brandon to the ground.

"Who hired you?" Sante growled, every muscle in his powerful body taut with murderous intent.

"I don't have to tell you anything," Brandon spat.

Sante opened his mouth, showing sharp fangs. He hovered over him for a moment, then struck like a snake. The flesh of Brandon's shoulder tore.

Brandon bellowed in agony. "Okay! Okay! I'll tell you everything." Hadn't taken much to convince him.

Sante disengaged his fangs—making Brandon yelp—and lifted his gaze, his eyes hooded. His lips curled back, giving Brandon a clear view of his most impressive weapon. Those weapons were already soaked with Brandon's blood.

Sante was only seconds away from losing control and killing him. That was clear from the cold sheen in the killer's eyes and his aggressive body language.

Brandon probably didn't know it, but Daria did—he wasn't getting out of this alive.

Brandon's breathing sounded labored and his eyes shone with fear. "When Richard Templeton learned I'd been assigned to work this case, he offered me money to kill his daughter." Brandon laughed. "Templeton bloody well set me up for life. He said do it any way I wanted, just make sure she died and no one knew who'd done it. Templeton knew if he accused you of the murder the entire universe would back him since you were already suspected of kidnapping her. He wanted to use her death to gain sympathy for his cause."

Alejandro took two threatening steps forward. *"You fucking bastard."* Daria put a hand on his arm to hold him back.

"I threw the bomb at the house from the other side of the fence, but the attempt failed. I couldn't get close enough to off her any other way," Brandon continued. "Tonight was my only opportunity."

Sante ripped out his throat.

Daria had seen lots of violence in her life, but this sudden and primal act made even her take a step back. Brandon made a sick, gurgling sound and then fell silent.

Sante bowed his head over the body for a moment, blood dripping from his fangs and mouth, his shoulders hunched. It was almost a position of regret, remorse, but then he lifted his head and fixed his gaze on Daria. In his eyes glowed savage bliss. He'd enjoyed what he'd just done with every fiber of his being.

Sante's mouth, neck, and throat were covered in blood and gore. Death smeared him, making his expression brutal in the starlight. "I know who you are, Daria," he growled.

27

ICY shock shot through her body at his words.

Alejandro immediately moved into a position to defend her, in front, but slightly to the side so she could still see Sante. "Back off," he warned. "You touch her and I'll gut you."

Sante never moved his gaze from Daria's face. "Calm down, Alejandro. I have no intention of harming her. Don't you think I would've before now, if I wanted that?"

"What *do* you want, Sante?" Daria asked.

His expression darkened. "To not have to deal with you, Daria. To not have to kill you. I am sincere in my wish to not hurt you. I have already done enough of that."

Alejandro took a step forward and snarled, "If there's any killing to be done, we'll be doing it."

"How did you recognize me?" Daria asked.

"The first time I saw you, I suspected. That night, when I came to your room, I knew for certain."

Great.

Sante smiled a little. "Did you really think you could fool me? Did you think you could disguise yourself from a man who once loved you, who memorized every move you made, every little gesture? You could have had ten plastic surgeries, Daria, I still would know you anywhere."

He'd known all along. God, he'd known when he'd allowed them into his inner circle, when he'd revealed the secret of Ari Templeton. He'd known when they'd rescued Ari from his house. He'd been acting the whole time.

"Why didn't you kill me?" The question sprang from her lips before she could stop it.

Sante rose slowly, and Alejandro shifted in front of her, ready to act if required.

Daria also shifted, balancing her weight on the balls of her feet in case Sante decided to rush them.

"Because I once loved you, Daria, desired to take you as my mate. Haven't you heard a word I've been saying? I know you and Alejandro are good people, and I have no will to hurt either of you. I wanted to wait and see what you would do before I made any decisions regarding your future."

Before I made any decisions regarding your future.

She shook her head, trying to wrap her mind around the words he'd spoken. Thoughts of murder she'd expected from him, but words of love . . . no, she hadn't expected those. He'd wished to take her as his mate?

"Yes, Daria," Sante murmured. "It's true I loved you. Not at first. In the beginning I only meant to use you. However, after I got to know you, I fell in love."

She put a hand to her head. "Stop. I don't want to hear that from you."

"Did you love me back?" Sante pressed. "I'm sorry I hurt you."

"Shut up! Just shut up." She paused, swallowed hard, and brought the conversation back to somewhere relevant. "It doesn't make sense that you wouldn't kill us once you'd revealed my true identity. We were a threat to you."

He smiled. It looked even more cruel and violent for Brandon's blood discoloring his fangs, face, and clothing. "You were never a threat. I wanted to know how you would react to the truth about Ari and me. I wanted to know if there was any way to deal with you two peacefully. There is an old Earth saying, 'Keep your friends close and your enemies closer.' That's what I was doing while I assessed you."

And, as his enemy, she needed to be closer to him now.

She took a step forward. Alejandro blocked her, but she gently pushed his arm away. "I need to do to this, Alejandro. If you care for me, you won't interfere."

"If I care for you, I won't let you take another step."

"Alejandro, I have come a long way to stand and face Christopher Sante. I have spent years dreaming of this, and have discarded my humanity to be here. *Please*. Do you understand?"

Alejandro hesitated, but then stepped to the side. "Don't do anything stupid."

She allowed a ghost of a smile to cross her lips. "Me? Do something stupid? Never."

Daria took another three steps toward Sante, coming close enough to scent the blood on him. She noted uneasily that the predator in her liked that smell a lot. She was a Chosen, a true vampire. Death was not something that she abhorred, as a human would. In fact, the smell of that blood made her hungry.

She could see that same hunger reflected in Sante's eyes, the eyes she once used to look into and glimpse love. An hour ago she would have said that love had been an illusion. Perhaps it hadn't been. That was a thought she couldn't follow at the moment, so she turned her mind toward the oddness of that violent hunger mirroring her own.

They weren't so different after all, she and Christopher Sante. The thought was chilling, but it was the truth. Daria preferred the truth, even when it was chilling.

She held his gaze. "I came here to bring you in, Sante."

"I know you did."

"I came to find Ari Templeton, nail you with kidnapping charges and anything else I could throw at you. Since you got out of punishment the first time, I came to make you pay for killing Julia any way I could."

"I understand that."

"You deserve to die for what you did." The words came out of her cold and bitter, like rusty water running from a pipe that had just thawed after winter. They made her feel sick because she meant them. She didn't enjoy meaning them, not even when they were directed at Christopher Sante.

"You're right. I do deserve to die for what I did. Afterward, I even tried to take my own life. In another time, in another place, I would let you kill me." He paused. "But I have someone to live for now."

Anger, hot and hard, filled her. "So, you're not going to come quietly then. Too bad." Just like she was in the gym back at headquarters, she pivoted on her right foot and brought her left leg up fast, kicking him in the side of the head.

He took it just like her punching bag, too, didn't even make a move to block her. His head snapped to the side and he staggered.

If he wasn't going to fight her, that was fine. It would make her job a lot easier. The fact she'd just engaged a Chosen male nearly four hundred years her senior was not lost on her. She knew she played lamb to his wolf, even though she felt better—stronger and faster—than she ever had in her human life.

Sante lurched to the side and put his hand to his face, where she'd added to the blood he already wore by splitting his cheek open with the side of her thick-soled boot.

Not giving him a chance to recover, she turned the opposite way and brought her other leg up to kick him square in the solar plexus.

He grabbed her foot before it could make impact and wrenched it, forcing her to twist in midair to avoid having her knee broken. She hit the ground unscathed and rolled away, spitting out sand.

She risked a glance at Alejandro to see him standing ramrod straight, fists clenched at his sides. Every muscle in his body was clearly tense from the effort to stop himself from jumping into the fray. She gave him a look of warning. This was her fight. She needed this, no matter the outcome.

"Do we have to do this?" Sante asked. "I don't want to fight you."

"Why?" she sneered as she pushed up. "Because you once *loved* me? Spare me, Sante. You don't know how to love. You don't have it in you."

His face became like stone. "Fine, you want to fight, little girl? Let's fight."

"Finally." She whirled in another kick and caught him right in the gut this time. The air whooshed out of him, and he staggered backward.

He came to a halt, holding his stomach and looking up with hooded eyes. Sante snarled and launched himself at her.

They met in the middle.

Daria ducked as he threw a punch, then spun to find him nearly on top of her. She crouched and elbowed his solar plexus, hitting the already sore area. The impact was like hitting a concrete wall. Sante hardly seemed to notice it at all. Kicks were more effective to his rock-hard stomach. Live and learn.

Daria stumbled backward, dodging another swing and feeling air brush her cheek. She whirled, but couldn't avoid the next punch. Pain exploded. She fell back, holding her cheek. *God, that hurt.* She only hoped it wouldn't swell too quickly, limiting her vision.

She heard Alejandro move near her. She should've expected him to leap to her defense. "No!" she yelled. "Back off, Alejandro."

"You're too weak for this, Daria," he answered. "You're newly Chosen!"

She fixed him with a grim stare. "I've dug my grave."

Alejandro swore loudly and colorfully, but he backed away.

Sante circled her, that eerie light in his eyes. This excited him. Clearly, the fight brought out the brutal part of his personality he'd been trying to suppress. That part that had led him to torture Stephen Miller for hours before he'd killed him.

This dome, his love for Ari Templeton, none of it fooled Daria. At the heart of him, Christopher Sante was a monster.

"You never could best me in the sparring ring at headquarters, Daria. Do you remember?"

She did remember. They used to spend hours training together there. Christopher had always been her favorite partner, since he never let her win. She'd always had to fight all out in an effort to best him . . . and had never succeeded. Now she knew that was because he was Chosen. She'd never had a prayer of beating him.

Nothing much had changed.

"If you're trying to psyche me out, it won't work," she replied. Knowing her best chance lay in her ability to move faster than him—maybe—she leapt up, whirled around, and caught him in the side of the head with her boot.

She may not be stronger, but she was quicker.

Well, almost.

With a roar, he turned and grabbed her before she could move to the side, slamming her to the ground. Her breath left her with a hard gasp. The loss of it stunned her into inactivity for a moment, giving Sante an opening.

The older Chosen hovered over her, that same murderous glee in his eyes that she'd seen after he'd snacked on Brandon's throat.

She snaked a hand up and palmed him hard in the Adam's apple. He yelped, released her, and she rolled to the side, as far from his reach as she could get.

She heard him come after her—his low growl and the shift of sand under his boots. Daria lunged to her feet and darted away before he could body slam her again.

Move met countermove.

Daria knew Sante wasn't giving it his all only because she wasn't dead yet. They danced their violent dance in the sand under the spread of glittering stars over their head, Daria gave everything, depleting her energy and grunting in exhaustion. Sante mostly just blocked her, wore her down.

She wanted nothing more than to kick his ass, but had to settle for just getting in a solid body blow once in a while.

Daria went down on her knees in the sand, her body aching from the continual hits and blood running afresh from the wound in her throat. She'd lost too much. Exhaustion suffused every molecule of her body. Hunger ached in her stomach and her head pounded. Her eye had swollen where he'd hit her, obscuring her vision.

Sante was winning, but at least she hadn't made victory easy for him.

"Give it up," rasped Sante, out of breath.

"Never." The word tore from her. She bowed her head, panting.

"I'll kill you before we're through." He leaned over, resting his hands on his thighs. "You have someone to live for, too." His gaze flicked to the pissed off vampire watching them.

Alejandro. It was true.

She realized she didn't want to die. It was jarring, since she'd spent the last seven years not really caring if she did or not. She looked up at Alejandro and locked gazes with him. He probably saw in her unguarded expression that sudden, undeniable truth.

She turned back to Sante, her gaze hardening. Yes, she thought she might love Alejandro, and she didn't want to die, but her bitterness for Christopher Sante was too much for her to deny.

"Fool," Sante sneered, seeing her answer in the hardness of her expression and the challenge in her gaze.

He lunged for her, catching her around the throat and pushing her back onto the sand. His big hands tightened and her airway closed.

Her gaze locked with Sante's. Brutal, joyful, light of death lit his eyes. This is what Julia had seen right before she'd died—Christopher Sante wanting nothing more than to take savage bliss from murdering her. Here was his monster in full rampage.

Alejandro moved on Sante like a striking snake.

Suddenly, Sante was just *gone.*

She rolled to the side, gasping for air and holding her burning, bleeding throat. Through her nauseous light-headed wooze, she watched

Alejandro and the older vampire. They fought, a tangle of limbs and growls.

Sante managed to push Alejandro away and lunge to his feet. Alejandro also rose. They circled each other.

Alejandro wore a murderous expression, but Sante didn't back away. Instead he snarled and attacked. They met in a flurry of fists and fangs.

Alejandro was much younger, but exceptionally strong. Probably even stronger than Sante. That strength made up for the discrepancies in their ages.

They dealt blow after blow, periodically circling each other with their fangs extended. Sante fought like a well-trained Chosen, but Alejandro . . . Alejandro fought like a bar brawler. He punched more than he executed any fancy kicking moves, brought his strength to bear on his opponent with brutal intensity.

Sante swung, but Alejandro blocked him and returned the punch, then swept Sante's legs out from under him, slamming Sante facedown onto the sand. He knelt on the small of Sante's back, in just the way they'd restrain any other piece of scum they'd arrested on the street.

One large hand gripped Sante's hair and wrenched his head back, exposing the vulnerable line of his throat. Sante growled and clawed the sand, unable to free himself from the press of Alejandro's weight.

"Kill him," Alejandro pushed out in a low, gravelly voice, breathing exerted. Blood streaked him. "Do it, Daria, if you want it so bad. Here's your chance to avenge your friend."

28

Her gaze dropped from Alejandro's face to Sante's exposed throat. Alejandro was giving her what she'd worked toward for years. It was literally almost within reach.

She rose, staggered forward, and knelt before Sante, her fangs already growing longer.

"Do you remember her, Sante?" she asked him. "Do you remember Julia?"

His eyes seemed to flash black for a moment. "I remember them all."

"Yes, but do you remember *Julia*? She's the one you were friends with before you murdered her. She's the one who probably met you at the door with a smile and a joke, the way she always did." Daria swallowed hard. "Right before you strangled her to death."

Sante snarled. "If you want me to say I regret what I did, I do. There hasn't been a day when I haven't. A day hasn't gone by that I don't remember each of those I killed."

"That's not what I wanted you to say, Sante. You murdered her. No amount of regret will ever bring her back, so I don't want to hear about it. It's done, and all that's left to do is make you pay."

Rage enveloped his face. "I liked it. Is that what you wanted to hear? It's true, I loved killing all of them even though I'm ashamed of it. Even though I'm afraid one day I might look for the thrill again." Something moved in his eyes. He held her gaze. "Daria, kill me. Do it."

Daria's fangs extended into sharp points in anticipation. She moved in to strike, her gaze focused on her target, her life's goal at hand.

Sante's gaze flicked to hers and she hesitated. Resignation shone in their depths now. Her mind flashed back to the unsettling sensation of herself mirroring Sante.

Daria rocked back on her heels.

Sante closed his eyes and grit his teeth. "I would have reveled in your death just now, Daria. Do it. Kill me." He sighed wearily. "I've lived long enough."

Julia's face popped into her mind, then the faces of the others Sante had killed that night. A part of her wanted to do it, to strike Christopher Sante's life just as he'd struck theirs, but if she did this, she would lose more of her soul than she already had.

She raised her gaze to Alejandro. Their gazes met, caught, and held. Hope glimmered in their dark depths.

Did he wish she wouldn't do it?

"Now is your chance, Daria," Alejandro said. "If you think killing him will bring you peace, then do it."

She looked down at Sante. Peace? No, killing him wouldn't bring her peace, or justice, and it certainly wouldn't bring Julia back from the dead.

"I don't want your blood in my body." She turned her head and spit in the sand near him.

Alejandro turned him loose with a shove and Sante collapsed face-first to the ground. Daria went motionless, watching him lie there and spit out sand.

From his back pocket, Alejandro extracted a zipstraint, strong plastic restraints that served as cuffs for law enforcement in more casual situations. She had let him keep his life, but there would be no way they'd let him go free. He secured Sante's wrists behind his back. Sante didn't even put up a fight.

But he didn't have to, did he?

Their cover was blown and they were on Sante's turf, with one hundred and fifty dome guards at his beck and call. Even cuffed, how would they arrest Sante and get him out of here? There wasn't much chance of them escaping the dome alive at this point, let alone successfully bringing Sante in.

She turned to Alejandro. "Of course, you do know we have a problem. By now Sante's probably contacted all one hundred and fifty of his guards on a pathway."

"No. I didn't." Sante lifted his head and stared at her, looking weary. "I'll go willingly."

"You? Go willingly? I doubt it, Sante," Alejandro answered.

"I mean it." Sante never moved his gaze from Daria's. "It's time to make things right." Her expression must have revealed her disbelief, because he continued, "I'll confess to the murders. I'll allow myself to be imprisoned."

"Why?" she asked. "You and doing the right thing have never been intimately acquainted. I find it hard to believe you'd want to make friends with it this late in the game."

Sante hesitated and swallowed hard. "I can feel the edge of age insanity. I wanted to dance in your blood just now, Daria. I lost control. I'll be dangerous when I go, dangerous to Ari. If you lock me up now, when I go I won't be a threat to her."

Daria considered him. She'd seen the edge of that insanity when he'd been trying to strangle her. His thirst to spill her life into the sand had been readily apparent, so it was jarring that he was now willing to incarcerate himself to protect another.

"But please leave Ari alone," Sante added. "Let her stay here, give her a portion of my assets to live on."

She frowned. "We have no charges to level against Ari. She will be left alone."

The double meaning of that was not lost on her.

He bowed his head and sighed.

Daria shifted and stared at the back of his bent head. "You're going in not only for the murders of Julia Harding, Vincent Almeda, Trudy Horowitz, Stephen Miller, and Brandon Nichols; you're also going in for distributing carmin, Sante." She regarded him for a moment. "And I know you have blood slaves under this dome somewhere. We'll find them before this day is over."

The murders would put him away for life, but she wasn't going to let anything else slide by when she had the chance to charge him. She'd add as much insult to injury as she could before the end of the day.

"Care to change your mind?" Alejandro asked.

He raised his head and held her gaze steadily. "No."

Not missing a beat, she looked at Alejandro. "Let's get the ABI and GBC in here immediately."

They had no time to waste. Just because Sante was willing to confess and surrender didn't mean his people would be. They were surrounded by three hundred and fifty hard-core Christopher Sante worshippers.

She started for her dune bike. "We need to get him out of here as quickly and as quietly as possible."

Alejandro nodded. "Once we get him back to the house, we'll make the calls."

"I ask one thing," Sante said. "I'll go without a fight, and I'll keep the others from fighting for me, but I ask you to allow Carlos to take over management of the Shining Way."

Daria stopped in her tracks, turned, and scoffed. "Carlos will just continue the trade of carmin, Sante. That's not a deal."

Sante shook his head. "He doesn't know about any of it." He gave a short, bitter laugh. "I had to hide it from him because he'd kick my ass if he knew." He paused. "He's protective of me and mine, Daria. To a fault. He is not corrupt. He's not the man you think he is."

None of them were, none.

She considered his words, considered what this place meant to so many people, people like Jia Ying, Rodrigo, and Emmet. This was their home, their one safe place in two galaxies filled with people who feared and hated them.

She licked her lips, hating to give him anything he wanted. "I'll research him. If I find out you're telling the truth, I'll see what I can do."

"Go ahead. You'll see I am."

"After I'm certain, we'll take it from there."

It was true that in the initial research into the histories of Carlos Hernadez and Eleanor Matthews, there had been few warning flags. There'd been no criminal histories for either of them, though Carlos's actions here under the dome made it hard for Daria to believe him clean. Anyway, Sante's word was not to be taken at face value. She would dig deeper.

He closed his eyes in relief. "Thank you."

"I'm not doing it for you." The words sounded like the lash of a whip. "I'm doing it for those who call this place home."

"That's why I want it done, too." Sante swallowed hard and averted his gaze from hers. "And Ari. Please make sure she's all right."

Daria started to say, "We don't owe you any favors," and then stopped. "I will protect Ari as much as she'll allow me to." Ari Templeton would hate her with the heat of a thousand suns by the time this was over. "Whatever I can do for her, I will."

"Thank you."

She turned on her heel and walked to her dune bike. "Don't thank me any more. It makes me want to kill myself."

~

As they approached the house, Alejandro watched Ari emerge and run toward them, a smile on her face. "Christopher! Oh, god, I was so scared! Did you find—" Her smile faded and her steps faltered. "What's going on? Why do you have him cuffed?" She came to a stop in front of them. "Christopher?"

Alejandro had one hand firmly on Sante's upper arm and wished for a weapon. Daria walked on Sante's opposite side, her expression grim. Sante's body stiffened in the face of his lover's bewilderment.

Guards poured out of the house behind her. He and Daria both shifted position, ready to fight if they had to.

The men took in the situation from afar—their boss cuffed and in the custody of two Chosen they'd thought were on their side less than an hour ago—and moved toward them, drawing their weapons.

"Sante," Daria snapped, her body going taut.

"Stand down!" Sante barked. "Guards, I'm giving you a direct order to follow the instructions of these two officers of the ABI and the GBC." He paused and seemed to gather his strength. "I'm being arrested."

The color drained from Ari's cheeks and the angry forward stomp of the guards died.

"Christopher?" Ari asked again. "What's happening?"

Sante studied the ground for several long moments before he raised his gaze to hers. "I'm doing this because I love you, Ari. One day you'll understand. You and I . . . would have been great, but the timing was bad." A sad smile flickered across his mouth. "Turns out I'm too old for you after all, baby."

Ari shook her head, trying to understand. "Too old for me?" She rounded on Daria. "What have you arrested him for?"

"At the moment, he's being charged with the murders of five people, plus the smuggling and distribution of carmin. I doubt that will be all, however. There might be a carmin field around here somewhere, so we can add drug manufacturing. Plus, I expect we'll be including the trafficking of blood slaves to the list soon."

If it was possible for Ari to go paler, she did. "Are these charges true, Christopher?"

"They are, but that's not the real reason I'm allowing myself to be taken in. I'm going age insane, Ari. I can feel it more and more every day. I need to be locked up . . . for your protection."

Ari's face twisted. She leaned in, a teardrop rolling down her cheek. Her voice shook. "If you did those things, you deserve to be locked up. I want nothing more to do with you." She sniffled. "I don't even know you!" She turned and ran back into the house, leaving Sante to sag where he stood.

"Allowing? Did you say you're *allowing* us to take you in?" Alejandro growled. His grip tightened on Sante's arm, rage surging through his veins. "Sante, from day one we were taking you, come hellfire or high water. We never would have backed down. You *allow* us nothing." He pushed Sante forward hard, making him stumble.

When they reached the clutch of somber, watching guards, Daria divested two of them of their pulse weapons and gave one to Alejandro. Then she ordered the men to disperse, and the three of them entered the house.

Daria cast Alejandro a look as they walked into the foyer. They were thinking the same thing. How long would it take for the guards to raise the other men and return? They'd been ordered by Sante to stand down, but the looks on their faces when Daria had taken their weapons had been anything but passive. They would have to make their call and move Sante somewhere else under the dome to await reinforcements.

The house was filled with the soft sound of Ari's tears. Alejandro herded Sante up the stairs and into the living room with the butt of the pulser he held. Sante's former lover was on the couch, curled up in a ball.

Daria stared at Ari for a moment, her expression sad, then turned to Alejandro and said, "I'll make the call."

Ari lifted her head. "You! This is all your fault. You came here, deceived us, pretended to be my friend. Now you're taking away the only man I ever loved."

"Would you rather have lived in ignorance?" Daria asked. "Would you rather have continued on, not knowing what a monster your mate is? Ari, really, is that what you wanted?"

Ari's lower lip trembled, but she said nothing in return.

"We came looking for you," Alejandro added. "Your father reported you kidnapped. We thought Sante had taken you against your will."

Ari's eyes widened. She sputtered for a moment and then her face melted into acceptance. "Bastard. He used my disappearance to fuel sympathy for his cause." She paused, closed her eyes for a moment. "I should have expected no less. He sent that man to kill me, didn't he?"

"I'm sorry, Ari," Daria said softly. "I really am sorry this happened to you."

"Don't speak to me. I don't want sympathy, especially yours," Ari snapped in response and turned away, her sobbing beginning again.

With a heavy sigh, Daria turned and left the room to summon reinforcements.

Alejandro guided Sante to sit on the couch and stood near him, one hand on his procured pulser, ready to fire. He didn't trust Sante, even if he had surrendered, not an inch, not with Daria . . . never.

Christopher Sante could say he regretted the murders all he wanted, and it might even be true . . . a little. But Alejandro had seen the look in his eyes right before stepping in to help Daria. Her death would have appeased some black, insane part of him that demanded death as a tribute to his ego.

Alejandro had no doubt he'd had fun that night so long ago, *fun* killing Julia and the others. The man might be capable of love, sure, but there was a savage portion that Alejandro suspected Sante had a hard time controlling.

Right now Sante looked far from dangerous. He slumped on the couch, about seven feet from Ari, looking defeated and oddly vulnerable. His zipstrainted wrists lay in his lap and his gaze rested on his sobbing former lover. He stared at her like he wanted to memorize every inch of her face and body, like a man knowing he would soon be walking into the desert wanting to store up as much rain as he could to last him awhile.

Alejandro recognized it, because that's how he felt about Daria.

From the corner of his eye, he caught movement. Daria entered the room, took a seat to the left of Sante, and gave Alejandro a thumb's-up. Everyone who needed to be contacted had been. The calvary was on its way.

By dawn the dome would be swarming with law enforcement, ABI and GBC alike. This mission would be over, and Daria would move on, taking a huge chunk of his heart with her.

He'd move on, too, just like he had the first time she'd left. He loved her, but he wasn't going to beg her. The woman loved him back, but she was too stubborn to see it. Alejandro knew he couldn't force her to open her eyes; she had to come to that on her own.

The truth could be so hard to see sometimes. Ari Templeton was learning that right now. She deserved the truth, though. All of it.

"What about the blood slaves, Sante?" The question fell like a rock into the silence of the room. Daria looked up at him from where she sat and then studied Sante. "Was Daria right about that?"

Sante shifted his gaze to the floor. "I'll bring you to them."

A disgusted look passed over Daria's face. "I knew it."

Ari leapt up, her face flushed bright red with anger. "Why?" She whispered the word. It came out hoarse and strangled. Then louder, "Why, Christopher? Why?"

Slowly, he moved his gaze from the floor to her face. "I learned how to manage the carmin and slaves from my blood mother. It makes money. It keeps the dome running. It provides a safe home for everyone who stays here. It was a little sin for the greater good."

Daria snorted. "A little sin? You call the enslavement and sale of human beings a *little* sin? I fail to see the little and I really fail to see any good."

Ari didn't respond, couldn't respond, perhaps. She stared at Sante like she'd never met him before.

"Humans are cattle," Alejandro interjected. "Only weaker. Right, Sante? That's what Lucinda used to say. Their value is minimal and they're fragile. You have to buy them in bulk and use them quickly, before they die."

Ari made a low gagging sound.

"Shut your mouth!" Sante snapped at him.

"That's it, though, right?" Alejandro pressed. "That's the prevailing attitude among many older Chosen."

"Yes," he hissed. "If they're stupid enough to get themselves addicted they deserve anything they get."

Ari turned her head away from him and closed her eyes.

Daria stood. "Well, on that cheery note, let's go."

"Ari should remain," Sante said softly.

Ari's head snapped around. "No! I want to see this. I want to see what you've done, Christopher. I have a right to know all of it." She stalked out of the room and down the stairs. The front door slammed behind her.

A few minutes later they mounted two dune bikes. Alejandro with Sante on one, and Ari and Daria on the other. With the pale gray fingers of dawn just beginning to spread over the roof of the dome, Sante led them toward the honey fields. Not a big surprise to Daria or Alejandro.

They set down in the restricted area about three miles from where he'd been working with Brandon, in front of a large metal warehouse.

Two tall, well-built guards snapped to standing position where they'd been lazing on either side of the door and picked up their pulse rifles. Once they caught sight of Alejandro helping the zipstrained Sante from the bike, they both bristled. The men glanced at each other and moved toward them, hands tense on their weapons. Alejandro touched his pulser, set to stun, hoping there wouldn't be trouble.

"Stand down," Sante commanded. "Stand away and let us through."

The guards, clearly aching with the desire to defend their leader, hesitated, but didn't lower their weapons. A tense moment passed in which both Alejandro and Daria charged their pistols, the soft whirring sound loud in the suddenly quiet air.

"Obey me," Sante snapped.

The guards immediately stepped away from the door and lowered their weapons. They clattered to a rest, the pulse lights at the top of their weapons, keyed to their brain wave patterns, still violently red. Their boss had told them to stand down, but they were pissed as hell he was being held and might just try and play hero anyway. These guards seemed even more likely to go vigilante than the ones back at the house.

Alejandro glanced at Daria, who gave him a knowing look. They would have to watch their backs with these guys. If they were going down, they were going down swinging.

They entered the warehouse and immediately darkness and stench enveloped them. Beside him, Ari caught herself against a wall and dry heaved.

Unwashed bodies. Blood. Urine. Fear.

It clung to the inside of their nostrils and curled into the back of their throats.

Noises filtered to them. Coughing to his left. Murmuring straight ahead of them. Somewhere to the distant right, low moaning.

"Illumination," commanded Sante in a hoarse voice.

Light flooded the building, making all the humans in the large area in front of them flinch and cover their eyes.

But not the Chosen, who had immediate pupil dilation in light changes. Alejandro and the others saw every detail right away, in its full, terrible reality. They stood in horror at the sight before them.

Daria's only reaction was a quick intake of breath at the cringing sea of enslaved humanity. There had to be close to four hundred men and women crammed into the small area, so close they probably had trouble moving. They were dressed in tatters, their bodies gaunt from hunger.

29

ONE piercing cry rose above the others. A small child, a boy of perhaps six or seven, pushed past the adult legs around him to the front of the crowd. He was dressed in ripped adult clothing. The boy turned a pale face up at them, his dirty cheeks tear-tracked. Hunger, not for food, but for veil, lay openly on his tiny visage.

Alejandro turned and caught Sante hard in the cheekbone with his fist. Taken unaware, Sante plummeted backward under the force of the punch, hit the wall behind him, and crumpled to the floor.

"You bastard," Alejandro growled and went down after him, taking him by his shirtfront and pummeling him with his free hand.

With rage thundering in his ears and the need to punish zinging through his veins, Alejandro didn't hear Ari and Daria screaming at him until both women were hoarse. Female hands pounded on his back and pulled at his arms.

When their protestations finally registered, Alejandro paused and looked down at his handiwork. Sante was still conscious, but barely. If he hadn't been Chosen, he'd be out cold. Sante's face was a mess, and blood marked Alejandro's knuckles.

Alejandro released Sante and rocked back on his heels. "Fuck."

"Anger management, Alejandro," murmured Daria. "You might work on that."

Ari rushed past them both and gathered Sante in her arms. The older Chosen male groaned and his eyes fluttered open.

"I wanted to kill him with my bare hands," Alejandro said, rising to his feet. He pushed a shaky hand through his hair.

"Past tense? Alejandro, I want that with every breath I take."

He and Daria turned to view the ravening horde again. Luckily heavy metal mesh separated them from the slaves, because once the slaves' eyes had adjusted to the flood of light in the room, they'd realized Chosen stood there. Normally slave traffickers drugged their stock to mute the drive to seek stimulus from the Chosen. Usually it was done through the food or water supply. It had to be close to dose time because these slaves weren't controlling their urges very well.

Like something out of an ancient horror movie, they moved toward the metal mesh separating them from the ones who could give them the dark kiss and the fix they so badly craved. They'd come to stand just inches from them, their grimy fingers threading though the barrier, trying desperately to reach them. All of them mewled, whined, and whimpered like nothing human anymore. The little boy was gone, lost in the crush.

"There's no way to get the child out," Daria stated in an emotion-laden voice. "We can't open those doors no matter what. They'd kill us trying to get a fix."

"Where there's one child, there's more children. We have to get all those people out of there."

The humans curled their fingers around the wire mesh and banged in an effort to pry it off.

Both he and Daria took a step backward, but it was clear their prison was too strong and the slaves too weak. They'd never get through.

The scent of blood and sweet, willing human infused Alejandro's nostrils, but not a wisp of hunger curled through his stomach. These blood slaves were too pathetic, too victimized to be looked at that way. Not even the hardcore animal part of him, the pure Chosen heart of him, could look at these people as food. They needed help, every last one of them.

Sadder still would be the individual stories. Alejandro had heard them all. Some of them would have courted the Chosen's dark kiss once, maybe on a whim or a dare, only to find they possessed the genetic makeup that made addiction instantaneous. Others would have been kidnapped and forced into the addiction because they were attractive, or simply in the wrong place at the wrong time. The children had perhaps been sold by their parents into slavery to pay off debts. Some of them had simply been careless, gone too far one night. No matter the reasons behind their addiction, this was wrong, pure and simple.

There had been a time, though, when he would have found them alluring no matter what. That time was not so long in the past. Understanding the reason why, he glanced at Daria. Having fallen in love with her seemed to have eased the dark need he had for human blood. She seemed to sustain him in so many ways.

Behind them, Ari and Sante had risen. Now Ari stood a distance away from Sante, having apparently regained her sense of outrage and grief.

"You're treating them like animals," whispered Ari. She was only barely audible over the rising clamor of hungry blood slaves and their demands for the dark kiss. "Like—like livestock."

Sante didn't turn, probably didn't want to meet her eyes, or maybe he couldn't turn his head after the beating Alejandro had given him. He only stared out over the swell of slaves. "They *are* livestock."

Ari flew at him, hitting him with her fists, screaming and crying. "How could you do this? How could you not tell me about it? You are not the man I thought you were, Christopher! How could I have ever thought I loved you?"

Alejandro took a step away and allowed it to happen. Sante took her pummeling calmly for a several long moments, then he turned and hooked his bound hands around her throat, pulling her against him and kissing her on the mouth. She protested at first and then stilled, allowing him to kiss her but not returning it.

Together they sank once more to the filthy floor of the warehouse, Ari with her arms around him. She sobbed against his chest as he told her over and over that he loved her and he was sorry.

Sante's blood now marked Ari's cheek and her tangled hair. His left eye was nearly swollen closed and his lip and cheek were split from Alejandro's fists.

Daria stared down at the couple, her expression mostly unreadable. She looked exhausted and completely unsatisfied with her snare of Christopher Sante.

He shared the sentiment. He just wanted to get this over with and obtain aid for these blood slaves.

Water popped on from spigots in the ceiling, drenching the crowd. Immediately, the slaves tipped their heads up and raised their arms, catching the falling water in their mouths. It was probably the only drinking water they ever got.

The dose was likely in the water, since soon the slaves quieted and began to settle back onto the floor, their expressions slack and the burning need to feed their addiction dimmed in their eyes. Alejandro searched the crowd for the little boy, but he was nowhere to be seen.

"There!" Daria pointed into the throng.

Alejandro spotted him curled up on the concrete at the edge of the crowd. He nodded. "I'm going in for him."

He went to the door and popped the lock. Slowly, he opened it. When none of the humans stirred, now sedated from the drugged water, he deemed it safe to enter. He did it quickly, scooping the limp child into his arms and backing out of the area. Daria locked the door once he was out.

The boy lolled sleepily in his arms and snuggled against his chest. He met Daria's stricken face over the top of his head. "He'll be okay."

She glanced at Sante with a gaze made of acid. "Yes, he will. *Now.*"

Outside the building came the sounds of commotion—shouting, pulse shots fired in hard blasts of air—and the noise of many approaching vehicles.

He and Daria moved toward the door, pulsers at the ready. It was probably the ABI and the GBC answering their summons.

Without Sante in command, they'd likely had no trouble knocking down the dome's defenses. After that, they would have been able to find him and Daria by the tracking implants they both wore.

Of course, it could be the dome guards come to rescue their lord and master, too.

Beyond the door, the clamor quieted.

"We're looking for Alejandro Martinez and Daria Moran," came a booming female voice.

Daria glanced at Alejandro and grinned. "That's Lucia Collins, my superior." She took the boy into her arms and pushed the door open, letting morning light flood the dank interior of the building. Alejandro gathered a stoic Sante and a sobbing Ari from the floor and escorted them out after her.

Outside the two previously hostile guards slumped against the building, the lights on the top of their rifles now out, signaling that their brain wave patterns had ceased.

Apparently they had tried to be heroes, but against a full force of ABI and GBC they never had a chance. Bikes and dune vehicles of both authorities surrounded the building, all weapons at the ready.

A tall black woman wearing riot gear approached them. She nodded. "Daria." Her glance strayed to the sedated boy she held. "Pick up a stray?"

"We picked up a whole bunch. I'm really glad to see you guys." Daria nudged Alejandro's arm with her elbow, her arms full of little boy. "Lucia, this is Alejandro Martinez."

He shook her hand.

"Nice to meet you," the ABI captain responded. "You both did exceptional work." She frowned, giving Alejandro a once-over, noting especially his bruised right hand, then glanced at Sante, who stood behind them with Ari. "What happened to him?" Of course, Lucia had already deduced that Alejandro's fist had repeatedly made contact with Sante's face.

Alejandro opened his mouth to explain he'd lost his temper. He could expect disciplinary action for what had happened, but Daria broke in before he could. "There are blood slaves in this building, upwards of four hundred." She paused, indicating the child in her arms. "We found this boy and got him out, but there are likely more kids. Alejandro became a little . . . upset when he saw that."

Lucia's gaze skated to Sante behind them and her lip curled. "I see." She nodded at Alejandro. "Christopher Sante needs to be more careful when he's riding his dune bike. It's lucky he only sustained those minor injuries during his recent accident. It could have been worse." Her expression turned dark. "Good thing where he's going there won't be any dune bikes to ride."

"I appreciate that," Alejandro answered.

Lucia nodded. "You both did a great job here," she finished. "The ABI is indebted to you."

"Have you tracked down Richard Templeton?" Daria asked right away, not bothering to even pretend to care about the praise. "Like I told you on the call, he sent Brandon Nichols in to kill his daughter so he could blame the death on Christopher Sante and garner sympathy for his cause."

"He's a powerful man, but we're working on it."

"What does that mean?" Alejandro growled.

"It means we've got a joint ABI/GBC team on their way to his residence. They'll give me full details once they've apprehended him. We need to get through his security first. The man isn't unguarded. Don't worry. He's not going anywhere, Alejandro. We'll get him."

"Christopher Sante would like to offer you a full confession for the murders of Julia Harding, Vincent Almeda, Trudy Horowitz, and Stephen Miller. Brandon Nichols is in the southwest part of the dome, in a sandy area," Alejandro said. "His body needs to be picked up." He hooked a thumb toward the building behind them. "The blood slaves in there need food, water, decent clothing, respect . . . help for their addiction. They need all that pronto."

Lucia nodded. "We're bringing in a special team for the blood slaves. The professionals will sedate them, load them into transport units, and have them into the city before noon. They'll all be placed in rehabilitation and their families will be notified of their whereabouts."

"Also," Daria passed a hand over her weary-looking face, "there's carmin in the teddy bear factory. Loads of it. There are probably plants somewhere around here, too. Have fun."

Lucia cocked an eyebrow. "Teddy bear factory?"

Daria nodded. "Not just a teddy bear factory, Lucia. It was a cover. Come on, you don't really believe Christopher Sante would be involved in something so wholesome? I suspected from day one he'd subverted it into something dark. He stuck the carmin in the teddy bears' stomachs."

Her gaze flicked to Sante, where the guards had taken possession of him like he was some dangerous snake ready to bite them.

"Good instincts."

"Not really. I was right about that, but I wasn't right about everything where Sante was concerned." She shook her head. "Anyway, obtain the records and follow the leads. If you keep it quiet, this could be a major carmin arrest." Daria paused. "Maybe I should head it up—"

"You're taking a vacation, Daria, and you're damn well going to enjoy it. We'll take care of the carmin factory."

"Vacation? Yeah, that sounds good, too." She rubbed her temple. "Before that, though, I need a thorough background check on a Chosen male named Carlos Hernadez and a Chosen female named Eleanor Matthews. I need a PComp and I need the information to the PComp by morning."

Lucia fished two small PComp units from her pocket. "I brought one for each of you. I'll have the information sent to you the first chance

I get, Daria." She handed them over and spread her hands. "Is there anything else we should know?"

Daria looked at Alejandro. "Carmin, check. Blood slaves, check. Sante's confession, check." She paused and licked her lips and glanced at Ari, who hovered near Sante. "I need Ari Templeton protected. She's traumatized and hates me for betraying her confidence. She probably won't let me."

"A female would be preferable, I would make a guess. I know just the agent."

"Good. That makes me feel better."

"We'll get Christopher Sante and Ari Templeton taken care of. We'll get to the teddy bear factory pronto, and take care of the blood slaves. The only thing you two need to do is get some rest. Your work here is done. Daria, take two weeks R&R and then report back to headquarters. Alejandro, your superior says you're due back to Earth for a vacation. Take it."

Daria licked her lips. "Thank you, but won't you need help with Richard Templeton?"

"Our job. You're finished." Lucia gave her a stern look. "Understand? Take a trip back and see your mother or something. Take some time to adjust to your new status as Chosen, because you have lots of work ahead of you. I would not be surprised to see a promotion in your future."

Daria nodded. "As you wish. One more thing, I would watch the locals. They're loyal."

Lucia nodded. "We'll move carefully. Now, both of you, go."

"And . . ." Daria drew a breath before continuing. "This commune is a good place but for the corruption of its leaders. No one but a handful knew about the blood slaves or the carmin. I would recommend the dome be allowed to continue to operate. I'm checking out Carlos Hernandez and Eleanor Matthews to see if they can take over in Christopher Sante's stead. If those two check out clean, they might be good choices."

Lucia pressed her lips into a thin line. "I'll take the issue under advisement. It may not be up to us, but I value your judgment and if you think this place should continue to run I'll do what I can to see it does."

Daria looked relieved. "Thank you. There are people here that call it home."

"Consider the issue looked after." She threw up her hands. "Now both of you get the hell out of here and get some rest! That's an order."

Alejandro and Daria shook Lucia's hand and turned away, allowing the captain to do her job.

Lucia barked commands and around twenty ABI agents mounted their vehicles for the factory. More agents poured into the building behind them.

From a distance, Sante, bracketed by officers, viewed the scene. Like Daria, his expression was unreadable.

Ari hovered near him, talking with a female ABI officer. Her gaze didn't waver from her former lover for a moment. She balanced on the balls of her feet, leaning in his direction. The female officer kept a restraining hand on her upper arm. Ari's face reflected her emotions like an advertisement. Confusion. Betrayal. Love. Shock. Her visage was an ever-changing tapestry.

Daria sighed and turned toward Alejandro. "I'm going to head back to the apartment. I'll sleep for the day and head out at twilight. One last day." They had to switch their days and nights around, since they were leaving the dome and its artificial light. She glanced up at him, and he caught a bit of hope in her eyes. "You coming?"

One last day.

"Yes. I'm coming." Daria would leave him in a few short hours and he would have to let her go. In the meantime, he'd take everything she had to give him.

They turned away to find their bikes. Ari glanced at Alejandro and Daria both in turn, but wouldn't hold their gazes. Pain flickering across her face, she just returned her gaze to Sante.

Beside him, Daria's breathing hitched.

"It has to be this way," he said softly. "You knew it would happen. Ari might come around in time, but right now she views you as a betrayer and the cause of her current pain."

"I know. Doesn't make it easy."

Just as they mounted their bikes, the pulse fire began.

30

PULSE fire always made Daria's eardrums pop. The two shots came from her immediate left and momentarily blew out her hearing on that side completely.

Alejandro jumped from his bike and onto her, rolling her to the ground and beneath the ample protection of his big body. From beneath him, she raised her head to see what was happening.

An unknown man dressed in an ABI guard's uniform—because surely he couldn't actually be ABI—had shot in the direction of Christopher Sante, hitting both guards to either side of him.

Daria lay stunned and staring, watching the shooter shift his aim a little. Realization bloomed like a poisonous plant within her mind. Sante wasn't his target.

It was Ari.

She pushed up from under Alejandro, understanding the guard meant to kill Ari, yet knowing she was too late to stop him.

Just as the man squeezed off another shot, Sante moved with the lightning fast reflexes of an older Chosen. He looped his bound hands around Ari's neck and pivoted her. From Daria's vantage, it looked like a dance move, an embrace. He hugged her, turned her, showed the assassin his back.

And took the shot meant for her.

Alejandro launched himself from Daria in the same moment Sante crumpled to the ground, the nerves of the older Chosen undoubtedly fried from the direct pulse blast. Daria would bet anything the setting had been on synap-cease.

With a loud growl, Alejandro tackled the fake guard. They struggled for possession of the weapon as Daria scrambled toward the fighting pair, looking for a way to help Alejandro. They were locked together on the ground, the weapon between them.

Another pulse shot rang out. Both men went still.

Alejandro wasn't wearing protective gear.

"No!" Daria's heart stopped beating. *Oh, please, god.*

In that one moment her entire life crashed and burned. Something hard twisted in her stomach. She couldn't lose Alejandro.

"No," she whispered, and then crawled to the two entangled men, oblivious to the commotion around her. In the background she could hear Ari wailing, Lucia shouting commands.

Her fingers closed around Alejandro's arm and she pulled with all her strength to roll his massive weight to the side, off the assassin. Alejandro's arms came around her as soon as she touched him, enveloping her. Together they both rolled away from the motionless killer.

Daria let out a sob of profound relief as Alejandro cradled her against him on the ground. "I'm okay," he whispered over and over. "Daria, I'm okay."

She closed her eyes and blacked everything out for a moment, reveling in the thump of his healthy heart, the heat of his body, and the comforting scent of him. She smiled. The world would be so much worse without Alejandro Martinez in it. *Her* world would be so much worse.

"Daria," called Lucia. "Alejandro!"

They untangled themselves and stood. The killer lay sprawled on the ground, a pulse-fire wound singeing his chest. He'd been a human male with no shot at survival at point-blank range and with the weapon's setting on synap-cease.

Daria forced herself to spring back into agent mode, rushing to where Sante lay on the ground and Ari knelt beside him, sobbing and rocking his body back and forth, her hands fisting in his shirt.

Sante was clearly fried. Immortality and a lack of aging could not protect even the Chosen from synap-cease. He lay sprawled where he'd fallen, his eyes dark with death.

A lump formed in Daria's throat, borne from so many emotions she couldn't separate them. They formed a big ball in her gut. Christopher Sante, the man she'd sworn as her enemy, was dead . . . and he'd died protecting someone. In the millions of ways she'd imagined that going down, this was not one of them.

She knelt and took Ari against her chest. This time, the woman did not push her away. She sobbed louder, turning into her and wetting Daria's shirt with her tears.

"I can't believe this is happening," Ari gasped.

"I'm sorry," Daria whispered. "I wish this could have happened differently for you." She paused. "Your father, Sante, all of it. You deserve better."

The killer had to have been sent by her father. Richard Templeton had paid that agent to shoot Ari, or he'd planted an assassin to pose as an agent.

However, Daria guessed that when they tried to connect the dots, they wouldn't lead back to Templeton. He'd probably lie and say it was someone with a vendetta against him, trying to kill his daughter to hurt him. Daria would make a guess he'd chosen the killer carefully. Perhaps he had family that was Chosen, or something in his past that would make it look like he'd had a reason to hate Richard Templeton and his daughter.

Or maybe Templeton had been so desperate to have Ari killed . . . silenced? . . . that he'd panicked and thrown caution to the wind.

"Why would he want you killed so badly that he would take this risk, Ari?" Daria asked. "What other reason would your father have to want you dead, other than your allowing yourself to be Chosen? Do you have information about him that he doesn't want made public?"

She turned red-rimmed, tear-filled eyes toward Daria. "I know things," she whispered. "Things he's done." Her expression hardened. "You'll know them, too . . . now."

"We'll get your father, Ari. There's nowhere in the Nabovsky Galaxy he can hide from the ABI. We already have enough to arrest him and put him away for a long time. He won't be able to hurt you anymore."

"Hurt me? I can't be hurt any more than I already am."

"I am so sorry," Daria said again. It seemed so inadequate.

Ari wiped away a tear. "I enjoyed it while it lasted."

The same words she'd uttered during the asteroid shower.

Ari pushed away from her. She stared down at Sante's body for a moment before turning and narrowing her eyes at Daria. "I blame you. I blame you for all of this. If it wasn't for you, Christopher would still be alive. You pretended to be my friend and then you killed my lover."

How familiar that sounded. Sante had pretended to be her lover . . . and then killed her friend.

Ari pushed up, her face red and tear stained. Lucia took that moment to lead Ari away from Sante's body and to the female agent who had been assigned to her.

Daria stared after her, feeling like shit, feeling her similarities with Sante even more acutely.

"No." The word came from behind her, low and powerful. "Don't do that, Daria."

She allowed her gaze to drop to Sante's body for a moment before fixing it on Alejandro's face. He held out his hand and she took it, letting him help her to her feet.

"Let's get out of here," she said wearily.

They turned and did just that. Daria could feel Ari's gaze on her as they mounted their bikes and headed out. She couldn't draw a breath until they were far from the site . . . from Ari's sight.

The dome was eerily silent, and ABI and GBC guards swarmed

everywhere. Daria knew that by now all of Sante's inner circle would have been apprehended and brought in for questioning. It was safe for her and Alejandro to stay until the next morning since the only people who had known their true identity had been Sante and Ari. Though Daria had every intention of finding Jia Ying in the morning and telling her the truth before she said good-bye. Daria felt she owed Jia Ying that much, since they'd developed a friendship during her stay.

The news, of course, would have spread across the dome like a highly effective virus. Carmin, blood slaves, Christopher Sante arrested. Daria was certain all were worried about the fate of the commune. She thought again of Jia Ying, who had nowhere else to go. Lucia may have told Daria to take a vacation, and she would, but she wouldn't take her finger off the pulse of that issue until it was settled.

They parked their bikes outside their apartment. Alejandro stopped and stared up at the blue sky of the dome, where clouds scudded lazily by. She came to a halt beside him and also looked up.

"I'll miss it," he said.

She hadn't had as much time away from sunlight as Alejandro had, but she closed her eyes and soaked it in for a moment, trying to store it up like a battery. "I'll miss it too. There are sunlight-for-pay domes in New Chicago, though."

"Yeah, but nothing as realistic as this. Nothing with blue sky and clouds."

They stood for another few moments and then turned and walked into the building. Daria looked forward to the comfort of her bed for one last night, well . . . day, as it were.

But even though she was beyond exhausted, she needed something more than sleep.

After thinking Alejandro had been killed by pulse fire, she needed to touch him, hold him, and kiss him. She needed to be one with him and reassure herself of their continued vitality.

Alejandro clearly felt the same way.

Once they'd cleared the threshold and closed the door behind them, they came together, all lips, tongue, and caressing hands. She ran her fingers over every inch of his body she could, assuring herself he was warm and alive and really here.

They kissed each other like they'd never kiss again, each pulling off clothes in a frenzy to feel skin on skin.

Somehow they made it to the bed, leaving a trail of fabric behind them. "You scared me," she told him between kisses. "When you tackled that agent and the pulse gun went off—"

"I'm okay. I'm here and I'm yours."

For some stupid reason the words made tears well in her eyes. He pressed her down onto the bed, his lips finding all the sensitive places on her neck, nipping and licking, until her cunt warmed and she let out a low moan.

"I want to show you how I feel, Daria," he whispered against her skin. "I love you." When she didn't answer, he cupped her chin and forced her gaze to his. His thumb traced a gentle crescent on her cheek. *I love you,*" he repeated.

She stared into his eyes, her response caught in a tangle of emotion somewhere between her heart and her throat. *Love.* She loved him back, she just couldn't get the words out. It had been so long, and he'd taken her by surprise.

God, she'd only just realized her feelings for him went that deep. "Alejandro—"

He made a frustrated noise. "I'll take what I can get from you." Then he sealed his mouth over hers again, swallowing any other sounds she might have made. Soon thereafter, she couldn't make any sounds at all beyond sighs, moans, and his name whispered and murmured.

His knee worked between her thighs, forcing them open so he could press his cock into her slick cunt. He slid inch by slow inch within her, making her teeth sink into her bottom lip and her muscles stretch until she moaned from the pleasure.

Alejandro placed his hands on either side of her head and forced her face to his. He held her gaze as he took her slowly, and then even slower.

The pleasure built swiftly and remained. On and on it went until he'd sent her into a long orgasm that stole both her breath and her thought. He stared into her eyes as he made her come, the intimacy of it bringing tears to her eyes. A moment after she'd climaxed he did, too, spilling himself inside her just as her name spilled from his lips.

After they'd drunk their fill of each other, they lay in a satisfied tangle on the bed. Exhaustion coupled with the events of the last twenty-four hours nearly overwhelmed her mind and body, but still Daria couldn't sleep.

Beside her, Alejandro lay with his eyes closed. She propped herself on an elbow and rested in the midafternoon sunlight pooling on the bed. It kissed the planes and hollows of his bare body, caressed his dark skin.

Even now, after they'd made love, she wanted more of him. She craved his touch, his warm breath along her skin. She needed the feel of his lips moving on hers and the sensation of their bodies melding together. She already missed his companionship and the sound of his voice, his easy way of being and his calmness . . . up until someone he cared for was threatened.

With a light touch, she traced the bulge of his bicep, his skin warm under the pad of her finger. His chest rose and fell as his relaxation deepened into sleep. Alejandro Martinez was a remarkable man. One of the best ones she'd ever had the privilege to know.

Like Ari had said, it was frightening to take your love and put it all into someone else, let them walk around with it like they held a fragile, expensive piece of china . . . and hope they didn't trip and drop it.

She'd done that with Alejandro.

He carried her love now—a delicate bowl brimming full of it. There was nothing she could do about it, no armor she could don to protect herself. The deed was done. The bargain struck. It had all been accomplished without her knowledge, without her consent or even her will.

Love was like that. Love was careless that way. It just wanted what it wanted and didn't think about what was best for it. She'd tried her best not to allow it to happen because she'd known from the start that Alejandro had been a threat.

Maybe she'd been doomed from the beginning; she didn't know. All she knew was now that she'd found him and realized how much he meant to her, she wasn't letting him go again.

"I love you back," she murmured, staring down at him.

His eyelids moved, but he didn't awaken. She brushed her finger over his cheek, then bent her head and kissed where she'd touched.

She almost woke him to make sure he heard her, but he was just as exhausted as she was and they had a long trip to make when dusk beyond the dome finally fell. When they woke up, she'd tell him again. Tell him that she didn't want what this was between them to end.

She snuggled down next to him, one arm thrown over his broad chest, closed her eyes, and fell asleep with a smile on her lips.

~

ALEJANDRO woke to the sweet, warm weight of Daria against his side. He remained there for a moment, cradling her in his arms and inhaling the scent of her hair.

This probably wouldn't be the last time they saw each other. They both lived in the same city, both worked for law enforcement authorities. Hell, now that Daria was Chosen there was a chance the GBC might recruit her from the ABI. Their paths would cross again.

But it would be the last time like this.

The last time they awoke from sleeping together after they'd made love, limbs entangled, drowsy, warm, and sated by one another.

He savored it for a moment longer, then slipped from beneath her body and looked down at her. Alejandro pushed her hair away from her face, regret for the circumstances filling his chest with a curious tightness.

He'd keep a piece of her with him always, though. A piece of pain, really. Alejandro would have to live with it for a long time, until he learned to deal with her loss.

He rose, took a shower, and packed a bag. He did it all quietly.

Daria still slept while he zipped up his duffle and set it near the door. He returned to her side and ran his fingers through her short hair, compelled to wake her to say good-bye.

But it would be easier this way.

"Have a good life," he murmured. "I wish you happiness." He leaned down and kissed her forehead. She stirred under the press of his lips, but didn't awaken.

Something hard twisting in his chest, he rose and left the room.

31

Daria entered the bar, the soft lighting revealing the rows of tables and short chairs. At the bar a group of people laughed and talked loudly, almost drowning out the smooth, female vocalist who sang low and beautifully in a classic song about wanting her lover to come away with her.

Daria had dressed in civilian clothing tonight, a short black shirt and a filmy gray blouse that complemented her eyes. High, sexy-heeled shoes even encased her feet; she almost never wore them.

She'd arrived in New York shortly after Sante's death. As soon as Daria had cleared her mother's threshold, exhausted from the long journey, her mom had known instantly that she'd been Chosen. Her mother had been shocked, but once Daria had explained the circumstances to her, she'd settled down.

Daria was also settling down, adjusting to her new life as a Chosen. It wasn't easy, but Daria had never shirked from a challenge. That's why she was here.

There were few people in the bar, so she spotted him immediately. He sat at a table by the large window, framed by darkness and softly falling snowflakes. The building was a temporary residence, condos rented for the short term. The bar was on the top of the two hundred and fifty-six floors. The view was nice.

But that's not what she'd come for.

Alejandro's head was bowed, his shoulders hunched. His finger-tips rested on the rim of a short crystal glass filled with amber liquid. His other hand cradled his head.

Daria walked to the table. Her insides shook with uncertainty. He'd left her that afternoon back at the dome, with not even a good-bye. She couldn't be sure how he would react to her appearance.

He raised his gaze to hers. It caught and held.

"Hey there," she said.

Alejandro blinked, shifted in his chair. "Daria."

"Can I sit down?"

"Of course."

She sat down at the table across from him.

He studied her with an expression made of suspicion. "Why are you here?"

She shrugged. "I figured you'd chased me enough. It was time I do the chasing."

He said nothing; he only pushed his glass at her.

She took a long drink, drained it to the dregs, in fact. She needed the strength for what she was about to do. Then she signaled the tall brunette cocktail waitress for another. How quaint. The wait people were human rather than droid. You didn't see that much anymore.

"You came all the way here to see me?"

"I'm also here to see my mother."

"New York City isn't anywhere near Madrid, Daria."

"Sure it is." She grinned. "If you hop an aerotram, it is. Do you not think you're worth the side trip? Should I leave?" Her throat tightened at the thought even though she'd managed a light tone. She swallowed hard and glanced away.

He leaned back in his chair. "How'd you know where to find me?"

"Just a little investigative work. The GBC gave me your mother's address. Your brother said you were staying here. I went to your room, and when you weren't there, I tried the bar."

The waitress arrived with fresh drinks for both of them. Thank god. He stared at her, his dark eyes piercing and his expression unreadable. "So again, I ask . . . why did you come?"

Damn. He wasn't going to make this easy for her, was he?

"I can do better than I have been, Alejandro," she said softly, looking down at the surface of the table that separated them. "If you'll let me, I want to try."

He said nothing.

She raised her gaze, found his intense, dark eyes and unreadable face, and blundered on. "Back at the dome Ari said something that made a lot of sense. She said, you have to love like you've never been hurt because life won't be worth much if you don't. I realized that life isn't worth much to me if you're not in it, Alejandro. In fact, I have trouble imagining a future that doesn't have you in it. I knew it before that last day under the dome, but it took thinking you'd been killed by pulse fire that brought it home."

"I told you I loved you, and you said nothing."

She shook her head. "I know. I was just tongue twisted and still shocked by the revelation I'd had." She paused. "And dumb. I was definitely dumb. I should have said it then, that day."

His eyes narrowed.

Oh, god. This wasn't going well. She babbled on. They said confession was good for the soul, at least. "So let me say it now. I love you, Alejandro, and I'm hoping that what you said back at the Shining Way was true . . . that you love me back."

He said nothing for several long moments, and Daria's face grew warm. She looked away from his inscrutable gaze and began to regret making the trip. No, that wasn't true. She didn't regret coming here and telling him the truth. That was something she'd needed to do, regardless of the outcome.

But maybe there was no hope for them as a couple. Maybe too

much lay between them. Maybe she was stupid for ever thinking this would work between them. Maybe Alejandro didn't want it to work and she'd misread him horribly.

Maybe she'd made too many mistakes.

His hand covered hers.

She looked up into his face and her breath hitched. His expression was inscrutable no longer. Love—pure, undiluted, like nothing she'd ever received from another human being—shone in his eyes. They held her in shining warmth. "I've been waiting a long time to hear those words, Daria."

"I'm sorry I didn't say them sooner."

"I think you just need practice."

She squeezed his hand. "I think I just need you, Alejandro."

They leaned across the table in the middle of the bar and kissed while laughter rang out around them.